"The author creates believable characters whose lives contain plenty of passion and tragedy but... history itself is the novel's best feature. The author has done her homework, infusing her work with convincing details of 19th- and early-20th-century city life."

—*Kirkus Reviews*

"This is the book you will carry around with you - on the porch swing and waiting in line at the post office – to see how our great-grandparents lived in these United States once upon a time...

— Rafael Alvarez, author of *Tales from the Holy Land*

"...a strong, serene, uplifting debut novel [from] a gifted writer with a firm grasp of American history, a fine way of turning a phrase, and a crisp sense of humor."

— Bryan Crockett, Ph.D., author of *Love's Alchemy: A John Donne Mystery*

Up the Hill to Home

A Novel

Up the Hill to Home

A Novel

Jennifer Bort Yacovissi

Apprentice House
Loyola University Maryland
Baltimore, Maryland

First Edition

Printed in the United States of America

Hardcover ISBN: 978-1-62720-039-4
Paperback ISBN: 978-1-62720-056-1
E-book ISBN: 978-1-62720-040-0

Design by Maegan Smith

Published by Apprentice House

Apprentice House
Loyola University Maryland
4501 N. Charles Street
Baltimore, MD 21210
410.617.5265 • 410.617.2198 (fax)
www.apprenticehouse.com
info@apprenticehouse.com

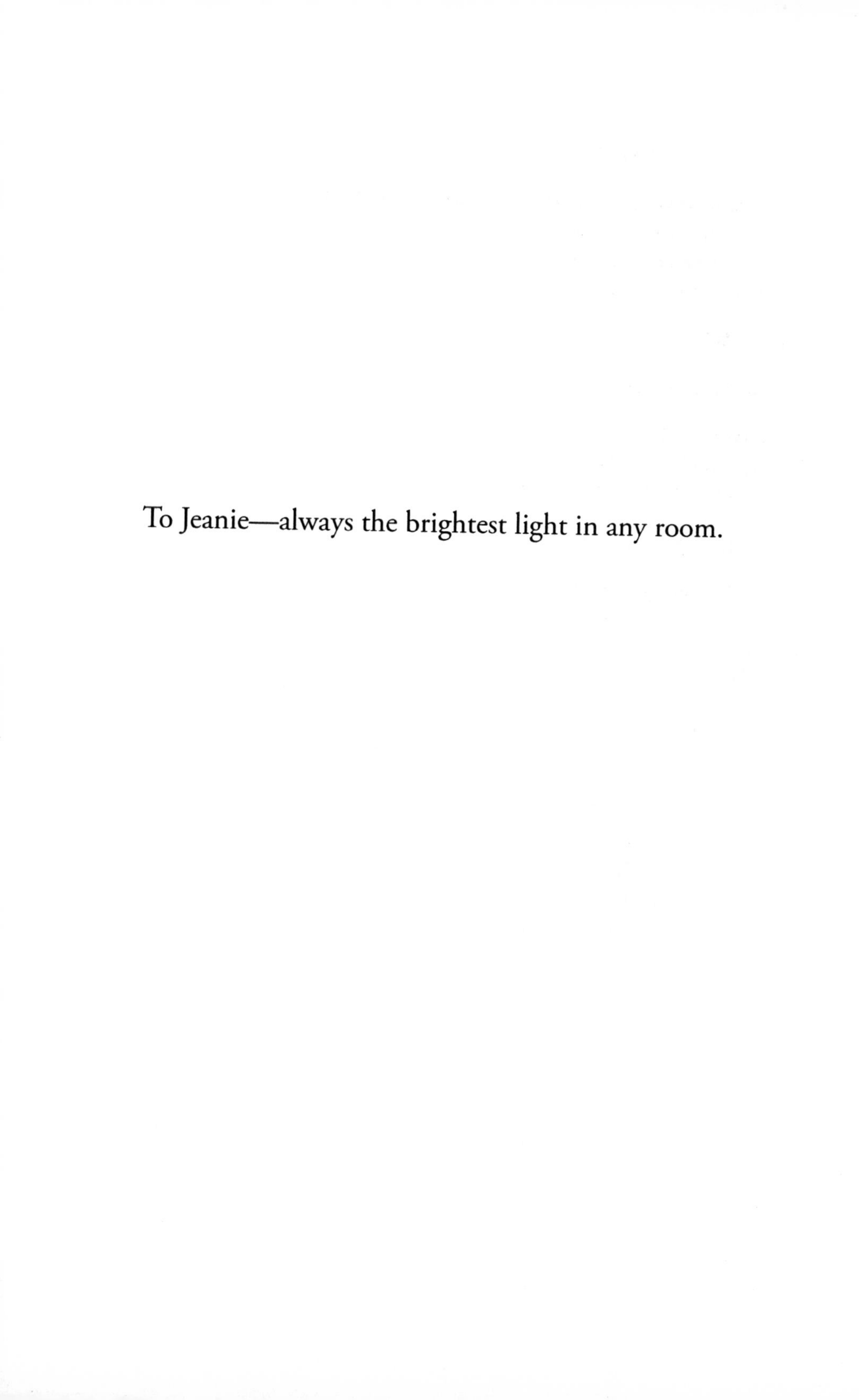

To Jeanie—always the brightest light in any room.

Table of Contents

Prologue

The first entry in the diary of Emma Lucretia Miller Beck, age 38:

Sunday, July 28, 1895, 9:15 p.m.: A beautiful day, a lovely bright cool night, when wee baby first came, only 7 ½ pounds, but lively as a little cricket, for she had not been in this world three hours when she put her little fist in her mouth and tried to suck it, for she was so hungry. The moon which was bright and clear was in its first quarter, Mercury as Morning Star and Venus as Evening Star were keeping watch over baby: Days length fourteen hours twenty-six minutes.

Morning, Passion Sunday, 16 April 1933

Lillie stands at the top of the cellar stairs feeling for the light switch, which is just out of convenient arm's reach. When Charley Beck makes the conversion from gaslight to electric—what, almost ten years ago now?—the work crew includes one tall gangly fellow who installs the box in a spot that's just right for him and his rangy relatives. In this more compactly built household, folks have stumbled on the steps more than once trying to find that switch.

Lillie remembers herself as a little girl being wary of the cellar. Dank, with low ceilings, it holds more dark corners than she can keep an eye on during errands to bring up canned peaches or green beans. She can clearly picture herself creeping down the steps, scanning for signs of movement, even then knowing that whatever is down there will hold still, until she is fully in the trap, before springing it closed. Pausing near the bottom step, she would take a deep breath, and then dash for the shelves, grabbing what she'd been sent for and scrambling back up the steps, propelling herself with a little shriek into the kitchen, triumphant once again in her escape. Charley would look from behind his paper and say, "Back again so soon?" and Emma, accepting the jar of peaches, would tell her, "Darling, you shouldn't scare yourself like that. It's just the cellar," and then Charley again, "Yep, we haven't lost a child down there in years," and Mary or Emma or both would scold him for teasing her. Maybe, Lillie thinks now, her young self enjoyed manufacturing that fleeting sense of danger, knowing that the rest of her world was so dependably safe.

This morning she is thinking of her childhood, of all of their collective childhoods and lifetimes, arranged and safeguarded in the trunk that again sits open next to the parlor secretary. She's taking advantage of the empty house and the few moments to herself, over hot tea and soda crackers, to dip in among the letters and photographs, diaries, and other treasures. Any keepsake she retrieves, words or image, she already knows by heart, and part of the sweetness is enjoying the layers of memories each item has itself accreted over the years.

There are only a few minutes to sit, though, and when the tea is drained, it's time to start the day in earnest. Her nausea is keeping her home while the rest of the family attends Mass; she's had to clench her teeth and breathe hard as she marshals the children into readiness. But the housework never gets done just by wishing, so she takes the teacup and crackers into the kitchen and then steps out onto the spring porch for the washing machine.

In its off hours, the Easy Wash stays out of the way tucked into its own designated corner of the porch, near the big canning stove. When it's laundry time, though, the washer needs to be wrangled from the porch into the kitchen, a tricky maneuver that requires both muscle and coordination. The spring porch is an addition onto the back of the house, and it encloses the original concrete steps that lead from the back door. There never was a railing, but there's a gentle slope meant to shed rainwater. With just enough space between the back of the house and the top of the steps to roll the washing machine, it's crucial not to miss that corner with the outside wheel, or the Easy Wash takes a header down the steps and just as likely takes the hapless pilot with it.

Lillie gets enough momentum up to carry the washer across the threshold into the kitchen. She rolls it into place next to the sink and is just about to connect the hose to the faucet when she thinks to double check the water temperature. She opens the hot side and waits a moment, then another. Cold. A disappointed groan deflates her shoulders; in the rush to get everyone off to church, no one got the task to run down and turn on the water heater. Her hopes of getting at least one load of laundry done before breakfast evaporate. Now she rolls the Easy Wash back out to its corner of the porch, this time needing to check it from picking up too much speed on the downslope. There's nothing for it but to fit in an extra load or two between breakfast and dinner. In a household of thirteen, staying ahead of the laundry pile—washing, wringing, hauling, hanging, plucking, ironing, folding, putting away—is a nearly continuous activity.

Which is why Lillie is looking for the light switch, so she can make the trip into the cellar and belatedly turn on the water heater in time to have post-breakfast hot water. But her mind, wayward this morning, marches past laundry and breakfast and right back to the trunk in the parlor.

Over the course of nine pregnancies, Lillie develops her own little rituals in preparing for a new baby's arrival into the family. One of the first things she does is to have Ferd go up into the attic and bring down her memory box. In fact, she sometimes breaks the happy news to him by smiling and simply saying, "It's time to get the box again." For his part, Ferd responds with some combination of a smile or laugh, a kiss, and a sweeping, feet-off-the-floor embrace before he heads to the attic.

How funny to think that little more than a month ago she catches her reflection in the parlor mirror and stops for a moment, Tommy heavy on her hip, Bernie and Dorothy combatively playing keep-away on either side of her. As she fingers a streak of gray in her hair, she says to no one in particular, "Look at how old I'm getting! It's sad to think that soon I won't be able to have any more babies." And here she is, already starting through the box once again.

She thinks of the photo she has just been smiling over, taken since Tommy's birth. What trick of nature causes the first five children to take so much after Ferd—tall, slender, with aquiline features—while the younger four are so decidedly from her Miller side—shorter, solidly built, round-faced? Will this next one complete the set?

Near the bottom step, with Lillie still distracted by the thought, a nail head lurking at the edge of the stair tread grabs the toe of her shoe. With no banister to catch, her arms pinwheel and her body twists as she tries to retain her balance, but her momentum continues to carry her forward. Two simultaneous thoughts go through her mind: *I need Dad to fix that before one of the children trips*, and *This is going to hurt.*

She lands hard and flat on her back, smacking her head against the concrete floor. The impact raises a great cloud of coal dust and other grime that, in the ensuing silence, swirls thickly in the shaft of light thrown by the electric bulb. Lillie watches it, unable for the moment to move or even breathe. Then, finally, she gasps hugely, pulling in as much air as her lungs can hold, eyes bulging, but still able to note with disembodied fascination how her breath has wheeled the flock of dust motes in her direction, like starlings streaming together in an autumn sky.

The spell begins to break. She hears a ragged gasping sound and realizes that she is listening to herself. Before she knows she can move, her arm draws up protectively over her belly, but her brain clamps shut against any forming thought. *Breathe* is all that it will allow.

She lies still for a moment, working to master her breathing, and then begins to take inventory. She starts by flexing and curling her fingers and toes, then the larger joints. She feels behind her throbbing head, but her hand comes away dry; she is not bleeding. Finally, Lillie sits up, which launches a coughing fit that hurts her ribs, and she concentrates on stifling it. She rolls to one hip and uses her hands to push herself first to her knees and then to her feet. She presses on her ribs—they seem sound—stretches her arms, and shifts her weight from one leg to the other. Gingerly, she takes one step and then another. It amazes her that not only is nothing broken, it seems as though she hasn't even sprained anything. *It's all right, then. Everything is all right.* Her head continues to throb, and she knows that she will be bruised and stiff. *Getting out of bed tomorrow is going to be a challenge.* But she laughs out loud in relief as she starts back up the stairs to the kitchen, triumphant in her escape.

ꕥ

"It was the silliest thing, Dad. I just caught my toe on a nail near the bottom of the steps and tumbled right down." Charley Beck is the only other person in the household who isn't at Mass, and he walks in from the garden before she's had a chance to get to the bedroom to change clothes and tidy up.

"Did you hurt yourself?" He looks her up and down, and takes her arm gently to turn her around; there is no trace of blood.

"Oh, I'm going to be sore, that's for certain, but everything still seems to be where it belongs. It's funny, though..."

"What is?"

"Well, it knocked the wind out of me for a minute, and now I can't seem to catch my breath again."

"Should I be calling Doc Cavanaugh to come take a look?"

"Oh, Dad, it's nothing. I'm fine. I just got my bell rung; isn't that what you used to tell me? And please don't say anything to Mother and Ferd, will you? I don't want them fussing at me."

He gives her a long look, then smiles. "Well, you'd better be fine, because you know I'll catch it from your mother if you pull up lame and I didn't say anything. And if you'd stop doing cartwheels on the steps, we wouldn't have to worry about any of this."

"Well, can you please fix the nail before anyone else goes cartwheeling down the steps?" She pauses and takes a deep breath, a hand to her side. "I need to go clean up before everyone gets home." At the threshold, she lets out a little laugh and looks back. "And while you're down there, can you please turn on the water heater? After all that, I completely forgot!"

By the time the children stampede back into the house after Mass, followed behind by Ferd and Emma, Lillie and Charley are finishing up breakfast preparations. After a quick kiss for Lillie, Ferd lugs the sleeping baby—solid at eight months and dead weight against his shoulder—up the long staircase to put him down in the crib, while Emma and Charley corral the stir-crazy and cranky children. The requirement to fast before the service means that everyone is ravenous by the time they arrive home. It is a challenge to quiet everyone down in their chairs long enough to say grace and to keep the boys from wolfing down all food within their reach.

Lillie is typically in the center of the throng, directing, commanding, or cajoling as the situation requires. At the moment, though, she is happy to leave much of that to the others. As Ferd lifts Jeanie onto the stack of books in her chair and swathes her in a dishtowel bib, Lillie sees Emma's silent look. Lillie gives her a weak smile and nods toward the soda crackers that are still sitting out on the counter. This satisfies Emma, who continues to ladle out scrambled eggs with a definitive smack of the metal spatula against each plate. "Frances, would you like to say grace?"

Francie, the beautiful child with golden hair, whose sweet nature matches her looks, blushes slightly with pleasure to be asked. She clasps her hands and bows her head, as does the rest of the table, and she recites in a clear voice, "Bless us, oh Lord, and these, Thy gifts, which we are about to receive from Thy bounty, through Christ, our Lord. Amen."

"Amen," the room choruses, as everyone makes the sign of the cross, and the chaos of eight children at one table recommences.

Ferd clears his throat loudly, which does the trick of quieting the rabble. He looks at his eldest son and father-in-law's namesake. "What was the gospel reading today, Charley Boy?"

He is ready for the question. "It was John, talking about Christ and the Jews."

"And Johnny, what did your patron saint say about Christ and the Jews?"

"Don't you remember, Daddy?"

Charley snorts and Ferd shoots him a look before turning back to Johnny. "I do, as a matter of fact. I'm wondering if you do."

Margaret and Francie are both straining for the opportunity to answer; Eleanor knows just as well, but feels no need to show off.

"Margaret, please remind us what Saint John told us today."

"He said the Jews were accusing Jesus of being a liar and possessed by the Devil. They didn't believe anything he said, and then they threw stones at him."

"And so what did he do?"

"He went and hid."

Ferd looks meaningfully at Johnny, who squirms in his seat.

"But, Daddy, she's the oldest. She remembers better."

"She has ears and uses them. You need to start doing that too."

Dorothy and Bernie look at each other, glad to still be too young to endure the Sunday breakfast catechism. Church is bad enough: being forced to sit still and quiet seemingly for forever in tight and itchy clothes, while the fearsome old priest stands with his back to everyone and talks in a strange language; and constantly standing, sitting, and kneeling for reasons that no one ever explains. After what seems like hours of this, it's finally getting close to the end when everyone stands up to get in the long, slow-moving communion line. At last at the front, the older kids and the grown-ups find an open place at the railing to kneel down, and it seems to Bernie that the priest must be saying, "Open wide and say *ahhh*," to make everyone stick out their tongues at him, just like the doctor does. One time, Bernie sticks out his tongue too, just like Emma is doing, and on the walk back to their seats gets a smack on the back of the head for doing it. Bernie finally asks Charley Boy—the brother whose explanations he trusts—what the priest puts on your tongue, and Charley Boy explains it's like a thin piece of cardboard, and you have to let it sit on your tongue until it's soft enough to swallow. If you chew it, you go to Hell. Also, if you eat before Mass, you go to Hell. If you miss confession, you go to Hell. If you eat meat on Fridays, or say bad words, or touch a girl who isn't your sister—the rules are endless, the outcomes identical. Bernie decides he is going to figure out a way to never have to eat the cardboard.

Thinking about this makes Bernie fidget, and Lillie reflexively reaches out to still him, as she gets up and goes to the pantry stove to put the teakettle on again. Standing is better than sitting anyway, and from the doorway she can see everyone collected at the table. Even Emma is finally sitting down, if only for one minute. Ferd cuts Jeanie's sausage for her and tries to get her to use a fork instead of her fingers. Eleanor describes a recent tennis match to Charley, who chuckles at her description of wiping the court with some braggart who thinks that girls can't play.

"Charley Boy, eat your eggs; they're getting cold."

"I am, Gramal," Charley Boy says, though his plate of congealing eggs begs to differ. He has smuggled a pencil and paper to the table and is diagramming a math problem that's due tomorrow.

Lillie's mind wanders off again, back into the parlor, and burrows once more into the box. Earlier this morning she opens her old diary to the first entry, written just as Ferd is starting to wheedle his way into the fringes of her affection, and laughs out loud at the coincidence that it is dated on another Passion Sunday, eighteen years before. Eighteen years that seem like a heartbeat, and yet here they all are.

The kettle whistles behind her on the stove, and she realizes that chairs are pushing away from the table as breakfast finishes. Charley leans back with a pick in his teeth, and pats his stomach with a sigh, content. "Thank the Lord for that small morsel. Many a poor divil would call it a meal."

Charley Beck's Happenstance

Charley Beck cracks himself up. He is perhaps the funniest person he knows. It doesn't matter that his grandkids don't always appreciate the humor of jokes they have heard practically every day of their lives. These days, Charley saves time by skipping over the buildup and going straight to the punch line; it's just as funny that way anyway. His all-time favorite comes from one of the Nativity minstrel shows he, Ferd, and the other fellows used to put on to raise money for the parish. Charley, in blackface, tells jokes and sings comedic songs. One year there is a courtroom scene that sticks with him such that, almost every night at supper and at dinner on Sundays, he declaims the final line: "Your Honor, he sopped his bread in my gravy, and I hit him!" This invariably causes him to laugh so hard that he leaks tears and sometimes spittle. Then, more dependable than grace, he finishes his supper with a sigh and says, "Thank the Lord for that small morsel. Many a poor divil would call it a meal."

A slightly built, sinewy man with a permanent walrus mustache, he is both quick and surprisingly strong, his grip impressive, even in an affable handshake. Charley is everyone's friend and nobody's enemy, and he is a wizard when it comes to building and fixing things. There is nothing he can't make out of concrete, and the house and yard at 741 is the proof of it: ponds, fountains, retaining walls, the foundations for the pump house and barn, the floor for the garages he rents out to the apartment dwellers across the road who have no other place to park their cars. At home, if Charley Beck isn't reading the newspaper, he is working in the garden; if he's not in the garden, he's building something new or fixing something that's broken. If he is doing none of these things, he is rubbing under his battered fedora at the divot in the back of his neck, considering what to do next. A born farmer, a natural mechanic, and a modern-day homesteader, Charley Beck is a self-taught Renaissance man.

There are a thousand stories of Charley Beck, worn smooth as river stones from the telling. Legendary is the time that he, working down in the cellar to coax a flywheel back into operation, finds himself stumped by its unwillingness to function. But what seems like reluctance on the part of the flywheel reveals itself to be pure meanness when, on finally unclenching, it bites the end off Charley's little finger, right up to the joint. Not one to hold a grudge, Charley admires the ragged wreckage of bone, skin, and blood, opens the grate to the furnace, kisses the fingertip and tosses it into the flame, saying, "So long, you son of a bitch, you're no good to me now!"

When he retires from the Bureau of Engraving and Printing in 1935, Charley receives a small corked ceramic bottle containing 52 shiny new pennies, one for each year of his employment. On more than one occasion thereafter, he remarks with a chuckle that he is surprised and touched by this outpouring of generosity by the U. S. Government. In contrast, the Voith children are always able to count on Charley Beck's largesse. He is forever a soft touch when one of them needs a penny, a nickel, even—if the situation demands it—a quarter, and he is never without change in his pocket. Any time he misplaces his pocketknife, there is twenty-five cents in it for the lucky finder. When Charley Boy once asks how he seemingly has an endless supply of change, he winks. "Why, at the end of the workday, I just sweep up the leavings," which causes him a good laugh at his own joke, since, of course, the Bureau doesn't mint coins. The youngest ones are stumped when he teases, "Got a hot date?" as he reaches into his pocket, but he often succeeds in making the older ones blush as they head out to the movies or the soda fountain.

Deaf as a block later in life, he mortifies the teenage boys when they go with him to Mass: as he marches up the center aisle between the seated parishioners, heading for the front while they hang back, he hollers, "Get on up here! No use dawdling!" Charley, of course, has no idea he is shouting in church. Nor does he understand that a comfortable volume for him on the big console radio next to his favorite chair means that neighbors three doors down are treated to Eddie Cantor or Ed Wynn whenever the windows are open. As they grow, and his deafness deepens, the kids adapt, standing close and bellowing to get his attention, keeping a hand against the closer ear when studying or reading in the parlor during Charley Beck's favorite programs.

Charley adapts too. Having raised only one child himself, he is bemused to find himself now surrounded by nine grandchildren, to the point that it is a puzzle to figure on where to put them all. He leaves that challenge to the women. Charley is one of a large brood himself, the product of another three-generation household, but those eons ago, he was one of the ones causing the bedlam, not ministering to it. The twenty-some years he and Emma spend in the big house with just Mary Miller, Lillie, and a nurse or maid effectively wash away the memory of what it means to pack that many bodies into what feels like a shrinking space. But these children have snuck into the house gradually over the years, so that Charley finds it something of a surprise when he considers the total numbers, though it's a hard thing by now to remember what the house was like without them. He finds it convenient that his deafness increases along with the family population: the chaos of the household typically reaches him as a low hum, a sort of pleasant background music, though admittedly punctuated every so often by a crash or a shriek.

Watching from behind the newspaper, he often wonders at Lillie's abilities as a mother to so many, herself an only child. From the beginning, it seems the most natural thing in the world to her, as though she has been practicing her whole life. She has an innate grace and cheerfulness that she's never lost, but that belie the strength and steadfastness that allow her to keep the machinery of the household running, and to keep the children from turning feral. He imagines that she has inherited the cheerfulness from him, the iron will from her mother.

ഇ൬

It's mid-winter of 1893 when he first sees her in Rock Creek Park, that huge green swath of paths, gardens, parkland, and wilderness that runs like a backbone down the center of Washington City. He loves exploring different parts of the park during his free time away from Engraving. Even if he walks the same path every day, there is always something new to see. This particular Saturday afternoon, enjoying the unseasonably mild February weather that has coaxed early narcissus to poke up through the leaf litter, he finds himself near the stables. Here are some other folks taking in the lovely day. A party of five or six people appear to be readying for a trail ride, men in boots and jodhpurs, women in long black skirts and riding hats. Charley folds his arms on the top of the rail fence to watch as the men joke among themselves and the women fuss about in preparation for mounting.

Then he notices one other woman, who holds herself separate from the others. While the rest of the party has clearly left the dirty work of preparation to the stable hands, this woman is doing her own final checks of the saddle, bridle, and stirrups. He smiles to himself when he sees that she knows the trick the horses like to play on an unsuspecting rider, of taking in air as he buckles the saddle strap, then exhaling after the rider mounts to loosen the saddle. Charley has seen novices slide completely underneath their horses after falling for that trick. This woman knows to wait until the very end of her preparation, after the horse has relaxed, to do a final quick cinch on the strap, catching the horse unawares.

It is not until the larger party is finally mounted and sauntering out of the fenced barn area that he's sure she isn't with them. Though she has done her own tack work, he senses that she is somehow of a higher social status and breeding than the rest of the riders, as though she has been raised to know the intrinsic value of doing some things for herself, a trait he sometimes observes in people who come from old money. She carries herself with a self-assuredness that gives her movements both grace and focus, but with a firm and unsmiling expression that makes her fully unapproachable. Finally, in one smooth motion, she fixes her foot in the stirrup and swings herself up unassisted and arranges her sidesaddle position. Without any noticeable signal on her part, the horse takes two or three steps and then breaks into a slow trot out of the yard. He watches as the horse and rider gain speed across the grassy field, break into a full gallop, and disappear into the woods.

It is not even a week later, taking a stroll after work toward the park at Judiciary Square, that he is brought up so short that the man behind him treads on his heel. A quick apology, forefinger to cap, and he turns to look again. It is the unique bearing that has caught his eye, the patrician way that she holds herself without any self-consciousness. Now she is wearing a starched white blouse with a rounded collar, a long tie, and a full gray skirt. It makes her look like an office worker, which thoroughly befuddles him. She is emerging from the Eighth Street side of the General Post Office building when he sees her. Another woman is beside her, and Charley can see that the woman is talking, apparently without pause, in that utterly self-absorbed way unique to the sex. She is oblivious that her companion is not listening. At the curb, his horsewoman stops, and he notices the way she seems to be looking over, or even through, the things around her—not in a haughty way, but as though she is absorbing the surroundings through more than her eyes. Finally, the other woman pauses for air, long enough to realize that this is where they are to part company. Disappointed to be losing her audience, she nonetheless takes her leave with a wave and a giggle, eliciting a brief nod in return. Charley waits to see which way his lady turns and briefly considers following. He dismisses this as intrusive. Instead, he simply glances at his pocket watch and heads toward home.

ຍ໑ଔ

A few times a week, he makes a point of lounging outside the building entrance at the time his horsewoman leaves from work. She rotates among three very similar outfits, and sometimes mixes elements of each. The only adornments she ever wears are a mother-of-pearl comb to hold up her hair, and, depending on the outfit, a cameo at her throat. He is glad for her that she is not always accompanied by the nattering woman. Often she is by herself, always with the same upright bearing and smooth carriage, the same distant look that appears to take in everything while giving nothing away. He has never once seen her smile.

One exceptionally warm day at the beginning of March, one that makes pedestrians roll their eyes at each other in speculating what this means for another suffocating Washington City summer, he stands upstream from her path out of the building. Today his horsewoman is walking out of the building with a man; the body language alone communicates that he is merely an acquaintance, probably a co-worker who happens to be leaving at the same time. A few steps beyond the door, they say a word or two in parting, and the man tips his hat. He turns and begins walking toward Charley, who takes his moment without a blink.

"Pardon me..."

"Good afternoon?"

"Don't mean to intrude, but the lady you were just speaking with?"

"Yes?"

"I feel sure I know her, but I just can't place the name..."

Charley can see the man's hesitation, but he combines a friendly smile with a sincerely befuddled look, and the man gives in. "That's Miss Miller, Emma Miller. She's a clerk in the office down the hall from mine."

Charley taps his chin and squints. "Maybe I know her parents from church."

"Not *parents*. I understand her mother's a widow. I'm not sure where they live."

"Well, it's a puzzlement. Maybe it'll come to me. Much obliged to you, though." The man touches his hat and continues on his way.

Emma. Emma Miller. What happened, Emma? Raised as a gentlewoman, but then Daddy died and the money ran out—or you found out it was never really there in the first place? And now you're a clerk at the General Post Office. He isn't laughing at her; he sympathizes, knowing the wellborn are so unready, so ill-equipped, when forced by circumstance to meet the realities of everyday life. *And yet you handled that horse with no nonsense, no worries of dirt under your fingernails. With a will.*

He waits another few days, then falls into the crowd behind her as she leaves the building. She heads north up Seventh Street and turns onto G, following the west side of the green space of the Pension Building, exactly where he'd been headed that first day. Half a block above the square, she turns onto Washington Street, one of the city's many alleys in which low-rent housing has insinuated itself. The alleys are originally cut through to remedy the problem of how to get essential services—garbage removal, coal delivery—to the residents of Pierre L'Enfant's fat city blocks.

And here again he is completely caught short. The row homes at the top of the alley are shabby but still neatly kept; farther down, he can see the progression into a jumble of shanties, some stacked precariously like building blocks, one on top of another. Far down the alley there is a group of colored children playing in the street, and Charley realizes that it is just beyond them, in the next alley over, that one of the city's last remaining slave pens has only recently been torn down. Of course, in Washington City, it's still common for the highborn and low to live cheek by jowl on the same streets, but there are clearly visible social distinctions, and there's no mistaking who belongs in which group. This is more like the rough and tumble of his own wharf-front Georgetown neighborhood, where the various races mix like so much stew. It's beyond him that she lives in similar circumstances.

Emma nods at a row house neighbor working on his tiny front porch, who has waved to her with his hammer. She mounts the three steps up to the adjoining porch and disappears inside. Charley stands on the other side of the neighbor's house and rubs at the back of his neck, no longer feigning befuddlement.

"I think she's already rented the room."

It takes a moment for Charley to process that the handyman neighbor has stopped to stretch, noticed him looking at the house, and offered a comment.

"Beg pardon?"

"I say I think Mrs. Miller already has a renter for the room. That's why you're here, yah?" His German accent is thick, but his English says that he's been in the country for some time.

"Oh, I see. Well, I thank you for keeping me from interrupting their supper for no reason." Charley smiles and tips his cap; the neighbor again salutes with his hammer as Charley turns and starts again for home.

ꙮ

"I tell you, Joe, I can't make sense of it. I'd've bet anything that she was wellborn, but I can't imagine a family falling that far in the space of a few years. I was thinking that they still had a big house and were just working to keep up appearances. You know how they do. But *that*?"

Charley and his buddy Joe are sitting on stools at their regular neighborhood bar, a half-empty glass in front of each. Joe and Charley share virtually their entire existence, since they work together in the Wetting Division at Engraving and Printing, and live in the same boarding house, sharing a room with each other and a bath with everyone.

"Well, I can't make sense of it either. You see this girl once at the stables, and now you're stalking behind her like an Injun hunting buffalo. And you were doing this when you thought she was *rich*? What exactly was your pitch going to be? You figured your natural charm and good looks would do all the heavy lifting?"

Particularly since Charley has no good looks to speak of, Joe knows perfectly well that there is nothing to recommend either of them to the fair sex. Today, as with every workday, they have changed out of their greasy coveralls into street clothes, taken a damp rag to their faces and a wet comb to their hair, and scrubbed their cuticles and fingernails with lye soap and a stiff bristle brush. Approximately twice a month, they take the work clothes home and, with their landlady's assistance, soak the coveralls in hot water and lye and scrape the grease out of them, if for no other reason than to make themselves less combustible. Even a poor woman might take pause.

"There's just something about her—not how she looks, but how she seems. Then when I saw her coming out of the post office, a worker! I just needed to figure it out."

"And now?"

"Well, I'm still figuring on it." He takes a drink. "I need to get her to notice me."

"Holy hell, Charley. What are you fixing to do? Set your hair on fire and get her to beat it out for you?"

"Naw. I think she'd just step around me and keep on going."

ഉന്ദ

She sees that he's not outside again today, and realizes that she's disappointed. For as much as he may imagine that he is being discreet, Emma notices him every time. At the stables, she understands that he has just happened by and is simply taking in the activity, this wiry young man with active, cheerful eyes and a big mustache. Outside of work that first time, it is the collision between the two pedestrians that catches her attention, but she would have noticed him anyway. His gaze then is intent, inquisitive. She sees him often after that, loitering at the curb, sometimes pretending to read the paper, sometimes chatting with a passerby while he continues to watch for her. Mr. Fredrickson describes him perfectly when he mentions a young man who asks after her outside of the building, with his made-up story of a church connection. And now that he has followed her home, she sees that her circumstances are below even what he is willing to accept, and he is gone. So now she feels disappointment, an old sensation that until this moment she is sure is boxed up and put away for good.

Emma has long since given up any thought that her life will ever be more than what it is: that of a spinster, living with her widowed mother who takes in boarders to fill the gaps in what Emma earns as a postal clerk, her position for the last sixteen years. By now, Emma has lived an entire second lifetime beyond what is normally considered a marriageable age. Her heart was broken once, long ago, by a boy who seemed interested in her for a time. In the end, though, his attentions were drawn away from her solid frame and unflinching demeanor by a big-eyed giggly thing with golden curls. From that point on, she's known her time is past. So now, seeing he is not here, feeling once again that empty hole in her stomach, she struggles to put her disappointment back into its dusty box and close the lid.

ꕥ

The Capitol Bicycle Club has set up on the Pension Building green this week, taking advantage of the lovely weather to put up a tent and some booths, and present a series of cycling demonstrations to encourage membership. Street vendors who know a business opportunity when they see one have also set up shop in the fringes, and the whole enterprise takes on the feel of a street fair. The club has an assortment of some of the very oldest bicycles alongside the latest models, and club members take turns demonstrating riding techniques and allowing game bystanders to try them out.

Charley stops by the first day and has a long friendly chat with one of the club's members, a Mr. Henry, who is very willing to discuss each type of bicycle and the challenges of riding each one. Mr. Henry is impressed with Charley's quick grasp of the mechanics. He allows Charley to take a few spins out of sight of the rest of the crowd. The bicycle Charley chooses, ridiculous-looking by the day's modern standards, is particularly difficult both to balance and steer, but again Charley takes to it naturally. Then Charley invites Mr. Henry into his confidence and asks his indulgence in helping with a bit of a plan. Upon hearing it, Mr. Henry laughs and says that if Charley promises to be careful, he agrees to be a willing participant in the scheme. And so it is that two days later, as Mr. Henry is using his best pitchman's banter to draw in the afternoon passersby to take a look at the bicycles, Charley is scanning the street, waiting to give the sign.

ꕥ

Emma is heading toward the knot of people that has been here all week, taking in the cycling demonstrations and browsing the temporary stalls that have sprung up. The square, with its wide expanse of grass, is a natural with couples, families, various organizations like the cycling club, and all manner of snake oil salesmen who regularly set up shop to sell their wares. Emma has looked on with mild interest as she passes by each afternoon, idly wondering what it would be like to ride one of the machines, which of course she would never do.

Suddenly, a collective whoop rises up from the crowd, then laughter and scattered applause. She glimpses a head, weaving among the onlookers, but has trouble making sense of what she is seeing. She slows down in time to see the crowd part, and in fact several people leap out of the way, as the laughter swells.

As soon as the cyclist is out of the knot of people, she sees who it is—*of course it is; who else would it be?*—and that he is heading right toward her. The contraption he is riding is one of the earliest models of bicycle, with the small wheel in front and the large one in back; it is a beast to control, and he is wild. She doesn't believe it for a minute, though; he knows exactly what he is doing, and she is having none of it. She strides forward in determination, but he begins to circle her even as she walks. The crowd loves it as he spirals around her, and hoots and claps to egg him on. On his third pass, she raises her head and fixes him with a hard look; it is the first time they make direct eye contact. In that moment, he realizes that he has been duped; she's been onto him all along. In the second before she breaks her gaze, he crosses his eyes and lolls his tongue from the corner of his mouth. He makes one more pass, and though her head is back down, he sees it: she smiles.

༺༻

The following Sunday afternoon, in the time between morning Mass and evening prayers, he knocks on the front door of the little row house on Washington Street. It is Emma who opens the door, and regards him without surprise. "I was beginning to think you would never come."

Without another word, she turns; he follows her in, taking off his cap as he steps through the door. She walks him the two steps into the little parlor where Mary Miller sits in the sliver of afternoon light at the window, tatting. "Mother, there is a young man here to see you." With that, Emma turns and leaves the room.

This stern-looking, white-haired woman looks up with some surprise, and spends a moment assessing him. "I'm sorry, I already have a boarder. We only let the one room."

"Yes, ma'am, I'd been informed of that. I have a room already."

"We don't welcome solicitors, then."

"I wouldn't expect you would, ma'am. I'm not here to sell you anything."

Mrs. Miller looks hard at him, and he plainly sees where Emma gets her bearing, if not her appearance. "What, then?"

"Ma'am, I'd like permission to court your daughter."

Charley can see that he'd have to think hard on it to come up with another sentence that would surprise Mrs. Miller even half so much. There is a long moment while she continues simply to stare at him. "Young man, how old are you?"

"I'll be twenty-six in September." There is an even longer pause now. He is wondering what combination of words he can put together that will prompt her to invite him to sit, and to offer him some tea. But he can see that it will be dashed hard to charm this woman.

"How do you know my daughter?"

He wants to be careful here. "We see each other from time to time outside of work."

"And where is that?"

"I work at Treasury, ma'am, in the Bureau of Engraving and Printing."

Of the next hundred questions wrestling with each other behind her gaze, the one that triumphs is, "Your name?"

"Charles Joseph Beck, ma'am, but everyone including my mother calls me Charley."

"German?"

"Yes, ma'am, on both sides."

"Emma?" Two beats pass before she walks back in, though both presume that she has been just outside the threshold the entire time.

"Yes, Mother?"

"I suppose you two have not been properly introduced. Charles Joseph Beck, this is my daughter, Emma Lucretia Miller."

He almost extends his hand, but hers are firmly clasped together in front of her, and he feels certain she will leave him hanging. Instead he puts his finger to his cap, which is of course not there, and smiles. "It's a pleasure, Miss Emma."

She simply nods. "Mr. Beck."

Mary Miller surveys the two. "Well, Emma, I suppose you'll need to make some tea."

She disappears into the kitchen, but still Mrs. Miller does not invite him to sit down. He is standing near the mantle, considering his next conversational gambit when he sees a picture of Emma. He has to stop himself from picking it up, but he can't help examining it closely. There she is, perhaps in her early twenties, in the fancy dress fashion of the day: heavy taffeta with a pronounced bustle, a nipped waist, and lace at the throat and down the bodice. She is standing at an open wrought iron gate set into a stone wall with trailing vines, an elaborate prop in the photographer's studio, no doubt. Her gloved hand rests casually against the stone doorway, and she is gazing just to one side of the photographer, which gives her an air of intrigue. Even here, she is no simpering ingenue, but it startles him to see her in so fashionable a pose.

"She had that photograph made a number of years ago, for a young man." He is now doubly startled that Mrs. Miller is sharing this confidence, one that he feels sure Emma would not appreciate. "My daughter doesn't like that I have it out, but I've always thought that it's the best photograph of her that was ever made."

"It's impressive."

There is a pause while he continues to examine the photo, and he can feel Mrs. Miller continue to examine him. He turns to face her. "You realize that my daughter is rather older than you—do you, Mr. Beck?"

"Yes ma'am, I expect so." They consider each other; he knows she is challenging him, and he feels it's crucial that he hold his ground.

"You walked through our neighborhood; this is where we live. You can see that we're not rich." The understatement doesn't require a response; he simply nods once.

He can see her trying to puzzle it out behind her sharp eyes, why he is here, why the interest in Emma. "Mrs. Miller, I can't say why no man has swept up your daughter to make her his own. It's clear to me that she's a strong woman who knows her own mind, and she holds a body steady in her gaze. Maybe that directness puts some off, but I see it as a mark of character. Something she's gotten from her mother."

It's an obvious currying of favor, and Charley can tell she sees the joke in it. They look directly at each other and exchange a smile.

Emma comes in with the tea tray and arranges it on the ottoman that squats in the tiny space between the sofa and easy chair. Mrs. Miller moves from her spot near the window to the chair, and Emma arranges herself at one end of the sofa. There is a brief moment in which Charley is unsure of his direction, but Mrs. Miller indicates the other end of the short sofa with a tilt of her head. He sits, realizing as he does that in the four weeks of seeing Emma perhaps three or four times a week, this is the closest he has ever come to her. She pours tea, adding sugar and milk without asking his preference, and offers it to him. "Mr. Beck?"

"Thanks kindly, Miss Emma." He holds the cup and saucer carefully, mindful not to slurp. It is a mighty fine cup of tea.

ꟷ

They settle quickly into a pattern. He waits for her outside the Post Office's main entrance in the afternoon and walks her home. She shows him her favorite spot, in the courtyard where the mail wagons come and go and the horses are stabled; they chat with some of the groomsmen Emma knows, who take great pride in their charges. When it becomes impossible not to, she finally introduces him to the chatty woman from that first day, to Mr. Frederickson from whom he has gotten her name—no hard feelings over a small mendacity in pursuit of romance—and a few others who can't contain their interest at hearing of Emma's new young man. This unexpected and improbable turn in Emma's fortunes creates quite a stir among the clerks, many of whom regard her with a newfound respect, as though she has suddenly revealed depths they have not known she possesses.

At Washington Street, Mary Miller invites him in for tea, and, on several occasions, dinner. During the visits, Emma remains almost mute, with her mother and Charley conducting most of the conversation. Eventually, Charley fills in the gaps by telling stories from his workplace, boarding house, childhood. Sometimes he inserts ridiculous, fabricated elements to see if she is listening. He considers it a victory when he gets her to roll her eyes, and several times to fully smile. His greatest achievement comes when he tells the story from work of the huge print roller breaking loose from its packing straps and chasing a whole herd of workmen down the corridor: she laughs out loud.

Early each Sunday, he picks her up at home and walks with her to St. Patrick's for Mass; afterward they might take a horse trolley up and go for a long walk in Rock Creek Park. It is on these Sunday outings that Emma is most engaged in their conversations, and Charley finds that she is a woman of ideas and opinions, simply rusty in sharing them. They enjoy competing to be the first to spot what's in bloom—Emma even knows some of the Latin names—or following birdsong to its source. She takes him on a hunt through the underbrush for some of the herbs she once gathered for her father's medical practice; she ends up on her hands and knees to get at a sarsaparilla root and uses his pocket knife to cut out a chunk for him to crush between his fingers and inhale the aroma. That she is unconcerned about the dirt or the spiders reinforces his sense of their rightness together. The day she sketches for him the device she has invented and patented, closely describing the operation of the roller mechanism now used throughout her office for assembling training pamphlets, he knows that there is no one else for him.

One Sunday they stop at the stables where he first sees her, and lean on the same railing, enjoying the warming scent of hay, horse sweat, and fresh manure. "Who taught you to ride?" Charley asks her.

"My papa. He kept horses all the time I was growing up. I did most of the stable work for him, too." She smiles at the memory.

"He was a medical doctor, was he?" She nods. "It must have been hard for you and your mother when he died."

"That's when I started working at the Post Office, certainly. But you know, we were living on Washington Street when he was still with us." She gives a baleful smile at his look of surprise. "There never was much money, and the times he was away, during the war and after, there was even less. Sometimes we were comfortable, but it was just as often we needed to move to find more affordable rent." She pulls a long blade of grass that is growing against the fence and plays with it. "Of course I didn't understand anything back then. For me, my father was Hercules, and I remember thinking that it must have been all Mother's fault that he wasn't there and we were poor." She pauses again and smiles to herself. "It's funny. I've never talked about this with anyone. I don't think I've even thought about it until just now. Anyway, I finally realized later how hard Mother must have worked to keep us all together. Imagine what those horses must have cost us."

Charley nods, able to see the picture clearly, and pleased that Emma has chosen to share so much. "Was there more than just you and your mother, then?"

"My brother John died before I was born; he was only a year-and-a-half old, and Mother said it hit Papa hard. Sister—my sister Mary—was born a few months before John died, and then I came about two years after that."

"So, where is Mary now?"

"She's not with us anymore."

"Ahh. I'm sorry."

Emma throws away the shredded blade of grass. "No, I'm sorry. I make it sound as though she's dead. She's not. She lives in a home in New York. It's very well kept and the people are kind to her. Mother makes sure of that."

Charley can see that this is not the time to ask anything more. They both lean against the fence, and Emma holds her face up to the sun and breeze. The moment passes, and they both relax again. Charley watches her as she smiles at the chestnut gelding she was riding that first day.

"Maybe you and I can go riding one of these Sundays," he suggests.

She gazes appreciatively at an Appaloosa one of the stable hands is exercising in the yard. "No, I'm done with riding. The day you saw me I had already decided was my last time." She reflexively touches her hair. Emma can't bring herself to say, *I'm getting too old to ride.*

Charley chuckles. "Imagine: if I'd been ten minutes later, or even just five."

Emma nods. "We might never have met."

They both push back from the railing, and continue walking. "Happenstance," says Charley, shaking his head, "pure happenstance."

ꙮ

Another Sunday in late April, Charley invites her to go up on the new electric streetcar along the Seventh Street Road to a spot above Florida Avenue. Until just a couple years ago, Florida was called Boundary Road, and marked the edge of the city. Here though, the large tracts of farmland are even now beginning to give themselves over to the radiating avenues and squares that echo the L'Enfant city plan, if only a tiny bit at a time. They alight at a stop on the section of the road that the city has lately named Brightwood Avenue, a small strip on the much longer Seventh Street Road that continues into the deep countryside of Montgomery County.

Charley guides her along the unimproved roads, grateful that the weather has been dry. At Eighth and Flint Streets, an unpaved intersection, he stops in front of a large, partially cleared corner lot, already staked with flags at the property corners. He sees that Emma understands immediately, though there has been no discussion of a formal engagement, let alone a wedding date; there is no need. He starts: "I've saved a good bit so far, about half enough to buy the property outright, but I'm figuring it will take another year to do the rest and have the cash to build the house...I know it's a little out of town, but I'd like to have room for a nice farm plot."

She turns to him. "I have some money. Mother insisted I save as much as possible so that I would be able to take care of myself."

He is vaguely ashamed to admit that he has calculated almost exactly this scenario to figure whether there is a hope of sealing this deal; it's her unblinking grasp of the situation and immediate partnership in it that prove he's been right about her.

Emma's eyes are on the property as she turns over the possibilities. "When can you sign the papers?" she asks.

Charley considers her as she considers the land. How different she is than any other woman he has ever encountered. By nature, necessity, and tutelage, she is thoroughly practical. He can clearly imagine her out on the frontier, breaking ground for crops or mixing mud to fill the chinks in the cabin walls. He has long wished to be out there, in the wide-open spaces of the endlessly possible. It will do, though, to make this half-acre of cleared farmland at the edge of the city into its own little frontier homestead. He's formed this vision in his head, and here is his pioneering woman, willing to pitch in and build it with him, who makes the vision complete.

☙❧

Mrs. Gamertsfelder sets the tray of lemonade on the small table in the kitchen garden and pauses for a moment. She loves to look at the neat rows of vegetables, thoroughly weeded, and the infant beans, sweet peas, and tomatoes already vining up the twig and twine trellises. They've already harvested some of the cool weather vegetables, like broccoli and cabbage. It's still early in the prime growing season—the tomatoes have only just gone in—but she has great expectations of how it will go: the tomatoes will inflate to bursting in their skins, their appearance on the dinner table followed by their immediate disappearance, devoured by boarders who sorely miss the fresh fruits and vegetables they associate with home. She will even be able to make a few extra dollars by selling the surplus produce at the farm stand on Wednesdays and Saturdays. Mr. Schultz always welcomes her selling at his stand, since her produce is top notch and helps to keep the customers coming back. And the best part is that she doesn't have to do a bit of it. It's all Charley.

"Can I get you boys anything else?"

"No, thank you, Mrs. G. Your lemonade never needs accompaniment," Charley tells her.

"Oh, go on with you," she laughs as he winks at her.

Her boarders are polyglot. She has Swedes, Poles, Norwegians, Dutch; Germans, of course—she especially loves the boys who are fresh off the boat, who bring news and stories in the native tongue, untouched yet by the English they so desperately want to learn, from a homeland she hasn't seen since girlhood. Every so often, she even rents to an Italian, as long as he is clean and comes with good references from an employer. But none of them are Charley, who immediately adopts her tiny garden as his own, expands it, and keeps it in sharp order. That Germanic instinct for military precision belies his easy-going cheerfulness and willingness to pitch in for her wherever he sees the need.

Mrs. G has taken in boarders since her husband died in the war, and her son in childhood from the whooping cough. So dashing as a young man, Niehls Gamertsfelder comes from a family of successful shipping merchants that builds the family home and business close by the bustling wharves of Georgetown's port, and makes its money on a succession of high-value products: tobacco, wheat, coal, lumber. But the port of Georgetown gradually loses its shipping channel to silt and flood, and its business to the railroad and the infringing federal city; and the Gamertsfelder family loses its fortune and its sons to war, disease, and bad luck, until Hedda Gamertsfelder, nee Sheckles, a mere in-law, is the last one standing.

She rents every spare room in the big house, two and even three to a room, and only has one hired girl to help out, so it is all she can do to keep up with the cooking and cleaning. But she looks after all her boys with redirected maternal pride, and Charley has never heard her say a cross word, even when Gretchen manages to tip the whole soup pot over on the wood stove, in a single motion not only ruining dinner but ensuring that another cannot be prepared. At the time, though, even Mrs. G has to bite her lip to keep the words back.

Charley pushes back from his knees to his haunches and stands up to stretch. Joe, who has been bending over, stands upright with a groan. "I told you not to do that."

"You always tell me not to do that."

"Pig head."

"Know-it-all."

Joe pours them each a glass of lemonade, and they drink in companionable silence. Joe knows nothing about gardening, but Charley has taught him to distinguish between the weeds and the emerging vegetables to the point that Charley trusts him with the hoe and the thinning trowel. Joe thinks of it simply as the difference between the good weeds and the bad weeds, but he certainly enjoys the final result. Plus, by helping out, he too gets to share in the profits from the farm stand—a jealously guarded secret, since he certainly doesn't want a crush of greedy lummoxes horning in on the bounty.

Joe has worked with Charley for a few years now, has been his roommate for only a little less than that. Younger by several years, Joe is happy to learn from his friend's greater experience in life, and grateful that Charley never lords that seniority over him, or laughs at the young country boy still new to the big city. The job at Engraving is the first he's ever had that's more than a mile from his family's home, and having to move into the federal city is overwhelming and, frankly, scary. Charley is the first person to find Joe the morning he shows up for work, looking pale and lost, and promptly takes him in hand. They are well-matched in temperament, both natural mechanics and self-directed problem solvers. They make a good team.

Charley surveys their work. "Need to finish up soon."

"Church *again*?"

"I can't help it that you're a heathen."

"Once a week is salvation enough for most of us...it used to be enough for you."

Charley gives Joe an exasperated eye-roll. "There's only so many places that are fit to take a young lady. I can hardly bring her down to McCreary's for a beer, now can I?"

There's a pause and Joe looks into the middle distance as he says, "So are you just waiting until the wedding to introduce us?"

He rubs the back of his neck as he considers this. So that's it: Joe presumes that Charley hadn't brought them together because he is somehow ashamed of Joe. Of course, that isn't it at all, but the plain truth of it is that he's afraid that Joe and Emma just won't like each other, and then what? Will he have to choose between his best friend and the woman he plans to marry? It's too painful to consider, and so he has simply side-stepped the issue. But now that Joe has brought it up, there is no sense delaying the inevitable, so it's just a practical matter of how to bring it about. An idea comes to him and without considering, he exclaims, "Crystal Spring!"

"What?"

"The racetrack up in Brightwood. It's right near the lot. We can have a picnic this Sunday on the grounds." Almost as he says it, he feels he should have thought of something less involved. Quicker.

They pick a spot to meet. Charley arranges to have Mrs. G pack a basket for them, and they decide that Joe will bring it, since Charley and Emma will be coming directly from Sunday Mass.

That evening, Charley waits until they are on her doorstep saying goodnight to tell her of the plan. It has taken him all evening to work up the courage, and even now he feels his resolve slipping. Once he finally gets the words out, she simply looks at him for a long moment and then nods. "Good night, then," is all she says.

And so, on Sunday, Joe sets off from the house, feeling conspicuous as he carries the picnic basket through the streets and onto the various horse trolleys he takes to get to the track. As he greets people along the way, he realizes from their smiles and nods that they assume he is headed off to meet with his own young lady, rather than that of his best friend. This is the part he doesn't like to consider, what his days will be like without Charley as a roommate. But now that Charley will be settling down and moving out of Mrs.

G's house, perhaps it's time he thinks about doing the same thing. Perhaps Emma has a friend. That way, he and Charley can still spend off-hours time together.

He is the first one at the appointed spot and considers what he should do. Lay out the tablecloth that Mrs. G has packed? But then what? There aren't many folks on the grounds yet, so at least there is no one right here to see him fidget. Finally, he lays the cloth so that he can put the basket down. As he straightens up, he sees them walking across the grass toward him.

Joe lets out a startled snort that he covers up by pretending to sneeze. If he'd been describing the scene to their buddies, he would have gotten at least one full-out, thigh-slapping guffaw. Charley and Emma are the same height, and while Emma is not at all fat, she is... solid. Substantial. Next to her, Charley, with his slight, wiry build looks for all the world like a broomstick with a mustache. It is a mighty comical sight. He forces himself to replace amusement with affability, but as they come even closer and he looks again, the smile slides off as he feels his mouth drop open, and he is not fast enough to cover that up. Joe has always imagined that Charley's girl is a *girl*. This is a *woman*—so much so that he can see gray strands salting her dark hair.

From his side, Charley's stomach hurts. He has watched keenly as Joe has gone from curious expectation to stifled laughter to open stupefaction inside of a minute. He can't bring himself to look at Emma; it's all happening just as he's feared. But as they finally reach Joe, a wondrous thing happens: Emma extends her hand, and in a warm, cheerful voice, says, "Joe, I'm Emma. It's a pleasure to finally meet you." Charley swivels to look at her, and he can't think he's ever seen a lovelier smile.

Disarmed by the friendly welcome, Joe responds immediately with his own genuine smile and says, "Me, too, Miss Emma. I was beginning to think we might never meet."

"I was beginning to wonder the same thing myself."

They both look expectantly at Charley, who spends a second with his eyebrow raised, looking back. Then he bursts out laughing. "Well, what a relief that we can all stop wondering now! My only wonder is what Mrs. G might have packed in that basket you've been carting around. Maybe we can take a minute and just see what, before the ants carry it off." He continues to chuckle to himself, and shake his head as he kneels down on the tablecloth. "My, my, aren't you two a pair."

Building 741

1893

The plan leaps out of the gate like horses at the track. The owner of the land is willing to hold the note, and recommends an architect, F. H. Kemght. In a happy coincidence, the builder that Charley plans to hire—George Dove, a childhood friend of his older brother Clarence—works with Mr. Kemght on a regular basis. Together, Charley and Emma sketch out the initial drawings, which Mr. Kemght refines into blueprints, and George fills in with the particulars needed to build the house. As the project evolves, Charley and Emma find that they work together well: their tastes are similar, they often see the same issues and possibilities, and each is willing to listen to the other when there is a difference of opinion. Eventually, Charley stops being surprised at how quick a study Emma proves to be concerning the ins and outs of designing and building a house.

This same partnership proves to be true in the matter of finances. Maybe if either of them had any acquaintance with how other people's relationships work, they would realize that money is not something that couples talk about. Unless she comes from a wealthy family, a girl typically doesn't have any money to speak of, and her intended doesn't speak of his at all, either before or after the wedding. Even if Emma and Charley realize any of this, it doesn't change anything. Neither of them harbor any romantic notions of the life they are undertaking; they need to be practical, and so they are.

Charley lives a frugal existence, and has saved since he began earning pocket change by threshing neighbors' fields or mucking stables. But Emma more than matches him in parsimony, and has a head start on him when it comes to savings. Because they aren't yet married, official paperwork demands that only one of their names show up on the deed, and because Emma is the one with the most earnest money to put down, hers is it. The landowner, Mr. Groff, is somewhat taken aback by this—even though plenty of surrounding acreage is held by women—but the check is good, which means the money is green, and that is all that counts. They work with Mr. Groff's attorney to set up a monthly payment plan that will eventually account for the full four thousand dollars plus interest that the lot costs them. The day they sign the final papers and officially become landowners, they celebrate by having a supper of cold chicken, potato salad, and apple-filled ebelskivers while sitting on a felled tree trunk near the front of the property.

The light of the spring evening is growing softer. Charley, his dinner only partially eaten, cannot stop scanning what is now his small piece of the earth. He paces in the clearing near the stump, and every so often puts together the steps of a little jig when he feels that he might otherwise burst. He is overwhelmed by a sense of pride that even he has not anticipated. "Oh, Emma, think of it! We'll put the vegetable garden over toward the southeast—good sunlight but not blazing hot in the summer—some fruit trees, flower beds in the empty spots. I know you'll like that, won't you? The house goes right here; we're practically sitting on the front porch! Since it's close to the street, we'll need to put in a little fence—something low so that it's friendly but still lends the necessary separation." He finally pauses, and lets out the long whistle of a happy man. "Can't you just see it?"

The truth of the matter is that Emma can't see it at all. She hears the words, and the excitement in Charley's voice, but she is unable to cast a vision in her own head. She finds this is true whenever she attempts to picture her future as it now presents itself. She is to be a married woman, the mistress of her own household, with a home and land that belong solely to her and her husband. *Husband.* None of these ideas resonate with her; after all, half her life has been spent in the certainty that these outcomes are unavailable to her. Picturing them has been pointless, even painful, when her future seemed fixed and unchangeable. Now, almost every day brings experiences she has never imagined, and she remains incapable of anticipating them. Sharing supper with her fiancé at the edge of their newly purchased property is but a small example. So she just smiles at Charley in his overflowing ebullience. "It's enough that you can."

ꙮ

Mr. Warner is a reasonable boss, fair and willing to look out for his subordinates, as long as they are punctual, put in a solid day's work, and remain respectful. He is among the many in the office who wonder aloud at the turn of events that sees Emma with a young man and an obvious intent to get married, quite beyond anyone's concept of feasibility. Mr. Warner can't wonder aloud among the office staff, since that would be fraternizing, so instead he shares with his wife the story as it continues to unfold. He can count on her eager attention to each new detail and periodic exclamations of amazement as he recounts the most recent developments.

Mr. Warner's agreeability makes it much easier for Emma to apply for the permit than it is for Charley, whose own boss Mr. Grimsley would never allow him to take leave during work hours, which is the only time the permits office is open. Mr. Grimsley communicates primarily in growls and barks, and sometimes in a full-fledged howl. The men in the shop presume that he hopes this management style intimidates his subordinates enough to keep them from noticing his thorough incompetence; the strategy is unsuccessful. "Old Grim," they say when they hear him gearing up again in the distance, "like nails on a blackboard." Charley chuckles and says, "Like sand in your boots."

And so it is that Emma asks and Mr. Warner gives his permission for her to leave the building for an extended midday lunch break so that she might apply for a building permit. She arranges in advance to meet George at the service counter of the office of the Inspector of Buildings to make application. A very pleasant older gentleman named Mr. Raymond meets with them to fill out the paperwork. George hands him a copy of the deed and a set of blueprints, and they walk over to a large drafting table that allows Mr. Raymond to unroll the plans; a leather-encased weight holds down each corner as he begins to fill in the permit form. From her vantage point, Emma is reading upside down, but she can still follow along.

APPLICATION FOR PERMIT TO BUILD
Brick and Stone

Washington, D. C. ______***May 15***______ 189___***3***___.

To the INSPECTOR OF BUILDINGS:

The undersigned hereby applies for a permit to build according to the following specifications:

1. State how many buildings to be erected: ____***one***____

2. Material: ____***frame***____.

3. What is the Owner's name? ____***Emma L. Miller***____

Mr. Raymond looks up quizzically. "My name is on the deed," Emma says, and nods toward the paper in front of him.

"So I see." He looks back to the form, and reads snippets aloud to himself in order to keep his place. "Architect...Builder...Location." His finger traces down the top sheet of the blueprints until he finds the notation. "Lot 8, Block 22, northeast corner Flint and Eighth Streets, Brightwood Park." He looks up at Emma and smiles. "Oh, that's a lovely area." He continues on. "Purpose? A dwelling...One family...26 feet front...28 feet deep...two stories...brick foundation... shingle roofing." He pauses for a moment, looking from the form to the plans and back again. "Hmmm. Flat, pitch, or mansard roof?" he asks himself.

"Well, it's not flat and it's not mansard, so I guess it's got to be pitch," George offers. "It's pretty steep."

Mr. Raymond smiles again. "*Steep* it is then. What means of access?"

"To the attic? We plan to put in a scuttle."

"Scuttle," Mr. Raymond says as he writes. His finger traces through the remaining questions, some of which contain words or phrases unfamiliar to Emma: what is an *oriel*? He draws a wavy line down through all of them, with the exception of, "What is the estimated cost of the proposed improvement?"

He looks up at her as he asks, and she realizes that she does not know the number that George and Charley have settled on. "Two thousand dollars," George says, and Emma coughs in order to cover up a small gasp. She isn't sure what number she has been thinking of, but it is not that.

Mr. Raymond scans the form one last time as he straightens up from the drafting table. Apparently everything is in order. He looks at Emma again. "That will be two dollars for the application."

Emma feels herself flush hot in a wave of panic. She hasn't thought to ask about a fee—why hasn't anyone mentioned it before?—and she knows she does not have that much money with her. She is so mortified that she almost doesn't see that George is already pulling the bills from his money clip to give to Mr. Raymond. "Thank you. Now, Miss Miller, I just need you to sign here on this line." He dips the pen, taps it against the neck of the inkwell, and hands it to her. Her hand is shaking, but she manages not to smudge the ink as she signs. He takes the pen from her and dips it again. "And Mr. Dove, here," he indicates. Then he blots the signatures, holds up the application to look at it one last time, and says, "If you wait here, I'll be back shortly."

"I don't have time!" Emma cries out before she can stop herself. On top of her surprise at the cost of the house, and the embarrassment about the application fee, Emma has been watching the wall clock with increasing apprehension. She can't count on Mr. Warner's goodwill extending into the afternoon; she needs to get back to work.

"Mr. Raymond, you don't need Miss Miller to sign any other forms, do you? I can wait for the permit myself." Mr. Raymond nods, and Emma breathes, "Thank you," quietly to George. She bids goodbye to Mr. Raymond and slips out the door, forcing herself to slow her steps as she walks back to the office. By the time she reaches the entrance, her composure is restored. She tidies her hair a bit, walks the two flights upstairs, and slips back into her chair.

By that evening, the episode has lost its sting to the point that she is able to make light of it during dinner with Mary and Charley, and again when George comes by the house. "When Mr. Raymond asked for the two dollars, I feared for a moment that I might faint."

"You did turn a bit pale there, Miss Emma. I'm sorry I forgot to tell you that I pay the application fee. But this might make up for it." With a flourish, he produces an envelope and hands it directly to Emma. She opens it and shares it with Charley as they take it in together.

No. ***2357***

PERMIT TO BUILD

DISTRICT OF COLUMBIA

OFFICE OF INSPECTOR OF BUILDINGS

Washington, ***May 15*** 189 ***3***
This is to Certify, That ***Emma L. Miller***
has permission to erect **one 2 story brick** building on lot **8**
Blk 22 Brightwood Park, Cor 8th & Flint in accordance
with application No. **2357** on file in this office, and subject to the provisions of the Building Regulations of the District.

She and Charley continue to admire the document long after they have finished reading it. In his happiness, he reaches over and squeezes her hand, and she responds with a smile. Charley folds the paper back up to look at the outside. The back of the document indicates that this permit had been recorded in the County Building Book, No. 13, Page 209. He flips it over to the front, and both he and Emma notice simultaneously. She gasps and Charley holds the document out to George. "This says the permit was granted on the eleventh. Today's the fifteenth."

George looks at it, surprised, and then lets out a good-natured laugh. "Well, whoever said that Government clerks aren't efficient? Here they approved the permit before they even got the application!"

ᘓᘏ

A hawk circling high overhead—in this region, almost certainly a red-tailed or red-shouldered hawk—wheeling effortlessly in the warm updrafts above the open farmland of Washington County, might notice, among the irregular and haphazard plots of cultivated farmland and uncultivated fields, a tiny grid superimposed on the land, an unnatural series of sharply defined squares stamped into the countryside. If such a hawk were to circle in for a closer look, it would soon resolve that the grid is formed by roads, to the extent that raw graded strips of land can be called such, that start and end abruptly for no reason that its hawk eye can discern, since, after all, man-made boundary lines are visible only on maps, not stitched into the countryside. Its curiosity piqued, it winds closer and closer to earth, until it glides past a sign that clearly states, "Welcome to Brightwood Park." Accepting the invitation, it selects one of the few trees in the grid to survive both farmers and land developers, settles in, and takes a look around. It considers that the food supply might be good here, since the land inside the streets still houses undergrowth of tangled brush, evidence of farmland that has lain uncultivated for some years. Finally, the hawk notices activity in one tiny section: hacking, chopping, a dragging out of vines and brambles. There's no need to hear it to know that under it all is the manic skittering of tiny, clawed feet, their owners shocked to be revealed in an instant naked to the world, and now scrambling for cover. Eons of instinct cause those red shoulders to contract automatically in preparation for flight, as an electrical pulse sends the signal: *Dinnertime.*

ᘓᘏ

Once the land deed is recorded and the building contract signed, Charley wastes no time. He and George have negotiated the price of the house based on the understanding that Charley is to contribute a significant amount of sweat equity to the project. It's also agreed that, if necessary, the house on Flint Street will take a back seat to George's other projects. The work will take longer, but the cost savings are worth it.

Evenings after work, when it's dry, Charley is out at the property. Every weekend, he has teams of helpers with him, at first clearing, then grading. Some of Charley's brothers come in from here and there, along with Joe and the other fellows from Mrs. G's boarding house, even Mrs. G herself, armed with tea, lemonade, and lunch. Emma does not hang back, but ties up her hair in a handkerchief, pulls on the leather gloves that Charley has given her, and sets to ripping out the vines that overrun the property. Mary Miller finally consents to come up on the cars once or twice to watch the proceedings—one of the boys produces a camp chair for her—though she grouses that she has no idea why they want to live all the way out here in the country. The shared labor establishes a fine camaraderie, and Charley watches as Emma laughs along with the others at the jokes and hijinks, and even joins in occasionally. When his little brother Billy shows off by balancing at the top of a huge brush pile, but slips and tumbles all the way down until he lands on his feet and cries out, "Ta dah!" as though he planned the whole thing, she laughs until tears roll down her sun-reddened cheeks.

Wagons pulled by massive draft horses trundle up to the lot to haul away the heaps of refuse, but it doesn't take long to open up the property enough to see it clearly. It is everything that Charley has hoped for: a few mature trees to keep the house and yard from baking in the sun, but good exposure for the garden plots, which he is already designing in his head. Most of the property is flat, but it slopes gently away from the spot where the house is to be sited; that will keep rainwater from seeping into the cellar.

It is that cellar that causes Charley some worry, since it has to be hand-dug; he needs the weather to be dry enough to keep the hole from becoming a mud pit, but not so dry as to become sun-cooked and impervious to shovels. George's crew is going to help, and Charley moves his week's vacation to coincide with their availability. If there's been a parade of vehicles to haul away the brush, then there is an entire battalion needed to remove the dirt that comes out of that cellar—and that's even after Charley and his pals nearly destroy themselves moving the rich black topsoil from the excavation site to the back of the property ahead of time. Below that is a rocky brown loam, followed by a thick layer of the heavy orange clay common throughout the region. At one point, even Charley despairs of ever being able to complete the excavation. Once they finally break through the clay, though, the digging goes significantly faster.

Finally, on a hot, muggy August day that drapes itself over everything like a wet wool blanket, Charley invites Emma to climb down the ladder into the ten-foot-deep rectangular hole that is now flat, smooth, and hard-packed. She navigates the ladder with some trepidation, but once on solid earth at the bottom, she breathes in the earthy smell and feels the delicious coolness of the space. Being here reminds her of a crisp autumn day amid damp leaves—more like the end of October than the middle of August. Charley tells her, "The cellar will always be the coolest place in the house in the hot weather, but also won't be freezing in the winter. Being underground moderates the temperature."

She touches the walls, fascinated by the distinct layers of sediment that make her think of a vast sliced petit four. "And next is...?"

"We'll pour the floor and then start the brickwork. That will take some time, but after that things should go quickly."

Quickly, of course, is a relative concept. The floor is poured and has time to cure, but then a long rainy stretch moves in that delays the masonry work into autumn. George and his men are putting up a commercial building downtown that competes with the Flint Street project. Nonetheless, George is determined to get the house under roof before the first snow. That way, his men are able to work inside when they have time over the winter.

ജ്ഞ

Joe and Charley are in McCreary's after work, and Charley is closely narrating the saga of the roof installation, which is just finishing up. It is a week or so after Thanksgiving, which Charley spends with Emma, Mary, and the boarder, Mrs. Klingelhoffer. Joe, meanwhile, has the rare opportunity to go home to spend some time with his family and boyhood friends, and to sleep in his old bed, which he finds blessedly peaceful. Charley is a fine roommate, but snores to rattle the cotter pins. It is this thought that puts a comical but indelicate image into his head of a Mrs. Emma Beck sitting up in bed next to a gap-mouthed, unconscious Charley, her eyes aghast and her hands clapped over her ears. The image makes Joe snort beer out of his nose, which, while painful, strikes him as even funnier, so he ends up spewing beer out of his mouth also.

"What the hell...?" Charley demands as he mops himself off.

"Charley, you talk about that house all the time. When are you going to talk about a wedding?"

Charley cups his palm behind his ear, "What? What's that you say? Oh, wait." He makes a production of cocking his head to one side and hopping on one leg while he knocks on his other ear. "Oh, that's got it. Yep, I think it's draining out now." He sits back on his stool. "Lummox."

"Priss."

"So tell me how the thought of a wedding makes you spew beer all over me."

"I'm just wondering who gets to warn your Emma that she'll never have another minute's sleep once she finds she's stuck with you and your snoring."

"I don't snore."

"You snore like a tornado kicks up wind."

"That's not me; that's the mouse in my pocket." They both have a good laugh at this, knowing it is Charley's standing excuse for any socially unacceptable noises he makes. "And at least *he* doesn't spit his beer all over me." It's Charley's turn to be tickled by the image in his head and Joe has to wait for him to stop chortling to himself.

"So it's the mouse in your pocket that's keeping you from getting married?"

Charley takes a drink and considers the inside of his glass seriously. "It's a hard thing, Joe. I'm trying to do the calculations in my head of when I think the house will be done. I need to propose a date that overshoots the finishing, but not so much that feelings are hurt."

Joe nods sagely at him. "I see. And are you factoring in distance and windage to figure how far to lead the target? Good Lord, man, you're getting married, not hunting geese!" Joe rolls his eyes. "*Calculations.* What a piece of work."

Charley fixes him with a look. "Imagine for a minute, against all possible odds, that some girl ever agrees to marry you."

Joe does imagine for a moment—a girl with long golden curls, fetching blue eyes, a pert nose, and a light, tinkling laugh—and almost sighs out loud.

"Yes, well, you hold onto that picture, for all the good it will do you. Now, consider—you and she, freshly pronounced husband and wife, arm in arm, gazing stupidly at each other—how far you would go to avoid moving in with your in-laws." Joe's image of his twinkling angel shatters in front of him at the horror of such an idea. He even turns a little pale. "Right. So now you're not above running a few calculations of your own, are you? Windage! If only it was that easy!"

Joe's beautiful vision now wrecked beyond repair, he gestures to the bartender. "I need another beer."

ꟷ

"We thank you, Lord, for the food upon this table and for the family who is gathered here in your name. Amen." As Mary Miller finishes saying grace, she, Charley, and Emma make the sign of the cross before they pick up silverware. Mrs. Klingelhoffer is already eating. She is a Lutheran, and the prayer is not hers. She doesn't typically participate during meals anyway; the others have learned simply to talk over or around her.

When Charley follows Emma into the house this afternoon, Mary looks at him shaking out his coat in the entry and remarks,

"Anymore, I don't need to look outside to know the weather, I just need to see Mr. Beck come through my door." It is true that Charley has taken to staying for dinner only when the weather makes it impractical to go out and work the new property. But she and Charley have developed an easy camaraderie, and Mary looks forward to the rainy days.

"Well, old Grim stepped in it today," Charley starts, in between bites of pot roast. Mary makes his favorite dishes when the weather foretells his visits, and the meals grease his storytelling machinery into a high hum. "He was supposed to order two gross of shearing collars, but he ordered twenty gross. The two would have lasted us most of next year as it is, but we figure that since he's got no idea what a shearing collar is, he just thought he should get a bunch." Another big bite of potato. "So here comes dolly after dolly of crates, and the delivery boys wanting to know where to put it all. Well, you should have heard old Grim howling. He's got us all lined up, figuring on how to make one of us the goat." Charley imitates Mr. Grimsley's bug-eyed, open-mouthed rage, which makes them all laugh. "Then here comes Mr. Graves into the shop, standing with his fists balled up on his hips just a few feet behind Grim, and more crates just keep getting stacked around them. So here's *his* face," Charley demonstrates, "eyes all squinchy and his mouth in a tight white line, and he's boring a hole into the back of Grim's head. And all the while, Grim's still snarling and snapping at us, just as clueless as a coonhound with a head cold."

Replaying the scene in his head, Charley can no longer eat, and tears bead at the corner of his eyes, he's laughing so hard. Emma and Mary lean in, anticipating the story's climax. Even Mrs. Klingelhoffer blinks into engagement. "So here's all of us, stuck standing there watching, and trying for all our lives to keep from dropping to the floor in hysterics. Smitty even let out a big old toot just from the back pressure." Charley pauses to drink in some air and wipe his eyes. "Oh, but then! Here's Mr. Graves: 'Mis-ter Grims-ley!'" the four syllables spoken like individual words, and then,"—a sharp snap of Charley's fingers—"instant silence. We're standing there staring at each other, us and Grim, and you could almost see him shrivel up. 'I will see you in my office. Now.' Icy. To watch him slink after Mr. Graves, why we almost felt sorry for him." The final carrot and a wink at Mary. "Almost." He wipes his bread around the plate to get the last of the gravy. "Only took about a minute before those dollies were turned right around in mid-delivery to wheel those crates away." The story over, Charley continues to chuckle to himself, toweling his fingers off, and pushing back a bit from the table.

Mary shakes her head as she rises to put the kettle on. Emma is up now also, clearing dishes and scraping plates. Mrs. Klingelhoffer drifts away from the table; they won't see her again this evening. "Nothing that interesting ever happens in my office," Emma says as she spoons tea into the pot and pours the boiling water in. "It's all just gossip and speculation." She sits the pot on a trivet in front of Charley and sees him grinning at her. Her face reddens as she glances down and smiles too. "Yes, I'll admit that sometimes it's appealing to listen in. Saturdays are always the most interesting."

"Juicy," Charley nods. "Friday nights get everyone in trouble."

"That reminds me," Mary says to Emma. "Make sure you have your bag packed on Friday. I'll bring it with me on Saturday, and we'll just leave from your office to go down to the station. We should easily make the one o'clock train." She sees Charley looking at her quizzically. "Emma must have forgotten to mention that we're going up to New York this weekend to visit Mary. We always try to fit in a visit between Thanksgiving and Christmas."

It takes Charley just a second to realize she is referring to her other daughter. Emma pours tea for them as she says, "I forgot to tell you that I won't be here to go to church on Sunday. But that doesn't give you permission not to go. I just know you'll use it as an excuse to spend the whole day on the house. Oh, and you said the roof is finished?" It's not hard to grasp that there's been a change of subject, so Charley leaves it alone until he's saying goodnight, when he says to Mary, "What time should I be here Saturday morning?" At her raised eyebrow, he explains, "You need someone to carry your bags to the station."

On Saturday, he's at the door on Washington Street at the

appointed time to pick up a valise in each hand and tuck a box under his arm. Mary walks beside him carrying a hatbox and another small bag. It's an easy walk to the Post Office and from there to the B&P rail station on the Mall, but having the extra hands allows Mary to pack just a bit extra.

This is the first time they've ever truly been alone together, but there's no sense of awkwardness.

"Emma explained to you about her sister?"

"Just that she's in a home. Not why."

Mary nods. "It's hard for Emma, I know. She's always been exceptionally fond of her father, and she was the apple of his eye." She takes a breath, as though steeling herself for an impact. "When she was very young, Mary started having seizures. Not the falling-on-the-ground kind, just where she would go into a trance. She couldn't help it of course, and we never knew when it was going to happen or how long it would last. But it enraged Christian. He thought she was malingering. He got it into his head that she was trying to make him look bad, as a doctor. He thought that he could…" She finds that she has trouble saying this out loud, and realizes it is the first time she ever has. "…that he could beat it out of her." She has to make sure her voice is steady before she goes on, so she doesn't terrify Charley with a threat of tears. "She had no idea why he beat her. To her, it just came out of nowhere, so she didn't know what to do to avoid it. Imagine," she says, almost to herself, "imagine one minute you're eating supper and the next you're being lashed with a horse whip." She exhales in a long sad sigh. "After a time, she just retreated out of herself. She's in New York because I needed someone who could do better with her than I could, and my cousin up there knew of the home. She's done better over the years, to where sometimes we have a lovely visit. Other times, well, no. The damage was too much for time to heal." They walk together in silence for a bit. "Anyway, I wanted you to know, in case."

"In case of what?"

"In case it makes a difference." This actually pulls Charley up short, and he can't even think of words to say. "I didn't imagine it would, but I just don't want you to think we're keeping secrets from you."

Charley shakes his head as they start walking again. "Ma'am, if you want to get rid of me, you're going to have to try a lot harder than that."

They see Emma standing outside the post office at her normal exit, and she raises her hand to them. Charley lifts a valise toward her in return. In their last moment alone, Mary says, "Charles Joseph Beck, I say a prayer of thanks every night that you walked into our lives. I don't want to imagine what it would be like if you walked back out again."

ᘓᘐ

It is just after the turn of the year that Charley shares his plight with the one person who might actually be able to help him.

"You can see my dilemma, George. I need to make a firm offer so that her relatives or those busybodies at her office don't jump to some damn fool conclusion that I'm not actually planning to marry her. I won't have her held up to ridicule. But I've sure got no stomach for moving into her mother's house, no matter whether it's just a month or even a week. I'm glad to have her come in with us, once we're settled, but not the other way. It would be a grim way to start out. Inauspicious."

A sympathetic man, George can understand Charley's position. He pulls out his annotated pocket calendar, held together with an elastic band and stuffed to overflowing with calling cards, jotted names and addresses, thumbnail sketches, and more. Not for the first time, he considers what it would mean to him if he ever had to replace this most irreplaceable object. On a scrap of paper, he does his own set of calculations, scribbling down the variables as he consults the calendar. He considers the ongoing jobs he has, the probability of others starting up, the size of his work crews, historical D.C. weather trends for winter and spring, and the list of primary items left to be done. He squints at the reckoning for a moment and makes a few significant noises. "July."

Charley's eyebrows shoot up in alarm. "July?"

"Yup. That allows a good buffer for any mishaps that might creep in. You can feel confident in a July date."

"July," Charley echoes faintly. May is so often a beautiful month in the area—tulips, azaleas, rhododendrons, tomato starts—though sometimes on the rainy side. June is typically drier and still cool enough, the most dependable of the spring months. But July? July can reliably be counted on to make the hellish descent into the insufferable heat and humidity of a Washington City summer, from which the area does not escape until well into September and sometimes not until October. "Early July?" he offers hopefully.

"Mid-July to be completely certain."

If the house manages to be done in the spring, he can hardly ask Emma to wait until the fall for a wedding. And if George feels certain that July gets them a finished product, then it will be better for them to suffer through a city summer in their own home rather than in someone else's. "July it is, then."

After Mass that Sunday, Charley and Emma join the other parishioners bundled against the January chill and visit for a bit with friends outside the church. While Charley exchanges news with some of the men, Emma chats with Mrs. Schultz, who holds her little Marta, the Clark family with their flock of children, and Lillie Dietz, a friend of Emma's from childhood. He watches her, noticing how different she seems now than when he first knew her. Her normal expression has softened and become more open, and she engages easily in the conversation. She laughs as two of the youngest Clark boys play hide and seek among the ladies' skirts. Marta reaches out to her, and Emma takes her from Mrs. Schultz to have a private, happy exchange of the cooing that always passes between an adult and a baby. When he considers for a moment the flush that he suddenly feels, he discovers that he is proud of her.

As they walk together back to Washington Street, Charley says, "George feels certain that the house will be finished no later than July."

She smiles, mostly to herself. "I suppose a year isn't really a long time to build a house."

He laughs. "No, not when you're at the bottom of the list." After a moment, he clears his throat. "So I thought, if you're agreeable, that we might get married in July. Possibly mid-July?"

She looks at him and, after a pause, nods with a soft smile and squeezes his arm where her hand rests. They continue walking, each one smiling out to the sidewalk. As he delivers her to her doorstep, she turns fully to him. "Thank you, Charley. I...thank you."

"Thank *you*, Emma. I know I'm a lucky man." Without thinking whether or not he should, he takes her gloved hand and brings it up to press against his lips. He looks up to see a flush of pink in her cheeks, deeper than from the cold. She lets him hold her hand for another brief moment, then disappears into the house.

Charley stands on the porch for a minute, then hops down the stairs and dances a little jig out to the street. He'll be heading out to the house just as soon as he changes clothes and grabs a bite, but at this moment his mind is elsewhere. He tips his hat back on his head as he strolls up the alley, hands shoved in his pockets, and whistles a wandering tune, a happy man.

ꙮ

Though the space between January and July may seem expansive, there is much to do. Charley redoubles his efforts to move the project along, both inside and out, laying out the planting beds as early as February. As soon as the exterior walls are up, he basically moves into the shell, tying up his bedroll in the morning, coming back to the property after work, and falling back into his blankets well after dark. He keeps a minimal toilet set with him, going back to Mrs. G's every couple days for a bath and proper shave, and changes of clothing. One evening after Charley leaves, having stayed only long enough to clean up and wolf down some dinner ("Delicious as always," he says through a mouthful. "How can you possibly tell, eating like that?" "I just know," he winks at her), Joe helps Mrs. G wash the supper dishes, since young Gretchen is still distributing the week's clean linens and towels to the boarders. Joe works the hand pump and adds hot water from the kettle at her direction, and dries as she hands the dishes to him. Mrs. G gazes out into the darkness through the kitchen window. "It's not going to be the same here when he's gone for good and all."

"Don't I know it. I'm going to have to break in a roommate all over again!" He grins at her, but they each know the other is taking the loss equally hard. Joe consoles himself that he and Charley will still be a team at work, but he clearly sees that their days of sharing virtually everything in their lives is coming to an end. Who will he drink that after-work beer with now? And here's Mrs. G, trying to smile at his lame joke. "Aww, Mrs. G, Charley said he'd come tend the garden for you still."

"I know he did, Joe, and I know he means it. But he'll be a married man. I think he'll find very quickly that it will take every moment he has to get his own garden in order."

Joe looks down at the dish he is drying, and says, "Well, he showed me a few things, Mrs. G. I'll surely do my best with it."

At the boyishness of it, Mrs. G's breath catches in her throat and for a moment she fears she might weep. She flashes on an image of her own Heinrich—Henry in their daily lives—gone so long now, and wonders whether he would have turned out as fine as these two boys have. She hopes so. "Which will be perfectly wonderful, Joe, I'm certain of that," she tells him as she puts a hand on his arm. He reddens but smiles at her. "Now get on with you, and go make up your bed!" She watches him leave the room, knowing that one day she'll be watching him leave permanently, too.

ꕥ

Initially, Emma plans to wear one of the dresses she already owns for the wedding; she has a navy one that's nice, but it's meant for fall and winter. Surprisingly, it is Mary who encourages her to splurge on a new outfit, and together they pick out a dove-gray cotton lawn for the wedding dress. They justify the expense by reasoning that she will wear it to church during the summers. Emma is not a seamstress, but her young cousin Lil does beautiful work, and quickly too. Lil brings the unfinished dress over to Washington Street one Saturday afternoon for the fitting, and helps Emma into it carefully, as much of it is still simply basted together. Lil stands behind and joins Emma in gazing at her reflection in the big mirror. "That's a lovely color for you, Cousin Emma. I think it fits you well, don't you?"

Emma continues to consider her mirror image. "I've never had as beautiful a dress as this in my life."

Lil blushes at the compliment. "Are you excited? Are you nervous?"

"It's all going to be so different. I don't know that I've ever even *been* in a new house; I can't imagine living in one."

"I can't wait to see it! I hear it's wonderful."

"Do you? Well, as it gets closer to being done, Charley wants me to see it less and less," she laughs. "I think he wants to surprise me with it."

"I think that's sweet. What will Aunt Mary do now that you won't be living here?'

"Oh, she'll be moving in with us."

"She will?"

"We planned for it when we laid out the house. It doesn't make sense to pay rent here when we have so much space now. Plus we don't want her living here by herself. So Charley will move her in the fall. That way, we'll have some time to make the new house ready."

Lil nods, appreciating the sense of it. "And time alone, too," she suggests, then turns scarlet at having said it.

"But you should have seen Mother the first time we took her out to the property. To start with, it was the first time she'd been on the new electric car that goes out to Brightwood, and she wasn't sure about that. Then, the longer we rode out, the wider her eyes got. By the time we were standing at the lot, she was sure we were insane." Emma puts her hands on her hips in an imitation of Mary. "'Mr. Beck, I am a city girl! I never planned to take up farming, and I'm too old to start now!' But you know Charley: he had her laughing over it in no time, and believing it was just this side of Paradise. I think she's starting to get used to the idea."

Lil laughs at Emma's comical and accurate imitation of Mary expressing a strong opinion. She places the last two pins that temporarily hold the lace against the bodice and steps back. "Oh, Cousin Emma, you're going to be a lovely bride."

ꙮ

As time draws closer, it's obvious that there are sizeable jobs that won't be finished by the wedding date: walls won't be plastered in two of the four bedrooms, shutters won't be hung, and paint will be missing from most of the outside of the house. None of that deters Charley. He presses both Mary and the busy seamstress Lil into procuring linens and making curtains; Mrs. G he doesn't even have to ask. The women use their combined feminine touch to smooth the rough-hewn edges of the brand new house. In the last few weeks, they bring many of Emma's things over so that they will be in place when she arrives as a new bride. Charley collects furniture from the house on Washington Street and from a storage barn his family still owns, far out in Bladensburg. The one thing he decides to purchase, his wedding gift to the two of them, is a new bed.

Finally, a bit less than a week before the ceremony, Charley and Emma ride out to the house. From the streetcar stop, they take the short walk to the intersection of Eighth and Flint Streets. Emma realizes that it has been almost two months since she's been here, and she is stunned at the transformation. No wonder she's seen so little of him lately. They stand outside the gate in front of the big house; as he promised, the gate is low enough to be welcoming, tall enough to definitively separate the yard from the street.

She can see that Charley is forcibly holding himself still, giving her a moment to take it all in: the wide front steps up to the porch, the offset front door that goes almost to the porch ceiling, the unadorned but still welcoming entrance. Finally she turns to him, which gives him permission to speak. "Do you want to see the inside or the outside first?"

"Let's look at the outside." She can feel her own excitement growing, and wants to savor the anticipation of the interior just a bit more.

Barely a breath interrupts Charley's narration of the yard, which is more about the plans he has for it than about its current state. Most of the property is behind the house, and Charley has grand visions for it. There will be no summer vegetables this year, of course, but he's still hoping to get some of the cool weather greens in before the season is completely over. Two of the beds are ready for planting. Here's where the fruit trees will go, over there the nut trees. He has laid out some of the pathways through the yard with stones excavated while digging the cellar and the beds; one goes all the way out to the back alley, and another ends at the water pump above their well. Immediately next to the pump is the windmill. Together, George and Charley engineered this marvel and together explained the concept to Emma with great enthusiasm. She remains lukewarm to the idea, but has deferred to their expertise. This is the first time she's seen the windmill, more than two stories tall on its spindly stork legs. Charley's grin is so big as she looks it over that the ends of his mustache fan out over his cheeks.

"Does it work?"

"Wait and see," is all he will say.

As they walk around the sides and the back, still unpainted, she admires the steps coming down from the kitchen, the storm cellar doors angled up from the ground to keep the water from seeping in and to make the entrance easier to navigate. There are big windows spaced evenly around the house. Having spent so many years in a row house in a back alley where the sun barely waves hello as it sails past, Emma longs for the luxury of sunlight in every room. Those windows are hers.

Finally, they arrive back at the point where they started the tour, and Emma stands to admire her favorite feature, which is primarily her own design: the turret, created by a set of three windows on each floor, angled in what looks like the first three sides of an octagon. On the first floor, the windows bump out onto the front porch from the parlor. Up from there, the bay is part of the main bedroom—theirs, of course—and beyond that is the attic. The turret ends in a tall cone of a roof that makes Emma think of a witch's hat. She sees that someone has climbed all the way up there to cap the tower with a simple weather vane that points into the breeze.

They stand together at the bottom of the wide steps. For the first time, she notices the house numbers, black forged iron against a white, mitered board that hangs on a diagonal by the entrance: 741. They take their time walking up the steps to the front door, savoring the moment, and he ceremoniously hands her the key—more symbolic than useful it turns out, since it spends virtually all of its remaining existence hanging on a hook in the entry. She unlocks the door, and he opens it onto the hall.

With the exception of the turret, and the pantry and bath bump-out in the back, the house is almost completely square and built around a central chimney. Each of the four rooms on the first floor has a fireplace, though the main source of heat is a coal-fired furnace in the cellar. Starting from the entrance and moving counterclockwise are the hall, the parlor, the dining room, and the kitchen, with its small bump-out for the cooking pantry. Immediately across from the front door is the staircase to the second floor, with its four bedrooms, bath, and access to the attic. The attic itself has big dormers and the turret, a full-height ceiling and the same footprint as the story below—an open, airy, light-filled space. In contrast, the cellar is thoroughly utilitarian and subterranean, squat and unattractive but vital to the operation of the household.

Even with the many trips that Charley and his friends have undertaken to collect, deliver, and arrange furniture, the big house is still sparsely furnished, but she can see the care they have taken to make it welcoming. The effort that her mother and the redoubtable Mrs. G have put into sprucing things up is not lost on her either. A lovely bouquet of gladiolus greets her from a small table in the hall, and there are lace curtains at the front windows. She walks slowly through the rooms, admiring the familiar and unfamiliar items. The parlor is bare, with the exception of a large gilt mirror above the mantle and an older velveteen sofa, still nice, both from the Beck's storage.

The dining room has but a small table and four unmatched chairs; however, Mary's Schlegel family's buffet and china closet are here, having survived every move of the Miller household since before Emma can remember. Mary's furniture has begun to populate the house in advance of her permanent arrival.

They reach the kitchen, and Emma takes her time walking around the room, letting her fingers trail over each surface. Charley has succeeded in finding an icebox that is secondhand but lightly used and good quality. The woodstove sits in the pantry, which is lined with shelves, cabinets, drawers, and a countertop. Finally, Emma stands at the enamel sink, looking at the handles and faucets for hot and cold water; this is where the windmill comes in. As Charley explains it to her during the design phase, the windmill pulls water up from the well and pushes it all the way up to a tank that sits on the roof; the head pressure that gravity creates guarantees a good flow of water from any faucet. It's all a new concept for her, having grown up thinking that a hand pump at the sink is the ultimate luxury. When he and George describe it to her, she rubs her forehead. "What if the wind doesn't blow?"

"I can hand-crank the screw for the windmill to pump it up by hand."

She shakes her head. "I still don't understand about the hot water. If it's not heated on the stove, where does it come from?"

George sketches out a picture for her, as he likes to do whenever he explains a concept. The water heater sits in the cellar and has its own scuttle for coal; the plumbers' name for it, *bucket-a-day*, comes from the fact that the heater typically consumes a bucket of coal each day to keep the water hot. A large coil containing the water wraps around the heated core; water from the rooftop tank is piped into the bottom, and hot water pushes out from the top. "So when you turn on the hot side of the faucet, out it comes!" he concludes with a flourish.

To ensure a successful demonstration for Emma, George had stopped by earlier in the day to light the heater. Now she and Charley stand together at the sink, but she hesitates. He takes her hand and puts it gently onto the right porcelain faucet handle. "This is the cold. Just turn it this way to get the flow you want."

With his hand still on top of hers, she slowly turns the handle. Water streams out, and pours more forcefully as she continues to turn. He holds his hand under the stream for a minute, and she copies his motion. In the heat of the summer, with the tank on the roof, the water will almost never be cold, as it is when it comes straight from the well. She turns the pressure up and down, fascinated by the expanding and constricting flow.

"Now on the hot side you need to be careful because it comes out hot enough to burn you." He puts the stopper in the sink and lets Emma turn on the second faucet. Both are running into the sink now, and she can see the steam rising from the left side. Her mouth is agape. Charley swirls the water in the sink to test the temperature. "See what you think."

Again she copies him to try out the temperature of the water. It is decidedly warm to the touch. Then she turns the cold water off and lets the steaming water pour in.

"Just be careful," Charley cautions, and it is a brief moment before Emma pulls her hand back to keep it from scalding.

She laughs out loud. "Well, isn't that just something! Everyone will want to try it!" She continues to look at the steam curling up from the water pouring out from the faucet, *her* faucet. It is not to be believed.

Charley finally turns it off, smiling at her obvious delight. "Let's just take a peek upstairs, shall we?" They walk back into the hall, completing the circle, then up the stairs to the first landing. There, a tiny table holds another vase, this time with yellow rose blossoms that Charley grows in Mrs. G's garden. They turn up the second set of stairs and end at the top landing, where the railing opens a view to the floor below. First, Charley shows her the finished bedroom that is to be Mary's, which faces out onto the side yard to the west. Then the plumbed bath at the end of the hall that holds a sink, a huge claw-footed tub, and a flush toilet; they try each fixture in turn, to Emma's continued delight. There is not much to see in the two unfinished bedrooms on either side of the main bedroom but, finally, he opens the door to their bedroom. He has arranged her things around the room: photographs, keepsakes, ceramic figurines, items that have been tucked away in her hope chest for many years. New curtains hang in the four windows that will allow the cross ventilation that might make summer nights almost tolerable. Finally, she looks at the bed, his wedding gift to her, knowing that he sees her redden slightly. The pillows and linens are new to her, freshly laundered and ironed, with a coverlet that touches the floor on three sides. The bed itself has a high headboard of dark wood and a central finial. At the foot of the bed, under a quilt, is that same hope chest, which for so long held no hope at all. And to have ever imagined this—all of this, *any* of this—well, she could never have stuffed it all into that chest and had room to close the lid. She slides her hand under his arm, but can't look at him. Just as when he proposes, she simply says, "Thank you, Charley."

ꕥ

As their present to Charley and Emma, and to stave off the sadness of the impending separation, Joe and Mrs. G decide to throw a party for the bride and groom. Three days before the wedding, they, Gretchen, and the rest of the boys scrub the common areas, string lanterns in the back, set up tables, and put the small beer on ice. Mrs. G outdoes herself in the preparation of the food, helped in the endeavor by her new great friend Mary Miller. Emma invites some folks from church, family who are going to be at the wedding, and some old friends. Several of Charley's siblings and buddies from work join the fellows from Mrs. G's to round out the party. It's not long before someone starts a sizeable fire in the fire pit, and a little band forms with an accordion, a Jew's harp, two harmonicas, and a few sets of spoons. Soon after that the dancing starts. Charley, of course, is the first one out, dancing a bit of a jig and then—after Emma laughs and shakes her head "no" at his wordless invitation, but continues to clap in time with the music—grabbing up Mrs. G to start a reel as the other dancers join in.

Later, within the general gaiety of the party, Charley notices his roommate staring ardently across the yard; Charley follows the direction of his gaze and at the other end of it discovers Cousin Lil, who is blushing prettily and keeping her eyes on the ground, except for when she feels emboldened enough to glance in Joe's direction. From a distance, Charley catches Emma's eye and nods first toward

Joe and then to Lil. Emma sees what he means immediately, and walks over to Joe while Charley strolls to Lil and stands beside her. "Are you enjoying yourself, my dear?"

Lil is startled from her surreptitious flirtation, and her color goes from pink to deep red as she is caught out. "Oh, very much so, Cousin Charley. It's a wonderful party."

"Well, look who we have here," he says in false surprise as Emma approaches with Joe beside her. Charley makes the introductions between the two, neither of whom is capable of coherent speech or even, with the distance closed, of making eye contact. "Emma and I are going to get a glass of lemonade, if you'll excuse us." Over at the refreshments table, Emma sips lemonade as she and Charley watch the unfolding scene with conspiratorial delight. Joe and Lil have found their tongues again, though both still appear to be fascinated by the ground between them. Joe glances over at Charley and Emma long enough to offer a look of pure thanksgiving, and Charley winks at him. She isn't blonde, and her nose is rather more round than pert, but Lil is lovely nonetheless and, indeed, has a light, tinkling laugh.

Charley takes in the music, the light from the fire and the lanterns, the yard filled with his friends and future relatives, and thinks he might burst. Instead, he slips his arm around Emma's waist, boldly proprietary, and squeezes. She leans in against his shoulder and he feels rather than hears her sigh. Heaven.

༺༻

The wedding itself is a small, mid-week affair. It is a rare day in July of low humidity and a fresh breeze. Emma, resplendent in her lovely new dress, carries a nosegay of white rose buds and purple violets. Charley is in his suit, cleaned and pressed for the occasion, his mustache freshly trimmed and his hair damp combed. Joe, of course, stands for Charley, and Lillie Dietz, her childhood friend, for Emma. Among those on the bride's side are Mary's sister Katie Schlegel, down from Baltimore, and Katie's freshly smitten daughter Cousin Lil. On Charley's side are several of his many siblings: his older sister Margaret and brother Jacob; younger brothers Harry, Louis, and Billy; and Lizzie, the baby of the family.

Father Mendelsohn celebrates the brief ceremony. When he asks, "Who gives this woman in marriage?" it is Mary who answers, since there are no male relatives to stand in for the late Dr. Miller. No one in attendance offers any reason why the two should not be joined in holy matrimony. When Father Mendelsohn at last gives his permission, Mr. Charles Joseph Beck, age twenty-six until September, turns to the newly minted Mrs. Emma Lucretia Miller Beck, thirty-seven the previous February, and, for the first time, kisses her.

Midday, Passion Sunday, 16 April 1933

The day started as a soft, cool spring morning with a pale blue sky and transparent wisps of clouds. After breakfast, changed out of church clothes, the children stormed out of the house into the warming day and a sky of stacked, sculpted cumulus clouds, edged here and there in gray. Emma brings Tommy down after his nap, freshly diapered, and puts him on Lillie's lap as she sits on the garden bench. Lillie nuzzles the top of his head, his hair still warm and tousled from his nap, and breathes in the scent of soap and innocence that babies exude. He alternately tugs at the covered buttons of her blouse and chews on his fist, drooling with the latest erupting teeth. She watches the children urging each other higher on the swings, or playing tag through the yard, and notices that the wind is picking up.

Charley somehow convinces Francie and Charley Boy to abandon tag and help him assemble some lattice for the vegetable beds. Every so often she hears his voice through the general ruckus: the Swede saying, "Vas dere any pie in de vagon?" or another rough-sounding character, "Hey, lady, there's a hole in your stocking!" accompanied by his own uproarious laughter. She knows without seeing that Francie and Charley Boy roll their eyes at each other with every freestanding punch line. Emma has already reeled Margaret and Eleanor back inside to try to catch up on the loads of laundry missed this morning. It should be Lillie in with Emma, but Ferd, seeing that she isn't feeling well, volunteers the girls and himself as her stand-ins, which simply makes her feel worse. *Thank heavens*

Chloe is here tomorrow. We'll be back on schedule in no time.

Jeanie wanders over, frustrated with the game she doesn't quite understand and keeps losing, and grasps onto Lillie's skirt, leaning back and then pulling herself forward. Tommy is entranced by this, and Jeanie starts blowing bubbles at him each time she pulls herself in close. Tommy just goggles at her as he continues to chew on his fist.

Lillie observes this with a quiet smile, but all she can think about is finding a comfortable position and being able to catch her breath. The solidness of Tommy leaning against her is just making it worse. She closes her eyes, breathes in deeply, and turns her face toward the freshening breeze.

Ferd comes out of the house lugging the first load of wet sheets to hang on the clothesline; when he glances over, he sets the basket down and goes to her. "Lillie?"

"Ferd, why don't you take these two, and I'll start hanging the laundry."

He leans over and takes Tommy from her. "Are you sure?" She nods as he continues to scan her face. "You look pale."

"I think I just need to stand up and stretch."

Ferd tucks Tommy under his arm like a football, which always makes the baby gurgle with a drooly laugh, and guides Jeanie away with a gentle hand at the back of her head. "Why aren't you playing tag?"

Jeanie pouts. "They're mean. They said I was too little to play right."

"Well, let's just go see about that."

Lillie almost groans as she stands up from the bench, and pauses again to take stock. Her ribs are just as sore as everything else, but no more so, and they all feel sound. But she needs to rethink the wisdom of trading children for laundry as soon as she bends to grasp the first heavy, wet sheet. Hanging laundry is a chore in the purest sense of the word, but it's something she regularly handles without assistance. Now she realizes that she isn't going to be able to do this.

Charley glances up and sees Lillie struggling. "Charles, wipe your hands and go help your mother with the laundry. Frances, you too."

Lillie is glad for the reinforcements. She has Charley Boy grab the other side of the sheet, while Francie hands them the clothespins. The wind has truly kicked up by now, making the sheets even harder to handle. They are on the third one when the first fat raindrops start to fall. This time, Lillie really does groan, knowing how far behind this will put the household before the week has even begun. Charley starts to herd the younger children toward the house, and Ferd hands Tommy back to her so that he and the two children can take the sheets down again and wrestle the basket back inside. As she hurries to the house, Lillie looks back at the dark, swollen clouds, surprised that she has not seen the storm coming.

ꙮ

Surviving a rainy Sunday afternoon in a houseful of thirteen people takes skill and cunning. The best strategy is to get as many children as possible up into the attic, where there are endless objects to rifle through and games to make up: forts to build out of old furniture and blankets, clothes to try on, odd equipment in wooden cases to wonder at. Emma sends Margaret and Francie up to keep an eye on the little ones; Ferd carries Jeanie up the ladder and puts her directly under Francie's care. Then he, Eleanor, and Charley Boy take the wet laundry down to the cellar to hang on the lines down there. It's not an ideal solution, since the laundry always picks up the dust and dirt that permanently hang in the cellar air, and the faint scent of coal dust, mold, and something feral like cat urine or mouse droppings. But it is far better than allowing the wet sheets and clothes to molder while waiting for nice weather. In the kitchen, Emma and Charley work together to complete preparations for Sunday dinner. The roast has been in the oven since just after breakfast, and while Charley Beck prepares his legendary sauerkraut, Emma visits the work crew in the cellar to bring up the last of the green beans they canned in the summer. The early season vegetables and fruit are already starting to grace the dinner table, a wonderful gift after a winter of preserved produce, but she may as well clear the shelves of last year's inventory.

Ferd leaves Eleanor and Charley Boy to finish hanging up the smaller items and goes to look for Lillie, who is notably absent. He finds her in the quiet parlor, just as she finishes nursing the sleepy, heavy-lidded baby.

"Can you take him upstairs for me?" she asks quietly. "I think I'm just going to close my eyes for a few minutes." She breathes in deeply and coughs.

He looks at her as he cradles his sleeping youngest child—youngest for now. His voice drops low. "Is it the baby?"

She startles before she realizes the source of his concern—that perhaps she is at the start of another hard pregnancy. Most go smoothly, but a few have been difficult. "I'm just not feeling like myself today. I'm sure I'll be fine tomorrow." He continues to look at her, unconvinced. "Truly, dearest." Resigned, he leans down to kiss her forehead, then takes Tommy upstairs to the crib in Charley and Emma's bedroom. Lillie leans her head back into the sofa, taking long, painful breaths, and closes her eyes.

She wakes to the clamor of children and pots, dinner preparation obviously almost complete and the pre-meal frenzy in full swing. She notes that the rain has slowed to a drizzle, but that the cloud cover makes the light of the early afternoon look almost like dusk.

"Mother?" Johnny is standing beside the sofa. He looks uncertain, never before having seen Lillie nap; he rarely even sees her sit down for more than a few minutes at a time. "Gramal said I was to come wake you for dinner."

She smiles at him, still drowsy, but the pain that radiates through her body as she shifts wakes her up quickly. When she draws in a breath, she actually makes a wheezing noise. Now Johnny's eyes are big and scared.

She smiles again in reassurance and says softly, "Come here, sweetie," as she takes his hand and draws him to her. "Give your old mother a kiss." He leans in and kisses her cheek, then sits down beside her and snuggles into her as she puts her arm around him. She works to keep her breathing quiet while they sit for just a moment, but then, gently, she shrugs him out of her embrace and says, "Tell Gramal I'm not hungry. You all go ahead and eat your dinner."

Disappointed at the briefness of the moment, he nonetheless stands up. "Yes, Mother," he says, and then runs back into the kitchen.

She tips her head back again—it seems easier to breathe that way—but lifts it up when she hears heavier footsteps through the dining room into the parlor. It is Emma; seconds later, she is followed by Ferd and then Charley. With some alarm, Lillie realizes that the children have been left with no adult supervision.

Emma and Ferd look at her with obvious concern, while Charley hangs back a bit, rubbing his forehead hard with his fingertips. He curses himself for not having gone for Dr. Cavanaugh this morning, and for allowing Lillie to make him promise not to say anything. *Well, there's nothing for it now.* He moves to sit beside her and nods once.

Lillie's shoulders slump, but she looks up at them as she says, "I fell this morning. On the cellar steps."

The noises of protest and alarm start almost at her second word, "Why didn't you tell me? Are you hurt?" competing with, "I *knew* there was something worse going on!" Emma has been duped, and she turns her outrage on Lillie's obvious confidante. "You knew and you said nothing?"

"Mother, I *asked* him not to say anything. Since I knew you would both make a fuss." She rolls her eyes at Charley to make her point, but then wheezes and coughs, holding one side to dull the throbbing ache in her ribcage. "Beside, I didn't hurt anything when I fell. I didn't even sprain my ankle. I'm just sore."

"Why have you been breathing hard and coughing all day, then?" Emma demands.

"I've obviously gotten a cough from one of the children. It's just that the coughing makes it all hurt worse." There is silence, until Lillie says, "*Please* go eat dinner. It's a wonder the children haven't set fire to the kitchen yet." More quietly, she says, "But Ferd, can you help me upstairs first?"

Charley pats her knee as he stands up; Emma isn't moving, but he takes her by the elbow and walks her back through the dining room. Ferd helps Lillie from the sofa, and she holds tight to his arm as they make their way through the hall and up the steps. They needed to pause on the landing for Lillie to catch her breath. Finally in the bedroom, she leans on Ferd as he eases her to sit on the bed, then he kneels down to slip off her shoes.

"I'm sorry I didn't say anything, dearest," she says quietly. "I just didn't want to worry you, and I truly didn't think it was anything. I still don't. It's just one thing to *know* you're going to ache all over, and another thing to actually *feel* it."

He looks up at her as he slips off the second shoe and she smiles at him. He wants to be stern because he is still upset with her, but cannot keep from smiling back. "Do you want to lie down?" He turns to get her nightdress from the hook, but she stops him.

"Maybe soaking in the bath with some Epsom salts will help, with both the cough and the ache."

He helps her back up again, and into the bathroom, where she sits on the closed lid of the toilet, wheezing a little and coughing every so often, while he starts the bathwater and retrieves the salts from the linen closet. He helps her out of her clothes and into the hot bath, where she lays her head back and breathes in the steam. She coughs hard several times, but then quiets down. Ferd sits on the rolled lip of the big tub, gently stroking Lillie's hair, which is still pinned up as it always is during the day. With her eyes closed, Lillie smiles, and feels her breath easing.

There is a sharp rap on the door as it simultaneously opens. Emma steps in, carrying the same nightdress that Ferd reached for. The immediate frigid silence between Emma and Ferd is palpable, and Lillie feels herself squeezed in the space between them. Ferd instinctively slides over on the edge of the tub, blocking Emma from Lillie, and rebuffing her calculated intrusion. To Lillie, the silence is so deep that it pulls her backward, and takes all the air with it.

"She needs her mother."

"She *wants* her husband."

Lillie slides her hand up to rest on Ferd's; she feels him flinch at the signal, and that makes her chest hurt worse. "It's all right, dearest," she says, as softly as possible. Rigidly, Ferd stands, brushes past Emma without a glance, and shuts the door behind him.

Unconcerned, Emma takes Ferd's spot on the edge of the tub and also begins to stroke Lillie's hair. After a long silence, Emma asks quietly, "Have you passed any blood?"

"No. I haven't noticed any."

"That's a good sign."

"I know. I've been worried since it happened." She is caught in a brief coughing fit, and realizes that her nose is running. Emma hands her a cloth, and they both see that it comes away dark, a sooty color. "I've been seeing *that* all day, though." She breathes in the steam. "Well, I certainly kicked up a cloud of dust. It was almost as bad as beating the carpets!" Emma smiles back, and Lillie slides down farther in the tub. "I think this is helping a little."

They sit in silence except for the rasping of her breath. Emma puts the back of her hand against Lillie's forehead; it is an automatic gesture, since the heat from the bath renders any diagnosis invalid. "The cough came on awfully fast, though."

Lillie's laugh makes her cough. "Mother, in this household, it's a true wonder that we're all not sick in our beds every day of the year."

Emma smiles. "It's that hardy German stock. It takes a lot to keep us down."

The water is cooling, so Emma helps her up and out of the tub and wraps her in a bath towel, just as she does when Lillie is a child. "I'll turn down the bed for you."

When Lillie comes into the bedroom, pillows are stacked against the headboard; lying flat with a cough only makes it worse. The linens are turned down, and Emma draws the shades. She helps Lillie in and pulls the covers up.

"I'm committing one of the seven deadly sins. It's nothing but sloth to be in bed at three o'clock in the afternoon."

"You just need to rest up a bit. I'll bring you some tea and the hot water bottle."

"Thank you. But Mother..."

"Yes, darling?"

"Please have Ferd bring them up."

Emma pauses with her hand on the doorknob, meets Lillie's matter-of-fact gaze, and finally nods as she closes the door.

Baby

1894-1902

The Becks of 741 Flint Street, Brightwood Park, quickly fall into a routine. Their day starts earlier than before the wedding, now that they take the streetcar all the way into town. Charley is in charge of packing the lunch pails, typically from supper leftovers of the night before. They ride home together also, often stopping at the market for the evening's groceries. Early evenings typically consist of Charley's gardening or finishing another item on the house's to-do list while Emma makes supper. On Saturdays, when Emma works until noon, George lends Charley a small work crew so he can finish the larger remaining jobs. Once again, there is a sense of urgency in the work, as Charley continues the preparation to move Mary into the new house. Saturday evenings and Sundays after Mass are their times to socialize with friends and family.

There are, of course, a few surprises on both sides for the newlyweds. For example, Joe's prediction of Emma's disrupted sleep, courtesy of Charley's snoring, proves true. More unexpected, though, is that Charley experiences the same problem.

One morning before breakfast, Charley stands at the window gazing out at the backyard, and starts to chuckle. "It's a surprise we have any trees left in the mornings at all, what with all the wood-sawing we're doing around here."

Emma smiles to herself, relieved that he knows the problem, until she realizes that he said *we*. She is stunned into horrified silence.

When he notices her lack of response, he turns to look at her and immediately realizes his mistake; she is as red as a ripe tomato. "Oh, Em, I'm sorry. I was just teasing. I wasn't meaning to hurt your feelings."

She can hear that her voice is thick. "Is it horrible?"

"Of course not. I'm just so used to Joe always giving me a fit about snoring—well, about all sorts of things. I just forgot you don't have a Joe."

"Well," she says slowly as she finds a smile, "I guess you're my Joe now."

From then on, they each know that the first asleep gets the better rest. Eventually, the tacit understanding develops that either party can give the other a tap—or a shove, as the occasion demands—to prompt a shift in position. In the end, though, Charley comes out far ahead in the bargain as he grows increasingly deaf.

Emma is most surprised to learn that her husband reads the newspapers every day from beginning to end. Though he has little formal education, Charley sops up knowledge like soft bread through gravy and is always greedy for the next bite. It's helpful that he has no particular political bent, since as a resident of the Federal City he has no voting rights whatever. "Politicians are like bad relatives," he likes to say. "You get no say in who they are, and there's no getting rid of them." So he finds as much humor in the foibles and general idiocy of all politicians as he does in the funny papers, which he likes to save for last. Emma enjoys that he reads snippets to her while she prepares supper, or in the evenings when she mends by the gaslight. Sometimes the item he's reading strikes his funny bone with such force that he loses his breath from laughing and can't finish.

For his part, Charley finds himself fascinated by Emma's hair. With few exceptions, he had never seen a woman with her hair down, and Emma's falls almost to her waist. That it is salted with gray is of no concern to him. Before they retire for the night, he watches her brush it out as she sits at her dressing table, fifty times on each side, until it shines. Occasionally, he asks if he can brush it for her, and that sweetly intimate act will sometimes lead to others.

Perhaps three months after the wedding, they meet Mary at St. Patrick's one Sunday for early Mass. She is within a week of moving in with them, now that they have met all the terms of the curmudgeonly landlord to ensure he doesn't hold them up for money. After Mass today, they intend to settle the plans for the final move. Mary is chatting with another parishioner and turns at Charley's call. He bows over her extended hand, the unserious greeting they have created between themselves, and Emma kisses her mother's cheek. Mary notices her pallor and looks closely at her. "You're not feeling well."

"It's nothing. I've just been under the weather lately."

"Have you gotten sick?"

"Only once or twice. But it passes. I'll be fine by dinner time."

Mary puts her hand to her own brow and shakes her head. "Lord, child." The church bells start to ring, summoning the parishioners in for Mass, and they all turn to walk inside. "Do you not know that you're expecting?"

Charley nearly stumbles, but they are across the threshold already, and all conversation ceases. Though they maintain the proper decorum during the Mass, Charley's little finger seeks out Emma's to give it a reassuring brush. Expecting? Who would have expected that?

ഇ ര

The memory box holds so many treasures, but chief among them is Emma's diary, which Lillie reads for the first time when she is pregnant with Margaret and Emma presents it to her. Whenever it's time to open the box again, Lillie is drawn to the diary first. Though she will settle in later to read in earnest, initially she simply skims the twelve years recorded there. She stops at entries as they catch her eye, and even though each one is long since written in her memory, there is always a sense of discovery, as though the recorded days are the glass pieces in a kaleidoscope that arrange themselves into a new image with each successive turn.

From Emma's Diary

Sunday, September 1, 1895: Sunday at 3 p.m. we had the baby christened in St. Patrick's Church by Father McGhee. It was a cool day, cloudy nearly all day, but the sun came out while baby was being christened and set a beautiful ray right across the font. We named her Lillie for the beautiful flowers of that name, and May for the lovely month of flowers, and the month dedicated to the Mother of God.

Tuesday, October 1, 1895: Mamma left baby for the first time to go back to the office. How hard it seems. I sit here at my desk and think all day of baby and how she is getting along without me, but she is too young yet, to know me or to miss me. It is only mamma that feels the loss of the sweet little face and the touch of her little warm hand.

Thanksgiving Day, Thursday, November 28, 1895: Baby is four months old today, a very pretty day. After dinner we took baby out for a walk. We had not gone two squares when baby went to sleep, as usual. She was perfectly happy to be out and laughed and cooed until she went to sleep. Then I tucked her under my cape and she slept until I got into the woods in the rear of the house. Then baby stretched herself, looked around, up at the trees and the sky and laughed as much as to say, *Well I declare, here I have been asleep and dreaming under mamma's cape, when I ought to have been sitting up looking around and enjoying the beautiful sunset and the lovely woods.*

Wednesday December 24, 1895: Warm as a spring day and baby's first Christmas Eve. Papa and Uncle Louis went to the woods Sunday evening and brought greens to decorate the house and a pretty little tree for baby. We brought baby down Christmas morning and put her in the large rocking chair in front of the tree. She looked at the bright things and was very much taken with a little Chinese baby that was hung up by its neck. The little thing would go around and baby would laugh.

୨୦ଓ

January 12, 1896: Baby is very bright and has been laughing and romping all day, but it is Sunday and that accounts for it, for Sunday is baby's day. Mamma is home with her all day and baby just has a good time.

Monday, August 3, 1896: Mr. Claughton sent his carriage over this evening for grandma and baby to go out riding, so cousin Lil, Joe, grandma, mamma and baby went out riding. Baby enjoyed it very much.

Friday ,August 14, 1896: Today baby walked for the first time alone. When I came home she walked to me, then hid her little head in my lap and laughed, she thought it was fine fun. Now I think baby will have a gay time, and oh my, won't she be getting into mischief. Papa says he will have to tie her to the windmill to keep her from getting away.

Sunday, December 13, 1896: A beautiful warm day. A friend came out to take baby's picture, and oh such a time as we had trying to keep baby quiet for just a second. She would not keep still, so I guess we did not get a good one of her. We wanted to have the cat's picture taken, but Tom was nowhere to be found, but just as Mr. Heilman was getting ready, here comes Tom up the road. We hustled him up on the porch by the side of the baby, then baby began hugging Tom. Well, that would not do, so we gave baby a graham cracker to eat to keep her quiet. When Tom saw the cracker, he wanted it, so we gave him a piece, then baby would stoop down and get the cat's cracker, and so, between the baby and the cat, we had a perfect show. The cat would sit still a minute, then the baby would move, when the baby was still the cat would move, we laughed and laughed, and it was about an hour before we had the picture taken.

ജ൫

Sunday, January 10, 1897: Papa and I took baby out to the zoo. It was a beautiful day. The park was very crowded, everyone noticed baby, and said what a cute, lovely baby. She would laugh at everyone, go up to all the children she would see, and want to kiss them, or shake hands with them. She was just as happy as could be. We got home about dark, but baby did not even get tired. When we got out of the car at Flint Street, papa said to baby, *If you are tired and sleepy, Lillie, lay your head on papa's shoulder and go to sleep.* She laid her little head down and sang to herself all the way down to the house. Then when we got in the house, she played a little with Cousin Lil and Joe, I nursed her, and she went right to sleep.

Tuesday, February 2, 1897: Groundhog Day, and such a day: rain, hail, snow and wind, all day and all night, so that the little fellow did not see his shadow, and if he stepped out that day he got pretty cold and wet. Baby is well and at night when I go home I do nothing but romp with baby, and she enjoys it. I tell you, Uncle Henry was out last night, he played the mouth organ and I took baby under the arms and danced with her in the dining room out into the kitchen and hall, until mamma was nearly exhausted, but baby thought it was fine fun, and cried as though her little heart would break because I did not keep it up. Then we went upstairs and played hide and seek until nine o'clock. Oh, but we have lots of fun, baby and I. She is just beginning to say little things: *mamma, papa, Harry, ice, pap*, but she understands every word that is spoken to her, and is a sharp, cute, sweet little rascal that laughs and romps all day long. What would I do without her? What if I should have to leave her? It would be terrible.

Sunday, April 25, 1897: Papa and mamma took baby for her first long walk in the woods, over in Browns woods. Baby had her supper, then we gathered some violets. Papa carried baby home, we planted the violets, and today they are holding up their little heads, as bright and happy as can be, although I think they would rather have stayed down in the violet dell, where the ground was just covered with them. I guess they had a real jolly time down there, and at night, I expect the little fairies would come out to dance and have a good time with them, so it does seem a shame to bring the little things from their sweet home to adorn baby's garden. But then baby is so sweet and loves them so, and waters them and cares for them, that I am sure when they look up into her sweet baby face, they forget all about their fairy dell and think she is one of the little fairies that has come up from the dell to minister to their wants.

Thursday, October 28, 1897: A rainy day, has been raining

for eight days, and I have been home sick for eight days. Baby was perfectly happy and wild with delight, she never left me for a minute. She would sit on the bed and have her breakfast and lunch with me. Sometimes she would sit in her little rocking chair, but she would always put it close to the bed, then she would say, *Right here, where mammie can see baby.* Ma taught her to say Rock a Bye Baby, I wish anyone could hear her. After she had said it two or three times, she insisted that baby could do it, in this way: I would tell her a line, she would say it after me, then when I was about to say the second line, she would say, *Baby dood it.*

Sunday, November 28, 1897: Baby is twenty-eight months old, still the same happy little darling. When I leave her in the morning she will kiss me and say, *Mammie go away and lead the baby all day,* in the most woebegone little voice. She can help me do everything, her little hands are in everything. She can make bread, she can cook, clear off the table, set the table, wash the dishes and wipe them, in fact baby can *dood* it all. She is a perfect picture with her little apron on, her sleeves rolled up, and standing on a chair by the sink, turning on first one spigot then the other, to get hot water or cold just as she wants it, washing her hands, washing out the dishcloth, washing off the table and other things too numerous to mention.

ꟷ

Monday, February 7, 1898: A beautiful day. I guess baby is out walking with Aunt Lizzie. I wish I could be with her everyday. She said to me this morning as I was leaving her, *Don't lead the baby, mammie, stay with me.* And so it is every day.

ꟷ

Saturday, January 28, 1899: Baby is well, and such a sweet little romp, still as happy as a bird, and three years, six months old. How very fast my baby is slipping away from me. Sunday when I am home with her, she says, looking out of the window, *Sunday, you must stay longer, the other Sunday wasn't long.*

Sunday, January 29, 1899: Took baby out for a walk. She insisted upon a car ride, she wanted to go to the city, to her new green house, to see her children that were sick. Well, we took a short ride and came back, when we got out of the car she burst out crying and said, *Mamma you did not take me to my new house.*

June 3, 1899: Saturday I was swinging baby in the hammock when she said, *Ain't I growing mamma?* Stretching herself out. I said, *Yes, you are darling.* She said, *Ain't you sorry? Indeed I am,* said I. *Well, never mind, mamma, when I grow up I will get you another baby.* W*ell, I may not love that one as I do you,* said I. *Oh, never mind, mamma, yes you will. I will get you six of them. Ha!ha!ha!* Poor little darling, and so she thinks it is all right, and so she chatters away. She says she doesn't want her new mamma, she loves me, and I am so good to her. I said, *Where is your new mamma? Oh!* she says, *Down in my new house.*

Monday, October 30, 1899: A hop will be given for the purpose of raising money for the Catholic church to be built at Brightwood. Baby doesn't know what a hop is, as she has never been to anything of the kind, but she hears everyone talking about it so she says she is going. So of course that settles it. When papa and I go Monday night, we will take her up for a little while. It will be given at the hall over the hotel.

Well, we went to the hop, and I will tell you we did hop, baby and I. She kept me dancing all over the hall. It did not make any difference to her whether anyone else danced or not, she could dance. She had me skipping in and out and dodging in among the dancers like fun, and she was so tired and sleepy she did not know what to do with herself.

Friday, November 17, 1899: Baby told Christie today all about her family in Maine. She said she had so many children, and they were so bad and self-willed. *Why,* said Christie, *who do they take after, their father or their mother?* With a sigh, *I guess they take after me.* Christie asked her where she got so many children. *Oh! I borned them all, and had them christened,* she said. *Well, how did you do that?* said Christie. *Oh! I took them around to Father McGhee's and he poured water on their heads.*

Tuesday, November 28, 1899: Papa is home with baby painting the roof, fixing the chimney, and finishing up the painting of the house that he started in September. Baby has a fine time playing in the garden, especially while papa is home. She is wild for a baby sister, and she says she is going to buy one at the Palais Royal, she has money enough. She will tell the man that is all she has, and he will give it to her cheap. Bought baby a beautiful pair of patent leather shoes at one of the finest shoe stores on F Street, Hoover & Snyder's, price $1.50, another pair of stockings thirty-five cents. Now baby is all fixed up. Little white coat looks beautiful, little cap with lovely new pink moiré ribbon, quite wide, so when she gets it on she will look very sweet, I am sure.

ꙮ

Saturday, January 27, 1900: A bright clear cold day, and my baby is well, and still a very happy, jolly little girl. Her home is now in Maine. She has the most wonderful things there, including 300 children.

Tuesday, May 15, 1900: Bought baby a pair of tan lace shoes, she wanted them lace, $1.00, tan stockings, twenty-five cents, drop stitch. She had them put right on, dressed, and her hair braided in two little pigtails, tied with pretty pink ribbon. And she thought they looked fine and went up to see Lydia McElwee, to show her shoes. She looked quite like a little girl, and my baby has gone. How terrible it seems, to lose the sweet baby so soon, but she still has the sweet little baby face.

Saturday, July 28, 1900: A very hot day. Baby is five years old today. She is growing tall, but is still the same little baby, happy and a great romp and tease. We have had the city water put in the house, cost of putting it in $50.00. She is wild over it. She will go into the garden, turn on the water, pick the hose up and turn it full on her father. This she thinks grand fun, then she drops it and runs, then her father will turn it on her. They have jolly times together. I am home on leave and baby thinks this is fine, to come downstairs every morning and find me home. But I am painting all the walls of the rooms, and she paints too, but she is always saying, *Mamma, please play with me*, and so the time passes quickly.

And now August is here, and I am back at the office, and baby misses me so much and feels so lonesome.

ഊ

Monday, January 28, 1901: Baby is five years, six months old, a sweet lovely little girl, that wants a little baby sister. And when we told her we would buy one for her, said she didn't want any bought ones or made ones. So what shall we do about it? She says she doesn't want any boys around the house, because they are a nuisance, and if one came she would send it back.

Sunday, February 10, 1901: A beautiful clear cold day, a little windy. The new Catholic church was opened for the first time, Mass at 10:45. Rev. Dr. Elliott preached the sermon about the church and the Catholic Church. We took baby. She thought it was fine, but she got tired of the sermon. It was too much for the first time.

Thursday, February 28, 1901: Baby is five years seven months old, is very well and as happy as the days are long. She said yesterday, when I got home, that she had something to tell me, then she whispered that on Sunday morning at half past six she was going to have a surprise party. She was going to have a little baby one year old and a little girl past five. She was going to get them out of the Asylum. There were lots there, the sisters would be glad to get rid of them, and she could take care of two.

Wednesday, August 28, 1901: A very pleasant day, not too warm. Baby is well and growing tall. She is losing her little baby teeth, and getting her new ones. Of course she does not look quite so nice, but the new ones are coming in nicely. A little boy by the name of Felix Daily that waits on the altar has attracted our baby's attention. She thinks he is a cute little boy, and watches everything he does. She did not know his name for a long time, and would say, *Mamma, can't you find out his name?* So I did, then she would say, *Mamma, don't you think Felix would come down to see me and play with me?* She is the sweetest baby, and so cute about it. She has always said that she did not want a baby brother, but now she wants one just like Felix. It is too cute to hear her talk. She is so lonely, she longs for someone to play with.

ꙮ

Sunday, June 1, 1902: Lillie has been looking forward with a great deal of pleasure and excitement to the coming of her little cousin Theresa.

Friday, June 6, 1902: Lil went over to Baltimore today to bring her over. Baby waited up for them until 11 p.m., but they did not come, so she went to bed tired and disgusted.

Saturday, June 7, 1902: As I was going to the office in the car, Lil and Theresa passed me, so I suppose today the baby is happy with her little playmate.

Monday, July 28, 1902: A very hot day, but clear. Baby is well and is seven years old. We gave her a party. Twenty-three children were there, Chinese lanterns were hung all around the garden, the table was set under the English walnut tree on the west side of the house, lanterns were hung over the table, and everything was very pretty.

Tuesday, August 5, 1902: Bought a very pretty Jersey cow, $30.00. Baby named her Blossom. She gives nearly two gallons of milk a day. She is very gentle, and the children just played with her all day, and in the evening when papa milked her, baby and little Theresa kept the flies off with palm leaf fans, while Gertie held her. She had quite a reception when she came; Gertie, Lil, Mr. Blade, Lillie, and Theresa were at the gate to meet her, and we did nothing but pet her all evening.

Monday, September 22, 1902: A beautiful bright warm day. Baby started to school, and a sad day it was for me, I can tell you. She did not know whether she would like it or not, but I went with her and stayed in the schoolroom with her until school was dismissed at 11:30. Miss Byrne her teacher is a very nice sweet girl. Lillie was very much pleased with everything, and as Lydia McElwee and the two little twins of Mrs. Wertmueller, Hortense and Selma, went, she did not feel lonesome. The second day, I let her go up with the twins alone. I followed shortly with her lunch, stayed a few minutes, came home, went back at recess, saw that she had her lunch. Then when the bell rang for them to go in and she was seated at her little desk, I left her. Went back again at 12:30 when the little ones were dismissed, and brought her home, perfectly happy and delighted, and she said, *I had the best day at school I ever had*, and this was only her second day. Oh, how I wish that I was home, and could go up with her every day, and watch over her. But such is life, and she must take it with all the rest.

Monday, November 10, 1902: Today at noon, Lil and Mr. Blade were married, a perfect almost-summer day. Baby went from school to see her married.

Thursday evening, November 13, 1902: Baby was vaccinated by Doctor Loseham on Tennessee Street. The weather so far this month has been perfectly beautiful, they say it is Indian summer. The days are as warm as summer, the nights are perfectly lovely, the moon as bright as day, the air balmy and hazy. A pair of shoes, $2.00.

Sunday, December 28, 1902: Baby is well and is seven years, five months old. Lillie has had a pretty blue cheviot dress made with Duchess pleats in the skirt, waist, and sleeves, very becoming. A pink all-wool crepe, lined with pink silk, a little drop skirt of pink silk, with fine knife pleating at the bottom, yoke of pink silk, trimmed with cream lace.

The Barn out Back

1902

Washington City is unique in America for the full equality of its citizenry, the entirety of which is disenfranchised. Women, men, coloreds, whites: none of them have the right to vote for so much as the city dogcatcher, or even the President. It's an odd thing for a town to live hip-deep in everyone else's elected officials, without having a single one to call its own. The city is Congress's plaything, and since not a single one of the esteemed gentlemen hails from the District, it's an easy thing for them to bat the city back and forth across the aisle like a shuttlecock.

The one governor the city has ever known, Boss Shepherd, was good for the city but bad for Congress. Once appointed, he tore off on a three-year spending spree to bring a level of sanitation and basic services heretofore unknown to the population. Clutching L'Enfant's city plan in one hand, he used the other to direct the installation of paved streets and streetlights, water, sewer, and the beginnings of the National Mall. Without his intervention, the city might still be living with the open sewer that long ago was Tiber Creek. But Congress was alarmed at the price tag and quickly showed the Boss the door, slamming it shut on the experiment of the Territory of the District of Columbia and any form of Washington self-government.

In its place, the neighborhood became the primary organizing force for demanding, cajoling, hectoring, or enticing individual Congressmen to coax their cohorts into delivering some minimal level of services. Of course, the new, tonier areas like Kalorama or

Cleveland Park, with their built-in connections to wealthy senators, are awash in parks, sidewalks, and regular garbage pick-ups. Others have to try harder. Brightwood, one of the oldest of the uptown neighborhoods, grown from its days as the tollbooth on the Seventh Street Turnpike, learned this lesson early and well. It was the muscle of the neighborhood association that got Brightwood one of the earliest streetcar lines. Before electric was available, the hill up from downtown into the neighborhood proved a hardship on the horses, earning the car line the nickname *G.O.P.*: get out and push. But the electric to the cars arrived just in time to support Charley Beck's dream of living on a farm plot out in the country and still being able to make it to work on time every day.

Brightwood Park is the scrawny little brother to beefier Brightwood, but benefits from the association. For example, when city water starts flowing into Brightwood at the turn of the new century, the Park gets to drink from the fountain too. Though the city water is never as sweet and clean-tasting as it is from the well, and the change from gravity to pressure-fed delivery blows apart a few solder joints in their old water line, Charley is happy to say goodbye to hand-cranking water up to the rooftop tank when the summer doldrums hit and there's no wind to turn the mill. The galvanized bones of the old mill, disassembled bit by bit, serve for many years to prop up Charley's laden tomato plants.

Another boon from pressurized water delivery is the sudden ease of transporting irrigation to where it's needed, even into the far reaches of the back planting beds. This helps to smooth out the vagaries of the weather and bumps up production considerably, allowing Charley and Emma to squeeze an even more impressive yield from their slice of earth. Though the seasons are unpredictable—winter often comes and goes sporadically or never shows up or never leaves, and there are years when spring misses them entirely—Charley has a farmer's feel for knowing when the season has settled down to business and it's time to plant. No matter how beautiful the weather, Charley cannot be fooled into putting the tomatoes in ahead of schedule. For the vegetables, it's produce or perish; no one has the space or time to waste with a balky or demanding plant. Even the flowers, for which both Charley and Emma have a weakness, are expected to provide payback: the lilies-of-the-valley that grow by the thousands in the side yard are picked, tied in fist-sized bunches, and sold for a quarter apiece to Cammack's, the wholesale florist known citywide for his big greenhouses and excellent produce. The income is enough to pay the winter coal bill for the big, drafty farmhouse. Peonies go to the May altar in the new church, ants and all, but roses are allowed to exist for themselves alone, as long as they consistently bloom. The mystery of the wisteria is that in decades it never once sets a bud; Charley only tolerates it for the shade it offers the porch.

The Becks are not the only agriculturally minded residents to appreciate the rural character of Brightwood so close to the city. John Saul, who gains fame as a horticulturalist with a hand in landscaping the National Mall, has a forty-acre orchard just up Fourteenth Street that supplies the fruit and nut trees that Charley plants the second year at 741. There are apple and peach trees, walnut and butternut trees, all expected to earn their keep. Five Noir de Schmidt black cherries and three Montmorency sour cherry trees are breathtaking in the spring, but it's their fruit that allows them to hold onto the real estate. The garden grows in size every year, finally pushing beyond the boundaries of 741 and demanding that Charley lease the farm plot far out of the city in Hyattsville. But it is Blossom that makes them build the barn.

They've been considering the barn since they bought the property. Long ago, to dissuade himself from putting it under cultivation, Charley stakes off the spot, levels it off, and tamps it down. They calculate the cost of upkeep of various animals against the savings on milk, butter, eggs, cheese, and dinner's main course. That last may prove problematic, given that Lillie tries to adopt and mother every living creature she stumbles over.

They start with the chickens in the spring, but it isn't until Charley pulls a trailer up to the gate and coaxes out their new tan-and-cream Jersey dairy cow that Emma gets around to applying for the permit to build. She asks permission to put up a two-story stable and chicken house, to be built by one Charles J. Beck. As with the main house, the permit for the barn is approved the same day, though this time it's stamped with the correct date: August 20, 1902.

Initially, Charley plans to ask Joe to help him put up the barn, but circumstances conspire to make that awkward, so it is Mr. Reddy who steps in to lend a hand.

The barn is complete, fully outfitted, and snug against upcoming cold weather just in time for a fine stretch of Indian summer in late fall. But once it's done, Charley's evenings are free once again, so he has the luxury after work one particular day to stop with Joe at their old watering hole and reminisce.

"Oh, I think I knew I'd lost her almost as soon as she started working for the family. Her letters dropped off, and when she did write, it was all about them: how sad it was that the little infant's mother had died, and how bad she felt for the handsome, heartbroken young father, heir to the family business and whatnot." Joe smiles into his beer. "I know I'm not the sharpest knife in the drawer, but when she stopped coming down on the weekends and didn't want me to come up, it wasn't too hard to see where things were going."

Charley laughs. "But it sure took a long time to get there! How many years?"

Joe nods in agreement. "I know. Four. It took that long to get the family to agree to let him marry the hired help. Poor Lil."

"Well, even so, I didn't know whether it would be uncomfortable for everyone, with Lil and little Theresa here all summer, and Morgan Blade coming by so much. I just figured better not to poke at that."

"Well, no bad feelings on my part, for sure. But it was probably easier for Lil not to have me around. What time is it? I guess the big party's over by now."

Charley pulls out his watch. "Going on six. They're probably headed for the train; Em said they were leaving directly for New York City to start the wedding trip."

Joe lifts his glass. "Well, then, every happiness to the bride and groom. May they prosper."

"Here, here." They each drain off the last of their pints, and

Charley beckons to the bartender for another round. "And how is our own little Master Joseph doing?"

"Cutting through a few more teeth, so noisier than usual. Anna rubs brandy on his gums at night so that we can all get some sleep. But I tell her I used to room with you, and if I can sleep through that, a little squalling out of our squirt isn't going to bother me."

"Still with the snoring."

"Can't imagine how Emma puts up with it."

"She's only tried to suffocate me a few times. Nothing drastic."

The beers arrive, and Joe lifts his glass in another toast. "Here's to a man's own family, the greatest comfort that God ever invented." He takes a big swallow. "But back to where we started, at the finishing of the barn. So how is the cow, anyway?"

"Oh, she's a sweetheart. Good producer."

"When do you figure on breeding her?"

"Done already. Last thing before they put her on the trailer. We ought to be seeing a calf sometime in mid-spring. We're going to add a few pigs, too. Maybe some ducks."

"Lord, look out, it's Farmer Charley! You plan on doing your own butchering?"

"I don't think Lillie will let me get away with that. We've already had a scene or two over the chickens. I told her she could stop naming them or stop eating them, her choice, but they'd still show up on the table. But for the big livestock, I can see I'll need to ship that off somewhere else for the dirty work."

"Oh, but she takes after you. I remember she used to drag that big watering can around the yard. She couldn't lift it, but she'd tip it over to water the plants. A little farmer girl."

"She loves it. Even in the cold and wet, she'd still rather be outside in her slicker and *muddy boots* she calls them. I'm glad to see it. I hope it's an antidote for the other nonsense."

"What other nonsense?"

Charley rubs at the back of his neck and considers his beer. "It's the oddest thing, Joe. It's like Emma's afraid of Lillie growing up. She's miserable that Lillie started school this year, because that means she's not a baby anymore. But her solution seems to be to treat her like she's a doll. At least once a week, there's some new outfit she's had made, and I swear each one is more elaborate and ridiculous than the last one. You should have seen this creation she was parading around in the other night. It was all ruffles and lace and ribbons and beads, and to me it looked exactly like she was being swallowed. And there's Emma, all proud of how much money she's spending, ticking off to me what everything costs—the more expensive the better—as though that's the most important thing! She's like a human abacus!" Charley seems a little taken aback by his own outburst, and downs half his beer in one swallow. "I reminded her that vanity is a sin, and she draws herself up and says, 'Our baby isn't vain!' and I say, 'I wasn't talking about Lillie.' She's never had an ounce of vanity for herself, Joe, but with Lillie…good night! I can't stand to think that she's going to encourage her to become one of those empty-headed girls who flounces around in all her finery, acting superior! It's, it's…!" Charley takes a breath and sips some of his beer to calm down, then chuckles. "Well, it's enough to make a fellow stammer."

"It does seem surprising. I remember you telling me that you married the most practical, level-headed woman on Earth."

"I did; she was. Now it's like the whole world has shrunk down to this tiny circle with Lillie at the center. When McKinley got shot and died, she never once even remarked on it. If you asked her the most important thing that happened all of last year, she'd say it's that the church opened in Brightwood." He chortles into his beer. "The old Emma would at least have had something to say about T.R. being younger than she is. 'When did they start letting schoolboys be president? I've got stockings that are older!'"

Joe laughs with him; the imitation is a good one. "Well, you're still Lillie's papa; she'll listen to you if you tell her you don't like flouncy, superior girls."

"Well, and I've got her grandmother in my corner, too. She's the second most practical woman on Earth, and she and Lillie spend a lot of time together. Maybe between the two of us and her being in school now, we can fight the flouncy." But his laugh is half-hearted and his gaze is distant.

"Charley, you're actually worried."

"Maybe I'll just add to your toast from before." He raises his glass. "A man's own family: his greatest source of comfort. And upset."

Jubal's March

1902

"Be careful, Lillie. Don't fall. And don't spoil your dress." Mary watches from a few feet away as Lillie negotiates the decaying earthworks, scrambling up the steep slope using the toeholds that have been carved out by others before her. At the top, she laughs in triumph as she looks out from her high vantage point to the streets below. If it were Emma, there would have been no climbing at all, at least not in her school dress. Charley, on the other hand, would have been right behind her, watching in case she slips and egging her on to try the steepest part.

Mary has been waiting for Lillie at the school doorway. She often walks up to the Brightwood School as it lets out for the day so that the two of them can walk home hand-in-hand while Lillie tells her all the latest classroom drama. Today is so beautiful that Lillie has dropped Mary's hand to run the circumference of the big grassy area behind the school, to consider the unnaturally uniform hillock jutting up to surround the grass semi-circle, and finally to clamber up onto the highest point. Mary stands on one of several crumbing stone platforms that are arranged at points along the earthworks and is looking over the hillock now, too.

"What's that, Grandma?" Lillie asks, pointing to the platform.

Mary's gesture includes all the platforms. "These are where the cannons used to be."

"Cannons? Why?"

"Because this was a fort, Lillie. Fort Stevens."

Lillie is confused. She and Charley make snow forts in the winter and tree forts in the summer. This is nothing like either of those. None of her forts have cannons. "It's a fort?"

"Yes. There are forts all around the city. Soldiers used to be here during the war."

"Oh." She still doesn't understand but is afraid that she is supposed to.

"Do you remember we told you that your Grampa was a surgeon in the war?"

"He was here?"

"No, not right here. The war was everywhere. But do you know who *was* right here? Almost right where you're standing?"

"Who?"

"President Lincoln! He was right here during the attack on the city."

"President Lincoln," she echoes in wonderment. She knows about *him*: he was ten feet tall and the smartest and best man ever for *saving the union*. The meaning of that last part is still fuzzy to her, but she knows it's somehow very important.

"He got his tall hat shot off because he kept standing up to see what was happening during the battle." Mary stands on her tiptoes at the earthen wall and cranes her neck to scan the landscape, mimicking what the president might have been doing when the hat was attacked.

Lillie laughs at the pantomime, but still feels confused. "Who was shooting at him?"

"The Confederates. The Johnny Rebs." It's clear that Lillie has no concept of what she's talking about. "Here, let me show you. Can you get down by yourself?"

Mary walks to an open spot of dirt near the end of the semi-circular hill, picking up a stick along the way. She rests herself against the earthworks while Lillie crouches down to see the map that Mary starts to draw. First, she pokes dots to outline a large circle. "See, there are forts that go all the way around the city. This is Stevens, but there's Totten, Reno, Marcy, DeRussy. Many more."

"Why?"

"Well, this city is the capital of the whole United States. When bad people want to hurt the country, they attack the capital. So it's important that we defend the city against those people." She draws a line straight down the center of the circle. "And this is the Seventh Street Road," pointing from the line in the dirt to the road below, to indicate that they are one and the same. She continues to draw. "When your Mamma was just a little younger than you are now, Jubal Early's army came marching down that road from the north, planning to claim Washington City for the Confederates. And our army, the Union, came marching up from south of the city to fend them off."

Lillie's eyes are big. "Did they come to our house?"

"Well, our house wasn't even there yet. This was far out in the country back then, all farmland. That's why they put the forts all the way out here, away from the city. But I'll tell you," Mary pokes a dot next to the road almost in the center of the circle, "your Mamma, your Aunt Mary, and I were living *right here* when all this was happening, and I can tell you we were mighty afraid that they were going to march right into our house."

ꟸ

Jubal Early, triumphant in his last several encounters, has marched his army down from Frederick, having swept up and around from West Virginia. Washington City, until only recently well-defended by an army of eighteen-thousand men and nine-thousand guns, is down to about four-thousand irregulars—so irregular, in fact, that some of their number is made up of invalids rousted from the local hospitals—to defend the thirty-seven miles of fortifications that circle the city. General Grant has pulled the real soldiers from Washington into the siege of Petersburg, where the Union has General Lee holed up and increasingly cut off from his supply lines. When the news comes of Early's intention to march on Washington City, Grant dispatches seventeen-thousand troops to the capital, but Early gets there first. Some of his officers, who ride in advance of the Confederate force, find points along the breastworks that are entirely unmanned. Washington City suffers from a surfeit of generals and dearth of fighting men. In the very best tradition of the seat of U.S. power when confronted with a crisis, many important people independently declare themselves in charge, issue conflicting edicts, and remain comfortably above the ensuing chaos.

The city has lived in fear of a Confederate invasion since the disaster at First Manassas, and now, in the run-up to the fight for the city, her residents are infected by rumor, wild speculation, and general hysteria. Old Jube breathes hellfire, they say, and his vast army has burned Pennsylvania and Maryland to the smoky nub. Mary hears the breathless tales from the customers at her little dry goods counter at the back of the yard, the talk swirling around her. *Soon he will have shot lightning bolts from his eyes and leveled armies by pointing his finger.*

That's not to say she's sanguine; she comprehends the danger, especially given that their house is only one square back from the Seventh Street Pike. It's obvious that the Pike is to be the main thoroughfare for Union movement, and for the Confederates, should they break through the northern line of defense. She has two children to protect and care for, and her weak-eyed, spindly boarder, Mr. Briggs, has fled to his parents' farm on the Eastern Shore to avoid whatever is coming. He surely would be of no help in the crisis; his entire body twitches whenever he hears the talk. She is completely on her own. On this point, she finds herself angry rather than fearful. Where is Christian but hundreds of miles away and far from any fighting? Taking his ease, as he likes to say. He has left them to this, to fend for themselves as best they can.

To add to the misery, it is the hottest summer that any of them can remember, and in Washington City that is saying something. The oppressiveness of knowing the battle is coming is overmatched by the oppressiveness of the heat and the suffocating, wet-wool tent of inescapable humidity. Tempers flare amid the misery and speculation, but any threat of fistfights peters out in a lack of energy to engage. Decorum does not allow for any unpinning of high collars or sloughing of jackets for the decent folk, so the adults slowly boil inside their civilized clothing, waiting for the city to be overrun by southern savages. In the heat and anxiety, Mary closes her door to customers, unable to maintain her composure.

"Can you hear it?" Mrs. Slocum from next door asks Mary in the wrenching noon heat of July eleventh.

"Hear...?"

"The gunfire. It's coming from their skirmishers. They're harassing the picket line in front of Fort Stevens." Mrs. Slocum's husband is a veteran of the Mexican war, and the impending battle gives her an opportunity to display her knowledge of military tactics and terminology. She dabs her face and neck with a wet cloth while they both stand in the sliver of shade offered by their adjoining porches. Nighttime offers no relief; in fact, it often feels as though the thickened air wraps even more tightly in the dark, like a tangle of wet bedclothes that cannot be kicked off. No one has slept.

"But that's miles away. I wouldn't think..." Even as Mary starts to protest, she picks out the faint pops that come in bursts of five or six before trailing away. In her exhaustion, she feels tears pressing behind her eyes, and she retreats into the house before she humiliates herself.

She feels stupid from lack of sleep, disconnected and off balance. She has left the girls at the table in their damp underclothes; they both have heat rash, and, every so often, she stands them in the washtub and pats them down with cool water from the pump. To distract them, she has given Little Mary a chalk tablet to practice her letters, and Emma a square of muslin, a needle, and a length of embroidery floss for stitching. While Mary is out sweeping the porch, Emma has climbed down to lie on the cooler floorboards; she is asleep. Little Mary focuses closely on her tablet, rubbing off each set of letters with her rag before beginning another. Mary has coaxed her out of the habit of making a fist around the chalk, showing her how holding it in her fingers makes it easier to form the letters. While she watches, Little Mary wipes down the tablet and picks up the chalk to start the next set. There it stays, poised above the tablet, one second, two, three. Without thinking, Mary begins to count how long the seizure lasts. The heat seems to bring them on more frequently than usual, but it's impossible to predict how long any of them will last. This time, after twelve seconds, the hand finishes its movement toward the tablet; Little Mary writes a capital H, sees her mother watching from over her shoulder, and holds it up to her proudly. Mary smiles and strokes her daughter's head, but looks at the permanent red marks that show through the damp muslin against her back. She blinks again to push back pointless tears. At least without Christian here, Little Mary needn't fear the lash. Now they just have to survive whatever is going to come storming down that road.

As though on cue, she hears a commotion outside and steps onto the porch to see. She is surprised that the wave of dust and noise billows up from the south, when the threat comes from the north. Every one of her neighbors is outside, along with many others she doesn't know, and the undercurrent of urgent voices finally resolves into an understandable message, "Union." These are Union soldiers marching up the Seventh Street Pike, heading up to the northernmost forts of the city to engage the rebels.

Mrs. Slocum's war-veteran husband, Henry, rushes up their street from the Pike, faster than Mary might have imagined he could, given the heat and his age. Mrs. Slocum sees him coming and fetches a cup of cold water fresh from the pump. He gulps it down and hands it back for more before he's able to provide an update. Henry and a number of his cronies have formed a loose communications network that stretches all the way from the lines at the fort, through town, and down to the river. They are better informed than virtually all of the Union commanders who are feverishly working at cross-purposes. "It's the Sixth Corps! They came into the wharves by steamer, just now. These boys have been in it, Ida Mae; they are hard-fired, I promise you. Not office clerks and derelicts." He turns and spits, then drains his second cup. "We got to fill some buckets and get water down to them. Elsewise, they still might buckle under this hell's breath inferno, no matter how tough they are."

Little Mary comes out behind her, and then Emma, rubbing sleep from her eyes and tucking herself under Mary's arm despite the heat. For the moment, Mary is too distracted to shoo them back inside in their undressed state. Henry comes staggering out of the yard with two filled buckets, and Mrs. Slocum trails with a cast iron cook pot. It contains tomatoes she has harvested over the last two days, some overripe but still edible. She's been planning to can them, and finds herself relieved that she will not have to labor for hours over the fire now. "Mrs. Miller, perhaps you could take these down to the boys. I don't know that I can carry the pot all the way in this heat."

Mary glances down at the girls and back up at Mrs. Slocum, who tells her, "I'll keep an eye on them, don't you worry." Mary casts another glance at Little Mary, and Mrs. Slocum says quietly, "It's fine, dear. I know about her...spells."

"Go inside, girls. I'll be right back. Mrs. Slocum is going to stay with you for a little bit." She takes the pot, surprised that it is even heavier than she expects. She follows behind Henry, who again is moving with surprising speed back toward the column, even as he takes care not to slop too much water from the buckets. She is afraid she might lose him in the crowd, which grows thicker as they get closer to the soldiers marching up the Pike. Finally she falls in behind him and takes advantage of his ability to part the throng in front. When they break through, the dust is so thick that it is difficult to see and even harder to breathe. The afternoon sun is relentless, and the humidity squeezes everything in its hot, wet grip. There are the troops, moving by in an unbroken column, dressed in their battle-worn wool uniforms; it is a wonder to Mary that they do not simply collapse like a row of dominoes, one rank behind the other. Were she to understand what the Confederates have just been through—hundreds of miles of marching in just a few days, with back-to-back battles and now the march to Washington, all in the same unflagging heat and humidity—she might be thoroughly amazed, before hardening back up and saying, "Good riddance."

She and Henry are not the only ones who have thought to bring refreshment to the troops. There are many people rushing along beside the column, handing in food and drink. With a practiced gait, Henry moves with the soldiers, offering the ladle, which is passed hand to hand and then back again for more. Mary struggles to catch up, gasping, her arms numb and, she can feel, vast growing welts where the pot has been swinging against her. Suddenly the pot is taken from her; she looks up into the face of a lanky, sad-eyed man who holds the cook pot while handing out tomatoes to his comrades, who bite eagerly into the fruit and suck in the juices, careful not to waste any on the ground. She cannot keep up with the soldiers, so Mrs. Slocum's pot is handed through the ranks until it gets back to her. Even though the blond young man who gives it back has not gotten a tomato, he still touches his cap to her and says, "Thank you, ma'am. Very kindly of you."

She stands back with the pot at her feet, staring blankly as the column passes. With the excitement over, she fears that she is going to crumple where she stands. Her face is burning, but she isn't even sweating anymore, which Christian told her once is a bad sign. Even if she is capable of walking, she knows that she will never be able to lift that pot again.

Henry has fallen in beside her to watch the troops also. He looks over at her, picks up the cook pot in the same hand as the two empty buckets, takes her by the elbow, and guides her into the shade under a nearby tree. She sits down heavily, spots popping in her field of vision. There is a puddle of water left in the bottom of the buckets, brown with dust and already warm, but enough to wet Henry's handkerchief and hold against her forehead. Henry stands in front of her to help block the glances of passersby and continues to scan the scene, giving her time to recover in private. She is not the only one overcome in the heat; many onlookers have retreated to the shade, and some have truly collapsed. "They'll be engaging right soon now. Rebs would have been over the walls already if they'd been able to form up. No one there to stop them. Let's hope the rest of the Sixth and the Nineteenth make it here by suppertime." He pulls out his pocket watch to check the time and sighs. "We'll know soon enough." He looks down at Mary; the bright red splotches against unnaturally white pallor have evened out somewhat. Her eyes seem clear, and sweat beads have formed along her hairline. She nods up to him, and he takes her hand to help her up; she holds tight to his arm as they slowly walk home.

In Washington City, the afternoon and evening are an agony of waiting and listening. Sound does not travel well in the heavy air, making the boom of occasional cannon fire even more ominous; the echoing reports of musket fire continue to thicken. The shifting sound tells the tale of air movement that is imperceptible on human skin.

For the second night in a row, no one sleeps. The heat and humidity continues unabated, and Mary spends the night sitting up in the rocking chair. Though the sounds of gun and cannon fire slow in the twilight and finally stop in the full dark, they are replaced with what Mary now knows is the sound of troop movement. During the night, columns of men continue to march north up the Pike toward the front line. Henry has said that more troops would be arriving, and here they are. She finds the rhythmic sound comforting somehow, and she prays that these boys will be able to keep them all safe, and that they will be safe themselves. That young blond boy, so polite to her this morning: he deserves to have his turn to grow up into a man, to have a wife and a family.

She must have fallen asleep at some point, because she is startled into consciousness by the sound of cannon fire. Dawn is peeking in the window, and the air is the faintest bit cooler. It is perhaps nearing six o'clock. She dresses quickly and steps past the girls, sleeping on a pallet on the floor, cooler than their bed, out onto the porch. Henry is already outside, drinking coffee, with his foot propped up on the railing. She can tell from his boots, dampened with dew, that he's been out already. They nod to each other, and Mary realizes that she hasn't heard more cannon fire since being jolted awake. She waits for an update.

"It's too bad for old Jube that he couldn't form up yesterday. He'd have walked right in and had his feet up on the desk by now. But since the Sixth is here, I think he missed his chance."

Mary feels her heart flutter. "Is it over, then?"

"Over? Naw. The Johnnies never give up easy. It's just that it took 'til daylight for Early to see what he's up against, but now that it *is* daylight, he can't retreat." Mary blinks at him, not following. "We'd go after him. He'd lose more men by running than by standing." Henry scans the street, finishing his coffee. "No, it's not over. It's gonna be a long day."

The Millers and the Slocums spend most of it together. It calms Mary to be with folks who seem better prepared to deal with this; she feels as though she and the girls are under their protection, this battle-hardened old couple who as late as yesterday morning were arm's-length neighbors. Throughout the morning, she and Mrs. Slocum—Ida Mae—constantly listen for the sounds of artillery fire, and wonder aloud to each other whether the relative calm is a good or bad sign.

They are eager to hear from Henry when he makes it home for dinner, and wait in the shade of the back porch as he washes up and cools off at the pump. He is toweling off his face and hands before he finally speaks. "Say what you want about the Rebs, at least their generals are fighting men. Seems like ours are hoping to wait until everyone dies of old age and boredom. It makes a body wonder how we've held out this long."

Over dinner at the Slocum's kitchen table, Henry describes how some of the well-to-do have come out in their carriages to picnic and watch the excitement. "Guess they've all forgotten Bull Run," he snorts in disgust as he bites into a slab of bread and butter. Mary has not. The first time the war is this close to Washington, back when everyone thinks it's going to be a quick and easy victory for the Union, people do the same thing: consider the battle a form of entertainment, and go out to watch. In the bloody rout that ensues, picnickers are trampled, and the carriages of senators and bankers clog the river bridges so that there is no clear path of retreat for the hopelessly unprepared Union boys.

Henry leaves again right after dinner. Over the next several hours, the sound of gun and cannon fire pick up, but remain sporadic. It is perhaps four o'clock when he comes with the story about President Lincoln. Henry has been up near Fort Stevens himself, and says that the tall, gaunt figure in his signature hat and a long tan coat was unmistakable. "He was like a rube seeing the big city for the first time. He kept leaning over the wall gawking, and they kept yelling at him to get down. Bullets were flying everywhere, and here he was, just taking in the view. One of the men next to him was hit in the leg, and they still couldn't get him to stay down. Whatever damn fool let him up there in the first place is a bigger idiot than the president."

As afternoon wears closer into evening—to Mary, the day seems without end—the gunfire thickens. Suddenly, there is a resounding boom of multiple cannons being fired at once. Distant though it is, Mary thinks she can feel it through the floorboards. Little Mary shrieks and claps her hands to her ears; both girls begin to wail. The gunfire is now thick and continuous. Mary gathers the girls to her, trying to comfort them, but she looks wide-eyed over their heads at Ida Mae, who is pale but calm. "There's the root cellar, if it comes to that," she says. "I think we can all fit." Mary feels her mouth drop open. "But I'm sure it won't come to that."

"I wish Henry were here," Mary whispers.

"I know, dear. So do I."

The fire is continuous now, underscored by frequent cannon salvos. As Mary sits in Ida Mae's rocking chair with the girls huddled against her, she pieces together the rhythm and timing of the cannon bursts, which seem to be taking turns in strict order. The consistency of the sequence gives her something to hold on to; as long as the rhythm holds, the Union boys are still by themselves on top of the wall at Fort Stevens, holding the Rebs at bay.

The light is finally softening at the edge of the afternoon, though the heat hasn't fallen off. Mary manages to settle the girls down and get them to eat some snap peas and cold boiled potatoes for supper, but she and Ida Mae have no thoughts of eating. They both startle at the sound of steps coming up the front and onto the porch—Henry would come in through the back. The voice comes along with the knock on the door, "Miz Slocum? It's John Carter, Jack Carter's boy."

Ida Mae breathes out in relief as she goes to the door. "Jack is one of Henry's old friends." She leads the young man into the kitchen; he is grimy and has sweated through his shirt. The girls stare up at him from the last of their supper as Ida Mae sits him down and gives him water and his own plate, with some salt pork on top of the potatoes. He wolfs it down.

"Mr. Slocum asked me to look in on you on my way into the city. I'm bringing news to my daddy."

Mary and Ida Mae exchange a look. Finally, Ida Mae is able to ask, "And what *is* the news?"

"The Johnnies are fighting hard, harder than we thought they could. But Mr. Slocum said to tell you he surely believes that General Early will still have to fall back once it's full dark. He'll head back out the way he came in." In the long Washington summer, it won't be completely dark until after eight o'clock; a glance outside shows the shadows haven't yet melted into twilight. "Mr. Slocum says to say he's staying up at the fort until he's certain they're turning back, then he'll be home directly." He stands up, even as he gulps down the last of his water. "I need to get these messages to my daddy. Thank you, ma'am." There is a stillness after he leaves, and wordlessly the women sit, the girls between them, and watch as the light draws back up into the sky, leaving the land in muddy darkness even as the colors of the sunset linger above.

"The cannons."

"Yes. They've stopped."

"Mamma, what's happening? Is it bad?" Little Mary's voice has a quaver in it.

"I don't think so, dearest. I hope not."

They both strain to listen; the faint pop of gunfire is still there, but sporadically now. Soon, Mary can't tell whether she can still hear something, or if that is simply the after-image of the sound echoing inside her. And then even that fades. They continue to sit and listen as the darkness draws in, until Emma begins to whimper; Mary lights one of the lamps.

Both women hear it together and jump up: boots on the back steps and then the creak of the porch floorboards. There is Henry standing in the kitchen doorway. For a moment, the three are frozen in place. "It's over. They're gone."

Ida Mae takes two steps toward Henry and he closes the gap between them as she throws her arms around his neck, and he hugs her tightly to him. Mary sits down hard in a kitchen chair, and has to press her handkerchief tight against her eyes to hold back tears, her breath coming in uneven gasps. She feels like someone has caught her frayed end and she has unraveled in one pull. Henry puts a hand on her shoulder, including her in their shared release.

That night, with the girls pulled close against her in bed, she sleeps.

Happy as a Bird

1903-1908

From Emma's diary:

Monday, March 16, 1903: Lillie came from school today and told me that her teacher had said to the children in the school, *If you all would read as well as Lillie, you would do well.* She is very proud of this and works very hard. She says, *I am not afraid to work.* The days are beautiful and warm, and Lillie is working out in the garden, making her garden. She enjoys it so much, the cow and chickens are a source of great pleasure to her. She calls Blossom a spoilt baby, and says I am Blossom's mother and papa is Blossom's father.

Thursday, June 18, 1903: Blossom's little calf came to town on Monday, May 18th at 5:30 p.m. Looks just like her, marks just like her. Baby was sick with measles when Blossom's baby came, and we told her nothing of it until she was more than a week old. So one day I carried her back in the garden where Blossom was standing. The baby was lying down on the other side of her mother and Lillie did not see her immediately. Finally Blossom moved aside, then Lillie saw the little brown heap with her little head resting on her feet, and her bright eyes shining at us from under the honeysuckle. I think I never saw anyone so surprised. *Oh! mamma what is that?* And before I could answer, she said, *Blossom's dear little baby, why you dear little dot of a thing. Who brought her mamma?* So she has petted her and fed her, and now she is one month old today. And we tie her in the garden, let her eat grass and feed her, but as she still sucks her mother, she is not very particular about eating. She is a beautiful baby, and Lillie calls her Dimple.

Tuesday, July 28, 1903: A lovely day, baby is eight years old, and this evening she has had her party. About twenty-four children were there, the bale was set on the lawn, we had the lanterns all around the garden. Mr. Dorisey came out and took the pictures of the group, Mr. Brown came down with the Graphophone, which the children enjoyed very much. Lillie's spoon is very pretty and quite heavy, bought at Mr. Hines on F Street between 9th and 10th, cost $1.75.

December 16, 1903: Wednesday, looks like snow. Lillie wrote a letter to Santa Claus at the request of her teacher Miss Cole. She said in her letter that she had everything she needed, all she wanted was a baby sister. Dear little Lillie, she is so lovely and such a sweet baby herself, so well and so full of life and romp, just the happiest little thing in the world, and her cheeks are just as red as red roses.

ഊ

Thursday, July 28, 1904: A hot day, cloudy and showery. Lillie had her party, thirty-five children, but a storm came up just as the children were having their pictures taken, then such a scramble for the porch and house. Then, after the party was all over, the moon came out beautiful and bright. The children had a good time however; plenty of cake and cream, peanuts, caramels, peanut brittle, bananas, chocolate cake, jelly cake, coconut cake, and white cake iced for the birthday cake with nine little candles. Nine years old, dear little baby, just the same sweet child, and just as much a baby as ever, but she is growing so tall.

Thursday, September 8, 1904: Charley, Lillie, and I went to N.Y., had a nice time. Arrived in N.Y. at one p.m., went over to Brooklyn to see Sister. She is living at 365 Hoyt Street. Went down to Coney Island that night, saw the beautiful ocean, and all the many things that are to be seen at Coney.

Thursday, October 6, 1904: Charley and Mr. Reddy are building a small addition to the kitchen, and a covering for the cellar and kitchen steps.

Monday, October 31, 1904: Lillie started in with music, the Fletcher system. She is getting along lovely, and her teacher says she is the most delightful child she had ever taught. She is very fond of music, and I hope she will make a good player.

ꙮ

Friday, July 28, 1905: A cloudy uncertain day, but we had the party, which went off very nicely. There were forty-four children, and they all had a good time.

Monday, September 18, 1905: School opened and I went up with Lillie. She looked very sweet in her little baby blue suspender dress of linen and silk and a very pretty embroidery, and white goods for a waist, and her hair in curls. She went to the fourth grade, her teacher is Miss Alice Clark.

Thursday, September 21, 1905: A beautiful day. Lillie started her music with Miss Payne again, lessons $1.00, or $1.50 for two lessons.

Monday, November 27, 1905: Had Lillie's piano brought out, a Knabe, $500.00. It is lovely. She knew nothing of it until I took her into the parlor after dinner, then she smiled her sweet little smile, and buried her little head in my arms. She was delighted, and sat down and played her little exercises for us, but she was so nervous and excited. She did very nicely. Grandma came down to celebrate, Gussie was there, Charley and myself.

ꙮ

Wednesday morning, June 6, 1906: A lovely morning. Lillie was not feeling very well. I remained home from the office and sent for the doctor, Dr. Waters. He is one of the finest men I have ever met. He talked and joked with Lillie, and when I asked him if he thought that milk made her bilious, he laughed and said, *Did you ever hear of a bilious calf?* This amused Lillie very much. While the doctor was talking with her, Father Mackin came in to give mamma communion and when he had finished with her, he came downstairs, and as the doctor had left, he sat down to have a chat with my little girl. And there in the hall, as she lay on the couch, windows and doors open to let in the lovely June breeze laden with honeysuckle and roses, Lillie made her first confession to Father Mackin of St. Paul's church. She is ten years, eleven months old, and Father Mackin was so lovely to her that he quite won her heart. She is a sweet, lovely child, pure and untouched by the world, and always good and obedient to all.

Monday, June 11, 1906: Lillie is better and has returned to school. Last week was quite an eventful week for Lillie. She moved out of my room into her own little room, and I slept with her for two nights until she got used to it. She was rather timid, but she loves her little room so much and keeps everything lovely.

Saturday, July 28, 1906: It was a lovely evening. There were fifty children, and they all had a lovely time. We had the little donkey pinned up on a sheet on the west side of the house, and they had great times over that, then the peanuts were hidden in the bushes and the flower beds, and the children had a grand scramble for them.

Tuesday, November 20, 1906: Began exray treatment for my hand.

Tuesday, November 27, 1906: Second treatment.

༄

Friday, March 1, 1907: A cloudy, cold, raw day. Lillie went to confession to Father Rosensteel for the first time. This was her second confession. She is just as lovely and sweet and pure as ever. We have our own little chats every night and she tells me all of her day's fun and troubles.

Saturday, July 27, 1907: A beautiful day and night. We had the party, thirty-eight children and about twenty grown people. Ice cream was furnished by Freund and was very nice. We had nine large cakes, a half-bushel peanuts and seven pounds of candy.

Sunday, September 15, 1907: A perfectly beautiful day. Cardinal Gibbons came to Forest Glen to confirm the children of that church and the children from the church of the Nativity at Brightwood. We had fifteen girls and seven boys, there were about fifty in all.

Father Rosensteel, Father Mackin from St. Paul's Church, and Father Dougherty assisted the Cardinal. The children looked very nice in their white dresses and veils, and Lillie looked particularly sweet and innocent, which she is. After the services, the Cardinal stood on the porch of Father Rosensteel's house to welcome those that cared to see him. It was a beautiful picture, the Cardinal in his beautiful scarlet robes, the children dotted here and there on the lawn, in their white dresses and veils, people standing around in groups, the lovely lawn, the beautiful flowers, the birds singing and everything in harmony for the occasion. Lillie chose Cecelia as her confirmation name, Lillie May Cecelia Beck.

Sunday, September 22, 1907: Father Bischoff said Mass for the first time in our church. It rained all day.

ꕤ

Wednesday, March 11, 1908: Lillie is well and happy, is twelve years, seven months old and eleven days, and the dread time has arrived. It seems so soon, as she is still a baby in knowledge. Mrs. Hazzard, Ethel and Frank came over today to see us. Ethel and Frank went up to the school to see Lillie. She was as happy as a bird.

Evening, Passion Sunday, 16 April 1933

Ferd, in his outrage at being dismissed from Lillie's bath, is at the staircase before he hears the baby crying. He circles back to pick Tommy up in time to avert the eruption of a full-body wail. With the bathroom occupied, Ferd has no choice but to leave the full diaper, unrinsed, in Emma's chamber pot.

Downstairs in the parlor, the children have been firmly instructed to find something quiet to do. The older ones are reading, listening to the big radio, and completing schoolwork. Francie is having Dorothy read out loud, and is helping her to sound out unfamiliar words, while Jeanie naps curled up on the sofa with her ragdoll Sally, comforted by the lingering scent of her mother. Ferd interrupts Margaret's reading, another weepy romance novel, and deposits Tommy with her.

In the kitchen, Charley is just putting the leftovers in the icebox to be available for Sunday supper, which is always an informal event. He inherits today's meal cleanup when Emma disappears upstairs. Ferd takes over the last of it, freeing Charley finally to pull up his chair at the kitchen table with the *Post, Herald,* and *Star*. He chuckles over some pointless little senatorial scandal as Ferd finally joins him at the table, sitting heavily.

Charley looks up from his paper. He doesn't need to witness the episode to know what's happened: the four of them have lived together in the same house for sixteen years, and the addition of a new child every eighteen months has done nothing to dampen the hostilities. Early on, Charley knows, Ferd gives it his best, but

Emma, a self-contained force of nature, is implacable from first to last. Charley is a neutral party, incapable by nature of being drawn in and fully unwilling to take sides. But it pains him to see the toll that it takes on Ferd, who almost always comes out on the short side of any skirmish, and on Lillie, the prize for whom the war is being fought.

He is fully re-engaged with his paper when Emma comes back in. Wordless, she sets about putting the kettle on, slicing bread, and putting the toaster on the stove. While she's in the pantry, Ferd pushes up from the table and walks out of the room.

He is sitting on the sofa, narrating a picture book to Jeanie, who is still groggy and snuggled in his lap, when Emma appears in the doorway carrying the tea tray. "Take this upstairs."

Ferd looks at her for a long moment, then kisses Jeanie on the top of her head as he picks her up and sits her down on the other side of Francie in order to take the tray. He passes the secretary but then steps back, considering. He sets the tray on top of the memory box and smoothly lifts it all up, spilling nothing on his way back to the bedroom. Lillie lies against a bank of pillows that keeps her almost entirely upright, and her eyes open as he steps in. Ferd sets the box next to her on the bed and arranges the tray over her lap. He watches from the dressing stool as she drinks the hot tea, using its heat to warm her hands and soothe her throat. She dips the toast into her tea to soften it before taking bites.

She puts her head back against the pillows for a moment and smiles softly at him. "Thank you," she says, a myriad of meanings encompassed in two simple words.

When she is finished with the tea, he moves the tray and sits down against the headboard next to her. She settles into his shoulder, then lifts her head to look at him. "Have you had any dinner?"

"I'm not hungry."

She leans back into him again, closing her eyes. "Don't you worry about me, dearest. I'll be bright as a new penny in the morning."

He sits back farther, feeling the warmth of her against him. He leans down to kiss the top of her head and linger for a moment, breathing in her natural fragrance. Unconsciously, he strokes her arm, and listens as her raspy breathing settles into the rhythm of sleep.

As an hour passes, and then another, Ferd drifts in and out of sleep himself, waking at changes in her breathing, which seem to him to become more labored as the time passes. But she remains asleep and he does not disturb her.

He is startled from a light doze by a spasm next to him. Her arm has flailed involuntarily as her own gasp for air pushes her completely awake. He snaps up in bed and put his hand up to support the back of her head, which she has tipped back to help open her airway. After four agonized gasps, she is able to calm her breathing into long deep pulls for air, each of which is exhaled with an audible rattle. She looks at him with something approaching alarm. "I think I do need the doctor."

ഇ൦ഗ

Leo Cavanaugh, whose extended family sits down to Sunday dinner at seven o'clock, is just pushing back from the table when the telephone rings. It takes him less than thirty minutes to reach the house. Charley Beck stays downstairs with the children, while Ferd and Emma attend the doctor during his examination. Lillie is still working hard to breathe, but not gasping. Dr. Cavanaugh takes in the sometimes overlapping accounts of the day's events, which help to direct his examination. He feels for the soundness of her bones, focusing on the ribs just as Lillie has done, but finds no obvious fractures. The makings of ugly bruises have already appeared on the backs of her arms and on her shoulder blades, and the knot on the back of her head is the size of a hen's egg. It's obvious that she landed squarely on her back. He checks her temperature and blood pressure, and uses his reflector to check that her pupils dilate and contract appropriately; she does not appear to have a concussion.

He is forced to agree with Lillie's own assessment that she seems not to have done serious harm to herself in the fall, and even so he is at a loss to see a connection between the fall and her obvious respiratory distress. He does not need to tell her to take deep breaths as he listens with his stethoscope, which gives him a clear auditory picture of constricted lung function, but he hears none of the telltale hissing sounds of a punctured lung. He considers the suggestion that Lillie has picked up something from one of the children that has simply taken hold. When he asks, "Which of the children has been sick lately?" they each realize that, beyond Jeanie's chronic ear infection that's flaring again, there are no obvious candidates.

Softly, Lillie asks, "The baby?"

Dr. Cavanaugh sits back a bit in surprise. "How far along are you?"

"Not far." She barks out a sudden cough and has to catch her breath.

"Something under two months," Emma finishes for her. "She already told me that she hasn't bled since she fell."

"That's good. We'll keep an eye, though. First thing is to get you feeling better." He turns to Emma, and says, "Can you fetch me a teaspoon?" Ferd starts moving first and says, "I'll go," knowing it will take him far less time. Dr. Cavanaugh takes a medicine bottle from his creased back leather bag—the bag that always fascinates the children, with its hinged mouth that forever seems to be responding to the doctor's familiar command to *Open wide!* He takes the spoon from Ferd and feeds Lillie two spoonsful. "This will help you to rest easier, yes?" Lillie nods at him. "Stay propped up like that, too. Don't lie flat." He looks up from Emma to Ferd. "I'll stop by early, but call me tonight if you need to."

Dr. Cavanaugh stops on his way out to confer with Charley, who understands immediately that they're going to need reinforcements. He finds the number in the notebook on the phone table. "Chloe? Charley Beck here."

"Mr. Charley? Is everything all right?"

"It's nothing catastrophic, but Miss Lillie took a tumble on the cellar steps today…No, no," he hurries to assure her at the sound of her gasp, "nothing's broken. It's just that the Doc wants her to take things easy for a time, so I'm wondering if you can come a couple hours early tomorrow."

"You know you don't hardly have to ask. I'll just need to shift some things around here, but you tell Miss Lillie I'll be there bright and early and she's just to work on feeling better."

People are talking and laughing in the background behind Chloe; a deep, resonant voice is relating a story that has its listeners laughing with hoots and claps. "Okay then. I won't keep you; sounds like you have a houseful."

"We always have a houseful, Mr. Charley, just like you. We all just got back from Sunday night meeting."

"How's that gospel choir sounding?"

"Just like angels!"

"Well, you're one of the angels, too, Chloe. We'll see you tomorrow."

After that, it's time to start herding the children to bed, youngest to oldest. Emma and Ferd consider the alternatives for moving Bernie and Jeanie into another bedroom for the night, but Lillie insists they stay in their normal spots: Bernie in a small trundle bed under the window, and Jeanie in the crib against the far wall. Now that she is three, Jeanie is allowed to climb out of her crib on her own—though she gets a stern rebuke if she does it too often during the night—and she uses the little set of steps Charley made to get in and out. Tommy, of course, is in the other crib in Emma and Charley's room, and Dorothy is in with the older boys in the back bedroom, tucked into her cozy nook in the former closet. Only the older girls have a room free of young children. Tonight they help to supervise the bedtime activities of washing and brushing, pajamas and toilet.

In the Voith family, the one ritual that drains much of the eternal childhood resistance to bedtime is Lillie's tucking in of each child. The incentive of having a few uninterrupted, unshared moments with Lillie is enough to get each one into bed, under the covers, with lights out, waiting their turn. There is palpable disappointment as each realizes that there will be no such visit tonight.

Ferd turns the bedside lamp down low and settles into the chair next to Lillie. Bernie is already asleep, but Jeanie is standing up in her crib expectantly. "Mamma. Mamma." Her voice is neither loud nor demanding, just reminding that she is here and still untucked.

"Jeanie, be quiet," Ferd scolds her. "Your mother needs to sleep now."

"But—"

"Lie down and go to sleep."

"Ferd, let her come up here," Lillie says softly, already heavy-lidded with the laudanum.

"Lillie."

"It will do us both good."

Ferd sighs, but walks over and picks Jeanie up out of her crib and puts her down on the bed next to Lillie. "You be quiet and be still."

Jeanie snuggles up close against Lillie, tucking against her side and under the weight of her arm, breathing in her familiar, comforting scent. It is the first time she has ever been allowed to do such a thing. They are both practically asleep already. "I love you, Mamma."

"I love you too, sweetie bug."

History Lessons

1910

Mary hears the footsteps on the front walk, up the front steps, and onto the porch. *Lillie's home.* The door, however, doesn't open, and after a moment there is the faintest creak from the front porch swing. She can't quite see Lillie's face through the window, so Mary pushes herself up and makes her way through the parlor, through the hall, and to the door. She rests for just a moment at the threshold, then steps out onto the porch and finally to the swing. If she sits down here, she will need help getting up, but a glance at Lillie makes the decision for her.

"Dearest, what is it?"

That tiny little nudge opens the floodgates. "Oh, Grandma!" Lillie wails, and actually buries her face into Mary's shoulder. "What am I going to do? It's horrible!"

Mary takes Lillie's hand in hers. "Tell me."

Lillie's two words explain everything. "Dorcas Hines."

Only two weeks into the school year and the name is already notorious at 741. *Dorcas Hines, Queen Bee.* Lillie's high school career, so hotly anticipated, is not starting well.

༄༅

Holy Cross Academy sits on a lovely campus far uptown in the wilds of Chevy Chase, just off of Connecticut Avenue among trees and rolling hills. Founded after the Civil War by the tender Sisters of the Holy Cross, the girls' school has been located for many years, up until almost this very moment, in fact, by Thomas Circle on Massachusetts Avenue. The boarding and day school proves so popular that the forethoughtful Mother Superior makes the leap of faith necessary to acquire a larger property and expand the school. Chevy Chase, being marketed by its developers as an exclusive neighborhood for the well-to-do, has been slow to entice its selected demographic, and Mother Mary Angelica is able to capitalize on the soft market in a shrewd land deal.

It's taken years since the acquisition to see the new school built, but it's finally ready for occupation in June of 1910. Lillie, member of the class of '14, starts her high school career in the first freshman class to cross the new threshold that September.

A week before school starts, the Sisters hold an open house for all the students and their families, since this year the school building is new to everyone. It's a Saturday morning and Emma has to work, so it is Charley who accompanies her. This is good practice: because the Academy is on the other side of Rock Creek Park to the northwest, it's a long ride and she'll need to change cars. Of course at fifteen she's a veteran of traveling the streetcars by herself—Emma finally allowed her to start riding alone when she turned thirteen—but she's not familiar with Chevy Chase.

Lillie has trouble sitting still on the trip up, shifting in her seat, fiddling with her new parasol, until Charley squeezes her hand. "Lillie, there's no reason to fret. You've always loved school, and school has always loved you."

She smiles, but looks out the window before she says, "I've only ever gone to Brightwood. I knew everyone there. And, well…it was nice last year finally to be the oldest." She blushes a little bit at the admission.

"All the little ones looking up at you and your friends with big eyes, like you were all some species of fearsome creature?"

She laughs at that. "Yes, I guess so. But now I'm back to being the youngest again."

"And you'll be the one who's all bug-eyed," he says, and demonstrates. They both laugh, and he puts his arm around her. "You'll own them all. You'll see. By the end of the first week, the school will be yours."

He and Lillie walk from the car stop to the school grounds, freshly landscaped and manicured, surrounding the beautiful new buildings. They both give a long look to the handful of fancy automobiles parked on the gravel driveway, and Lillie immediately notices several family groups in expensive finery. She wears one of the beautiful new dresses made for her by Cousin Lil; next to her, Charley is in his one suit, made shiny by many pressings over the years, and a straw boater that's in its third season. The wicked thought pops into her head, unbidden: *Why can't Daddy dress any better?* She turns red, mortified at herself, even as she edges a little away from him. *Now I'll actually have to* confess *at confession.* Two minutes here and she's already committing the sin of vanity.

Her spirits lift when she finds the two friends from Brightwood School who are also starting at Holy Cross, Lucinda Mills and Gwendolyn Kramer. The girls exchange hugs and exclamations over hair and clothes, while Charley stands with the girls' parents and chuckles with them over the unfolding tableau of high school. Groups are forming, with sophomores, juniors, and seniors gravitating toward their own kind, self-organizing in an established hierarchy that is, as ever in nature, focused on the alpha. Only the freshmen remain scattered about, knowing no one, not yet having formed a herd. Vulnerable.

The day progresses well enough. The freshmen and their parents are collected up so they can start to recognize faces even if they don't at first catch names. They have their own tour through the school, and are treated to a group introduction to the nuns who will be their instructors for the year. Each one says a few words, describing the class she teaches, and each woman sounds warm, encouraging, and enthusiastic by turns, except for the last. Sister Justinia is younger than the rest, strikingly so, in fact. Her delivery is smooth, chilly almost, and it causes Lillie a little shiver. Sister Justinia's cool smile is not for them but for herself.

Then they are back among the larger population, free to explore from inside to out, where a tent is set up and light refreshments are offered. Now, mingled in among the junior and senior girls, able to see them up close, Lillie is stunned as she grasps that in fact these are practically grown women. But while approaching them feels out of the question, some of the older girls actually smile and nod to the newcomers.

The girls start to relax. Their little group has picked up two more girls, who fall in with them during the orientation tour and seem to fit well into the established dynamic. At one point, Lillie is relating a brief story and gestures out with her arm, accidentally knocking into the girl standing just behind her. She sees a splash of punch miss the front of the girl's magnificent dress by a hair's breadth.

"Oh, I am *so* sorry," Lillie begins to say, until she looks up into the cold, hard eyes of what would otherwise be a beautiful face, and her words strangle in her throat. The moment is frozen, and it feels as though every head has turned to take it in.

Beyond the look, Lillie remains unacknowledged. As the girl turns with her companion to stroll away, she remarks, "It's a shame, Beatrice. It seems they've started admitting the rabble."

The prickles of heat tingle at the base of Lillie's spine, then sprint up the path to her neck and overspread her scalp, igniting her face in a crimson flash. None of the other girls move, only their eyes darting to each other in sympathetic mortification. Finally, though, Lucy remembers herself enough to slip her arm through Lillie's and walk purposefully out to an open space away from the crowd. It's exactly what Lillie would do if the tables were reversed. Gwendolyn falls in beside them, and the other two trail behind.

As a group, the girls turn to watch the casual progress of the two young women through the crowd, where they fall in with several smartly dressed, impossibly handsome young men. "Well," Gwendolyn huffs, "who does she think *she* is?"

"Oh, she *knows* who she is," comes the retort from Mary Treadwell, who, along with the other girl, Maddie Montgomery, is from St. Patrick's parish downtown, where Emma and Mary used to attend Mass. "That's Dorcas Hines. Her daddy is the richest man in the whole school. He helped to pay for the new campus." She meets the amazed look of her new friends. "My sister's a junior. I've been hearing about Dorcas Hines for two long years."

They continue to watch in silence. From this distance, they can just hear Dorcas's coquettish laughter as she slides a possessive hand onto the arm of one of the men, who is saying something to her. She leans in to share a comment with the group, and then smoothly turns to look directly at the five girls gathered at the periphery. The rest of the group turns to follow her gaze. Lillie's group, in a collective show of backbone, holds its ground and continues to look back. Dorcas and her acolytes erupt into laughter. The young man whose arm she holds smiles briefly, but then continues to look their way for another moment, not unkindly. As quickly as that, though, the older group moves on to other topics, dismissing them completely.

Mary says, "That's her friend Beatrice Gainsboro, whose daddy is almost as rich. And the boy is Edward, Beatrice's brother. Dorcas has already claimed him. The other two are Dorcas's brothers."

Once it seems safe to move, they make their way to the refreshments table, but then find themselves reluctant to reach for anything. "May I offer you ladies some punch?" Glasses are being handed around to them even as they realize who is doing the handing: it's Edward, brother of Beatrice, trophy of Dorcas. "Be careful, though. I understand it's particularly dangerous this afternoon." He smiles mischievously at Lillie as he says this. He holds his own glass up to them. "Ladies, to a successful year. Cheers."

They echo him uncertainly and drink. He looks around at them and is about to ask a question when an imperious feminine voice cuts through the surrounding conversations. "Edward!"

There is male laughter coming from the same direction. "'Oh, Edward!'" comes the one voice, in a comic female falsetto, and the other calling, "Dory can't go on another moment without you!"

He rolls his eyes at the girls and smiles. "It seems I'm being summoned." He tips his boater to them, his eyes going one last time to Lillie. "Until we meet again, then. Ladies."

After he walks away, they all have to restrain themselves from breaking into giggles. To imagine: a handsome, rich young man seeking them out, coming over to speak to them!

A few minutes later, a voice calls out from the other direction, "Lucinda!" They turn to see Lucy's mother waving to her, with Charley and Gwendolyn's father standing nearby. "Time to go!" Charley beckons to Lillie.

The girls put their glasses down and turn to leave the tent. Just then, a group of senior girls, talking and laughing amongst themselves, jostle through them, and there is a definitive *snap*. The seniors stop, and one of them reaches down to pick up Lillie's parasol, which is flopping over on the now-broken handle, a shoe print embedded in the creamy silk. "Oh. What a shame. Is this yours?" She hands it back to Lillie and they all continue on without another glance. The glance comes as the girl draws even with Dorcas, who has been watching from just outside the tent, and the two of them exchange a smile before they both look at Lillie.

ꕥ

It's a cruel and bewildering turn of events for a girl who has always loved school, which, as Charley says, has always loved her back. Word of the afternoon's events spreads quickly to those who aren't there or don't bear witness, and of course the story sprouts embellishments in the liberal fertilizer of retellings. She feels eyes on her wherever she turns, and hears the whispers of "That's the girl." To be marked as a curiosity at the very moment she starts her new school career is an ugly burden. It saps her of her natural resilience to weather the ordinary setbacks that high school delivers wholesale: Neither Lucy nor Gwendolyn, or even Mary or Maddie, for that matter, are in any classes with her. The school buildings remain a labyrinthine mystery, and it's hard to get used to having to change classrooms, to dash to far-flung rooms before the late bell sounds. Adapting to the teachers' different styles and rules demands study in its own right, and it sometimes seems as though one or another nun thinks her class is the only one her students attend.

In large measure, the nuns are sympathetic. They too have heard the gossip, and even paring it down to its most realistic bones gives the women a sense of what Lillie is suffering through, and the Lord

Himself knows the challenge that Dorcas represents to them all. They see that Lillie is a sweet, well-behaved girl, conscientious in her schoolwork, whose one mistake has been inadvertently to cross the girl who brooks no crossing. ("For Dorcas to go after a freshman! It's like using a stick of dynamite to swat a fly!" Sister Marie Therese observes to Sister Bernadette, who can't help laughing at the apt observation.) So the nuns do what they can to smooth things along for her, though some of them are the ones who see an extra load of schoolwork as the best remedy for any unhappiness.

There is, however, a singular exception in the person of Sister Justinia. Fate has served up the lion's share of Lillie's school day to the Sister, and she has wasted no time in becoming the source of Lillie's daily torment. For no possible reason that Lillie can divine, Sister Justinia does not like her. The young nun is cool and level with everyone, never once raising her voice to them, but her manner is unsettling. For one so young, Sister Justinia wields inflection and expression with a surgical precision that normally takes years to master. And she uses that skill consistently to convey to Lillie that she, Lillie, is a hopeless idiot. Lillie is not at all an idiot, but Sister Justinia has decided to treat her as though she is; the question is *why?*

Today has provided the answer, and that answer is *Dorcas Hines*.

"It's so unfair! What did I ever do but bump into her, and now everything is ruined! Lucy and Gwendolyn already have new friends, and I can't make any because now I'm *that girl*! And no matter what I do or say, Sister just looks at me in that way of hers and says, 'Well, Lillie, I suppose you'll just have to try again.' But then I saw them together! There they were this morning before first bell, the two of them, sitting on a bench in the garden, talking just like they're friends!"

Mary is having trouble following the narrative. "Who was together?"

Lillie gestures out, as though they are out in the yard somewhere. "Dorcas and Sister!"

"Sister Justinia and Dorcas were sitting together talking?"

"That's what I've been saying! And then Sister looked up and saw me, and nudged Dorcas so that she'd see me too. Oh, Grandma!

How can they be friends? Is that even allowed?"

"I don't know. It certainly doesn't seem like a good idea." As though she is a little girl again, Lillie curls herself up on the swing and puts her head in Mary's lap, weeping bitterly. Mary strokes Lillie's hair, at a loss. "Lillie, no matter how hard you try, not everyone will always like you. And sometimes the fact that they don't doesn't even have anything to do with you, even though it seems it must. I know it's not fair, but sometimes that's just the way it is."

"But," Lillie sits up suddenly, angry. "But she's a grown-up! She's a nun! She's supposed to be..."

"Better than that?"

"Exactly!"

Mary can't help but smile. "Oh, dearest, I wish that's how it would work." Lillie sniffles and Mary gives her a handkerchief. "It seems to me that if Sister Justinia has decided she doesn't like you, then you shouldn't spend another minute worrying about whether she does or doesn't. All your other teachers like you, you've said so yourself. Maybe they're the ones you should spend your energy on."

Lillie considers this for a moment, sniffling. "You mean care more to prove them right instead of trying to prove Sister Justinia wrong?"

It's Mary's turn to say, "Exactly." She can see the wheels turning as Lillie considers this.

"I guess that makes sense."

"Who's your favorite teacher, so far?"

"I really like Sister Bernadette," and Lillie smiles for the first time since she's been home. "I like that she's so excited to teach us. She loves history and she wants all of us to love history too. That's what she told us the first day. How everything that's gone before has worked together to make things the way they are now. I never thought about it like that before."

"That sounds like someone you'd like to spend more time with."

Now Lillie actually laughs. "And I'm going to have to. She just assigned us a huge, year-long thesis. She wants us to choose a subject from history and draw a line from it to ourselves. She used European emigration as an example. She wants us to start from the general, the different causes based on when and where it was happening, and then get more specific until we trace all the way down to what it means to our own family. She says, 'History conspires to make us who we are.' That's what she wants us to show."

"Well, how wonderful!"

"You should have heard the girls groan when she explained everything she wants us to do. But that's why she gave us all year to finish it."

"Have you thought of any ideas?"

"I was thinking...I was thinking about Grampa, and that he was in the war. Maybe I could use that as a subject?"

Mary is quiet for a moment. "You know that not everyone in the war was a hero, or even fought in the battles, right?"

"I know. But the Civil War was one of the other examples Sister used. I remember you said he wrote letters to you when he was away." She laughs. "I remember you read me the letter about the Indians and the buffalo."

"Well, that was when he was in the Dakota Territory. But you're right, he wrote letters during the war too." Mary looks over at Lillie, who seems almost back to her old self, save some lingering puffiness around her eyes, and squeezes her hand. "Lillie, I think that's a marvelous idea. You should get started right away. But first, you're going to have to help me get out of this swing!"

That evening, Lillie sits at the secretary in the parlor puzzling over math problems and thinking that she'd rather be practicing her piano lesson, when Charley comes into the parlor carrying a box and something wrapped in a sheet and tucked under his arm. Emma is upstairs with Mary, to make sure she can make it into bed for the night.

"I have something for you," he tells Lillie, as he puts the box down. He unwraps the sheet from around the other item, and hands her the mended parasol.

She takes it from him and opens it up; a new wooden center post replaces the broken one, and she cannot see a trace of dirt anywhere on the fabric. She closes it back up slowly. "Oh, Daddy."

"I don't suppose you really want to use it anymore, but thought

I'd fix it just in case. Funny how things you think are broken beyond all repair can be fixed. Just takes time and patience."

Lillie has been attending Mass all her life, and knows a moral when she hears one. It makes her laugh. "Oh, am I the parable of the umbrella now?"

"You realize that we've had to physically restrain your mother from marching down to that school and taking hold of that girl by the hair."

Lillie shakes her head, even as the image makes her laugh. "Then I *really* could never show my face anywhere ever again. I'd never set foot outside the house!"

"The way I figure it, you should be proud of yourself." Lillie looks at him, obviously not following. "Queen bees like your Dorcas reserve games like this parasol meanness for the girl that scares them, the one that might knock them off their throne."

"Daddy." Eye-roll, head-shake, heavy sigh.

"Well, then, think about it this way: after this year, Queen Dorcas graduates on to making her future husband miserable, and Sister So-and-So stays behind to torment a fresh crop of students. You're rid of them both in one blow." That earns him a laugh. "In the meantime," he picks the box up and sits it on the secretary next to her, "your grandmother sent me up to the attic to bring this down for you. Says it's for your school project."

"Thank you, Daddy."

He leans down and kisses the top of her head. "Don't stay up too late."

As Charley walks through the other rooms closing up for the night, turning down the gaslights, Lillie opens up the box, takes out the first bundle of papers, and begins to read.

ꕥ

WAR DEPARTMENT,
Washington December 9th, 1863

Sir:

You are hereby informed that the President of the United States has appointed you Assistant Surgeon in the Eighth Regiment U. S.

COLORED TROOPS, in the service of the United States, to rank as such from the Eighth day of December, one thousand eight hundred and sixty-three.

Immediately on receipt hereof, please to communicate to this Department, through the ADJUTANT GENERAL of the Army, your acceptance or non-acceptance; and, with your letter of acceptance, return the OATH herewith enclosed, properly filled up, SUBSCRIBED and ATTESTED, and report your AGE, BIRTHPLACE, and the STATE of which you were a permanent RESIDENT.

You will report for duty ~~to~~ in person to the Commanding officer Camp William Penn, near Philadelphia Pa.

Edwin M. Stanton
Secretary of War

Seaford, Delaware
January 9, 1864

Dear Wife,

I received your letter of the 6th last evening and it was welcome, for I had the blues bad. I am glad to hear you are all well and doing plenty of business. You need not worry about the notice to move, I will be there to see to it. I think it is because I have become an officer in the U. S. Army. I will see when I come on a visit.

Dear Mary, we have had very rough, bad, cold weather ever since we started out. We are encamped in tents always and I have felt it very severely, but I am getting used to it. We expect soon to march again. It will be fully a month before we get back to quarters. This is the very worst season of the year, and when all other soldiers are in quarters we have to camp and march in all kinds of seasons—march, march—I am sorely tried, but I will stand it. I have had a great many sick and have had a row with the commanding officer, who said he could put me under arrest, but he did not do it. I know whose fault it was, but if he ever gets sick I will be even with him.

But our whole trip will be just enough to initiate me, all in all it will do me good. I have not seen a woman yet that I had any desire for, what do you think of that? I am not as bad as you had thought. No, dear, I am not so bad as you think of me; so don't fret and worry. When we get back, if I can leave, I will come home to see you. I am still in good health and getting fat in camp life.

Kiss little Mary and Emma and tell them I said to be good. You need not write for nearly two weeks as we won't stop anywhere long enough for a letter to reach me until we get to Wilmington.

Hoping this will find you all well, I am

Your affectionate husband,
C. Miller
When you write again, address me
Dr. C. Miller, Ass't Surgeon
8th Reg. C. Troops U.S.
Wilmington, Delaware
N.B. I did not laugh over your letter. I don't laugh so much now.

ଓଓ

Hilton Head, S.C.
January 29, 1864

Dear Wife,

I am well excepting a very bad cold, the nights here are very damp and the days as warm as summertime, but for all that I attend to my duties and am getting fat on hard living and hard work, for we had a great deal of fixing up to do. I have vaccinated twenty men. A grand dress parade is going on and we will have more to do after it is over.

I haven't got a horse yet. I have had some hard words with Dr. Gasshaus, but I am going to see it through. As for the carriage, if Georg wants to give $90.00, why let it stand, that is all. I will soon have money and care for nothing.

I hope this will find you all well. Kiss Mary and Emma for me. We had a big dress parade and I was the only doctor who had good clothing, sash and sword to wear. I hope you are well and doing enough business to keep you.

This is the sunny South.

Affectionately your husband,
C. Miller

ଓଃଃଓ

Hilton Head, S.C.
February 5, 1864

My dear Wife,

I take the pen in hand to write you a few lines of news; this is a great sandy place, we have been here ever since the 24th of last Month. I have a great deal to do, most of the time. We have had for two days a little cold weather, and a great northwest wind, and oh the sand flying in your eyes and the clothing, through the boots even, and the feet get black in 2 or 3 hours. But with all, this is a great country and we are about to see more of it. Last night at half past twelve o'clock midnight we were called from our slumber, and had to get Medicine ready, operating case bandages, and everything for a fight, to go off to Florida. We packed up everything, went to bed at three, got up at six o'clock and examined all the men that were complaining. Those that were not fit to go were to be left behind, because we only need fighting men now.

I picked out about 30 of them besides what were in the Hospital, which were 17, and got ready, packed my duds, and was going to see a battle, but no! I was ordered to stay and take care of all the sick. And of course I didn't get scared? I would rather have gone to the field and seen balls and shells flying! Not for me, I must live and what for? An exile. Yesterday we had a grand Division Review of Infantry, Cavalry and Artillery on a place about 3 miles long and 2 wide. General Gillmore inspected the troops and ours looked so well that the order came last night, for to fight. That was so much for looking well. I did not turn out, but only went to see, as I had no Horse; the Doctor had to borrow my sash and belt, it was so nice. We get along. He is beginning to treat me more like his equal. I know my duties and he sees it. So, dear wife, I hope this will find you all in good health, as it leaves me. I am well and getting fatter every day and blacker too, from the sun and sand. I will carry my pipe, you know my pipe, smoke all day long when I tend to the sick, when I go to the offices or anywhere else, always my pipe, in my mouth.

ଃଓ

"Here it is!" Professor Dettweiller emerges from behind one of his bookcases, white hair mussed and bowtie askew, brandishing a folder. "I knew I had it." He hands Lillie the folder and together they step to his large document table and lay out the contents.

"I remember reading this article and thinking it an excellent contemporary account of the battle of Olustee. And here it is, written by our own Dr. A. P. Heichhold."

Professor Dettweiller has evolved into Lillie's thesis advisor, introduced by Sister Bernadette as her *colleague*, which strikes Lillie as odd coming from a nun. He is a pre-eminent scholar of Civil War history, and he maintains a vast, meticulously kept library, in his row house, which has become a primary source of Lillie's research. He helps to organize her source material into chronological order and to map it against a larger timeline. Not only does she have Christian's letters, she also has sets of orders from the War Department and various commanding officers, reports, contracts, and other records. Together, they discover that her documents represent three distinct episodes: there is the service during the war, a contract with the Army to serve in the Freedmen's Bureau, something she has never heard of before, and then another Army contract to attend the soldiers posted at Fort Rice in the Dakota Territory, out on the frontier. On the surface it all sounds very adventurous and exotic.

Sister Bernadette goes with her to the first meeting with the professor, Lillie clutching a portfolio that contains all her documents. The two adults exclaim over the items that Lillie offers, and the professor immediately begins to sort through them. It's easy to see that these two have worked together before, and in this setting the historian in Sister Bernadette trumps the nun. In the middle of their excited discussion, Lillie asks sheepishly, "You don't mind that he was just a doctor to the colored troops?"

That is enough to stop their conversation in mid-stream. "Just? Oh, Lillie." Sister Bernadette looks at her with something like disappointment. "We are all God's children, aren't we?"

Lillie sits back a little. "Well, yes. I guess so."

Professor Dettweiller looks at her over his glasses. "Think of it this way, Lillie. The North was fighting to keep the country together.

Crucial, of course, but you could say it's a philosophical reason—political, economic. The colored troops were fighting for a very basic personal reason: their right to be free people. They had the biggest stake of anyone in the outcome, and your grandfather was seeing that firsthand. Perhaps that's an element your thesis can explore."

Since then, she has learned so much: That Professor Dettweiller teaches at Howard University, just down the block, a school founded by a Civil War general, Oliver Howard, to serve both white and colored students. That General Howard was also put in charge of running the Freedmen's Bureau, where Christian later served, because of his reputation as *the Christian General.* That Howard has only recently died, and that the professor considered him to be a great man as well as a great friend. More particularly, there is Professor Dettweiller's muster list of the Eighth U.S. Colored Troops, a unit organized in Philadelphia and mustered out of Delaware, which serves as a sort of Rosetta stone, pointing them to firsthand accounts of people who were with the Eighth in the battles that Christian references in his letters. Here is the book of collected letters of Oliver Norton, which describes the brutality, incompetence, and failure of leadership, along with soldierly bravery in the face of a far better prepared enemy force, all represented in the single Battle of Olustee, which is the first that the untrained Eighth faces. Christian, who first wishes to be there, later describes this as "the battle where we got whipped so bad, the Col. was killed and a great many others, and everything was in terrible confusion." Norton's and others' accounts are heartbreaking, and Lillie finds them difficult to read. Now, Professor Dettweiller has unearthed his files from the *Christian Recorder* of Philadelphia, a weekly newspaper published for colored readers, who, of course, have a particular interest in the Eighth. Among the back issues is a letter written by Dr. Heichhold, the chief surgeon of the Eighth, under whom Christian serves.

Together they read through Dr. Heichhold's letter as they trace the action through a detailed sketch of the Northern order of battle that the professor has previously drawn. He has hundreds of similar sketches; he creates multiple illustrations of each battle using different contemporary accounts from both sides, and hones them over time to achieve a comprehensive and possibly accurate account. In Dr. Heichhold's letter concerning Olustee, General Seymour is still feckless, Colonel Fribley still doomed, the men still unprepared, the battery still abandoned, and the flag of the regiment still lost, despite many brave attempts to hold it fast.

Lillie sees that there are many people who speak with clarity, sympathy, and passion about these events and people. Christian is not one of them.

ഇര

Jacksonville, Fl.
March 23, 1864

My Dear Wife:

I received your letter of the 9th March on the 17th and I was glad to hear from you. I am well and getting fat oh! Quite an alderman, because the Rebels are in our front and the beautiful river in our rear and the birds and all around us, five nights. But a few nights it has been cold enough to have five blankets to cover, to just be a little warm, especially last night. The days are pleasant, but you know I don't like getting up early, well just think of it.

I have to get up every morning before day, at five o'clock and tend to the sick call, oh! How delightful—only think, and nobody to console me. Oh! Dear, but I have nothing to do all day, only read papers, books and shall I tell you, I always keep the last letter you send me to read pretty often till I get the next one, and then I burn the others. You know I can't keep your letters, because the Rebels might capture this little Dutch Doctor, and then they might read and make fun of yours.

My dear, pay Mrs. Phillips and sell some of your Gold. You can get 65 cents on the dollar or at least 62. For instance $20.00 gold would give you $32.00. I will send you some money as soon as we get paid, I have not received a cent as yet, and all the officers are in the same fix. I had some trouble with my mustering, and on account of the battle where we got whipped so bad, the Col. was killed and a great many others, and everything was in terrible confusion, but it is alright and I hope we will soon be paid. I have no horse as yet. I *have just wrote a letter to Georg about the carriage, to let me know yes or no about it for $85.00—to pay you cash, not otherwise. Don't be too anxious, everything will come out right. When I get started right I often wish you were here, the birds, the landscape, the river and everything is lovely, but this Cruel War. Oh! How delightful, I often think we might spend a few happy hours in this clime with you and the children but no—it is all a ruin, nothing but gun batteries and gun boats. They captured two boats up the St. Johns River and brought them to this place this morning. A great many houses, wharfs and five or six saw mills have been destroyed by fire at this place, which must have once been a very pretty town, with orange trees and a great many other kinds around the houses and gardens. Some few are good yet, but look dreary. Only a few people remained here when we came, nothing to drink here but water. Oranges we buy the very largest for one or 1 ½ cents a piece by the dozen, but no eggs, fresh meat or good butter for neither love nor money, so we often live on hardtack and get fat. For all I am well, and hope these lines will find you and the children the same. Kiss them for me and tell them I want them to be good or I won't bring them oranges. So goodbye till next time.*

Your affectionate husband,
C. Miller

❧❧❧

Yellow Bluff, near Jacksonville, Fl.
June 6, 1864

Sir:

I have the honor herewith to resign my position as an Ass't Surgeon in the 8th Regiment, U.S.C. Troops for the following reasons, viz:

Having passed a thorough and satisfactory examination before the Medical Board in Washington, I was appointed Assist. Surgeon of the 8th Regt. U.S.C.T by the President, and having discharged my duties to the entire satisfaction of the Surgeon of the Regiment, Dr. Heichhold, I was ordered before a second Board at Beaufort, S.C. without the assignment of any reasons whatever. I appeared before the Board and underwent a second examination, the result of which

has never been forwarded to me, having waited nearly three months to know why I was ordered before the Board, and what was the character of my examination. I cannot, with respect to myself, as a Physician and Officer, longer remain in the service of the U.S. I state upon honor that I am not indebted to the U.S. Government.
I am, with much respect,
Gen., your ob'd't Serv't.
Christian Miller, M.D.
Assist. Surgeon 8th Rgt, U.S.C.T.

Endorsement:
War Department, Adjutant General's Office
Washington June 29th, 1864

Respectfully returned, disapproved.

The fact that Asst. Surgeon Miller's military superiors saw fit to satisfy themselves in regard to his qualifications to perform the duties of his position, is not considered a sufficient cause for tendering his resignation.
By Order of the Secretary of War:
C. W. Foster
Asst. Adjt. Genl. Vols.

ઉଊઉ

Headquarters, Dist Florida
Jacksonville July 18, 1864

Approved & respectfully forwarded:
Dr. Miller is reported wholly incompetent, was before a Board where decision has never been received.

Wm Birney,
Brig. Gen. Camp

Medical Directors Office D. S.

Hilton Head S.C., Aug 1, 1864

Respectfully returned to Headquarters D. S.

The Army Medical Board before which Asst. Surgeon Miller was sent for examination reported that he "was competent for the position of Asst Surgeon of colored troops." The alleged reasons for resignation do not seem sufficient to recommend acceptance of resignation at this time.

Meretilth Clymer
Asst. Med. Director D. S.

ꕥ

"*Dr. Miller is reported wholly incompetent,*" Lillie reads softly, and blinks up at Professor Dettweiller. "*Wholly incompetent.*"

The professor tilts his head and quotes back to her, "*Competent enough for the position of assistant surgeon of colored troops.*"

Lillie gives him a little smile. "Yes, I guess I should feel sorriest for his patients."

"So far, then, we have Dr. Miller attempting to resign twice, his commanding officer attempting to have him relieved of his commission, and the Army Medical Board deciding that his skills are good enough for the colored troops so that he has to stay. What happens next, I wonder? See, Lillie—drama, conflict, suspense. All the elements necessary to a good story. We just have to put it all together to reveal the ending to the mystery."

And at first it is something of a mystery to Lillie, as she tries to make sense of what she has. With practice and Professor Dettweiller's help, Lillie learns how to decipher the various endorsements that accumulate on military correspondence as the orders pass from hand to hand. There are many terms and abbreviations that are baffling at first but soon as easy to read as plain English: *A.A.G.* is Assistant Adjutant General, *Vols* is Volunteers, *Reg* or *Regt* is Regiment, *D.S.* is Department of the South. A *brevet* is a temporary field promotion, often demanded by mortality among the officers, so that someone noted with the rank *Bvt. Maj.* means that they have been temporarily promoted from Captain to Major. She learns that *N.B.*, which Christian sometimes uses as a postscript, means *nota bene*, or *note well.*

As they transcribe letters and orders into a more readable form, he shows her his standard notations to indicate different sections, illegible portions, and those that are missing. Some of these missing pieces are simply victims of time and the elements. There are several letters, though, from which sections have been carefully removed, as though by a scalpel. After she starts this project, Lillie quickly learns not to ask Mary questions about the letters or their contents, as it is immediately obvious that the memories are painful to her. Lillie finally decides to ask about the excised passages, though, and Mary stares into the middle distance during a long silence before she says, "I cut those out to use when I applied for my pension. I had to prove your grandfather became chronically ill while he was in the Army." She looks away with a tight smile and says almost to herself, "One boon from his willingness to complain."

ഊര

Jacksonville Fl.
July 25, 1864

My dearly beloved Wife:

I sit me down and take up the pen to write a few lines of love and words of consolation to you my dear wife, having heard in this distant clime, through Rebel newspapers that your City has been attacked by the 7th Street road, and that you are in danger and might be in trouble. It makes my heart ache and my bosom heave, to think that I, who ought to be there to protect you and our children, am not there. Oh my dear! I hope no harm will befall you, and dear don't get alarmed at any time, but trust in God and hope for better times coming.

I am now sitting quietly in my room, and while writing to you, a <u>*Regimental Band*</u> *is* <u>*discoursing sweet music*</u> *nearby, but all is sadness* *in my bosom, to think that you are or might be in danger. I have been in some, but thanks to a kind, overruling Providence I am safe and well. They, or our Regiment, is gone with another expedition and our Dr. Gasshaus had to go with it this time. He tried very hard to make me go. He even went to the Genl. Commanding to have me returned to the Regiment so that I would have to go, but no—here I am, rusticating, very busy, but easy, as Post Surgeon, for a little time at least. Oh dear! I wish I were with you and the children. We have no mail yet and I hope that you received the $140 dollars which I sent to you on the 27th of June.*

We will soon be paid again, I hope, and I will send you more, if everything is safe around Washington. Write to me often, so that I have something to read and dream over at least.

I hope these few lines will find you all safe and well. I hope I will soon hear of my Resignation and that I will be able to come home and be happy with you and the children.

Your affectionate Husband
C. Miller

Kiss the children for me, and tell them to be good.

ꟲꟲꟲ

Hilton Head S.C.
August 4, 1864

My dearly beloved Wife:

Your letters of the 9th, 20th, and now received another of the 24th July. My dear I would have answered before, but my dear I have had no time. I have been so busy, and three days ago we received Orders to pack up and be ready to go to Fortress Monroe and join the Potomac Army. So you see we are on our way now and I sit down in haste to answer your letters and let you know that I am coming nearer home if not home, for the last few days.

I am sorry to hear that your Landlord bothers you. Pay him the $5.00 extra, which I have always paid every year, but on an extra bill as balance due for rent, but don't pay the $25.00. Tell him that I am willing to pay $15.00 dollars a Month, and if he don't stop bothering you my dear wife, why just get Georg Miller to have him arrested for disturbing and entering unlawfully into your house, while your

Husband is absent in the Union Army.

Kiss the children for me and address me at Fortress Monroe until further news.

Your loving affectionate Husband
C. Miller
Asst Surgeon U.S.C.T.
Fortress Monroe

ↀↀↀ

Adams Express Company
GREAT EASTERN, WESTERN AND SOUTHERN EXPRESS FORWARDERS.

Fortress Monroe, VA August 13th 1864

Bermuda Hundred

My dearly beloved wife,

I send my trunk home to you, you may open it and clean it out. We are going to the front and I cannot carry it along. My dear, I enclose a five dollar bill to pay for it, whatever it may cost. I hope soon to be able to come home. Oh dear, while I am writing these few lines, they are firing continually with heavy artillery. It is quite noisy, but with God's protection I may get safely through it all.

Kiss the children for me. Goodbye my dear till next time.

Your Affectionate Husband
Miller

ↀↀↀ

Field Hospital 10th A. Corp.
near Petersburg, Va.
September 8, 1864

My dearly beloved Wife:

I received your letter of August and I am glad to hear you are all well. But I am sorry you have had so much trouble, but never mind dear, better times are coming. I am glad you have moved and I hope you will like your new house and be patient until such time *that I may be able to come home. I am at present very comfortably located, a fine position, some work, plenty good things to eat, and I take a ride on my horse of two or three miles every day. Ah, he goes fine and rides easy. If I could only get home for a few days to see you, I would be happy and perfectly content with my place in the Potomac Army, but dear at present not one Medical Officer can get away for we expect some hard fighting soon, somewhere near here. My dear, I am in no danger as we are some distance in the rear, and if we should have to leave why I have a good, trusty and fast horse to carry me to City point, one of our landing places, but I don't apprehend any such thing. So you must not be uneasy and do the best you can to get along. If you know any nice person, say a man and wife, why, rent two of your Rooms out to them for $15 or 20^{\underline{00}}$. My dear as soon as I get paid I will always send you all I can spare. So be as careful as possible, how you live and you can get along. I am glad you are away from the shanties, and when I get back I will have a nice Office as Doctor on 6th Street. I am careful and don't spend a cent, only what I must have, and dear a horse I had to have. I could stand the fatigue of marching no longer. So you see how it is.*

My dear I hope you are fairly settled in your new home. It is too true my dear, it is hard to leave that old house, but after all, it was very unhealthy there, and we have been living long enough in it under cheap rent. I am only too glad that you got a house at any price.

Oh dear! Last evening I rode out to the front and there I found my two Doctors with my resignation in their hands and with a great many things written on it, but not accepted. The Government can't let me go—no—I am a slave and must stay, that is hard. I send you the paper and you can see for yourself. I tried all kinds of ways and yet—no—I am too good a something—I must stay.

My dear I am enjoying excellent health and I sincerely hope that these lines will find you and the children enjoying the same blessing. Yes dear we have a fine place here. Of course I may have to leave tomorrow but I have learned to make the best of everything as I find it and enjoy all I can get, eating, drinking and sleeping, operating on a wounded soldier, et cetera----

So we go. I would be willing to give half a month's pay if I could only go home for two weeks, but I can't. The poor soldiers need me—

yes—and you and I must wait till other times come. I have two wards of sick men, besides wounded to attend to here, all white soldiers, and they all think I am a good Doctor. One man made me a present of a 10th Army Corp badge, a silver one, and I wear it on my cap, a pin, like a bastion Fort, they call it, so you see I am somebody after all. My dear again hoping that you will have no more troubles, kiss the children for me and write often, for your letters, from one time to another are my prayer book. yes----
Your affectionate Husband
C. Miller

ഇ ഢ

"You can follow the path here in this series of letters, where Dr. Miller describes the preparations for the various actions in Deep Bottom and Bermuda Hundred. His regiment moved by sea all the way from Jacksonville to Virginia, which was faster and safer than over land, certainly. There, the Eighth joined up with the Tenth Corps of Virginia and the Army of the James. The whole of them played a part in the siege at Petersburg. Then, in General Butler's letter here," he clears his throat, knowing this is hard for Lillie, "the action that he describes is the Battle of Chaffin's Farm. The colored troops were widely recognized as having fought very bravely there, but they suffered horrible casualties."

He can see that Lillie is only half listening, nodding and murmuring but absorbed by the next two items in the chronology. Professor Dettweiller touches her hand. "Not every man can be a hero, Lillie, however much we'd like them to be."

Lillie nods again. "I know. That's exactly what my grandmother said."

ഇ ഢ

Headquarters
Department of Virginia and North Carolina
Army of the James River
In the Field, October 1st, 1864.
General Orders}
No. 117.

Asst. Surgeon Christian Miller, of the 8th U.S. Colored Troops, having been put in charge of the transportation of one hundred and fifty, as he admits, wounded men, who had had nothing to eat all day, as he reports, left Deep Bottom without making any preparation for their comfort or providing for them food, and when reaching Bermuda Hundred was found personally intoxicated from, as he says, a grain and a half of morphine, and a half gill of whiskey, as to be unable to do his duty, is ordered to be and is hereby dismissed the service of the U.S. with the loss of all pay and allowances, subject to the approval of the President.

By Command of Major General Butler

☙❧☙

Special Orders} Extract 19
No. 527
War Department,
Adjutant General's Office, Washington,
October 4th, 1865

By direction of the President, General Order No. 117 of October 1st, 1864, from Headquarters, Department of Virginia and North Carolina, dismissing Assistant Surgeon *Christian Miller*, 8th U.S.C.T. from service of the United States, with the loss of all pay and allowances, for drunkenness on duty, and neglect of wounded men under his charge, is confirmed, except so much thereof as directs a forfeiture of pay and allowances due.

By order of the Secretary of War:

E. D. Townsend
Assistant Adjt. General

ജര

The professor makes a notation in the timeline they're detailing: *End of field duty. Six-month break until next correspondence.* He chuckles, though, as he makes the note. "I guess we can take heart that everyone makes mistakes. Even on formal government documents."

"What do you mean?"

He hands her the letter—the letter from the War Department, sent by order of President Lincoln himself, cashiering Christian from his post. "They've made a rather important mistake here. I wonder if anyone caught it. Can you find it?"

She scans the letter, but shakes her head. "I don't see—oh!" She squints at the paper, then glances up at the timeline. "Well, that's funny. They dated it with the wrong year."

Professor Dettweiller pulls a face at her. "Oops!" he says, and they both laugh. But he becomes thoughtful as he taps at the next item in the chronology. "And yet, here's what's curious: When next we hear of Dr. Miller in March of '65, he's reporting for duty to one Captain Loral of the Baltimore 13th at Camp Relief, right here in the District. And then these next two items: in April, here's Dr. Miller demanding information from the sergeants of three companies about their men being assigned to the Veteran Reserve Corps, and in May, the good doctor is being ordered to report for duty to Emory Hospital by a U.S. Army colonel. And through it all, he is still Acting Assistant Surgeon C. Miller, U.S.A."

"How is that possible? Could they have changed their minds?"

"I think, Lillie, we've found the point at which Dr. Miller becomes a contract surgeon with the army."

Lillie shakes her head in disbelief, even though they've read through some of Christian's contracts already and discussed this apparent contradiction. "How can it be that he's not fit to be a doctor *in* the army, but he's fine to be a doctor *under contract* to the army?"

"It does seem problematic," he says with an arched eyebrow. "And even so, being under contract was obviously not good enough for Dr. Miller, since here he tries to argue his way back in."

ꙮ

June 12, 1865

Sir:

I respectfully submit, this late day, my case, with a succinct statement of my own position of who I am and what I am, what we call a self-educated Medical Doctor and Surgeon.

I left my father's home when near twenty years old, with nothing. I earned my living in a very short time with cupping and leeching, which I learned from a German like myself in Baltimore City, Md.

In the year 1851, I came to Washington City and established myself as Cupper and Leecher. Through the kindness of Drs. Saunders and Holmead (who are now both dead), I studied in their offices while following my own business. In '58, I received my diploma as M. D. from the Medical College attached to Columbian College. I attended Lectures for five years according to German custom. In '52, I married. Now nearly thirteen (13) years since during all that time, I paid my own expense at college and supported my family, paid high rent et cet. in this expensive city. In '63, I volunteered my services to the Surgeon General U. S. A. as a surgeon of Colored Troops. I was the only one from this city to sacrifice home comfort, to brave the jeers and taunts of friends and enemies alike, to face the danger and horrors of being an officer of <u>negro soldiers</u>, but my adopted country needed my services, and my qualification before two different U. S. A. Medical Boards (not political recommendations) placed me where I was when General Butler found me.

I never occupied an office of any description whatsoever, nor swayed I ever to quackery.

When in South Carolina, Florida, or in Virginia's campaign, I never was an hour or day off duty. In Virginia, I was detailed to the

10th Corp. Field Hospital in front of Petersburg, and just previous to the Corp being ordered to the advance on Richmond on the 25th.

I volunteered and rode to near the front of the 18th Corp, found a great many wounded and only two Ass't Surgeons on the ground.

[Lines missing.]

Well, sir, we advanced on Richmond and on the 29th, this to me an ever memorable day, word came to the 10th Corp Field Hospital that in front of the 18th Corp they were losing heavily a great number wounded and scarcity of Medical Officers. I went to work and worked hard all day, in spite of the pain in my bowels from my complaint. Late in the evening when all the wounded on Chapin's farm had been attended to and sent to the rear, I returned about seven or eight o'clock to Deep Bottom on the banks of the James where the 10th Corp Field Hospital was. I had scarcely arrived when I was ordered to load the little miserable ferry boat the George Washington, which used to run for a great many years between this City and Alexandria, with as many wounded men, "walking cases", that is slightly wounded, as I could put aboard her to be taken to some Hospital down the river. After placing one hundred and fifty men on the floors with straw and some officers in the cabin, at half past nine or ten oclock we started.

[Lines missing.]

I felt physically exhausted and mentally depressed that I took my own remedies to quiet pain and exhaust, thinking I could get at least some three or four hours rest, but no. Thus by me not getting the rest which I ought to have had I certainly appeared to strangers and those who had it easy as one intoxicated.

[Lines missing.]

at my duty everywhere was reported drunk. I was condemned without being heard. I felt it too keenly to stir or say one word until now. My Regiment is gone to Texas and during all my absence has never been about one skirmish and I have been urged to present my case. I beg in all, to be seen and heard personally, where in an interview I can better explain, as I am a bad penman.

Your obedient Servant,
C. Miller M. D.
late Asst. Surg. 8th U. S. C. T.

ꙮ

"I'm guessing this is a draft of a letter he wrote, probably to the War Department, to be reinstated. I wonder if he ever sent it."

Lillie's brow furrows. "But he spent so much time trying to resign."

"Ah, yes. There's a big difference between quitting and being fired. It's easy to see that his pride was gravely wounded. When he wrote this, the Eighth was already down in Texas, which is where it mustered out, so he never joined up with his unit again. He is a contract doctor from here on. And the next chapter in his story takes us to the Freedmen's Bureau." The professor straightens up from leaning over the table and stretches. "Perhaps it's time to make some tea before we tackle that."

Equilibrium

1911

Professor Dettweiller has already walked Lillie though much of his material on the *Bureau of Refugees, Freedmen, and Abandoned Lands*, an agency the Government hastily establishes in the aftermath of the war to address a problem that the Lincoln Administration perhaps fails to anticipate and that seems to take the Johnson Administration by surprise. "Imagine, Lillie: slaves are prohibited by law from owning land, or anything of real value. Then, in one stroke of a pen, they are declared to be free. What then? They have no property, no money, no resources of any kind. Much of the South is a burned-out wasteland, and its white populace has just suffered a humiliating defeat. Colored people still have no defined legal rights beyond their freedom and are an easy target for blame and abuse. Exactly what are they supposed to do now? And yet it seems as though no one in the Government spent the five minutes it would have taken to anticipate that outcome."

This is the only time that Lillie sees Professor Dettweiller become heated in discussing any of this history. Even the name of the bureau irritates him, since it is the refugees—dispossessed white Confederates—who take top billing. He has counseled her about an historian's responsibility to remain disinterested in the events she researches and reports on, and to leave aside partisan or personal concerns. "An historian's job is not to judge, but to try to understand." On this particular topic, though, he admits to taking a personal interest. "General Howard and I spent many an evening discussing this. He did the best he could to rectify that lack of forethought, but it was a huge gap."

"Here's General Howard, first thing!" Lillie is sketching a timeline that notes the dates of military orders, personal letters, and any other artifacts they have from Christian's archive, which will then overlay a larger timeline of the Freedmen's Bureau. "The orders come from him on October third of sixty-five. Then here is a letter of introduction from Arthur West to Thomas Cox of Montgomery, Alabama, asking him to show Grampa, I mean Dr. Miller, around the city." It still feels clumsy to refer to him as Dr. Miller, but she agrees that the distance helps to numb the sting of her growing disappointment. "This first paper doesn't look like a letter; it's more like some journal entries."

"Oh, that's promising. Let's hear what Dr. Miller has to say about his experience."

ꕥ

Demopolis, Maringo Co., Ala.
October 12, 1865

I started from Washington City D.C., 4th at night; arrived at Annapolis Junction, started in western train, arrived at Belair next evening, 5th. Cross Ohio River on a boat, started again for Cincinnati, arrived next day, 6th afternoon. Started for Louisville, Kentucky, arrived next day, 7th. Started again for Nashville, Tennessee, arrived next, 8th. Laid over one day, looked through the town, a miserable, dirty, filthy-looking place, accommodations everywhere miserable, from Nashville to Chattanooga. Passed Murfreesborough and Stevenson, almost (in the latter place) everything destroyed, not a vestige left of it. Saw Cumberland Gap, Lookout Mountain, arrived at Chattanooga at night; everything destroyed but building up again. Started for Atlanta, Georgia, arrived next day noon, 10th. Here everything was destroyed. Started for Montgomery, arrived same evening. Here I stopped in the Center Hotel, reported next day for duty to Surgeon Kipp, Chief Medical Officer. Was ordered to this place to take charge as Medical Officer. No Medicine, no quarters, no boarding houses. I took camp fare with

Capt. Haptenstall, who is in charge of the Freedmen here and seems to be a gentleman as Assistant Superintendent. Oh what a wild, God-forsaken country this seems to me, who had a bright vision of the Sunny South, how they have vanished like a beautiful panoramic view or a cloud before the noonday sun. Ignorance and common language is prevalent, "Chaotic Confusion". 10 o'clock; I will stop and retire to dream of happy times coming. Serves me right.
Miller, Surgeon

October 23 & 24. Visited Linden Colony and inspected "Linden Village Jail", bad place for men to be kept. Returned to this place, began to feel very sick myself; 25th a little better, went to "Green Oak Colony"; while there at night, was taken the second time with cramps, worked round 27th. Came back to the town 28th at night, taken with the worst "Bilious Cramp Colic" I ever had. Lasted with such intensity for five days as almost to destroy my mind. My system is shattered, death would have been a relief, but no, not in a strange land amongst strangers. O no! Thank God this 5th day of November I am able to be up and shall soon be going about my duties again. O how I want some fruits and to be home again, poor me——

Started 11th in an Ambulance which I requested (rather than wait for a steamboat, as the Alabama River is very low and boats uncertain). My driver nor I knew the way, however, after driving all night, next day morning the river came to my view, which I crossed on flat boat. Started for the Mississippi depot at Selma but came too late, had to stay all day and night at the Gee House. Prices here are exorbitant and nothing fit to eat, "oh for a good table." Well, 12th I started for here, arrived safely at noon. Selma is all dust and so is this place. This evening it rained and I waded through mud to come to this hospital, where through the kindness of Dr. Hawley, Surgeon of the 10th Mississippi Infantry, I am now lodged, dark prospects and hard labor before me. What a fool I was to leave a comfortable home and accept this position offered. When will I become wise? Never, I fear. I have to visit two Colony of Freedmen and attend to them here in Hospital, not where I am penning these lines, but in some frame shanties not a great distance off, say ten (10) squares. Everything in beautiful confusion and disorder, nothing—

ꕥ

A little cry escapes from Lillie as she realizes this is all there is. The words simply stop on the page, and there is nothing on the back. Christian never leaves a page blank; he simply writes larger to fill the space. When she and Professor Dettweiller realize this is the start of a journal, they are equally excited at having an account of daily life in a Freedmen's hospital. But they find nothing more than this. "I wish he'd kept up with the journal," she tells the professor with a sigh.

"It held a great deal of promise as a primary source. The mention of Dr. Hawley, a Confederate doctor there in the hospital, is tantalizing, so it's a shame if we're not going to hear any more of him."

That isn't what Lillie is thinking about though. "I like it much better than his letters. He seems…nicer." Professor Dettweiller looks at her over his glasses, and she starts laughing. "I know, I know! Detachment! I'm trying!"

ꕥ

Freedmens Hospital
Demopolis Ala.
November 27, 1865

Surg. C. J. Kipp
Chief Medical Officer
Freedmens Bureau, Montgomery Ala.
Sir:

I have the honor, most respectfully but positively to decline rendering further service at this post after the second (2nd) day of December "65" as a "Contract Surgeon". (Though I will attend till 5th or 6th for which few days I do not wish recompence):

For the following reasons:

Viz. four weeks since I was taken with "Billious Cramp Colic" which terminated after severe suffering in a "Congestive Chill" from which I narrowly escaped with life, but ever since I am subject to severe chills at midnight. My system is prostrated and needs recuperation, I am weak and scarcely fit to attend to my duties; I must therefore return to the bosom of my family, where I will be able to procure such "Tonics and Chalybeates" as I need.

Second: I have been Insulted with every application either to the Assistant Commander Capt. Haptenstall, Post Quarter Master, or Post Commander for anything needed for the Hospital, even for fuel. "Get it the best way you can, we can't furnish you with anything." Fine indeed. Even the Post Q.M. refused to deliver the "Medical supplies" and Capt. A. C. Haptenstall Asst. Cmdr. agreed with him. The provisions are often not of the best; when I complain, as I have had to do, I am insulted by telling the man who carried the request for better food "tell your Dr. to go to h—l, et cetera, it is good enough for negroes."

Thirdly: I have not been furnished with suitable Quarters nor fuel, unless the room I occupy in the Building used by the 11th Regiment Infantry Volunteers for a Regimental Hospital, on all sides sick rooms surrounded by malarious atmosphere and sickly exhalations. Truly fine quarters for a Doctor in charge of Freedmens Hospital and numberless sick that I am called to attend in the "Log Cabins" around this Village, but as the Asst. Cmdr., Post Q.M., and Post Cmdr. say "it is good enough for such as you, only a Doctor for Negro's". Well sir, with these surroundings, the first law of nature is self-preservation; with the precarious state of my health and insults heaped upon me. Profanity and Immorality with Gonorrhea stalking abroad and with those that should, as Officers, set a better example. I cannot longer submit to remain in this irksome position. I hope my successor will meet with better success as to what is due to a Medical Officer and a Gentleman.

Respectfully your obedient servant
Christian Miller, M.D.
A.A. Surg. U.S.A.

ଔଔଔ

Office of Surgeon in Chief State of Alabama
Bureau of Refugees, Freedmen &c
Montgomery, December 1, 1865

Sir:
Your letter of the 27th last is at hand.
I will relieve you from duty as soon as I can obtain a medical officer to succeed you in charge of the hospital. Your contract expires January 2, 1866.
I regret that you have not been kindly treated by the Officer at Demopolis. I hope however that you and Capt. Haptenstall will soon come to a better understanding in regard to the wants of your Hospital, as this is absolutely necessary for the welfare of your patients.

Very Respectfully
Your Obedient Servant
Charles J. Kipp
Surgeon U.S. Vols
Surgeon in Chief

ঙঝঙ

Freedmens Hospital
Demopolis, Ala.
December 13, 1865

My own darling Wife:

I sit here in my room attached to my own Hospital and feel like one alone and yet not alone, for my thoughts are far away with my dear ones at home, thinking how you all might be getting along and whether you miss <u>me very much</u>, hoping that you are well and comfortable around the warm stove and wishing I were there, <u>so do I wish it</u> but my duty seems here. I am (thanks <u>to God</u>) very well and getting every day stronger and hearty, I have been very successful with my patients and had only two to die during the whole of last month, and only one as yet this month. I have at present thirty (30) smallpox *patients and more coming in every day. I am doing so well that they all wish me to stay here and not go home, what say you? Shall I stay? Everything looks up, and after awhile they promise me nice quarters and all I ought to have. My Chief Surgeon Dr. Kipp wants me to stay. I guess I will not, I am almost tempted to stay and disappoint you a little longer hey? How are you grass widow!*

Well for the last ten days it has been raining and we have a northwest wind blowing like forty all around here, coming through every chink and crack of the wooden building. I have a nice little hot wood fire in my little fireplace and feel very cozy. I am again indulging with my pipe and smoke for the first time for six (6) weeks, so you can judge I must be quite well again. Just think for me to be so long without smoking. I can eat and I do eat, and what is more it don't cost me anything now, for I eat of what I draw for my patients, fresh beef et cetera. I get a plenty for them and live well myself. I have a good cook, who also does my washing without cost. In fact the "Freedmen" I have in this Hospital all want to work and do something for me, they think I am such a good "Gentleman" and nice "Doctor." They never saw such a good one, don't you think so too! You see I will blow as I always did hey! But this has been a cold blowing day and I must blow a little bit— just a little but it is the truth "but I am a good little husband yet"—so don't get alarmed my dear. I do my duty, stay at my hospital nearly all day, go to the Bureau Office, look for letters, and look at the pretty w---n, oh I meant to say the houses, "Log Cabins" and what! Well, to think of you and the children all day long and a little at night, when the mosquitos don't bother me, shall I stay? Don't you think I am in danger of loving some pretty Southern beauty hey? Not yet I guess.

Well my darling I am coming home if I can (providence permitting) that is if you say so. I am well and hoping these few lines will find you all well and cheerful. In anticipation of soon seeing and being with you, I wish you all a merry Christmas.
Yours affectionately devoted Husband
C. Miller

ℬ

Lillie can't hold back a little shriek of indignation as she reads this, and her expression is incredulous when she looks over at the professor, who is writing at his desk. "He submits his resignation in disgust on November twenty-seventh, and just two weeks later he wants to stay, *and* he's joking about other women? How dare he?"

"Lillie..."

"That's my *grand*mother!"

"Lillie." He's looking at her over the top of his glasses.

She exhales the outrage and laughs at herself. "So much for remaining detached. I guess I'm not making a very good historian, am I?"

"We all have our sore spots. But as to your skills as an historian, you have a fine eye for detail and a talent for research." In fact, only just today that talent has saved them both from the embarrassment of Lillie having to ask and the professor having to explain the meaning of *gonorrhea*. "Well, as we know already, Dr. Kipp took his resignation at face value and here he is back in Washington by the end of January sixty-six."

Lillie shakes her head. "All that fuss and bother, and he was only away four months."

"Which takes us to the final installment in Dr. Miller's travels, out in the Dakota Territory. This is outside my area of study, Lillie, but I'm interested to see what you have here. I might have some references that can help to fill in the gaps."

Lillie still isn't sure whether she'll use these letters as part of her thesis, though Sister Bernadette endorses Lillie's incorporating the theme of post-war westward expansion, but she welcomes the professor's help in organizing the documents: laying them out chronologically, categorizing the elements, and sketching a timeline that eventually captures the various threads of information woven through the material. Eventually, all of this will be tied into the larger historical perspective.

Once again, they are able to construct a telling narrative from the papers that Christian has left behind.

"What have you been able to discover from these first few artifacts of the Dakota adventure?"

"Well, let's see: Dr. Miller's last communiqué was in February of sixty-six, when he came home from Alabama. Then an associate of his writes a letter of recommendation to the Surgeon General dated in August, six months later. The letter offering the six-month contract is dated April twenty-fifth of sixty-seven, so that's fourteen months since he'd been back home. Plus their address has changed since then. It looks like they've moved a little farther up Sixth Street." Lillie can't help herself from adding, "I hope for Grandma's sake it was to a nicer place."

ꕤ

Missouri River on board Steamer
"Ida Fulton"
June 14, 1867

My dear little darling wife:

I take the pen to write you a few lines of greeting and thanks to God for our safe deliverance from danger that hung over us yesterday 13th. 8 ½ o'clock we struck a sand bar, and the wind was blowing terrible, which swung our boat completely around at the mercy of the storming "elements" and almost doubled the steamer up. One side, upon which Lt. Chance and I were standing, commenced crushing down, the very large iron hold bars and pillars crushed together like so many little wires, and for about (4) four hours things looked very squally. At last after a great deal of anxiety and labor, kind providence landed us on "terra firma" the shore, where we, that is the Capt. of the boat, sailors and soldiers soon welted and put the boat in running order again, by 12 o'clock last night. Strange to say the boat does not leak a drop and the hull remained firm. At three (3) o'clock this morning we started up the river again, rejoicing. We are now taking wood on board, near a place called "mosquito bend." Truly so for the mosquitos will scarcely let me write, they fly around and on a fellow by the thousands.

My darling I am well and hearty. Last Sunday evening I received some good Medicine, in the shape of a letter. We landed opposite "Fort Sully." Capt. Smith and myself went over to the Fort in a small boat and had the mail hauled out, where I found the first letter that you wrote on the 14th of May. We had quite a time getting to the "Fort" as it was after night and cloudy. We lost our way and I became very tired scrambling through bushes, mud, and stumbling over fallen trees. I was bruised, but when I grasped your letter I forgot all about it. I was so glad to hear you were well for a "grass widow" but sorry that Mother was sick. I hope these few lines will find you all in good health. Yes dear, I dream and think of you sleeping or waking, and I hope soon to see you again by the help and blessings of God, say some six, eight, or twelve months hence, so darling take care of yourself and our two darling children. In about two more days [here is a kiss from your truant husband, more anon---Miller] I shall be at Fort Rice.

Saturday Evening everything is pleasant and tomorrow night I may sleep at Fort Rice. Here is a good night salute for you from your loving husband on the broad Missouri River.

Sunday morning: rainy disagreeable weather, more like March. I feel well, but O! how I miss you my dear. I have arrived 16th 3 o'clock all mud and rain.

I am your devoted loving Husband
C. Miller
Fort Rice

ଓଷଓ

Fort Rice, Dakota Territory

June 17, 1867

A Sketch of the Grand Pow Wow held by General Sully and Colonel Parker of General Grant's Staff held on the above date at Fort Rice on the said 17 of June 1867:

Some 50 to 60 Chiefs of various tribes or Lodges assembled within the enclosure of the Fort at General Sully's request. They all seated themselves in front of Headquarters. Some on the platform, some crouched on the ground, all in various grotesque costumes. The laboratory of nature and art had been called into requisition to disfigure their faces and body, with various colors containing black, green, yellow, blue, purple, white, gray, sprinkled and intensified as only the aborigines can compound, feathers decorated their heads; charms, their throats and breasts, various colored ribbons decorated their bodies and limbs, with the invariable tomahawk, pipes of peace, and blankets of various hues. Such a "tout ensemble" can only be appreciated by ocular perception; pen is weak and feeble to describe such a gathering.

There were in this assembly six (6) principal Chiefs representing the Hunkpapa, Black Feet, Grand Tetons, Cut Head and any quantity of minor importance. The Very Rev. Father Smith, a Roman Catholic Priest belonging to the S.J., opened the "Pow Wow" with a very appropriate prayer to the "Great Spirit" which was interpreted to the Indian Chieftains, to which they all said "How" which means "Amen," of course.

General Sully then informed them through an interpreter that he came here amongst them for the purpose of assuring them that their Great Father at Washington would do all manner of kindness for them, but if they did not behave well and did go on the "War Path," the Great Father at the White House would be angry and punish them by sending a great army and take them prisoners, et cetera (of course they believed every word of it). They all said "Hmmmmm" like the sound of a half-angry Buffalo (to us outsiders). Then he told them that what they would now say would be all put on paper (at the same time a very fine specimen of a reporter appeared on the scene, who with his portfolio, placed himself against Headquarters Building and commenced writing very earnestly).

Colonel Parker then had his say, that all they said would be put on paper and reassured up in the Archives of the U.S. Government, which he assured them that their conditions would be considered and they properly treated by the Great White Father at Washington.

About this time the God of Pluvius put a stop to further outdoor parlavous, to which the Indians all said "Ugh" and General Sully, Colonel Parker, Father Smith and the Big Indians, all adjourned to the fire and Canadian Steamer, General Graham, which was lying at the river bank. There they finished the "Pow Wow."

The Big Indian Chiefs' reply was that the white man must let them alone, leave them their country, their antelopes, buffalo and other game, not send any steamboats up the Missouri River or any soldiers in their land.

There is really nothing in this country very attractive. The Missouri River is a grand circular stream, crooked as an old maid, one elbow after another, something like the folds of a rattlesnake, sometime travelling twenty-five miles, when you find that you are only two miles by land from where you started. As to the banks, they are irregular, some places high, precipitous, slatey strata, others low, with here and there the banks washing away, some cottonwood in various places along the river; around this "Fort" we have very little timber or wood that can be used. The scenery is very monotonous and almost painful; nothing to relieve the sight, but plains and hills, some scorched and ashy, like an upheaving of a volcanic nature, for miles not a tree or even a bush to soften the aspect.

There are at present on the east and west sides of the river at this point, somewhere about a thousand lodges or "Tippys" as they call an Indian tent, around us. They nearly all claim to be friendly, but we do not know, nor do we believe it, as long as they got plenty of fat meat, well, but the "Indian" cannot be trusted. He considers the "Pale Face" an intruder so that at any moment they may scalp and murder us if they can surprise the garrison. They had one of their celebrated war dances lately, which lasted five days; during this dance the braves, or those who wish to be counted as such, undergo all kinds of torture and pain, cutting their flesh in strips, passing belts through them to lift heavy weights and pull till the flesh often gives way.

ജ൴

Professor Dettweiller's eyes have been bothering him lately, and he asks Lillie to read this lengthy report to him. He sits and listens with his eyes closed, his glasses perched on his forehead. When she's finished, he shakes his head. "Now, isn't that a treasure? A first-person account of treaty negotiations with the Indians. How exceptional!" He has a sad smile on his face. "Doesn't sound like the Hunkpapa were very agreeable. They probably knew the Government isn't good at keeping promises."

In their time together, Professor Dettweiller has already shared tales from General Howard's leadership in campaigns against many Indian tribes, both before and after the war, the most famous against the Nez Perce. Though some of the stories are funny or exciting, many are brutal, ugly, and sad, and the professor seems sad when he tells them.

Lillie's brow wrinkles. "How do you mean?"

"The U.S. Government has made many treaties with the Indian tribes over many years. There isn't a single one it hasn't broken, often through force. And this isn't ancient history, you know. Skirmishes with the Indians still break out every few years."

"But…they *are* heathens. Aren't they? They don't believe in Christ." Even as she says it, though, she feels certain that she is somehow disappointing Professor Dettweiller.

"Is that what makes it acceptable?" She has no answer, and after a long pause, he says, "Lillie, why are you Catholic?"

"Why…?"

"It's because your parents are Catholic, isn't it? And because you're surrounded by a Catholic community. What if your parents had been Jewish?"

She actually has to suppress a gasp.

"I will tell you: you would have loved whatever God they taught you to love. That's how cultures are formed." His eyes are closed again, but he says, "When people are different from you, it's easy to think that they are less than you. Then it doesn't seem like a bad thing to treat them in a bad way." The pause is long enough that Lillie is almost certain he is asleep, but he isn't. "Remember what Sister Bernadette said, Lillie. We are all God's creatures."

ꕥ

Fort Rice, D.T.
August 24, 1867

My dear little sweet wife:

I received your letter of the 30th July last mail 22nd. I am very glad to hear from you, that you are better and doing well, both you and the children. Thank you, darling, I am well and hearty, though yesterday I had to bleed myself. The weather has been very hot out here, as high as 99 Fahrenheit and 120 in the sun, so I took about one quart of blood from my arm, and today I feel quite light and easy. I did it myself, not wishing to trust the other "Dr. P. McShane" who is here with me as "Post Surgeon." I do not know yet when I can come home. I wish I could do so now, for I am completely disgusted with everything here, even the "Post Surgeon." He is no man at all, as I have told him several times. He has neither knowledge nor manhood to stand up for his professional opinion. Whenever he has a case to attend to, he gets his old "family Doctor" called "Vade Mecum," printed about 35 years ago, and hunts up a prescription in it, to write down for his patients. He cannot write one prescription scarcely without it. He is quite an old man, gray haired and a regular "Irish Fool." Every one of the officers think they know as much as any Doctor, not to me but to Dr. P. McShane.

We had two men killed on Thursday, mail day 22nd, one that shot himself through the chest and another took a dose of poison. Both were dead in less than twenty minutes. I could do nothing for them. So we go.

Well my dear, I not being able to come home at present, I will send you three hundred dollars, by our Sutler, Mr. Gregory, who is going East. He will send you a "check" on some bank in Washington City D.C. and you can go and have it cashed and use it as you need it. God bless you darling.

ଓଃଓ

Fort Rice D. T.
Nov. 1st 1867

I have the honor to report that I performed duty at this post as A. A. Surg. U.S.A. by order No. 56 from Dept. Headqr Dept. Dakota, Bvt Major Gen Terry comdg.

I have had my contract annulled this day, for two reasons.

Viz. 1st: I came here last June with the impression that I were to have charge as Medical Officer of this Post, but no! by some maneuver one Patrick McShane, A. A. Surg U.S.A. was created Post Surgeon, one whom I do not respect as a Gentleman, still less as a Surgeon and Physician. I therefore sacrifice my position to principle.

Second: The Post Comdr. refuses to furnish me with a servant or orderly. I therefore resign my place to be filled by another more pliant. If my services are in demand anywhere near Washington City or St. Louis, Mo., I will serve my address hereafter at my Office.

Dr. C. Miller
No. 388 6th Street
Washington D. C.

Very Respectfully
Your Obedient Servant
C. Miller, M.D.

ഇഢ

With Christian once again safely home, Professor Dettweiller and Lillie are relaxing with a cup of tea to celebrate finishing their survey of all of his artifacts. "Well, what an adventure this has turned out to be! I must tell you, Lillie, I am thoroughly enjoying myself. I'm so glad you chose to embark on this project."

"I am, too. Even though it's not turning out exactly like I expected." He cocks his head and waits for her to elaborate. "Grampa died way before I was born, and Mother always has such wonderful stories about him, and she loved him so much, that I always wished that I knew him. Well, now I kind of feel like I do."

"And you're disappointed."

"He just seems so…selfish."

"Why do you say that?"

She knows the professor well enough now to know that he's not arguing but prompting her to provide evidence to support her statement, and she enumerates. "He burns all of her letters, he insists that she needs to save and he doesn't spend a cent but that *a horse I had to have*, he's always teasing her about other women, and he keeps going away and leaving his family when he doesn't need to."

"And yet your mother loved him very much." Lillie nods. "In my experience, Lillie, very few people are wholly bad, and no one is wholly good. Consider our own General Howard, the *Christian General*, whose generosity of spirit so helped the coloreds but did not extend to the Plains Indians. They would never describe him in the terms of respect and friendship that so many of us use. And yet it's all the same man."

"It does seem odd that talking about Grampa makes Grandma

sad but makes Mother happy."

"Consider that your grandmother bore the brunt of his self-absorption because she was responsible to her children, but perhaps your mother brought out the very best in him—a generosity that other people didn't often see. But no matter what, he'll always be your grandfather. Remember, Lillie: good and bad both, our history conspires to make us who we are."

ꕥ

It is halfway through the school year, and Lillie has regained some of her equilibrium. While she hasn't forged any close friendships, her peers warm up once they realize she's not some freak of nature. History class is, of course, her favorite, and her classmates are eager to learn how she has tamed this vast and intimidating assignment. Their monthly oral presentations describing the progress of their research is a source of dread for most of the girls, either for having to speak in front of the class or for having to scrounge up something to report, but Lillie is willing to coach them through the preparation and presentation, as long as they've actually worked on their project.

Her source of dread is still civics and government, not for the material but for the teacher. Sister Justinia's undisguised disdain for Lillie warns the rest of the class away from her. She understands their reticence and wonders whether she would be any braver in their place, but the isolation is draining. She keeps her head down and her mouth closed as much as she can, which earns her poor marks for class participation and written comments about an uncooperative attitude. The times that she is forced to contribute usually end badly.

One day, as part of a lesson on the formation of the nation's capital, Sister Justinia asks each girl to say where she lives and to offer an example of how her neighborhood is somehow touched by the Federal government. Lillie's mind scrambles to come up with something, and her stomach clenches as her turn approaches. She hits upon describing the wholesale change in street names suffered by all of upper Northwest in 1905, mandated by Congress to match the city's street-naming convention. She quickly coaches herself through three sentences that describe the issue and feels ready. *Wouldn't it be horrible if I said I live on Flint Street?* "I live in Brightwood Park, on Flint—" She almost groans out loud as she has to correct herself. "On Longfellow Street." She keeps her eyes on her desk, not bothering to continue.

"Well, that's interesting, Lillie. Most people know where they live by the time they're in ninth grade."

An irritated voice breaks in from the other side of the classroom. "They changed all the street names, Sister. Mine was Des Moines, but now it's Jefferson. Lots of people still say the old names. And now they've changed the Seventh Street Road and Brightwood Avenue to Georgia Avenue, and that messes everyone up even more."

Again there is a significant pause, and Lillie's eyes cut over to see who is speaking. She has only talked to Eugenie Lieutand on a few occasions. Eugenie is pretty and bright, but this is their only class together, and, unlike Lillie, she has an established circle of friends here at school.

"I'm sorry, Eugenie, are you lecturing me?"

"Oh, no, Sister Justinia!" Lillie sees Eugenie's wide eyes blink innocently. "But since we were talking about our neighborhoods, well, that's one of the very interesting things about Brightwood Park."

"I see. Perhaps next time you'll remember to contain yourself until you're called on to share."

"Oh, yes, Sister. I certainly will." The words are so emphatically virtuous that Lillie has to clamp down to keep from snorting.

Lillie waits until lunchtime to approach Eugenie, who is eating with some of her girlfriends. She hesitates a moment, but then Eugenie sees her and hops up to meet her halfway.

"Thank you for that."

Eugenie smiles and rolls her eyes. "She makes me tired. Why is she always so hateful?" It's a rhetorical question, and Eugenie imagines that there's no knowable answer. "Today I was so aggravated that words just started coming out of my mouth. I guess it's a good thing I didn't actually say what I was thinking!"

"Well, I was thinking, *Don't say Flint!,* so of course I did. Anyway, it was very brave of you."

"Or foolish."

"I guess we'll find out." They laugh together. "I never knew you lived in Brightwood Park."

"I didn't know you did either, 'til today. And I wasn't kidding that everyone on my street still calls it Des Moines. And Erie—"

"And Flint and Genesee! My mother complains about *Longfellow* every time she has to write it out, since it's twice as long."

"And what sort of name is *Quackenbos* anyway?"

"Eugenie!" one of her friends calls from their lunch table, beckoning her back, and she waves in acknowledgement.

"Well, I just wanted to say thank you."

"Are you having lunch with someone else?" Lillie usually eats her lunch in Sister Bernadette's classroom, even though she's not supposed to. "Why don't you come sit with us?"

It is thanks in large measure to Eugenie, Professor Dettweiller, and Sister Bernadette that Lillie finally regains her former confidence. In civics class, she begins to keep her head up and eyes level, and answers Sister's questions pleasantly and with poise. It's an effective strategy to parry the jabs, and when the blows fail to land, Sister Justinia starts to tire of the contest.

Eventually, the mystery of Sister Justinia and Dorcas Hines is solved, or at least plausibly explained. Lillie is relating to her new lunch group that the source of Sister's bias is somehow rooted in a connection with Dorcas, when Imogen Harris says, "Oh, they're cousins." Heads snap to look at her, none more sharply than Lillie's. "I heard Sister Betina and Sister Mary Lawrence talking about it at the beginning of the year. Sister Betina kept gasping what a scandal it all was, and Sister Mary Lawrence kept gasping that it was too horrible to talk about. But they kept talking about it." She laughs, but the girls need more.

"It's a scandal that they're cousins?"

"No, no, that Sister did something so horrible that her father disowned her and sent her off to the nunnery." She can see they're waiting. "No, they didn't say what it was. I guess it really *was* too horrible to talk about. Anyway, she decided to act like she's saved to prove she's learned her lesson and maybe her father will reown her again—is that a word? *Reown*? Anyway, put her back in the inheritance. So Sister's trying to convince her father to let her leave, and Dorcas is trying to convince *her* father to convince Sister's father."

"Let her leave what? Being a nun? Do they even let you do that?" Eugenie is amazed.

"Maybe when you're rich as Croesus and you can buy your way out."

"Imogen!" The girls are horrified.

"I didn't say it! Sister Betina said it."

So: cousins cut from the same unattractive cloth. After that, Lillie doesn't give a thought to either one of them.

Her thesis presentation and defense, given to a board of three nuns, two Jesuit brothers from Gonzaga, and two Howard University professors, is articulate and incisive, and she never falters, even under the hard questioning of one of the brothers. At the year-end school assembly, Professor Dettweiller makes a special appearance to present Lillie with the Outstanding Scholar award, one of the few times it has been awarded to a freshman. Afterwards, accepting congratulations from some of the girls and their parents as she cranes to find Charley and Emma, there is a tap on her shoulder. She turns and looks up into the face of that impossibly handsome young man. "Miss Beck, perhaps you'll remember me? Edward Gainsboro. We met informally last August. At the school open house."

"Of course I remember. How do you do?"

"Very well. I want to offer my congratulations on your achievement. It seems you've had a fine year."

She sees Dorcas approaching from behind him, all thunder and lightning. Lillie laughs, entirely comfortable. "Thank you. It got off to a rocky start, but it ended well."

"Edward, we're leaving now."

"Dorcas, hello. You must be thrilled to be graduating next week." Even Lillie is surprised to hear how evenly these words come out of her.

In true Dorcas fashion, she offers no acknowledgement. "*Now*, Edward."

Edward tips his head to Lillie even as Dorcas firmly takes his arm to pull him away. "Best of luck to you in the future, Miss Beck."

"And to you, Mr. Gainsboro." As she turns away and finally sees Emma and Charley, she murmurs to herself, "You're going to need it."

Morning, Monday, 17 April 1933

Ferd snaps awake at five a.m., pushing himself partly out of the chair in a dream-addled urgency to be somewhere. It takes him several confused seconds to remember where he is and why. He sits down again in the muddy shadows, gazing at his sleeping wife and waiting for his pulse rate to subside. He thinks that he has startled because of some movement from her, but she is sleeping quietly, her breathing more even and easy than it was before.

Jeanie is back in her crib, moved there as soon as she was fully asleep. Ferd learned early in fatherhood that a sleeping child can be handled much like a sack of potatoes without any concern that she will wake up. He also knows that the youngest wake up the earliest, and he wants Lillie to sleep as long as she needs to. But neither child is stirring yet, so he lifts his work clothes from the far chair and leaves them all sleeping as he slips out of the room for a quick shave and change from pajamas while no one is clamoring for the bathroom. Charley has already been in ahead of him, and is at the kitchen table with a cup of coffee and the newspaper, dressed for work. Ferd pours himself a cup of coffee and sits. "She's still asleep."

Charley nods but then sees that Ferd needs more from him than that. "She took a hard fall. It will just take time for her to get her wind back."

They sit. The paper rattles as Charley turns the pages and shakes them back to see the articles. Normally by this time, Emma and Lillie are starting breakfast as the household prods itself awake; Ferd presumes he knows where Emma is now. Breakfast will not make itself, so he pushes up from the table. In the pantry, he pulls out the big cast iron skillet, lights the burner, turns the flame to just above guttering, and greases the skillet with bacon fat from the jar. Charley has already brought in today's milk. Ferd cracks eggs into the big glass mixing bowl, splashes in some milk, adds the pepper, and whisks it into a yellow-orange soup. As the cast iron continues its slow absorption of heat, Ferd sits the toaster on another burner to let it warm up.

When he looks out from the pantry again, Jeanie is climbing into a chair and dragging her doll Sally with her. She kneels up so that she can see above the tabletop and rubs her eyes. "Jeanie, what are you doing out of bed?"

"Gramal told me to. Me and Bernie. She doesn't want to hear a peep. Not a peep."

Normally, hearing Jeanie innocently mimic an adult's words and inflection makes him laugh. This morning he turns back to the stove and pours eggs into the skillet.

A few minutes later Bernie appears, and climbs into another chair. Charley pulls his newspaper down. "If you both got tossed out together, where have you been?"

"Pooping."

"All righty then." He goes back behind his paper.

Ferd pulls a chair in front of the sink and points at it for Bernie. "Then get up here and wash your hands."

"Did already."

"Then you get to do it again."

Bernie climbs up on the chair as Ferd turns on the faucet and puts a cake of soap in his hands. Bernie idly splashes the water in the sink as smoke starts to leak from the pantry. "Daddy, your bread's on fire again."

Stepping back into the pantry, he runs the spatula through the setting eggs once or twice, then, with wetted fingertips and a practiced hand, flips each piece of bread over to toast the other side. The side that has been facing the burner is black. He glances out at Bernie. "Use the soap."

"Am."

Ferd stalks over to the sink, picks up the soap, and scrubs Bernie's hands, front and back.

More children wander into the kitchen and sit at the table, the girls in various stages of school readiness, some hair still in rollers. Charley Boy is fully dressed; Johnny is in pajamas.

"Where's Mother?"

"She's resting, so all of you need to keep the noise level down."

"Daddy, your toast is burning."

"Where's Gramal?"

"I have no idea."

"She's in Mamma's room!" Jeanie informs them.

Ferd closes his eyes momentarily; he tells them, "Which means no one is waiting on you this morning." He turns the egg preparation over to Eleanor, has Margaret set the table, and lifts Bernie from the chair at the sink. "Go sit down."

He flips his black toast onto a bread plate and takes a bite as he sets it at his place at the table. Francie takes over toasting for the rest of them. When a few are finished eating, he sets them up on a lunch assembly line: bread, peanut butter, jelly, bread, wax paper, sack, apple, cookie. In the midst of it, he pours more coffee into his now-cold cup and sits down heavily. He finds himself glancing up at the noises he hears from the rooms above.

"Daddy, why d'you eat black toast?" Jeanie is leaning across him to look at the remains on his plate.

He sits her back down in her seat. "It settles my stomach."

"You got a stummy ache?"

He gives her a little smile. "Yes, Jeanie, yes, I do."

She strokes his arm in comfort. "Poor Daddy. I hope the toast makes it all better," though the expression on her face says that she is unconvinced. She looks past him to the hall doorway. "Mamma!" Jeanie starts to scramble down from her seat, but Ferd stops her with one hand.

"Sit down and eat your eggs."

Lillie is dressed, but looks pale and moves slowly. Her arm is tucked under Emma's as they enter the room. As he gets up, Ferd lifts his chin at Charley Boy, who vacates the chair closest to Lillie. Ferd is there, holding the chair for her and helping her to sit. She makes a small wincing noise. "How are you?" he asks softly.

Her voice is thick and low. "Still groggy from the laudanum. And *very* stiff." She grins at him at little. "You should see some of the bruises." She looks around at the expectant faces, all looking back; even Charley has come from behind his newspaper. "Well, I see no one needs me to make breakfast. It's good to know you can all manage without me." There is a flurry of children showing what they can do: A clean plate shows up in front of her, eggs are scooped onto it, and toast slices, nicely browned rather than carbonized, dressed with butter and grape jelly. "My goodness, I feel like a queen."

Emma sets a cup of hot tea in front of her. Lillie dips a point of the toast in and takes a tentative nibble, swallows.

"I'm glad you're feeling better, Mother," Francie says.

"Me, too, dear. But time to get ready for school, isn't it?"

The kids start to get up, leaving their plates. Ferd clears his throat significantly, and they take the hint to bring their plates to Emma who scrapes the remainders off into the garbage. Jeanie slides off her chair, making conspiratorial plans with Sally, and Bernie is intent on setting up toast sails on a congealed sea of eggs swirled with jelly.

Lillie breathes in deeply, considering another bite of toast. "I'll stay home today," Ferd tells her.

"Don't be silly. I just need to move, stretch. Stay oiled," she smiles at him. "Sleep helped." She keeps her sentences short, saving breath.

"Well. If you're sure."

"I'm sure."

Charley snaps his paper closed, folds it up at his place. "Come on, Ferd. Time to go earn our two bits."

Ferd leans down to Lillie and kisses her cheek. Her long, deep breaths seem to have an edge to them. "Promise me you'll take it easy today." She nods at him, smiling. "And eat your breakfast. You need your strength." They share a smile, then Charley knocks against him with an elbow to get him moving out of the room.

On the way out of the house, they see Dr. Cavanaugh pulling in along the Eighth Street curb, so they wait until he's out of the car, bag in hand, and heading to the front walk. "I wanted to stop by first thing to check in. Am I too early?"

They exchange notes on the patient's progress: quiet night, obvious severe stiffness, reported bruising, labored breathing observed moments earlier. The doctor nods and makes significant noises. "I'll do a more thorough examination and see what I need to prescribe. She's probably right that getting up and moving around is the best thing for it. Though I'm still stumped about the breathing." He squints off into the middle distance. "Well, let me go take a look."

Charley tips his hat and turns to go, but Ferd stays where he is. The doctor puts a hand on his shoulder. "I promise I'll call you at work if there's anything significant to report."

Over his shoulder, Charley tells him, "Just go on in. They're in the kitchen."

Dr. Cavanaugh knocks as he's opening the door into the hall, hearing as he does the stamping and braying of wild beasts on the floor above him. He stands for a moment looking toward the noise before he sees Jeanie on the floor staring at him with big eyes, her back against one of the armchairs, holding a rag doll. "Well, hello there."

Her lower lip is quivering a bit, and she pulls Sally in close. "I don't need a shot," she insists.

"No, I don't guess you do. I'm here to see your mother."

Jeanie's eyes narrow at him in suspicion. She has a fine memory of the many needle pricks administered by this man, all preceded by an assurance that, "This won't hurt a bit," which is always a lie. He bears watching.

The commotion from above has covered up the sounds coming from the kitchen, of gasping, ragged coughing. He is there in two strides, and finds Emma bracing Lillie at the sink, holding a damp towel against her neck. Lillie is in the midst of a coughing fit, but is also choking in her struggle for air. Dr. Cavanaugh straightens her up, and brings her arms straight up over her head, as though she is a child who swallows down the wrong pipe. Her eyes are wild from the sense of suffocation, and he stands in front of her, tilting her head back slightly to open the airway, but maintaining eye contact to coax her back to herself. "Sip the air, Lillie. Don't try to gasp. Sip. Sip." He does it himself, forming a little straw with his lips, for her to imitate. "That's it. That's the way." He waits a moment for her breathing to settle out, but he can hear the ragged edge of it. He helps her to a chair and looks at Emma. "Why were you at the sink? Did she vomit?"

"The coughing brought up phlegm."

He uses the dishcloth to examine the product of her cough. It's dark and thick, a greenish-gray color.

"The baby!" Lillie gasps, launching another, milder coughing fit. Piercing the general roar of the Voith multitude overhead is the insulted shriek of a hungry, soiled child being poked in the thigh by an errant diaper pin.

"Mother! Oh, I forgot—Gramal!" shouts a voice from above. "Tommy wants you!"

Emma collects up the lunch sacks to prevent the herd from storming into the kitchen, and meets the children on the stairs, doling out lunches as they gallop out the front door.

Chloe comes into the kitchen through the spring porch, removing her hatpin and hat, and patting her hair. Concerned after Charley's call, she is here almost three hours earlier than her normal Monday start time.

She and Dr. Cavanaugh nod to each other, and she touches Lillie's hand. "I'm so sorry you're feeling poorly, Miss Lillie. Mr. Charley told me about the fall."

Lillie gives a dismissive eye-roll as she smiles. "Clumsy! Thanks for coming early. Will you help Mother with the baby? They're upstairs." Tommy remains at full volume. Another touch in assurance and Chloe hurries out.

Alone together in the kitchen now, Dr. Cavanaugh conducts a second evaluation, using his reflector to shine light into eyes, ears, nose, and throat. He palpates her neck, and asks her to swallow. He pauses several times during the examination as she coughs. He has her unbutton the collar of her blouse, rubs the stethoscope on his coat to warm it up, and then: right front, "deep breath," left front, "deep breath," and again on the back. The rattle is distinct and worrisome, but again no wet hiss to indicate a puncture. He gently probes the lump on the back of her head, and sees bruises on her back, below her neckline. "Ferd says the bruises have fully blossomed, yes?"

She nods, coughing into her fist. "I'm one big bruise." She indicates upper arms, calves, thighs, across her hips, shoulders.

"But you can move everything?"

She nods again, but this time the coughing takes hold and doesn't let go. He gives her his handkerchief, stands her up, and tips her chin up again. "Try to breathe in through your nose." She holds the panic at bay this time, but it takes effort. Once the fit subsides, he lets her sit again and examines the results in the handkerchief: thick, gray, sticky. "We need to get you back up to bed."

"Don't you hurt my mamma, neither," Jeanie demands from the corner, arms crushing Sally tight across her chest. She and Bernie have come in through the dining room, unseen. "He wants to give everyone a shot," she informs Bernie, who rubs his bottom protectively and keeps his eye on the doctor.

"Bernie, can you please go upstairs and ask the maid to come down?" he asks.

"Who?"

"Chloe," Lillie tells him, through the gravel in her throat. "Go get Chloe."

Bernie barrels through the kitchen and out the door to the hall. Jeanie glares at the doctor, ensuring her mother's safety as they all mark the clomping progress of the expedition: stairs, landing, stairs, hallway, door, muffled words, hurried hallway footsteps, stairs, landing, stairs, hall, kitchen! Chloe needs no direction, offering her arm to Lillie on one side while Dr. Cavanaugh helps her up on the other. Jeanie follows the procession out through the hall, where they pick up Bernie again, then up the steps—slowly now—to collect Emma and Tommy from the landing.

Emma takes over command, issuing a steady stream of orders to the ranks on the march up to the hallway and at last into the bedroom, parade rest.

Endings and Beginnings

1912-1915

The last fall is a bad one, probably caused by a small stroke that leaves Mary partially paralyzed on the left side. Her voice is unaffected and her mind is as sharp as ever, but she can no longer attend to her own toilet and has no choice but to keep to her bed. They all understand that things are on a downward trajectory.

Lillie spends as much time with Mary as she can, reading to her after supper, sharing the latest gossip from school and the neighborhood, telling the story of how she and her girlfriends make a big snow fort in the backyard on the Eighth Street side and ambush the boys walking by, as though they are all seven and not seventeen. But under her stream of chatter, she wrestles with the unhappy concept of inevitability.

Facing the loss of someone close to her is a new and painful experience, but Mary's own unblinking acceptance helps her to maintain composure. "Oh, child, this is what we spend all our lives preparing for, you know that." She fingers her rosary beads, now never far from her good right hand. "Think of how long a time I've had here. Why, I'd be eighty in May!"

"Grandma! You make it sound like…like you're gone already!"

"Well, whenever it is, I hope I find the gates open when I get there. There are so many people I want to see again; I'd hate for Jesus and Peter to decide I don't belong." Lillie is horrified and starts to protest before she realizes that Mary is teasing her. There's a quiet moment while Mary looks wistfully at her. "I remember the day you were born. What a tiny little bundle you were! When I was cleaning you up and wrapping you in a blanket, I remember telling you, *Little baby, you are here to bring us joy*, and that's just what you've done. You've brought me more joy than I ever had a right to expect." Her eyes twinkle at Lillie. "I don't guess you remember that I told you that."

Lillie laughs with her. "No, Grandma, I don't guess I do." They smile at each other. "Grandma, what's your earliest memory?"

Mary closes her eyes for mere seconds, and feels as though she sees her entire life as a vast photograph, as though it occurs in a single instant. Perhaps it does.

She had no memory of home, of Bavaria, outside of a few crisp images that capture frozen moments—an orange in the toe of a Christmas stocking, a surprise litter of kittens. Even the wistfully repeated memories of her older siblings, of school and friends, skating parties and summertime wildflowers, she often hears as more nostalgic manufacture than actual memory. She can summon the general feeling of familial warmth, undercut by a shared wariness of Friedrich Schlegel, the cold and exacting husband and father who serves as an atmosphere more than a physical presence. But she feels sure that she has her own memory of the indelible episode of her childhood, the sudden and inexplicable decision by Friedrich to move his family to America. The word, *America*, spoken in whispers among the Schlegel children, evokes a sense of menace, like stepping into a dense and unknown forest that closes in behind you.

Not quite four, Mary, still Maria then, remembers being frightened by her mother's palpable panic. Still suckling one child and gravid with another, Clara Schlegel is given a deadline by which to pack up the household of seven in readiness for a transatlantic crossing, without any understanding of how to prepare. Used to a measure of material comfort, Clara thinks for a brief time that the family will have one of the few cabins on the packet ship, where there are beds with linens, and meals are prepared and served hot by assigned valets. Friedrich soon makes it clear that there will be no such luxuries.

Disobeying Friedrich's explicit orders, she speaks to some of her friends along the street, women with relatives who have already gone across, but the stories and advice offer a jumble of conflicting tales. The ones that depict America as a giddy and effusive host who stuffs money into the coat pockets of each new arrival seem, even to Clara, to be the embellished inventions of underfed and ill-housed relatives, cloaking their general misery from the folks back home.

The one consistent element of each story, though, is that the crossing is a trial to be endured. Each woman shares a staggering tale of woe from a friend or relative: weeks, a month, in over-stuffed, choking, and fetid quarters that roil into a soup of contagion; rations provided in the cost of the ticket that shrink to crumbs as the packet ship gropes its way across the ocean; furious storms or even rogue waves, arising from nowhere to scour the decks and empty a few of the unsuspecting into the trailing foam, like the sediment carried in the toss from a scrub bucket. They tell also of the speed with which any sense of shared community breaks apart into narrow-eyed suspicion, grappling, hoarding, and thievery, while the footings of allegiance erode from countrymen to townsfolk to neighbors to family, finally remaining only to self. When at last cries come of "Land ho!" and "There! There it is!" most are able to retrieve their crumpled humanity from the discard pile, shake out the creases and slip it back on. Neighbors once again greet each other with hearty backslaps and the laughter of relief as they gather at the railings for a first glimpse. Dressed in their fresh skins, it is easy to forget that each has seen the other naked and ugly. Together they stand, blinking into the glare of sunlight and opportunity.

For her part, Clara can only stare numbly at the approaching coastline, stupefied from exhaustion and in disbelief that she and her children have emerged whole after almost four weeks at sea. The trip is every bit as wretched as described, and more: they are forced to wait in Bremen for the onshore wind to turn, and what's more, they need to hide themselves, as it becomes clear that their hasty emigration is an attempt to outrun debts from Friedrich's failed mercantile business. Once onboard, he melts into the planking, invisible and untouchable. Clara hangs blankets to claim her family's tiny section of floorboards, and quickly learns to keep all valuables on her person. She attempts vigilance for vermin, both insect and human. Her huge belly and constant seasickness make it difficult to wrestle a turn at the one stove provided in steerage for meal preparation, the one whose fire is doused by crew members at every hint of impending weather. Between diarrhea and vomiting, the children shrivel. When Clara lies down in the darkness, she finds herself half-wishing that she will not get up again.

Mrs. Steinman is their angel. They meet when she sees Clara slump against a post and lose the week's potatoes she is carrying in her apron. She scoops them up before other grasping hands can get to them, and shepherds Clara back to her bunk. From there on, she takes over, and Clara surrenders with thanks. Mrs. Steinman is forcible in securing their turn to cook, and has herbs that help to staunch the children's fluid loss. Clara has been keeping them all huddled together in what she sees as the relative safety below; Mrs. Steinman insists that the entire family spend time on the open deck during the better weather to breathe clean air and escape the infectious confinement. It's during these turns on deck that they share their brief and unremarkable stories. Mrs. Steinman, newly widowed after twenty-five years in a comfortable marriage, is on her way to join her daughter and son-in-law in a remote outpost with the exotic-sounding name of *Milwaukee*.

When the baby comes—breach, followed by Clara's hemorrhaging—the situation demands every bit of Mrs. Steinman's skill as a midwife. She successfully marshals the press of curious women into making themselves useful, and soon enough there is a tiny, pink-cheeked bundle of baby girl, perfect from head to toe, tucked into Clara's elbow.

It takes a full day for Friedrich to show himself. In the gloom, Clara is propped up in her bunk while Rachel, the eldest, reads to them, and Mrs. Steinman paces with Baby Catharine tucked in her elbow. They all stop to look up when they realize he is standing there. He is red-faced in his fury. "You let my child be birthed by a Jew?" he hisses.

Clara stares directly back at him. "She saved our lives; all of us.

We would all be dead without her, if we had to rely on you." She touches Rachel on the shoulder to have her continue, dismissing him utterly. She doesn't see him again until they dock in the Port of Baltimore.

As time passes, it becomes clear that this incident is the fulcrum that shifts power in the Schlegel household onto a more equitable plane—that, and the thorough beating Friedrich endures when the cousins of one of his Bavarian creditors track him down. The family settles within the large German community in Baltimore, and this is the point at which Mary is able to pick up a consistent thread in her own personal narrative. She and the other little ones absorb English quickly, and help their parents toward a passable understanding; there is little to be done with the accents, which remain thick as porridge. At first, Friedrich has to accept manual labor, for which he is ill-suited, but then he tries his luck again at a small dry goods business. Clara insists on keeping the books herself. Mary loves spending afternoons at the store, sweeping, arranging displays, stocking shelves, eventually working behind the counter. At school, she is *Mary* and speaks English; at home, she is *Maria* and speaks German; at the shop, she speaks whichever language the customer prefers. In the neighborhood, their Lutheran family finds itself increasingly surrounded by Catholics, who, to Clara's thinking, seem to find passion in their religion, warmth in their church, and a hearty camaraderie among themselves, all in contrast to the chilly and tightly laced Lutherans she is used to. When she finally meets the charismatic priest who guides the local parish, Clara decides that they will all convert, and so they do.

Mary is seventeen when she meets Christian, another Bavarian immigrant who makes the trip in his mid-teens, as the packet trade shifts from sail to steam; his family makes the crossing in an astonishing six days. Even as he steps onto the ship, Christian changes his name from Mueller to Miller, slipping out of his old name as a snake slips out of a skin that has become worn and constricting, leaving it behind as though it never existed. By the time they meet, he is twenty and recently apprenticed to a German surgeon specializing in cupping and leeching. Mary is both drawn to and maddened by his proprietary and imperious manner. He insists that no one call her Maria anymore, and the one time that he hears her chatting in German with a neighbor, he raises his hand almost as though he might hit her, and then seethes at her, "English. Always English."

Friedrich presses for the match, pleased at the prospect of a doctor in the family, and a bit taken by the similarity to his own younger self. Clara sees it too, which is what gives her pause. She finally relents, having extracted a promise that he will convert, not knowing that Christian welcomes the idea as another opportunity to reinvent himself.

Contract made, Christian surprises them all by announcing his move to Washington City, where he sees that his future lies. He will establish himself as a cupper and leecher while he continues his apprenticeship under the doctors to whom the old German surgeon recommends him. Once established, he will send for Mary. How long? However long. There is no discussion; Christian has decided.

His last act as a resident of Baltimore is to become a naturalized U.S. citizen, having endured the mandatory five-year residency period. He gladly signs his name to the document in which he pledges that "he will support the Constitution of the United States, and that he doth absolutely and entirely renounce and abjure forever all allegiance and fidelity to every foreign Prince, Potentate, State and Sovereignty whatever, and particularly all allegiance and fidelity to *the King of Bavaria.*" Satisfied, "The Court thereupon admits the said *Christian Miller* to become a Citizen of the United States."

The next year is a series of Saturday or Sunday visits, made exclusively by Clara and Mary's boarding the train south, since Christian is, by his account, exceedingly busy. During this time, a young man from the neighborhood begins to work in the store. He and Mary are often alone together and develop an easy companionship. Between customers, they have wide-ranging conversations. Rolf plans a teaching career, with dreams of becoming a college professor. He is interested to hear her thoughts, and asks her questions that make her think about things in new ways.

Clara isn't blind, and while for Mary's sake she feels the pang of what might have been, she is resolute. The agreement has been made, and the Schlegels will never default on a contract again. Clara will make sure of that.

When Christian finally summons her for the wedding, he insists that she come alone, perhaps to hide the fact that he is not yet a Catholic and they are to be married in an Episcopal church. She spends the night before the final train trip weeping into Katie's shoulder. Katie, the baby, the sister with whom she has always had the strongest bond, strokes her head and makes soothing noises, even as Katie needs to catch her own tears at the looming separation. Rolf sees her off at the station, bringing his wedding gift of Shakespeare's collected sonnets, gripping her hand to tell her all the things that will never be said. The wedding is attended by two people she has never met before, acquaintances of Christian's. Much later, when Mary examines the image made on her wedding day, she sees the story of her marriage written there: Christian, dark eyes hard and resolute, lips drawn downward, a possessive hand on her shoulder; Mary, gazing out at something no one else can see, resigned, bereft.

The first year is a misery of homesickness and morning sickness, and of learning how to manage a household to Christian's specifications. Perhaps surprisingly, he is not unkind to her, especially once it's clear that she's expecting, but always somehow vaguely disappointed. When John is born in March, almost on their first anniversary, the pride that engorges him until it leaks from his pores softens him further. For the first time, Mary finds her footing in the marriage, and is hopeful for the little family. When their second child is born the following April, Christian doesn't even mind that it's a girl, and names her Mary. Mary chooses the middle name, Catharine, for her sister.

But then John dies—gripped out of nowhere by a fever that refuses to break, his father overmatched and impotent against the anonymous infection, Mary unable to watch as Christian raises blisters on John's tiny chest with the red-hot glass cups, and her son shrieks from the pain and the fever. It is a scant seventy-two hours from the first hint of sickness to the final shovelful of dirt on the toddler's coffin. Observing the aftermath, her brain somehow disconnected from her maternal misery, she is certain that whatever flicker of hope has shone for this family is now extinguished beyond any rekindling.

The next years are simply a hazy wash. Christian throws himself into his practice, his apprenticeship, and his study at Columbian College. Acceptance at the college requires that he show letters of good standing from the surgeon to whom he is apprenticed; that, and the price of admission to the lectures. The curriculum consists of six months of lectures presented twice over an eighteen-month period. The two terms are identical, the thinking being that repetition is a good teacher; Christian attends lectures for five years. By the time he receives his diploma in 1858, Emma, their third and last child, is more than a year old. Christian notes the birth date in the family bible with the spare comment: *another girl.*

Christian's practice flags. With the progress of medicine into the modern age, the practices endorsed by heroic medicine—cupping and leeching, induced vomiting and sweats, mercury purges—are increasingly seen as suspect tools of a less enlightened era. To help make ends meet, Mary uses her knowledge of the dry goods business to open a tiny shop in the shed by the alley. It helps, but not enough, and it is a further humiliation to Christian, who is given to black moods and sudden rages. He is certain he hears his fellow doctors' comments, sees their sideways glances. He is a man sorely aggrieved, unappreciated, besieged and beleaguered by lesser men, men of low quality who are nonetheless in positions of authority over him; it is not to be borne. This and more, punctuated with a fist slammed down on the table that makes the silverware jump. As the final ingredient in this roiling soup of discontent, Little Mary begins to have seizures.

Even now, Mary can't look those years in the eye with any sort of equanimity. Whatever other failures she is guilty of, her failure to protect her daughter is unforgivable. She is ashamed, too, at the relief that slowly creeps through her when the army camps start to form throughout the city and the demand for surgeons grows. How horrible is she to welcome harm to countless others in order to protect one, simply because she cannot?

But it's true that the run-up to and final outbreak of war shifts the mood in the tiny household. Some physicians and surgeons leave town entirely so they may support the Southern cause. Others are drawn into serving the needs of the encamped soldiers, which, this early in the conflict, are still the everyday complaints that any patient might suffer. No matter: scarcity of practitioners means that Christian's services are in high demand, and he spends most of his waking hours in his little office across the street. As the war wears on, though, the successful practice doesn't satisfy. He feels left behind, as more and more of his cohort enlist in the army to serve at the very front lines of the battles, selflessly saving lives even at the risk of their own, gathering the respect and honor of their peers and the thanks of a grateful nation. Christian decides he must go too.

This is not the outcome that Mary has bargained for. As things stand, their finances are finally robust, while his practice keeps Christian out of the house but still within arm's reach. He is, after all, the only one who knows the terms of the various leases and agreements, understands the accounting for the income and outlay, and negotiates for favorable terms with the local businesses. Mary is capable of doing at least that much, but Christian has never allowed it. The only area she manages is the dry goods shed.

Christian's decision is, as always, beyond discussion, but the speed of its execution stuns her. Only two weeks separate his appointment and his departure. The flurry of preparations may be a blessing, though, since it leaves Christian little time to stew over the injustice of being assigned as assistant surgeon to the colored troops.

Almost the moment he is gone, she receives the first in an endless series of dunning notices, this one telling her to vacate the premises. His response to her panicked letter that *you need not worry* and *I will see when I come on a visit* confirms that she is on her own. Her misery causes her to retreat further from her Baltimore family, though the retreat is hastened when relatives in their own straits presume that the wife of a doctor has means that she should share.

Meanwhile, Christian is kinder in his letters than he is in person, though his tender words and awkward attempts at humor can't overcome his natural self-absorption. It is an odd mix. She envisions him trying on different personalities as he sits down to write. Some letters are so manic, she wonders if he is drunk as he writes them. For her part, she knows that her letters become increasingly shrill and hectoring, but she can't stop herself when it's obvious that he does not understand: there is *no money*. The letter in which he asks why she doesn't send money to him causes her to collapse onto the floor in wracking sobs, frightening the girls.

Of course he learns quickly that he made a mistake in enlisting and seems genuinely puzzled when the Army won't simply let him go home. Desperate to leave home before, now he spends all his energy trying to get back there again, until the Army decides he isn't fit, and then he argues that he should be allowed to stay.

In ten months, he is back again, now to the latest shabby address that Mary has been forced to rent. His return is disruptive in so many ways: Mary has learned to run the business and financial end of the household, even in the face of poverty, and she and the girls enjoy a close bond. For his part, Christian is drinking more heavily, and the humiliation he has endured in his dismissal causes black and dangerous rages. Emma is the only one who can soften him, since she alone seeks his company and is genuinely happy to be with him. Though this means that Emma draws away from Mary as she embraces Christian, Mary welcomes the buffer.

Even with the continued shortage of doctors, Christian has trouble re-establishing his practice, but he discovers that the same Army that won't have him in its ranks will employ him under contract. For a time, he works at Camp Relief in the city, where the sick and lightly wounded are sent, and he watches as many of the boys find an exceptional opportunity to shed their uniforms and slip off into the countryside. It doesn't take long until he, too, is casting about, looking for another opportunity for reinvention.

He finds it in the chance to serve under contract to the Freedmen's Bureau, established at the end of the war to help the displaced and newly emancipated. And so, after a year at home, the cycle begins again: desperate to be away, regretful as soon as he is, unnaturally solicitous in his letters, always at loggerheads with his superiors. At home, though, things are different from before: Little

Mary at age ten is already irretrievably beyond Mary's reach, lost into her own world, and Emma, eight, is palpably resentful, sure that Mary is responsible for Christian's chronic need to escape. There is no comfort in togetherness anymore; they are simply in uneasy proximity, fully separate from each other.

This time, he is gone a mere four months; Mary is almost relieved when Christian returns, glad to have a focal point for her anxiety. It takes a bit more than another year for him to be off again, this time to join an expedition into the wilds of the far frontier, to serve as a doctor to the troops garrisoned at Fort Rice in the Dakota Territory. It's the third and final time though; when he returns home after just seven months, he does not leave again.

Old friends from medical school help to open doors as Christian rebuilds his practice, and he contracts with the city to provide health care to the poor in the area. Emma becomes his helper and constant companion. Christian softens to the point that the horsewhip goes back with the horses; perhaps Little Mary's utterly impassive response to him drains the energy from his whip hand.

But as time goes on, the drinking becomes more constant and more acute. He takes to his bed for weeks at a time, his rages replaced by a repetitive maudlin lament. He often threatens to harm himself, hoping to coax tender reassurance from his family that they love him too much to let him go. At other times, he makes a spectacle of himself in public, staggering out of the local saloons and bellowing at everyone and no one, attempting to pick fights with other patrons who simply stare at him and walk away, shaking their heads and laughing amongst themselves.

At the same time, Little Mary, hardly little anymore, rockets into a manic period in which she talks constantly, her eyes alternating between wide alarm and narrow suspicion. She takes to escaping from the house at night and prowling the neighborhoods, accosting strangers, grasping at them with clawed hands and whispering of conspiracy. Most shake her off and hurry away, but some badly mistake her intent. The night that Mary, once again combing the streets, comes upon Little Mary being pressed against an alley wall by some brute who has already bloodied her lip to get her to stop struggling is the final straw.

By the time Mary finds the home and makes arrangements, Little Mary has settled out of the worst of it, and is back to her quiet, sometimes clear-eyed self. She is attentive and engaged during the train trip to New York; she carries her own valise and shakes hands with the administrator, but then begins to twitch and bark out noises as she studies photographs on the walls. It is only Mary who cries at their parting. When she is shown out and the door closes behind her, Mary is alone. She sees, finally, that this is a lasting condition, and it saps her over years, pulling at her like the ivy that strangles an oak.

Christian dies at forty-six, after his practice has shrunk once more to the point that they are living in the alley that is Washington Street. There is nothing for it but for Emma to find a job. At age twenty, she heads off to the General Post Office to become the family's breadwinner. Sometimes it isn't enough, even when Mary takes in boarders, and they find Emma a tiny room to rent while Mary is now the one begging charity, living for a time with relatives in Baltimore. When one of them suggests she apply for a pension against Christian's military service, she embarks on a hellish, two-year battle with the federal Government over her application for a stipend of seventeen dollars a month. The Government demands she prove that Christian's death is caused by a condition he contracts during his service, and spends impressive resources in gathering depositions, sworn statements, and the reports of a hired investigator to prove that it is not. On the claimant's side, Christian's own voice is the most strident in making the case, since his old letters are filled with complaints of his declining health; Mary's lawyer chooses *chronic diarrhea* as the most likely and best documented. In the end, though, the thorough humiliation of the allegations that Christian killed himself, that Little Mary was a loose girl whom the family abandoned, that Mary or possibly Emma was cohabiting with a man not her husband—a kindly boarder of perhaps eighty-five who helps Emma build the model she includes with her patent application—snuffs out the last bit of will she has to care about her life. That the pension is finally and inexplicably approved simply means that her death will not come from starvation.

For both Mary and Emma, this begins a long trudge through pointless existence: days, weeks, months, years, each one utterly indistinguishable from its predecessor, save for the face and habits of whichever boarder is on hand. There is a brief, bright period when Emma is courted by a young man from her office; it ends soon after another, prettier girl begins to work there. They find themselves once again and finally in the old shanty on Washington Street. The women evolve a necessary symbiosis, one that is pared over time to its most basic elements, stripped almost of the need for words.

Is it possible then to overstate the magnitude of surprise, the sheer jaw-dropping improbability, when after sixteen years—sixteen!—Charley Beck one day crosses her threshold, upending her existence like a lightning bolt wrapped in an earthquake? How can the impossible still be true? But here she is, practically twenty years later: twenty years of every single day being different from the one before, twenty years of lively companionship and the shared, enduring love of this most beautiful girl, now practically a grown woman, who has brought her more joy than she thought there was in the world. How could she not find full contentment and peace in that?

Her eyes flutter open again. "Kittens," she smiles at Lillie. "I remember kittens."

ഇഗ

Dr. Darling stops by every few days to check in, accompanied by the young doctor he is grooming to take over his practice one day. Dr. Cavanaugh has a charming, easy manner that puts his patients at ease, but Emma stiffens a bit when they are introduced, and Dr. Darling pulls Charley aside. "Does it bother you that he's Irish?"

"Is he a good doctor?"

"Yes."

"Is he a good man?"

"Certainly."

"Can't imagine what else matters."

Mary obviously loves him, lighting up in a smile whenever he comes in to see her. But it is to Dr. Darling that she speaks in confidence, away from anyone else's hearing. "Don't let me drag on."

"Now, Mary— "

"No," she tells him, gripping his arm with a surprisingly strong hand. "We've known each other too long for you to pat me on the head. You and I have both seen it, and I won't do it. I won't be an endless, hopeless burden on this family. There are things you can do if it comes to that. Promise me you will." They look squarely at each other, and Dr. Darling's jaw clenches. "Gottfried. You have to promise."

Finally he nods. "I promise."

Mary spares Dr. Darling the pain of a Hippocratic conundrum by seeing herself out. The next stroke renders her speechless, causing her and him to exchange meaningful and worried looks respectively, but the final one just days later does the dirty work.

It takes Lillie a long time to recover from the blow. She drifts through the last few months of her sophomore year, and has to force herself to fulfill her duties as class president and to keep her studies up. Summer offers a welcome set of distractions, but the start of the new school year brings a fresh shock of loss, as Lillie returns each day to an empty house. Her solution is to spend most of her time at school, volunteering to help out in the classrooms of her favorite teachers, tutoring the younger girls who struggle with the harder curriculum. She enjoys taking on the big sister role. Especially after her painful freshman year, she is glad to offer the kindness and encouragement that means so much to the underclass girls, and to be to them the one who has lived through it all but is still approachable, the one who is almost like them but also practically an adult.

For the second year in a row, she is voted class president, and those duties keep her busy too. Being engaged, absorbed, helps to pull her back into her normal self: happy, confident, on solid footing. As the winter semester moves into spring, the warming weather brings a fresh round of social engagements. The junior class is responsible for executing the senior girls' plans for their graduation formal, and that demands every planning and coordination skill she can muster. Her way of coaxing cooperation and action causes Sister Marie Therese to dub her the *gentle general.* Some of the girls take to snapping to attention and saluting when she walks into the grand hall for more decorating, causing Lillie to laugh as much as anyone, but then it's back to work!

As Charley has predicted, once out from under the malevolent thumb of the Dorcas clique and Sister Justinia, Lillie thrives. Besides being elected president of her sophomore and junior classes, she remains in the top three or four students with the highest marks, and makes close friends of girls who match her in wit and temperament. She participates in the Holy Cross theatre group, enjoying both backstage and onstage roles. Now eighteen and nineteen, the girls in her group have a full calendar of parties, visits, outings, and church socials. More and more, of course, the activities involve boys.

They have materialized almost from nowhere, to Lillie's surprise, and she finds herself tossed about in a sea of possibilities, both at school and in the neighborhood, without the tools for proper navigation. She tries to keep her wits, especially when she sees how some girls fully abandon theirs. She has no plans to simper, but sometimes she feels as though she's playing at being someone else, while her normal self stands to one side and watches in disbelief.

At school, juniors from Gonzaga and St. John's are sent over to help prepare for the formal, since their seniors represent a majority of the escorts for Holy Cross's graduating girls. Some senior boys even come by, curious and perhaps wanting to get their bearings ahead of time, the better to take masculine command during the big event. Lillie finds that she has little trouble attracting attention from either group, even when she's not trying.

At the same time, as the school year winds down and her circle makes the annual shift from Holy Cross back to Brightwood Park, that circle expands more and more to include the boys. Some of these are boys she has known from her first day in school, but now they seem almost foreign, suddenly, somehow, exotic.

Without any discussion, the girls choose to go out only in groups. Lillie hears the shocking stories of boys who try to take liberties with girls while they are alone together, and, beyond her desire to maintain a spotless reputation, a group allows her to practice being around boys without having to make a choice, or tip her hand too early in showing preference. Still, it's inevitable that pairs start to form.

As school starts up again—seniors at last!—some girls don't even bother to pay attention to their studies. Lillie is aghast when Loraine Lancaster flips her hair in that annoying way and says, "What are they going to do, throw us out? We're seniors! And who needs school anyway when there are boys?"

Possibly to prove the Loraines of the world wrong, or possibly because she has no answer to give, she focuses more on school and less on "the gang": the collection of boys and girls that underpins her social life, that for the first time contains members from both her home and school circles. As the year wears on, though, and winter makes the turn toward spring, everyone around her is gripped by graduation fever. Soon enough, she is infected too.

Emma feeds it, taking Lillie shopping for all manner of exquisite fabrics and trims that Cousin Lil transforms into gowns for the May Procession, the formal, the graduation itself. She encourages Lillie to participate in the full range of social events, hosting several gatherings at 741 and dismissing complaints from some of the nuns about disappointing and slapdash schoolwork as "whinging from a bunch of old hens." Emma delivers this pronouncement in the middle of a long and wide-ranging soliloquy as she and Cousin Lil sit together at the kitchen table sewing buttons onto two of Lillie's gowns. Charley and Lillie are at the other end of the table, he reading the paper and she addressing invitations. At one point they make eye contact and Lillie pulls an exasperated face. Charley looks over at Emma and back at Lillie. "Do you know, when I first met your mother, I had to work hard to get her to talk at all?" He winks at her just as a well-aimed pincushion hits him in the chest. He chuckles and continues to read.

Emma is happy to have Lillie spend time with the boys who seem so eager to spend time with her. Lillie remains unwilling to commit to any one boy, but allows one or two of them to walk her home from church on occasion. Bill Kilerlane is handsome and charming enough, and she is impressed by his skill as a pianist. When he hands her up to her door one Tuesday evening after church club, he says, almost to himself, "I wonder what a fellow needs to do to escort you to your graduation ball."

Lillie can only laugh. "Perhaps a fellow can start by making the offer."

Those last few weeks in May and June are like a fairytale of beautiful dresses and handsome escorts, dances and dinners, benedictions and processions, academic awards, yearbook signings, and vows of continued connections. But then, amidst the laughter and tears of an inevitable parting, she graduates. After all these months of constant attention and activity, the abrupt silence leaves her askew, and the beginning of the summer finds her drifting through the house and yard, unmoored. She has been in school for twelve years, and she realizes now that she has never really considered what happens after this. What's next?

She isn't left alone with her thoughts for long, though, as she is swept up once again by the gang, now fully released from any scholastic obligations, in fact from obligations of any kind. With school over, the church club becomes a primary focus of weekly activity, with club meetings, elections, entertainments, socials, and dinners. There are Saturday visits to Glen Echo, Sunday walks to Peirce Mill or through Rock Creek Park, and midweek shows at Keith's.

While she hasn't been paying attention, some of the faces have changed in their little group, and alliances have formed, shifted, and broken, some amicably, allowing both parties to remain in the group, others in an uglier way, which teaches lessons both useful and painful to everyone involved. At the moment, though, as summer gets underway, things are quiet and without drama, which Lillie appreciates. The group usually includes the Lynch sisters—Mary and Phoebe—Dorothy Gibson, Stella King, Margaret Donovan, and Eugenie Lieutand; then there is Edgar Laake, Garrett Miller, and of course Bill. She is willing to walk out with Bill even though he always tries to talk her into a kiss, until the day that she is forced to turn her head and plant a palm firmly on his chest to push him away. After that, she is polite but unavailable, and he gravitates toward Phoebe. Margaret is going with charming Frank Voith, whose family lives in the neighborhood and attends Nativity, so he has joined the circle, along with his gangly older brother Ferd, who is introduced as Fred.

There are others on the fringes, some known through church, others who are friends of friends. Among these is a handsome young man named John McGraw, a distant cousin of the Dentz twins, Edwin and Florence. He lives with his land-speculator father in a posh house in Kalorama. She meets him only briefly, but he holds onto her hand and looks straight at her for longer than is entirely proper, and she feels her cheeks turn red and warm under his gaze. After that, she usually sees him only in passing, but he is always sure to tip his hat and grin rakishly.

Lillie turns nineteen in late July, meaning that there is yet another flurry of activity in preparing for her party; Emma has hosted one every year since Lillie was able to walk. Lillie tries on a succession of dresses to decide which one to wear, coming down to the parlor in each one to have Emma appraise its suitability for the occasion. Emma keeps up a running commentary about the different young men who might be there, until Charley finally looks from behind his paper. "Tell me, will these fellows be drawing lots for our child, or is it pistols at thirty paces?" A strangled shriek of aggravation gurgles in Emma's throat, but this time there is nothing unbreakable within arm's reach for her to throw.

ꕥ

It's a beautiful night for the party, with lanterns strung through the backyard and guests milling easily between the house and yard. There is an awkward moment right at the beginning, when the first guest to show up is Frank Voith's brother, whom she doesn't know particularly well. He doesn't seem to find it awkward at all. As she introduces him to Charley and Emma, he reminds them that they have seen him and his family at Mass often. He offers to help with last minute chores, and then attaches himself to Lillie as though he is co-hosting the event as her steady. He tells her that he will also turn nineteen in just five days, which makes her, to him, "an older woman." He raises his eyebrows to indicate that this is meant to be scandalous, and it's obvious to her that he has practiced this, possibly in front of a mirror.

She's vaguely irritated by his attentions but remain gracious, until she sees Edwin and Florence arrive with their cousin, John McGraw. After that, her attempts to shake herself loose are matched by his obvious commitment to remain close by her, as he keeps baleful watch on John. Emma finally sees that Lillie needs to be rescued, and enlists Charley to engage young Mr. Voith in a conversation about something that demands a walk to the far side of the yard. For all that, though, Lillie spends just enough time with John—"My friends call me Jack"—to understand that he has only stopped in to wish her a happy birthday before escorting a young lady of his acquaintance to the theatre. In taking his leave, though, he sweeps off his hat with a flourish and, saying, "If I may be so bold," he takes her hand and raises it to his lips, as his eyes flash at her. "My best wishes to the birthday girl." He leaves her, the back of her hand where he kisses it burning as hot as her cheeks.

After that, she resolves to remain unattached, determined to enjoy the company of all the fellows equally and show no preference for any of them. Emma cannot help herself from asking after the handsome (and rich) Mr. McGraw, but there is no information to be had. Lillie is glad for the opportunity to get out of the city and spend a week with Dorothy and the rest of the Gibson family at the shore, in North Beach on the Chesapeake Bay.

Once back at home though, in late August, she finds herself drifting aimlessly, directionless without the rudder of an upcoming school year. At some point, she drifts into the kitchen where Charley sits in his usual chair, drinking coffee as he reads the *Evening Star*. Lillie sits down opposite him; without really hearing herself, she sighs heavily. Charley lowers the paper and looks at her, waiting. It doesn't take long.

"I just don't know what I'm supposed to do now, Dad."

"Now?"

"I mean, now that school is over and done. What am I supposed to be doing?"

Charley nods thoughtfully as he folds the paper, pushes back, and stands up. He continues nodding as he goes out to the spring porch and she hears him say, "Yup, we'll have to think about that one."

Lillie follows him onto the spring porch where Emma has a batch of tomatoes stewing on the old stove, with the canning pot simmering on the rear burner. He gives Lillie the pot hook as he opens the carton of sterilized jars, and nods at her to pull the pot forward to bring the water to a boil. He hands her jars one at a time and she sets them in the water. As it starts to boil, she uses the tongs.

"So you want to know what you should do now. Do you remember what you used to tell us you planned to do when you grew up?"

Lillie laughs. "I think I said I was going to have fifty babies."

"And now?"

"Well, I still want a big family. Just not fifty."

He hands her the ladle and she starts to fill the jars. "And what do you suppose that will take?" She frowns at him, clearly not following. "Lillie, what did your mother do today?"

"Went to work."

"And then?"

"She made dinner."

"And where is she now?"

"Out in garden. I think she's picking zucchini."

"And what did you do today?"

Lillie isn't dense; she can see where he's going with this now. "I read a book."

He leans against the counter. "And here we are, our little family of three." He chuckles, amused at the image in his head. "Maybe if you snare that McGraw fellow you and your mother have set your cap at, the only finger you'll need to lift is the one to direct the servants. On the other hand, if you see your way clear to a practical young man like, say, Fred Voith," she snorts when he says this, "then you'll need to do some heavy lifting. A household doesn't run itself."

He watches her as she continues to fill jars, and nods in their direction as he leans in to kiss the top of her head. "Maybe this is the school you need, sweetheart. Time to start learning."

He leaves her to go back to the paper, and she stays to finish canning the stewed tomatoes.

ꙮ

"Did you hear?" Mary Lynch leans in to them even as they are sitting down with their sundaes. "That girl Annabelle Hatch has *gone abroad*. You know what *that* means.

Stella rolls her eyes a little at the other girls, and says, "No, Mary. What does that mean?"

"Well, they say that she was sent away so no one would know that she's gotten herself into trouble."

Dorothy looks at Lillie. Annabelle Hatch is the girl that Jack McGraw has been squiring around town. A handsome match, says the prevailing sentiment, even if predictable: their fathers are business partners.

This time Stella sighs out loud. "Who is the *they*? How do you know that *they* know what they're talking about?"

"Well, it does seem awfully sudden. And who *goes abroad* anyway?"

"People with money."

Mary starts to retort, when Phoebe touches her hand. "Stella's right that we shouldn't be so quick to judge. None of us know Annabelle. We shouldn't help to spread ugly rumors."

Mary huffs as she sits back in her chair, stung at the rebuke. "Well, anyway, it probably means that John McGraw is available again."

Lillie pokes her spoon at her ice cream, her stomach suddenly cartwheeling as her throat clamps shut. Here it is, the middle of Lent, and the girls have decided to be brazen and go out for ice cream. Now she can't even eat it, but will still need to admit this offense in confession. But if Mary's conjecture about Jack is true, she will gladly say as many Acts of Contrition as Father Bischoff levies on her.

Bill, Ferd, and Edgar see them through the window of the parlor as they pass by, and stop in. Bill automatically stands behind Phoebe, a hand draped on the back of her chair. Lillie finds herself considering whether Bill has ever gotten a kiss from Phoebe, and then is immediately ashamed for doing exactly what Mary has just done.

Edgar sits down in the last empty chair and helps himself to some of Mary's ice cream, which is melting while she gets over her snit. He gestures with the spoon. "Ferd, pull up a chair."

"No, I'm fine here," he says, positioned as he is directly in Lillie's line of sight.

"What are you girls doing besides being naughty?" Bill asks, gesturing at the remains of the ice cream.

"We were just saying that it looks like John McGraw is eligible again, now that Annabelle Hatch has *gone abroad*," Mary says as she looks darkly at Stella.

Ferd holds himself steady but can't keep the color from draining from his face. At that moment, Garrett walks in with Frank and Margaret.

Garrett reaches for Dorothy's hand and lightly kisses her fingers; he dismisses the inevitable teasing, saying, "I'm just hunting for the last of the ice cream, boys." To Dorothy he says, "These two have been following me everywhere. I can't seem to shake them."

Frank says, "What's eating you, Fred? You look like your goldfish just died."

"Since everyone's here, why don't we take a walk?"

"Where shall we go?"

"We still have time to make it to Peirce Mill and back before dinner."

"We'll have to walk fast."

"*You'll* have to anyway, to work off that ice cream before trying to eat your dinner."

Lillie tries to think of a way to beg off, since she sees immediately that everyone else is paired up. The walk to and from Peirce Mill will probably take two hours. Right now she wants to be alone, and she knows that on this walk she has no hope of being left alone.

She steps in beside Dorothy and Garrett, hoping that this will dissuade other company, and she hears Edgar call out, "Hey, Ferd, tell Mary that story about the mansion you delivered to this week," which makes the footsteps closing in behind her pause long enough for Edgar and Mary to catch up.

Later, though, as they all sit on the grass by the creek, she listens to some of the stories Ferd's telling about his job. So many funny and bizarre things happen on his delivery route for Woodward & Lothrop, and his droll way of relating the stories makes her laugh until her jaws hurt.

On the walk back home, she allows him to fall in beside her and it is just the two of them. "Why does Edgar call you Ferd?"

"Ferdinand is my given name, so just about everyone in my family calls me Ferd."

"Your family? Edgar?"

"He's my cousin. My mother Dorothea and his mother Gertrude are sisters. The Bollinger girls."

"Oh, I had no idea! But...but your brother always calls you Fred."

Ferd laughs. "Yes, well, he's the one who started calling me Fred to begin with. Then the fellows at school started to, then pretty much everyone I know picked it up. So, I'm Fred to everyone except my family, except for Frank." He smiles at her. She decides she likes this side of him, when he's relaxed and hasn't been practicing in the mirror. "Besides, calling me Fred is lots better than what he calls our little brother Leo."

"Which is?"

"Feeney." At the look on her face, he says, "Don't ask."

When the group arrives back in Brightwood Park, Ferd insists on seeing her all the way to her porch. Charley is in the yard, fixing a few pickets in the front fence. He and Ferd shake hands, and he gives Lillie a little conspiratorial wink, which she ignores. "I need to help Mother with dinner. Thanks for walking me home, Fred."

She slips into the house. As Ferd tips his hat to go, Charley says,

"Make sure you don't give up."

Ferd's face is serious. "I don't intend to."

It's just a few days later when Charley finds Lillie in the backyard wrestling with the wet laundry, which seems to be winning. Her hair is up in a kerchief, her sleeves rolled back onto her forearms. "It seems you have a visitor, Lillie."

She turns and sees immediately that he's not delivering what he thinks is welcome news. That can only mean one thing. She lets out a little shriek, touching her hand to the kerchief. "Five minutes!" she exclaims, even as she breaks for the spring porch. "I just need five minutes!"

She needn't have worried. By the time she comes down again, her hair perfect, her freshly changed dress setting off her complexion to good effect, Emma has installed herself and John McGraw on the front porch swing, while Charley continues pruning the front hedges. It is obvious that John understands where to direct his charm, not that he has to work hard to make his case here. Emma is grinning like a schoolgirl, her own brand of charm on full display. They both look up as Lillie steps out onto the porch, and John stands immediately and doffs his hat to her.

"Why, Miss Beck, you look stunning as always."

She tips her head down prettily. "Thank you."

"Mr. McGraw is just telling me of his studies last year on the Continent." She says this as though the Beck family travels there regularly. There is a silence before Emma pushes herself up, saying, "Well, I'll leave you two young people to the porch swing. You're sure I can't bring you something, Mr. McGraw?"

"It's John, please. Mr. McGraw is my father," he tells her, and she almost giggles, as though no one has ever said anything so clever. "And no thank you. I'm here to see whether your daughter will consent to walk out with me. With your permission, of course."

Emma practically swoons. "Of course. By all means."

John offers Lillie his arm. With almost any other fellow, Lillie might have teased, "Oh, did I already give my consent?" But in this case, she slips her hand through his arm, and shares a backward glance of delight with Emma, who is pressing her hands together tightly. As the couple walks by Charley, he and John acknowledge each other with a nod. Charley joins Emma up on the porch and they both watch as the couple disappears down Longfellow. "By the way," Charley tells her, "there's a full basket of wet laundry moldering in the backyard."

Emma makes a dismissive noise. "As though that's important right now."

Charley rolls his eyes and goes back to his pruning.

ᘐᘓ

"Did you invite him to come to Rock Creek Park Sunday?"

"Yes, but he said he didn't want to intrude. I told him of course he wouldn't be, but I really think he just doesn't want to come."

"Well, when are you going to see him again?"

"I'm not sure. He says he doesn't like to plan ahead, and that he'll either send a postal or just come by here when he's free."

Dorothy makes a face. "Well, that doesn't sound very helpful. Is he expecting you to just wait around to find out if he's available?"

"I don't know." Lillie sighs and stares out the window at the rain that has forced the girls out of the yard and into the parlor. The weather has been lovely so far this spring, so different from last year with its three back-to-back snowstorms in March. So she's hoping this will clear up and dry off before their outing on Sunday. But if Jack won't come, she'll again be the odd potato.

"Well, are you going to?"

"I don't know."

"Oh, you've got it bad!" Lillie looks over at her in surprise. "With anyone else, you'd be up and gone and too bad for him if he can't keep up. This, well...I've never seen you like this."

"I know." She stares at the rain again. "I was just hoping that if he came on Sunday, he would hear us talk about the dance. Now how is he going to know?"

Dorothy huffs her frustration. "What happened to the Lillie who just would have told him? And you'd better figure out a way for him to ask you soon; otherwise, you-know-who will get there first."

Lillie gasps. "You don't think…?"

"That Fred will ask you when he gets a chance? I'm amazed he hasn't yet!"

Lillie sags a little bit. "He is such a bother." Then she feels bad for being unkind. "I mean, he's a sweet boy and everything, it's just that…he's always *there*."

Lillie is in charge of planning for the Easter dance. It's a fundraiser for the church group and it's the biggest event they've ever held. It has even been part of the announcements at the start of Sunday Mass, and they've already sold most of the tickets, with the dance still weeks away. And here she is, the chairman of the entire event, under threat of being escorted by entirely the wrong boy.

And then Providence intervenes: Dorothy, who can see the front walk from where she's sitting, says, "Well, I'll be. Here he comes now."

Lillie jumps up and lets out a little squeak. "Fred?"

"No. John McGraw."

She is at the parlor mirror in an instant, fussing with her hair, biting her lips and pulling at her cheeks before running into the hall.

"Oh, Lillie, you're beautiful as always. For heaven's sake, he's here, isn't he?"

Here is the knock at the door. Lillie takes a deep breath, waits just a beat to prove she hasn't been standing there waiting to throw it open, and does her best impression of pleasant surprise. "Jack! What a pleasant surprise! Come in! Here, let me take your umbrella and coat."

"Just point me to where I should put them. I don't want you getting wet."

He hangs them on the coat tree behind the door and then follows her into the parlor. "You know Dorothy, I think."

"Of course," he says as they nod at each other. Dorothy is still sitting and wearing a little smirk. "I'm sorry, I didn't know you had company. I don't want to intrude."

As Lillie hastens to say, "Of course you're not intruding!" Dorothy rises from her spot and walks toward the hall to gather her things.

"Oh, I was just leaving anyway. Remember I told you, Lillie? Mama and I are picking out fabric for my dress today." She looks at John significantly. "We're having a formal at the church on Easter Monday. It's going to be the biggest event of the year." She glances over her shoulder at Lillie with a mischievous glint.

John is surprised. "A dance? How come no one told me about a dance?"

ꟷ

Now that that's settled, Lillie feels free to be herself, and to enjoy rather than simply tolerate Ferd's companionship. He presses the advantage, even as he absorbs the blow of learning that John McGraw has beaten him to the dance invitation. Not only is Ferd now her normal walking companion on the weekend outings, he also escorts her home from Mass and Tuesday night church club, and they enjoy deconstructing the events of those evenings. There's always some kerfuffle among the members for them to discuss; she likes that he's observant, and he sometimes puts into words exactly what she has been thinking.

He still aggravates her when he sometimes acts as though they are a couple, but many times things are so easy between them that she forgets they aren't entirely on the same wavelength. When at some point she exclaims to him, "Fred! You haven't bought a ticket to the Easter dance yet!" he says to her simply, without complaint, "The girl I would have asked already has an escort." By now, she has enough respect for his dignity not to say anything more.

From Ferd's perspective, it is all to the good that John McGraw doesn't seem to like to be around any of the rest of them, when that's where Lillie spends most of her time. He shows up occasionally, but always seems surprised to find other people there. Lillie only mentions John as a matter of course, as she might chat about any of them, but Ferd hears Dorothy and Stella or Mary or whomever evaluating the situation in hushed tones.

"He just shows up when he feels like it. Just expects her to be there waiting for him."

"What nerve! I guess he's used to girls just being at his beck and call."

"Maybe he thinks her name is Lillie Beck And Call."

"I know Lillie wishes that he would join in more, but I think he just wants her all to himself."

That's fine with Ferd; more time for him.

"Well, he's certainly turned her head. He is awfully handsome."

Ferd feels confident that he can overcome this deficit.

"And rich, too."

That, on the other hand, is an issue. Ferd has nothing but himself to offer, and that may not be enough to win the day. But he believes that he has an ally in his quest to improve his circumstances.

ꙮꙮ

Master Charles Joseph Beck, fifteen and a half years old, reports for duty at 6:55 a.m., on Monday, February 5, 1883, to begin his duties as a helper in the Wetting Branch of the Bureau of Engraving and Printing, little brother of the Treasury Department, earning the princely sum of fifty cents a day. After his one-month provisional employment ends with a favorable report by the Examining Committee, he becomes a permanent employee. A year and a half later, on reaching his seventeenth birthday, Charley's honorific formally shifts to *Mister* and his compensation rises to one dollar per day. He remains a helper, then a skilled helper, for twenty-five years, until, in 1908, he is promoted to Custodian of Presses, a position of significant responsibility. A few years hence, he will be selected to work on a committee of three to argue for wage parity for the custodians of presses, a position that requires long experience, a level head, and skill with both people and equipment. The committee surveys other federal agencies for jobs of similar skill and responsibility to show that the custodians have chronically been underpaid. The brief they draft to present their case is read into the record during the 1921 Joint Congressional Hearings on Reclassification of Salaries, and Charley is surprised at the twinge of pride he feels to know that his name is now in the *Congressional*

Record.

At the moment, though, Charley has been Custodian of Presses for seven years, comfortably situated and well-respected, when Ferd decides to seek him out.

It's after Mass one Sunday when Ferd sees Lillie home, only to have her and Emma immediately depart with a bouquet of jonquils tied in a pretty blue bow. They are off to visit one of Emma's friends whose daughter and son-in-law are just welcoming a new baby boy. Ferd is able to catch Charley's eye with a significant look, and Charley stays out by the walk to see the ladies off. Once they disappear down the block, Charley leads Ferd up the porch and into the kitchen. This is the first time that Ferd has been beyond the hall or parlor, and he feels a little electric jolt of accomplishment.

Ferd accepts the coffee that Charley pours, and they sit together at the table. It's obvious that Charley is happy to wait until Ferd is ready to explain his purpose. Charley's ease in this situation helps to calm Ferd's naturally peptic stomach, and he feels his nervousness drain away.

"Mr. Beck, I think you know how I feel about your daughter. You probably also know that she doesn't feel the same way about me. Yet. I'll be twenty in August, and it seems to me that if I'd like Lillie to be serious about me, then I need to be serious. About the future. What I need to do, I mean. For a wife and family." He has clenched up after all. He sees that there's a difference between thinking the words in his head and saying them out loud.

Charley is nodding, unconcerned over the delivery. "Well, you sound serious. Not many young men are willing to take the long view. Most don't even know there *is* a long view."

"I know that other fellows have more to offer." The reference is obvious. "I probably should have stayed in school longer. I know my dad wanted me to, but once I got a job, school just didn't make sense to me anymore."

Charley nods again. "I didn't spend much time in school either, son. I've managed to do okay."

Ferd looks up at Charley earnestly. "I'm not afraid to work hard. I'll do what I need to do. It's just that, well, I can hardly build a future driving the livery wagon for the department store."

"You need something better," Charley suggests, "more like a career than a job."

"Exactly!"

"What are you thinking?"

"Well, it needs to be something dependable, stable. Where I can count on being able to work a full week and get paid for it, too."

Charley knows what Ferd means: sometimes the work is spotty, and sometimes the employers are shady. "Have you considered civil service?"

"Well, yes, sir, that's exactly what I was thinking. I understand that it helps to have someone put in a good word for you once you make your application."

"It doesn't hurt. Your father's with the government, too, you told me?"

"Yes, and he'll do what he can, but I thought it would go a long way with things if you could…" Ferd trails off, embarrassed.

Charley can't help but laugh. "You're thinking that if I were the one to help you find a job, say, at Engraving, well that would get you one step closer to being part of the family. Is that right?" Ferd forces himself to nod, but can't make eye contact. "Lillie's going to choose who she chooses, son. I'm not going to be making up her mind for her."

"Of course not! I mean, of course Lillie makes her own choices. It's just that her mother is pushing so hard…" This time he cuts himself off, fearing he may be saying too much.

"Ahh, yes, Mrs. Beck does seem to have her eye on Mr. McGraw, doesn't she?" Charley sits back in his chair, gazing at Ferd for a moment. "In that case, it really only seems fair to try to balance the scales a bit." He appraises Ferd for a moment before standing up and extending his hand. Ferd leaps up too and shakes Charley's hand. "Let me see what I can do for you, son. Truth be told, I'd rather be in the kitchen with you than in the parlor with him."

Fred for Friends, *Ferd* for Family

1915

Nestled in the memory box is Lillie's own brief diary, started in the excitement for Jack and the Easter dance. And yet, whether he is Fred or Ferd, in this diary there is only ever one main character.

Sunday March 21, 1915. Bright & clear.

Peace Sunday. Pope Benedict XV has granted a plenary indulgence to all who will receive Communion today with the intention that the war in Europe may stop. Mother and I went. Dad could not because he had to go down to the office and had to get his breakfast before he went. Nearly everyone in church went so there was quite a large crowd to receive.

We went to church tonight and the usual crowd went home together, but we did not go to anyone's house afterwards. Fred came home with me and I asked him about Stella, if she had said anything about John being here last Thursday. He said she hadn't said much, but Fred had a good deal to say on his own responsibility. He liked John alright, but did not care particularly about his being here. When he said "goodnight" he remarked that I had not stood so far away from John when I said "goodbye" to him. I asked him why he knew. "Why, I turned around and looked."

"What right did you have to do that?" I asked.

"Well," said Fred, "I thought I had the right."

Tuesday March 23, 1915. Clear.

Rehearsal tonight for the play, "The Girl from Porto Rico," by Joseph Le Brandt. Gertrude refused to take the part of lead, so Mr. Hunter asked me if I would take the part. I said yes, I would try and would endeavor to do my best. After the meeting we rehearsed by reading the first act. We had a good deal of fun of course. We drew the curtains so the rest could not see but some of them peeped around anyhow.

Cast

Jack Jenkins – Bill Kilerlane
McGinty – Hugh Fegan
Robinson Dodd (Robin) – Jimmie Schrider
Abraham Mite – Fred Voith
Dina Mite – Lillie Beck
Violet Waters – Phoebe Lynch
Vacant – Phil Huck
Sara – Marie Huck

Wednesday March 24, 1915. Bright & clear.

Went to Mass this morning. Margaret, Mary and I went down together afterwards and decided we would go walking Sunday, the party to include Mary, Margaret, Phoebe, myself, Edgar Laake, Fred, Frank, and Bill.

Friday March 26, 1915. Cool & clear.

Went to church. Fred came home with me afterward and stayed a little while. He told Mother that as "Dina Mite" I was quite a success, that the rest of the cast had gone at their parts like amateurs but I had done mine like a professional. He also said that some of the girls had said I was very good and that Bill who had come out to his house the night before said the same thing.

Saturday March 27, 1915. Cool & clear.

Went downtown. Am having a new hat made for Easter Monday night.

Sunday March 28, 1915. Palm Sunday. Clear & bright.

We had a wonderful time today. Went to early Mass, then Sunday school. We were supposed to meet at the Lynch's at two o'clock, so I went down about quarter past. Bill arrived next, then Frank and Margaret, then Fred and Edgar. We started out about quarter of three.

Went over to Fourteenth Street, down Colorado Avenue, past the reservoir, down through the woods and out to Military Road, then down that to Peirce Mill. Mary had her camera so we stopped and took pictures every once in awhile. We had a lovely time, for everyone was in a good humor and the weather was lovely. When we got to one of the bridges, we took pictures of each couple. Arrived at another bridge. We wanted a picture of the whole group so we asked a little boy to take it for us. When we got to Peirce's Mill, Bill took a picture of us out on the rocks by the dam. The last picture, I took of the group, standing near the mill. We went home by way of Blagden's Road, to Sixteenth Street. We finally reached Brightwood Avenue, but as we saw some children playing rope, we had to stop and play awhile too. We reached home safe, tired and happy, where we had supper, then we all met at church again.

Wednesday March 31, 1915. Clear.

Went downtown to see about my hat.

Thursday April 1, 1915. Holy Thursday. Cloudy.

Went to Mass this morning and church tonight. Hour of silent adoration. Fred came down with me after church. He gave me a dozen films for my camera as we intend going walking Sunday.

Friday April 2, 1915. Good Friday.

Went to the Mass of the Presanctified this morning then downtown. Bought two hat pins, silver, and a pin for my hair. Also got pictures.

Went to church tonight. Fred came home with me. I told him I was not going to ask him in as I was sleepy and my throat hurt me, so he said alright.

Saturday April 3, 1915. Holy Saturday.

Went to Mass this morning. It was snowing quite hard and kept it up all day. Did not stop until late this evening.

My throat is much worse, so I suppose I have another attack of tonsillitis. I don't like the idea one bit with the dance Monday night, club Tuesday, and theater Wednesday.

Received a postal from Claudia this morning and a card from John McGraw.

Sunday April 4, 1915. Easter Sunday.

Beautiful bright clear day with the snow melting nicely. We all went to early Mass and Communion this morning.

Monday April 5, 1915. Clear.

We had a perfectly lovely time yesterday. The bunch arrived here about a quarter of three and as we had to wait for Margaret and Frank, Bill played for us and we sang. Then when they arrived we started out. We were going over to the Soldier's Home, but on account of the snow making roads muddy, we decided not to go there but to walk to the District line through Rock Creek Park instead. We arrived home about half past six, and had supper. They all seemed to enjoy it very much, especially the boys. We were just about finishing when John McGraw came. He did not want to stay when he saw the crowd, but at last we prevailed upon him and I took him into the dining room and introduced him to those he did not know. Bill and he know each other very well, otherwise I am afraid Bill would have gotten grouchy as he usually does when there are any strangers. When we had finished supper, we went into the parlor where we played, sang and danced, Bill with Phoebe and Jack with me. Jack is a lovely dancer. They left about half past ten. Jack was the last to leave and he stopped a few minutes to say what time he would be out tonight and to ask about his wearing apparel.

Tuesday April 6, 1915. Clear & warmer.

Had a wonderful time last night. Jack came at half past eight and we got over to the hall about quarter past nine. I wore my graduation dress and my new pink hat. Dorothy had on a dress of orange satin trimmed with shoulder straps of purple velvet and purple velvet pansies around her waist. She looked lovely. Jack filled up my program and I danced every dance with the exception of two that I sat out with him as he was rather tired having been up to Great Falls all day. We had a lovely time and enjoyed ourselves very much. We left about quarter past twelve. Coming home on the car we met Jimmie Fegan, Hughie's older brother. He is very nice and is a great deal like Hughie. Arrived home about quarter past one. John said he enjoyed himself very much.

Thursday April 8, 1915. Clear.

We went to see "The Rose Maid" last night, a musical comedy at the Columbia Theater. Wednesday night was given as a benefit performance for Holy Cross. Bill, Phoebe, Edgar, Mary, Frank, Margaret, Fred and myself, Mother, Dad and Aunt Annie all went. We eight came home together. Fred and I were down in "E" row but the rest were all back on the Orchestra circle.

Fred brought the pictures, but only eight came out. However, he is going to have the rest printed anyway as I think some of them will come out all right.

Sunday April 11, 1915. Rain.

John came out this afternoon about three o'clock and stayed until nearly five. He wanted me to go to the Sousa concert down at the National Theater this evening with him, but as I already had an engagement with Fred, of course I couldn't. I told him if he wanted to he could come out tomorrow evening as Dorothy, Louise, Joe and Garrett are coming. He said he was afraid of interrupting, but I said oh no, he wouldn't.

Friday April 16, 1915. Clear

Fred and I went to Pali's last night. "Rebecca of Sunnybrook

Farm." I have seen it before but I enjoyed seeing it over again. Fred said he would be up Sunday night but we would not go out with any crowd.

Sunday April 18, 1915. Clear & cool.

Mrs. King (Stella's mother) celebrated her twentieth wedding anniversary last night, so Stella asked Fred and myself to come down, which we of course did. We had a very nice time.

ꕤ

Lillie comes to think of the moment when she stops saying *Fred* and instead shifts entirely to *Ferd* as *The Crisis*, the phrase coming to her with an exasperated eye-roll. How grown-up and sophisticated Lillie thought herself back then, and yet here is a clear picture of her manufacturing drama like a petulant schoolgirl. It did, however, serve to move things along.

ꕤ

Wednesday April 21, 1915. Clear.

Had a kind of a stormy meeting last night at the club. We also decided to form an athletic association. After the meeting we danced and here's where I got into trouble. I danced once with one of the boys, then I played a waltz, then Ferd asked me to dance and I refused. I knew he must be provoked with me, so I did not dance with anyone else but went up and talked to Lana who was playing. When we reached home Ferd said to me as we came up the steps that he was sorry I did not think he was good enough to dance with. Of course I apologized and asked him to forgive me and then he changed the subject and told me not to make a friend of Mary Lynch, as she had made several remarks about me and was probably trying to make trouble between us. I told him I knew she talked about me and so I said I would never say anything to her again. The remark was about John McGraw and the invitation to the concert.

Between Ferd's call down and the knowledge of Mary's remarks I started to cry. That upset Ferd and he said he wished he had not said anything.

We stood on the porch talking for about half an hour. We spoke of many things. He said he cared more for me than for any other girl he knew, though I had told him that I did not care any more for him than for any of the other fellows I knew. But he said no matter what happened, he would never let me go home from club by myself and thereby give them a chance to talk. By "them" I mean the bunch from the club.

Thursday April 22, 1915. Clear & warm.

We had our club social last night and had a splendid time. In the afternoon Margaret, Mary and I decorated the hall and fixed things up. We danced for awhile before the entertainment and of course afterwards. We had refreshments and then we stayed until about twelve. We had a circular fish walk and Bill really danced with me for a wonder. Hughie and I had two dances together, one before the entertainment and one after. The second one was a one step and the two of us acted like idiots as Hughie did not know the steps and was trying to learn it. Anyhow we amused ourselves. Altogether we had a dandy time.

Tuesday April 27, 1915. Hot.

Church again and again Ferd. He said he thought that was a pretty good record, Sunday, Monday, Tuesday, tomorrow club and then where do you want to go Thursday or Friday? We decided to go to Keith's.

Wednesday April 28, 1915.

At the club tonight we decided not to give an excursion but to give another minstrel show next winter.

Saturday May 1, 1915. Cool.

Went to Keith's last night. Show was fine.

We have got to go to church tomorrow night. Ferd says he'll lose his religion if this keeps up.

Sunday May 2, 1915. Clear & cool.

Went to Church last night, to "Holy Hour." Father Currier, or rather Bishop Currier, preached a sermon on the Blessed Virgin. It was really a sermon on "Peace" as he called the Virgin our "Lady of Peace."

Ferd came home with me, of course. He stayed until eleven as we did not get home until nearly ten. I am beginning to like him much better than I did at first. He is really a dandy fellow and will do anything for me.

Thursday May 6, 1915. Clear & cool.

Ferd came down tonight as usual and he had not been here long when John McGraw came. John stayed until about half past nine, and Ferd insisted upon staying longer than usual, because he said John had taken up part of his time.

Ferd was very much put out with Bill Kilerlane, as it seems he has been talking about me. Ray Crogan told Ferd that Bill had said to him that he did not see why Ferd came around here; he used to come up here, but he did not like the way I acted. No, I guess he didn't, I told Ferd, because I wouldn't let him kiss me. Frank said Bill seemed to be a h - - - of a lot concerned about Ferd coming around here. Case of jealousy on Bill's part. I wonder if he thinks all the girls he used to go with should think only of him and never go with anyone else?

Ferd is going to take me to see "Robin Hood" tomorrow night. He brought me a lovely box of candy tonight.

Saturday May 8, 1915. Clear & warm.

Ferd and I went to the National last night. Play was very pretty and the songs were beautiful. Phoebe and Bill went down on the same car with us, so we walked up to the theater together. Bill was very amiable last night. Ferd and I talked ourselves to death coming down on the car so Bill wouldn't have a chance to accuse us of fighting, which he said we always did. Ferd said maybe he would think we were squabbling when we talked so much, but I said no he couldn't because we were smiling or laughing most of the time.

Sunday May 9, 1915. Clear & warm.

I went to confession yesterday evening as Mr. Hunter asked the club members to go to Communion for Frank Schrider. He was operated on Friday for ulcers of the stomach, and of course we are all anxious to see him come through all right. They say he seems to be getting along very well now though he is still weak and sick from the ether. A good many members of the club went to Communion this morning, so I think Frank will come through all right.

Monday May 10, 1915. Clear & cool.

Stella and I went up to Church last night, to May devotions.

Ferd and I had a little talk after we got home and were seated in the porch swing. He said that he was becoming very much attached to me, and I told him I liked him much better than I used to, and he said he was glad.

Sunday May 16, 1915.

Ferd came home with me from church this morning and stayed a little while, wandering around the garden.

About half past two I went down to Stella's and we went down to the hospital to see Frank. Annie, Mary and Phoebe were there when we arrived. Frank is getting along nicely and looks very well despite the operation. He expects to go home in about a week's time.

Monday May 17, 1915.

Went to Club tonight. Strictly business meeting lasted until about eleven o'clock. We had nominating of officers. Mr. Hunter for president and Frank Schrider for vice-president, renominated with no opponents. Several nominated for recording secretary, financial secretary and executive committee. I was nominated for the first and third offices.

Wednesday May 19, 1915.

Went downtown this afternoon to buy a suit and gloves, then stopped by the hospital to see Frank and then took the car and went up to church to rehearsal for the May procession.

Friday May 21, 1915.

Ferd and I went over to Dorothy's last night. Helen Shaw, Willie Murphy and another fellow were over. Dorothy and Garrett have had a falling out. I hope they make up soon because while Willie is alright I don't like him as well as I do Garrett. We spent a very pleasant evening and did not get home until about half past twelve.

Sunday May 23, 1915.

The children made their first Communion this morning and the rest of us marched up with them. The little ones all looked very sweet and pretty.

This afternoon we had the May procession. Everything was beautiful and the children looked lovely.

Ferd came up to see it and afterwards he came home with me, stayed for a little while and then went home. He came up again about half past seven and we went down to moving pictures which were very good. We walked down but rode out. Dorothy Voith, Ferd's younger sister, was on the car so we took her home first. As we came up Illinois avenue we met Bill and Phoebe coming down.

Ferd stayed until eleven o'clock. He often asks me if I like him just a little and tonight I asked him how much he liked me. He said he had no right to say how much he cared for me because he did not have anything to give.

Tuesday May 25, 1915.

Went to the club tonight. Ferd caught up to Stella and me as we were going into the drugstore so he treated us and then we went on up to the club.

We got home about eleven o'clock but it was nearly twelve before Ferd left as he insisted upon our sitting down in the swing for awhile.

Friday May 28, 1915.

Ferd and I went to Keith's last night. We met Margaret and

Frank over at Fourteenth Street. They were going to Pali's. I wore my new suit, my pink hat and then I pinned on a big pink rose and Ferd said I looked very nice.

The show was good and as we arrived home early Ferd and I sat down in the swing. Ferd very often teases me for kisses but in accordance with commands I've never let him do it. But alas for good resolutions, last night they got smashed and Ferd kissed me. Then I started to cry and Ferd almost had a fit. He is awfully good and really never takes advantage so if I hadn't let him do it he wouldn't have, so I blamed myself and Ferd blamed himself. He asked me not to be angry with him and please not to tell anyone.

Sunday May 30, 1915. Rainy & cold.

John McGraw came out this evening about half past seven. He wanted me to go to the country club with him next Sunday but as I intend going out to school for class night I told him I could not go.

Ferd came about eight and John left soon after but Ferd stayed until eleven. It's developing into quite a serious case with him.

Wednesday June 2, 1915. Rain.

The officers of the club for the ensuing year were elected last night. Mr. Hunter and Frank Schrider were reelected unanimously for president and vice-president, Eunice Connor, recording secretary, Phoebe Lynch financial secretary, Mr. Mitchell, stage manager, and the executive committee, Mr. Boyle, Edgar Laake, Edwin Dentz, Mary Lynch and myself. Then the executive committee met after the meeting to elect its chairman and I was chosen for that.

It rained quite hard when we came home so we got on the car and then Ferd and I ran the two squares home. I loaned Ferd an umbrella so he brought it back this morning.

Sunday June 6, 1915.

Ferd and I went out to school this evening to class night. It was splendid and we enjoyed it very much. The girls looked very pretty and all of them read well. Claudia had the class poem.

For the first time since I left it I was homesick for Holy Cross last night and wished I was back again.

Tuesday June 8, 1915.

We had our social tonight and had a very nice time. The entertainment went off fine with the new chairman of the executive committee in charge. She got lots of compliments afterwards in regards to the entertainment and how well she took charge, how graceful and poised she was and etc. We danced as usual and altogether had a very pleasant evening.

Tuesday June 15, 1915.

Club night. Had a business meeting and Bill made a motion that Miss Beck be given a vote of thanks for the fine entertainment she had gotten up, the best they ever had. So Bill said. Ferd said he thought there must be a little spark still burning. And that reminds me, Bill and Phoebe have had a falling out, because they were reported engaged and Bill objected.

Monday July 5, 1915.

We have had a perfectly lovely time today. Ferd took me to Keiths this afternoon and the show was fine so we enjoyed it very much. Then when we came home Ferd would not stay to supper but said he would be around about half past seven. Dorothy and Will came soon after Ferd left. They had been over to the races at the reservoir so they stayed to supper and then afterwards Dorothy played for awhile and when Ferd came he and I went down to the fireworks with Frank, Margaret, Edgar and Mary. We had lots of fun.

Saturday July 10, 1915.

Eugenie came out this afternoon to stay until Monday morning. This evening we walked up to the store and while we were gone Ferd came. He met us coming down the street. He came up to tell me something about tomorrow night.

Friday July 16, 1915.

Spent the day over at Dorothy's and Ferd came over in the evening. Of course Will was there and Pete (Will's brother) and his girl Virginia came over also. We had a lovely time.

Tuesday July 20, 1915. Club night.

My invitation for my birthday party was read tonight. Still squabbling over new members and visitors' night.

Saturday July 23, 1915.

Ferd's gift to me, a beautiful green parasol, came today.

I went up to confession this evening and of course Ferd was there and came home with me.

Sunday July 24, 1915.

Ferd and I started out to see Ethel but it was such a lovely afternoon and we were afraid she wouldn't be in, so we stayed on the car and went out to Forest Glen. We wandered around the seminary grounds for about an hour, sat down on a stone pillar for a long time talking and then took the car for home. We had a lovely time and it was just beautiful out there.

When we got home we sat in the porch swing for awhile and then I started to get supper when who appeared on the scene but Annie Reeves, her husband and three children. Supper was delayed until they left about eight o'clock, when Mother and I repaired to the kitchen. We had it ready in about half an hour so Ferd said we were some cooks. After supper, Ferd and I sat out in the hammock.

Wednesday July 28, 1915.

My birthday and I am twenty years old.

Thursday July 29, 1915.

Had the party this evening and had a perfectly lovely time. There was quite a crowd and outside of the club members there were Dorothy and Will, Eugenie, Ethel, John McGraw, and Ray Crogan. We had refreshments outside by the light of Japanese lanterns. Then we went in and danced and sang until about twelve when they all left. They all said they had a lovely time and I think they did.

Friday July 30, 1915.

Ferd came down tonight so we could make arrangements about his going down with us to Chesapeake Beach, Sunday. Dorothy asked me to spend the week with her at North Beach so I am going and Ferd is going with me.

We spent the evening out in the hammock and I gave Ferd the first installment of his birthday present (August the second is his birthday), which was a kiss, the only thing he wanted he said. Of course there wasn't only just the one, seldom is nowadays.

Saturday July 31, 1915.

Ferd came down again tonight. Dorothy made a mistake about time so she sent me a card. Mother met Ferd as she was going to work this morning so she told him to come around this evening.

We leave tomorrow on the nine-thirty train; that necessitates our having breakfast before Mass.

Gave Ferd his tie clasp tonight, which was the second installment of his birthday present.

Sunday August 1, 1915.

Ferd and I started out this morning right after Mass. We arrived over at Chesapeake Junction about nine o'clock.

Ferd got our tickets and we got on the train. The Gibson's came about twenty-five after, so there was a wild skirmish for seats. Finally the four of us Dorothy, Will, Ferd and myself located up by the door. It was a terribly hot ride and a very dirty one but we finally got there and settled in the lunch pavilion where we had our dinner and then the four of us wandered around and finally landed up near the hotel under the trees on the terrace where we stayed the whole afternoon. Then after awhile it began to cloud over so we went back to the pavilion and when the rest of them came we had supper. Ferd left on the six o'clock train and we departed for North Beach. There had been a right heavy rain when we got to the pavilion so the roads were rather sloppy. We finally arrived and Dorothy and I went on a tour of inspection. We sat out on the porch until about ten-thirty when we departed for bed. Dorothy and I have the middle room and as it has three windows in it we had plenty of breeze. Slept fine.

Monday August 2, 1915.

Got straightened up this morning and Dorothy and I went for a row, then Will took us out for awhile. After breakfast we fooled around for awhile then went in bathing. Spent the whole day very pleasantly.

Wednesday August 4, 1915.

Had a terrible storm last night. Wrecked the pier at South Beach and played havoc generally. Went in bathing this afternoon. The water was lovely and deep for the first time. Went down to South Beach this evening to dance.

Thursday August 5, 1915.

Usual routine of the day. Just came out of the water and were starting to dress when Ferd came. I was mighty glad to see him and he and I and Will and Dorothy spent the evening in one corner of the porch. He left about nine-thirty and we walked over to the car with him.

Friday August 6, 1915.

We are going home tomorrow so Will phoned to Owen and I to Ferd to meet us at the junction. We went for a long row this morning as it is our last day but didn't go in bathing as we got back right late from South Beach.

Saturday August 7, 1915.

Got up at five o'clock this morning. Had everything ready at eight. Left for south beach about nine-thirty. After many adventures we finally got the eleven-forty train. Got in about quarter of one. Ferd was waiting for me and he and I took the car for home which we reached about two o'clock. Ferd stayed to dinner and then left about six oclock. Altogether I had a very enjoyable week.

Thursday August 12, 1915.

Ferd and I intended to go out to Glen Echo tonight but as it had rained all day and was still threatening we decided to stay home. Ferd gave me a picture of himself tonight. I had asked him for it as I had only a tiny picture of him.

Wednesday August 18, 1915.

Ethel came down this evening to spend the night with me. After supper we took a long walk all around Madison Street, Kennedy, Sixteeth, Fourteenth, Emerson, Georgia Avenue, where we met Mrs. Voith and Mrs. Laake. Arrived home, we made candy and then went to bed.

Sunday August 22, 1915.

Ferd and I spent our evening out under the walnut tree. It is a glorious night, with the harvest moon shining. We had a lovely evening and enjoyed ourselves as usual even though we did not go out. Ferd did not leave until nearly twelve as we kept on talking after we went up on the porch.

Tuesday August 24, 1915.

We had our social tonight. The bunch said they had a good time. I did not, as my program was spoiled by two or three backing out and refusing to perform. Ferd and I left before the others. We are both thinking very seriously of resigning from the club.

Thursday August 26, 1915.

Ferd and I went down to moving pictures tonight. It is a lovely night so we walked down and back. We sat on the porch until about half past eleven and then Ferd started to go home. It always takes a long time to say good night and tonight was no exception.

Sunday August 29, 1915.

We went to nine o'clock Mass this morning. Met Ferd going up to "ten" as we came down the road. We stayed home this afternoon. When Ferd came this evening we took a walk and as Eugenie did not want to go to moving pictures we came home. We sat out on the porch for awhile and then as Ferd wanted a drink, he and I started around to get it. Of course the family thought it quite a joke and teased us accordingly and then when we went in there was powder on Ferd's shoulder. It got there when we were on the porch but of course I knew the family would hardly believe that so I was hoping they would not see it. But Mother and Claudia spied it and then good night! After the girls and Mother and Dad had gone up, Ferd and I went back to the porch where we stayed till after eleven. Then when I got upstairs, not wishing to wake the family I tiptoed around in the dark as it was then quite sometime after eleven. The girls go home tomorrow morning.

Thursday September 2, 1915.

I went out to Ethel's yesterday and spent the night. Ferd walked out with me so of course the walk was very enjoyable. We got out there about three o'clock. Ethel and I wandered around Takoma in the evening and after supper I played and then we went to bed. This morning we took another walk around and this afternoon I left about three o'clock and got home near four.

Ferd came down this evening and we spent it out on the porch. After the family had gone up we went back in the little corner behind the vines.

Monday September 6, 1915.

Florence Dentz, one of the girls in the club, was married this morning so most of us went up to the wedding. It was a very pretty one and Florence looked very sweet and happy. They were married with a nuptial Mass. Hereafter her name will be Florence Holubovich. After the wedding we all went out to congratulate the bride and groom and then went home. Ferd was there so he walked home with me.

Ferd and I went to Keith's this evening. We had a lovely time. Arrived home at twelve and Ferd stayed until nearly half past.

Tuesday September 7, 1915.

We had a business meeting at club tonight so of course we had a little argument. Supposed to start rehearsals next week.

Ferd and I left before the others. He did not feel very well. Ferd said when he left home that evening he was right sick but was better then. He thinks he will go to Baltimore Thursday and stay until Sunday. He asked me if I would miss him. I said "yes, of course," why did he always ask that. Well, he liked to hear me say it.

Friday September 10, 1915.

Got back from Eugenie's about three o'clock this afternoon. Found Dad up on the scaffolding burning and scraping. I put up some peaches and got dinner. Also found a postal from Ferd awaiting me. He did not go to Baltimore so he said he'd be around tonight.

He came about half past seven and we went for a walk. When we got back we sat on the side for awhile and then went around on the porch in our little corner.

Sunday September 12, 1915.

Ferd came down about seven-thirty tonight and we went for another walk, a longer one this time. We spent the rest of the evening on the bench under the walnut tree.

Tuesday September 14, 1915.

Went up to club tonight but as there wasn't much doing and I had a sore throat, Ferd and I came home. The folks hadn't gone to bed yet so we talked to them and then when they went in we sat in the swing for awhile.

Thursday September 16, 1915.

Spending the day in bed. The doctor was out this morning. Said it might be an attack of quinsy and to keep ice on my neck.

Sunday September 19, 1915.

Quinsy it is. Mother came home early Friday afternoon and as my throat was much worse she phoned for the doctor again. He came and ordered hot applications instead of cold and as the weather is extremely warm I had a very joyful time.

Ferd came up Saturday night and of course that was an oasis in the desert. He stayed until half past nine. He will be up again tonight as usual.

Monday September 20, 1915.

Stella came up yesterday afternoon, then Mrs. Elliott and then Ferd came about quarter of eight and stayed until ten thirty.

I felt much better last night and Ferd was rejoiced to hear it. The abscess broke yesterday morning so I can swallow a little tiny bit better.

Tuesday September 21, 1915.

Mary Lynch was up last night and Father Bischoff came in, in the afternoon. Throat is better but I am still confined to a liquid diet.

Wednesday September 22, 1915.

The weather has cooled off, thank goodness.

Ferd came. He stayed until nine o'clock.

The other evening he told me that he had two compliments for me. Here they are. Mr. Hunter told him that he had the pick of the organization and that I had more brains than any of the rest of the girls up there. Then Ferd said that a fellow had told him that if he could, he would come up here and cut Ferd out. After some coaxing Ferd finally told me that Johnny Labofish had said that.

I got up today. My throat is still on the "blink" but it is much better. The weather has taken a notion to cool off so it's very wintry out today.

Gertrude and Stella came up tonight. They almost came to blows up at the club last night. That is, two of the boys, so the two girls each gave me an account of it.

Saturday September 25, 1915.

Eugenie came out this afternoon. She will stay until Monday morning. Ferd and I stayed out on the porch talking until after ten, so when I got upstairs Eugenie was asleep.

Sunday September 26, 1915.

Ferd took Eugenie and me down to moving pictures tonight. It was nearly eleven o'clock when we got home so Ferd told Eugenie she need not expect me upstairs until at least 11:30.

Ferd asked his usual question tonight of how much I cared for him and I told him that I loved him. I suppose he could have sung an anthem of joy then but instead he hugged me extra hard.

Tuesday September 28, 1915. Club night.

We are going to spend tomorrow downtown as the Grand Army have their parade and the government clerks have holiday.

Sunday October 3, 1915.

Our mission starts today. It will last for a week. We shall have to go to church twice a day, in the morning to Mass and in the evening to Sermon and Benediction.

Sunday October 10, 1915.

Our mission ended this evening. We all enjoyed it very much as Father Schneider who gave it is splendid and his sermons were certainly fine.

Evening, Monday, 17 April 1933

Charley assesses the situation: it's a large crib, heavy, and it's not going to fit through the door. He wants to disassemble as little as possible to get it out of the room. What should he take apart?

They have already moved Bernie's trundle bed into his and Emma's room, after seeing that the second crib will not fit in there. So Jeanie's crib is going into the boys' room as soon as he figures out how to get it in there.

There is stirring behind him. "Hey, Dad."

He turns to Lillie, who has been sleeping propped up against a bank of pillows while he works to relocate the children. Her heavy-lidded eyes are half open, and her voice is raspy. "Oh, hey now, sweetheart. I didn't mean to wake you up." He is over at her bedside, brushing strands of hair up from her forehead with a finger.

"You didn't." She gives him a little smile, gesturing to indicate her current state. "Cartwheels on the stairs."

"Didn't listen to me, did you?" He continues to stroke her forehead. "Just be glad your Grampa Miller isn't here. He'd be bleeding you with leeches!"

She notices the disarray. "What's this?"

"Doc Cavanaugh wants to make sure you get all the rest you need, so we're moving the kids out. Bernie's with us, and Jeanie's going in with Dorothy and the boys." He sees her rising protest, and cups his hand against her cheek. "Just for now. Just 'til you're back on your feet."

Emma sweeps into the room. "I told you to let me know if she woke up!"

"Mother, I just this mi…" Her throat closes around the words. She tips her head back and breathes through her nose the way Dr. Cavanaugh has shown her, to ease her breathing.

Emma gives Charley an accusing look, which he declines to acknowledge as he leans over to kiss the top of Lillie's head. "Little girl, I've been in trouble every day since you were born. Don't you start worrying about it now." He pulls a screwdriver from his pocket and turns back to the crib.

Emma squeezes out the compress that's soaking in the water bowl by the bed, and dabs at Lillie's forehead and neck. "You need to eat something."

Lillie doesn't bother to protest. "Tea and toast?" she croaks, but it's an effort to speak.

Ferd appears in the room, knowing Emma's scolding voice signals that Lillie is awake; if Lillie were still asleep, she would keep her complaint to a hiss. He sits next to Lillie on the bed and takes her hand. "How are you feeling?"

She keeps her head tipped back into the pillows. "Muddled. Hot." She presses her free hand against her breastbone. "Sore."

"The doctor says you're running a low-grade fever."

Relegated to the far side of the bed, Emma fusses at the pillows and coverlet. She leans over to hold the back of her hand against Lillie's forehead, as though she wants to check whether the doctor knows what he's talking about. Indeed, she is warm, despite the compress, and her cheeks are flushed.

"Come, Mrs. Beck," Charley says to her as he takes her elbow in one hand, a railing of the crib in another. "We're making tea and toast, remember?"

Emma snaps her arm out of Charley's hand and marches out ahead of him. Charley winks at them and closes the door behind him.

Ferd has been home since mid-morning. True to his word, Dr. Cavanaugh calls to let him know of the reversal, catching Ferd almost as he walks into the shop. His supervisor, a terse but intelligent man, listens to the situation then makes a small motion with his hand. "Call me tomorrow if you need more time." On his way out, Ferd stops by to tell Charley, whose current supervisor is no more intelligent than any of his previous ones and does not offer the same latitude. It's only later in the day that Charley is able to secure his own work release.

At home, Ferd finds Lillie already in bed, drugged into sleep. He is used to the look of innocence she wears in her sleep, a half-smile, and her eyes as though she has only just closed them for a moment. This slack-faced, open-mouthed unconsciousness scares him.

Dr. Cavanaugh confers with him and Emma at the kitchen table, bringing Ferd up to the latest. "She's had several bad coughing fits, and her sputum is thick and gray. Since I've been here, her temperature has gone up." He reaches a bottle from his bag and looks at it as he turns it slowly in his hands. "I've made up a tincture of opium that's a bit stronger than what I gave her last night. That should help open her breathing passages and ease the stiffness. And it makes her sleep, too, obviously. I'll leave it with you, but you have to be very careful about the dosage. Too heavy a dose will depress her breathing."

"The baby?" Ferd asks quietly.

"It's too soon to know, but there's been no blood." He sits the bottle on the table. "For the fever, cold compresses should be fine for now. Make sure she gets plenty of fluids. Let her tea cool off before she drinks it." He leans back in the chair. "I've called a colleague of mine to come for a consult. He may not be able to come today, but promises to be here tomorrow." He is staring hard at the table, perplexed. "It makes no sense. Yesterday morning she was fine beyond some morning sickness. She took a hard fall, but no apparent injuries outside of normal bruising, and now, not much beyond twenty-four hours later, she has a fully developed case of pneumonia."

"Pneumonia?" Emma is incredulous.

"That's my diagnosis. But, as I say, I'm having my colleague Dr. Brandon consult on the case. He specializes in respiratory ailments."

Ferd finds that he has a dull buzzing in his head and he's having trouble getting his eyes to focus. The doctor is saying, "...move to another room, so they won't disturb her. I'll be back later this afternoon; I hope to have Dr. Brandon with me. Call me if I need to come sooner."

Now Lillie is saying to him, "Water?" and nodding at the pitcher by the bed, squeezed in between extra handkerchiefs, the medicine bottle and spoon, the water bowl with the compress. How quickly her nightstand has taken on the trappings of the sick room.

She sips from the glass, gingerly, as though she is testing for contaminants. "Trying not to cough," she tells him with a little smile. "Coughing hurts." She sips some more and tries a small throat-clearing. Another. "That's a little better." She rests her head back against the pillows and briefly closes her eyes. "I'm sorry to worry you."

"Oh, Lillie…"

"I saw you eating black toast." She looks at him through one eye and pats his hand. "Do you remember that time, when we were courting? The charcoal?"

He is baffled for a minute, but then Lillie makes a show of running her tongue over her teeth. Ferd rolls his eyes in old embarrassment as he remembers, and she grins at him: The young Ferd chews charcoal to settle his always-peptic stomach. One evening, after spending time with him in their little corner behind the clematis, she turns the gaslight up in the bathroom, and the mirror reveals her cheeks, lips, and teeth blackened from the transfer.

She gestures at the water glass again and sips carefully before handing it to him and leaning back into the pillows. "Thank you for the memory box. At least I can read a little." Her diary is open on the bed next to her. "You know, I feel I know everything in there by heart."

"I'm certain you do."

Her eyes close again. "This laudanum. I have the strangest dreams. Things from the box, but all these other things, too, jumbled. Things that aren't in there. Not my memories...possible?" She is starting to drift, but her eyes open at the solid steps of Emma on the stairs. Lillie's hand squeezes his arm. "Let the children come in," she tells him, clear-eyed. "She won't want them to. You won't either. But *I* want them. Let them come in. Promise."

He cups her chin in his hand, and leans in to kiss her forehead. "I promise," he says, as the door opens once again.

ᘓᘐ

Dr. Brandon may be an expert in respiratory ailments, but he is a menace as a practitioner. He pokes at Lillie as though she is insensible, talks as though she is not present. And he only speaks to Dr. Cavanaugh, ignoring the others more completely even than he does Lillie.

"Pneumonia, without question." he says, while the others startle that he is pronouncing this in front of the patient. "Inhalation."

Dr. Cavanaugh is appropriately mortified at his colleague, but the damage is done. "You think it's an outcome of the fall, then?"

"No doubt the cellar is filthy. Dust, mold, fungus."

Emma draws herself up in outrage, but Charley pulls her back. At Lillie's side, Ferd gapes at this creature, but feels Lillie's hand slide into his. "Well, then," she croaks, and smiles as they all turn to her. "At least I know. None of you would have told me."

"But for it to have taken hold so quickly," Dr. Cavanaugh presses.

"Mold spores, drawn deeply into the lungs, lodge in the alveoli and begin to reproduce immediately in a very conducive environment." He manages to sound simultaneously bored and irritated.

"Do we need to worry about contagion?"

Dr. Brandon stiffens and looks at Dr. Cavanaugh as though he has proved himself mentally defective. "I just told you it was inhalation pneumonia."

"I guess that's a *no* then," Charley says. "So what now?"

They all wait, as the callous Doctor Brandon carefully repacks his medical bag. Finally, Dr. Cavanaugh clears his throat and says, "What course of treatment do you recommend?"

He snaps his bag shut, as though that were pronouncement enough. "Not much to be done. It will run its course." As an afterthought, he says, "Keep the fever down."

"And for the coughing?"

"The coughing doesn't signify."

"It's painful. For the patient."

He purses his lips. "The tincture then. Or morphine injections if the patient declines."

"Well, that's enough, right there," Charley breaks in, picking up the bag and sweeping the doctor before him. "That's just as much expert opinion as we can stand."

Dr. Cavanaugh follows, turning to them before he leaves. "I'm so sorry."

ꕥ

Lillie opens her eyes, disoriented. It's late afternoon, and the soft spring light plays on the floor. She's not used to being asleep in the daylight. Her breath catches, taking her by surprise, and she starts to cough. The handkerchief clutched in her hand, even as she sleeps, goes to her mouth to catch what comes up; again, the other hand presses against her breastbone. It's hard not to panic in the struggle to breathe, but she coaches herself through. Ferd is there at the bedside, holding a glass of water for her. She waits until the coughing has fully subsided before sipping.

"Mother?"

Lillie hasn't even seen Margaret there, sitting in the light by the window, holding her sketchbook. She's standing up now, worried. "I'm okay now, sweetheart." Lillie looks over at Ferd.

"Your mother isn't happy at all. But a promise is a promise." They exchange a smile. "They've been peeking in all afternoon. You smiled and said hello a few times. Do you remember?"

"I thought I was dreaming." She sees that the crib has disappeared, replaced by one of the card tables to hold all of the sickroom supplies. Even so, the room looks so much larger now.

"Well, she only just dragged them out now to get ready for dinner. Margaret snuck back in."

She turns back to Margaret. "Come sit with me. Show me what

you're drawing."

Margaret is shy in the face of her mother's illness, but goes to her bedside. Lillie pats the bed, inviting her to sit down. "Let's see," as Margaret hands her the sketchbook, now flipped to the beginning.

Margaret sketches in pencil or charcoal things that she sees around her: flowers in the garden tipped with a butterfly or hummingbird, jack o' lanterns, the huge Christmas tree with the train running beneath it. They are beautifully rendered and realistic. But it is the portraits that truly reveal her talent, each one evocative of her subject's personality. Here is Tommy as a newborn, still wrinkled like an old man, squalling in outrage, his fists up; Charley, fedora pushed back on his head, poised mid-aim with a horseshoe up to his nose and a twinkle in his eye; Ferd with his sleeves rolled above his elbows and Jeanie riding on his shoulders, squealing. Lillie flips to the final page, and she sees a portrait of herself, standing in the same window where Margaret has been sketching, the softening afternoon sun casting light and shadows across her face.

"Oh, Margaret," she breathes softly. "These are beautiful. You have so much talent." Margaret blushes at the praise, tongue-tied. Lillie reaches out and covers her hand. "You have real talent," she repeats. "Be proud of that." Margaret is almost beside herself now, so Lillie pats her hand, and says, "Dinner. Before Mother notices she's one short."

Margaret catches up her sketchpad and beams at them both as she leaves. Lillie sinks back into her pillows, still smiling but spent. She presses a hand against her chest. "I think I'll just close...my..."

Ferd draws his chair in closer and sits back down, watching her sleep.

ꟷ

It's late and the house is quiet. Lillie is fully asleep, but in a leaden, immobile posture that is unnatural to her. Her breathing is rough. It makes his chest hurt listening to it, and he sees that he is mimicking the gesture that is now constant with Lillie, fingers pressed into the breastbone trying to relieve the ache. He checks again that she is not stirring, because he has waited as long as he can; he needs to use the toilet. He slips out without a sound, and is back just three minutes later.

Emma has taken his place. She is fussing over Lillie, fluffing the coverlet and arranging the pillows, pressing the refreshed compress against her forehead. It occurs to him that she is hoping to wake Lillie up. Unsuccessful, she sits down in Ferd's chair, her back to him. "You haven't given her any of the tincture, have you?"

"No."

"Good. I'll be the one to give her the doses. So there's no mistake." Lillie's ragged breathing fills the silence. "You *are* going back to work tomorrow." It is very barely a question.

"No, I'm not going to work tomorrow. I don't plan to go anywhere again until she's better."

"Hmm, well, you may as well go to bed. I'm here now."

He stares hard at her back. She is sitting in what was supposed to have been his bed. He stands, she sits, neither one moves. But he knows she has him; he cannot stand here forever, and he will not pull the ladder-back chair up to the other side of the bed like some secondary hanger-on.

He ends up in the kitchen, where Charley sits with a cup of coffee reading the paper. Except that he holds the *Evening Star* rather than the *Washington Post*, it would be easy to believe that he hasn't moved from the spot since five o'clock this morning.

Automatically, Ferd pours a cup of coffee and sits down. The day's milk is long since gone, and no more available for another five hours.

Again, the only sound is the rustling of the newspaper, the creak of the kitchen chairs. Ferd mindlessly toys with his coffee spoon, looking at it without seeing. "Sometimes I wonder. I wonder what it would have been like to live in my own house. Have my wife and my children all to myself." He finally looks up at Charley. "Is that selfish?"

"Guess it depends which side of the question you're on." He finishes the last section, last page, and folds up the paper, slurps the dregs of the coffee. Sits back. The two men look at each other.

"She had Lillie to herself for twenty-two years."

"Would that be enough for you?"

"But when do I get my time?"

"She won't be around forever, you know."

A derisive snort. "Are you sure?"

Charley stands and stretches. He puts his hand on Ferd's shoulder on his way out. "Lillie knows she's lucky, Ferd. You never tried to make her choose."

Alone, at midnight, in the kitchen of his in-laws' house, Ferd stares into his coffee cup. Finally, in disgust at himself, he stands sharply, the chair jumping back. He puts the two mugs into the sink and flicks off the kitchen light. There is a waning moon, still bright enough to cast milky silver shadows into the room. He wanders through the dining room into the parlor, running his finger over the big Victrola as he considers the sofa and two easy chairs there. He circles through into the hall and looks up, knowing that Lillie is sleeping in their bed above him. He chooses the armchair beneath the spot, eases himself down, and settles in for the night.

Lonesome Avenue

1916-1917

Tucked down in the memory box, carefully tied in a heavy pink ribbon, are the letters they exchanged during the one time in their courtship they were apart. Reading them always makes Lillie laugh and shake her head, sometimes even blush at the silliness; she and Ferd were so young.

Naneva Camp
Bluemont, Va.
Sept 7. 1916

My dearest Boy:

There is so much to write that I don't know just where to begin, but I guess the beginning is the best place to start, so here goes. We left Brightwood about 7:30, arrived over in Georgetown 8:30. Left there 9:04. We had a perfectly lovely ride, so nice and cool and clear, no dust or cinders to worry us. It rained quite hard along the line between Washington and Vienna, but after that it cleared off, the sun came out and it was perfectly beautiful. It is a very pleasant ride through rolling, wooded country, along cornfields and by little streams. It took quite awhile to get to our destination as the train was a local and stopped at all the stations, waited for trains to go by instead of making them get out of its way. When I caught my first glimpse of the mountains, you don't know what a thrill it sent through me and I was wishing my boy could be along to enjoy them with me. I believe they call them mountains but I would call them very large hills, but they are beautiful whatever they are. We reached Bluemont about 12:20, the train was an hour late, and then we had a three mile drive up the mountainside in a little "Ford" which was sadly in need of a shock absorber. The ride part of the way up was very dusty as they are scraping the roads preparatory to fixing them, and then there were two autos in front of us to kick up the dust. After we turned off the main road the dust was no more but the road was very rough. We reached here somewhere around one o'clock, just in time to get the dust off for dinner at 1:30. After dinner we roamed down to the spring, which they say is the second purest in the world. Then we went up and sat down on the porch and got acquainted with the other boarders, about seventeen I believe they have here. Mother left on the 4:10 train so her auto came for her about 3:30.

After she had gone I went up and unpacked my suitcase, undressed, put on my "nightie" and kimona and lay down to rest and take a nap if possible, which it did not happen was possible as the two dames who have the room on the left of mine are very talkative about politics and the war, which of course did not interest me and therefore was more of an annoyance. The reason I could hear the conversation is that the walls are of boards and the dame's voice was very penetrating. The persons in question are a mother and her daughter who is an old maid and thereby hangs a tale, for as with all old maids she is more or less perverse and soured by too much single blessedness. These two and one other old lady who sits at our table are the only funny ones here, the others are all lovely people and I like them very much.

I have a dear little room with a cute little porch outside the door. All I can see from the windows is woods but by looking out around my porch I can see the valley way over in the distance. This valley is the Shenandoah and way over in the distance are the Allegheny mountains. The view is wonderful and I do wish you could be here with me to enjoy it.

I slept nicely last night in my little bed and woke up early, then went back to sleep and woke up when the rising bell rang. We have breakfast at eight o'clock. Now I am down in the little summer house writing. It is lovely and cool and I came here for the quiet because the talkative element sit on the porch and I can't write when people are talking.

How is my boy and what is he doing with himself? How did the examination turn out? Was it hard? How are our numerous neighbors? Any particular news? How are all the family?

I am not real lonesome yet though I may be, but I do miss you honey and wish you were near so I could see you. Your picture is a great consolation and I can kiss it when I want you very much. There is one tiny spot on my arm so I kissed that last night and thought of our last moments together.

Well lovey darling I guess I had better close because this must go in the 12:30 mail. This letter will not reach you until Saturday I don't believe, as the mail of today does not leave Bluemont until Friday but the Washington mail takes only one day thank goodness to get here.

If Mother said anything to you about coming up Sunday be sure and call up the railway and be sure when the trains leave. I think the Sunday train leaves at 9:30 in the morning and leaves here 8:30 in the evening. Well my darling I shall say goodbye with lots of love and kisses,

Your loving sweetheart,
Lillie.

P.S. I was mistaken about the bath as we have all modern conveniences here.

ଓଉଓ

Naneva Camp.
Bluemont, Va.
Sept. 8, 1916

My dearest Boy:

You are not going to have a long letter this time as there isn't much to tell, except that we eat three meals a day, sleep nine or ten hours, walk a little, rest a lot and enjoy ourselves very quietly.

Last night was one of the beautiful nights; the moon was in its first quarter and very bright, there were some stars out and everything was lovely. We walked up to the gate so we could get the full effect of moon and stars then we walked around a little and after awhile went up and sat down on the porch.

This morning about two or three o'clock I was awakened by something and lay in bed looking out of my east window at Venus, the morning star. That is the one you said looked like the crescent moon. So I was trying to see the crescent, but whether I was too sleepy or because it has gotten over its crescent shape I could not see it, but just the star shape so I turned over and went to sleep and woke up in time to see the sun rise.

I am writing in the summer house again. I just had a visitor, a young girl about fifteen, nice little thing who is stopping at the house and we were discussing our fellow boarders especially the old maid of whom I spoke in yesterday's letter. It seems that nearly everyone has the same idea of her that I have. She is really very peculiar and I get so tired of listening to her talk because she is so decided in her opinions. The other people are all pleasant but she is the limit. I know if you should meet her she would exasperate you just as she does me. Well enough of the old maid. Why should I worry about such?

I am having a lovely time and enjoying myself thoroughly. The only thing I have left to wish for is that you were here to enjoy it with me.

I am beginning to have more respect for the size of these hills. As I look at them more I realize that they are a pretty good height. We are on the top of one a hundred and fifty feet up. I suppose that means above sea level. The view over the valley is lovely. Yesterday morning there was a very heavy mist that obscured everything, even the mountains nearest had a thick fleecy cloud over them, that gradually rolled away as the sun shone on them but the far-away mountains were still covered. This morning we had no mist but I can't
[pardon the half sheet. I am saving paper.]
see the far-away mountains except as a faint gray line on the distant horizon. But enough of this rhapsodizing.

Have you heard how the wedding on Longfellow Street came off? Several of the people up here know that I am going to be married so are duly interested. I had to tell them in self-defense because they thought I was nothing but a school girl. Think of that.
Well take good care of my boy and don't get too lonesome for your loving girl,
Lillie
Give my love to your mother and the rest of my family-in-law.

5405 Lonesome, Ave. N.W.
Washington, D.C.

Dearest Sweetheart:

Received your letter dated Sept 8, 1916 and am very glad to hear that you are still feeling good and not so lonesome, and probably after receiving my first letter, which you should have received Saturday you will feel still less lonesome.

I noticed that you did not expect your first letter to reach me until Saturday, that would have made it Monday before you would have heard from me. I would have been very disappointed if that should have been the case, because as I stated in my first letter I somewhat expected to receive one Thursday. And just think what a long time that would have been for you to wait to hear from me. According to that you must have been surprised to hear from me Saturday. How did you like my first letter? Could you read it or was it like shorthand to you?

Well dearest I must say that that was over three times as long a letter as I have ever written and although it gave me pleasure to be able to write so much to my dearie I must admit that I had a pain in my back and a kink in my arm.

Now sweetheart I will attempt to give you an account of myself beginning with Friday night after mailing that ten-page letter. I hope they did not charge you any extra postage. Well Friday night after mailing the letter I returned to 5405 Lonesome Ave., and helped Mother, Dorothy, Frank, and Raymond Crogan dispose of a nice red watermelon, which reminded me of that one we had around to your house, and I could have enjoyed it as much had my darling little sweetheart been there to share my part with me. Saturday being our last half day, that's unless the President opens up his heart and grants us next Saturday; and a double-header being scheduled at the Ball Park between the Nationals who are at present playing dandy baseball and the Boston Red Sox, who are the prospective World Champions, I thought I would loosen up and take in the bargain. The first game was won by Boston, the score being 2 to 1—the great Walter Johnson going down to defeat. The second game lasted ten long innings, Washington winning out after a grand finish—score 4 to 3.

Both games were very interesting and it really proved to be a

"Bargain Day" as they call a double-header in baseball talk. When I returned from the games I was hungry as a bull, for I had not eaten a thing since breakfast, unless you would call ice cream cones something to eat. I bought two of these, one for you and one for myself and as you were not here to eat yours I ate it myself.

When I returned, I noticed that it was too late for me to eat my supper, write a letter to my lovie dovie, and get dressed and go to confession, so I decided to put that off until next week so that I could write to you and get it in the box before nine o'clock.

I have not heard a thing about the Longfellow St. wedding, but I notice "Dear William" has another write up in this morning's Herald, for his valuable assistance in helping to obtain a pension for Fireman and Policemen's widows.

Well sweetheart, I have not been as lonesome as I could have been for I have had a little something to do every night, visiting, writing these two letters and several other things which I have already told, but even at that I have been very lonesome, and just to think dearest, Sunday will be the first Sunday that we have not been together since we have been going together, I guess that will be the most lonesome day I have ever spent so far or will spend in the near future. Well sweetheart I will not write again until Monday as you say there is no delivery on Sunday, and that will give me more to write about. Did you get all of my kisses, especially that long one? Take the best care of the sweetest little girlie in the world for I would not have anything happen to her for anything in the world.

XXXXLots of Love & sweet Kisses. Ferd
XXXX XXX

ଓଓଓ

Sept. 10, 1916

My beloved Sweetheart,

Your dear letter came yesterday and I was so happy I almost stood on my head. Why dearest you write a perfectly lovely letter, whatever made you say you could not? It was certainly a lovely letter and it came when I was feeling right lonesome so it was doubly dear. There really is very little to write about because so little happens up here. The arrival of the mail carrier with his bag is the greatest event of the day. But sweetheart don't think I am not enjoying myself because it's so quiet. I am having a lovely time with only one exception and that is because you are not here to enjoy it with me. And now sweetheart I'll tell you why I did not call you up and tell you to come up anyhow regardless of the bank account. While the people are very nice up here they are a very straight-laced set and there are a couple of old hens at our table that I would not want you to meet. I don't mean that there is anything wrong with them, but they are just plain cranks and I am afraid they would spoil a good deal of our enjoyment in each other, and as we could be by ourselves so little I thought it would be better to wait until I got back to enjoy each other's society. You understand don't you lovey? You know I would love to see you and love to have you see this beautiful place, so some time after we are married we might be able to come up and enjoy it together. (I have changed pens because mine does not write dark enough to suit me.) Miss Wolverton said she thought I was right too and that this bunch of people was too prudish to suit either of us, so sweetheart mine, please don't think it was because I did not want you. And now I'll tell you the news, which isn't very extensive.

Yesterday morning one of the ladies and myself gathered flowers and filled all the vases, dressing up for Sunday, you know. Then I strolled around and then we had dinner. After dinner Effie Wolverton and three other boarders and myself went down to the summer house. They served, and I got the caretaker's little youngster to play with. She is a cute little thing, blue eyes and fair hair. I am afraid both she and the baby will be sadly spoiled when we leave because Effie puts the baby to sleep and we all play with Edna, the little girl. But she does not like men, she seems to be afraid of them, and when the husband of one of the ladies came down she put her little arms around my neck and held on tight, refused even to look at him. When she came to go she condescended to shake hands with him, but that was all. We went back to the house about four o'clock to take a rest, and after supper we took a walk up the road to the gate where we stood and gazed at the moon, then Miss Dill, who is interested in astronomy, and myself stood in the middle of the road discussing the moon and stars. Miss Dill is very nice but she is very homely and she is a school teacher. Miss Barney and Miss Crippen, the two ladies who own the place, came up yesterday afternoon and stayed until this evening. Miss

Crippen and I had quite a long chat last night, and she was asking when we were going to be married.

Were you looking at the moon last night, dearest, between seven and nine, because if you were I was also!

This morning I woke up early and found that the comforter I had put over me last night had very unkindly slipped down on the floor, so I hauled it back and went to sleep again. After breakfast I said my Mass prayers (no church up here), and then while the Presbyterians were having their prayers in the living room Effie and I started up to Raven Rock which is on the next mountain. We went up the road, then up a path, then up a road again, into the woods and finally out on the rock. And then, Dearest, one has a wonderful view of the mountains and Shenandoah Valley for several miles, and it is just beautiful. The valley is spread out below and the mountains tower about. There are mountains near and mountains off in the distance as far as the eye can reach, all a soft grey like fuzzy down on chickens. That doesn't describe it very well, but it's the best I can do, so you will have to use your imagination, beloved. The mountains near are densely wooded. I made a mistake in the height above sea level, it is 1750 feet not 150 feet.

I am glad you got through the examination alright and could take a day out of your annual leave. Tell your boss he had better be careful with my boy while I am away.

Dearest, please tell Mother to send up some more writing paper, I am running short. I forgot to put it in her letter today and I am afraid if I wait until tomorrow it will get here too late. Tell her just to send the paper not envelopes. The writing paper is in a box in my room on the bureau.

No more to write at present, dear heart, so will say goodbye with lots of love and kisses from your loving sweetheart. – Lillie

༺༻

Ferd walks to 741 and is relieved to find Charley Beck in the side yard, digging at something with a shovel.

"Evening, Mr. Beck."

"Well, howdy do, Ferd." Charley pushes the hat back on his head, rests his arms on the shovel handle. "Are you holding up under the strain? How many days has it been?"

"Six."

"Stopping by to look at the house helps the time go faster?"

"Oh, I'm not as sad off as all that. Though I'll tell you, with her away, there's a big hole where she normally is."

"I'm right there with you, Ferd. There's surely something missing."

Ferd and Charley contemplate this for a moment before Ferd remembers his errand. "Lillie asked me to have her mother post some blank stationery out to her. She's running out."

"That didn't take long. Let's see, that's six days with posts twice a day...Guess there's been a flurry of letters out to some young man hereabouts." He gives Ferd a wink. "Well, come on inside. I'm thinking there's blueberry pie from dinner." Charley sees Ferd hesitate. "Not to worry. She's out at some hen party with the biddies from church. It's just us."

In the kitchen, Charley cuts them each a generous slice of pie and pours coffee from the pot. "So how have you been filling your time?"

"Work. They had me take some kind of aptitude test this week, not sure why. That worried me, but I think I did all right. I went to the ballgame on Saturday. The double-header against the Red Sox."

Charley gestures at the papers on the table. "I read about that. It's a darn shame; Johnson keeps losing to that kid, Babe Ruth."

"Yeah, we sure don't seem to be able to hit against him."

The pie slices are disappearing. "How's the saving coming?"

"Pretty well. I try to bank every bit I can, outside of courting Lillie."

"I hope she's not too pricey." Charley smiles over his coffee cup.

Ferd laughs. "No, your daughter is not terribly demanding, not like some girls. You know Lillie's friend, Dorothy? I don't know how Will can put a cent by. It seems like she's not happy unless he's spending money on her. I'm afraid to see what this wedding of theirs in a few weeks is going to look like."

Charley chuckles as he carries their plates to the sink and pours more coffee. "Have you talked about a date yet?"

"We're thinking the spring, but there are a few things I want to take care of before we say for sure."

Again they sit in companionable silence. Not for the first time, Ferd considers that, outside of Lillie, he's never found anyone easier to talk to than Charley Beck.

"You know, Mr. Beck, I will always try to be the man she deserves."

Charley rears back a bit in surprise. "Son, I don't think there's ever been a question of that."

"Oh?" Ferd glances at an empty chair. "I don't always feel as if I measure up."

Charley follows his glance and bursts out laughing. "Oh, Ferd, you can't take it personal. Against that yardstick, we *all* come up short!"

"You don't think that the idea of Lillie spending ten days out in the country was to give her a chance to reconsider?"

There is a long pause while Charley takes a slow drink from his cup and sets it back down. "Well, now, Ferd, even if that's true, we both know it makes no difference. There's only one opinion here that counts, and she's made her choice."

Ferd finally nods once and brightens again. "I really do appreciate everything you've done to help me, with the job and everything. I, well, I wonder if you can help me with one more thing. Then I'd feel comfortable picking a date for the wedding."

"What do you need?"

"Well, advice, I think, more than anything. I want to buy a house."

Charley sits back and appraises the young man who will soon be his son-in-law. "Well, that's the ticket, Ferd. Good for you! Yep, I think I know just the folks you'll want to talk to." They smile at each other in this collusion. Then Charley claps the table. "Before I forget. Where's the stationery?"

"Lillie said it's on her bureau."

He is gone and back in a flash, carrying a stack of heavy rag paper. He hands it to Ferd. "Here, you send it. We'll let you be the hero."

ഊഌ

Sept. 11, 1916

My dearest:

Just a short letter this morning as there is not very much to write about and I want to get this to town with some people who are leaving.

My darling how are you getting along without your wifie? Is he very lonesome for his girl? Last night I looked at the beautiful moon and thought of my boy and wondered if he were looking at the moon, too.

Yesterday, after dinner, we took a short walk around the place and then sat down in the summer house and talked and then the only man on the place (he is married) came down and we amused ourselves by teasing him and then he threw some apples at one of the girls so one of them threw one at him and hit him in the face and so then we fled. He leaves this morning so we shan't have anyone to tease. We worry him to death! After supper we took a walk up to the gate and amused ourselves by howling like cats and other foolish things like that to let off excess energy which we don't dare let off down at the house for fear of worrying the old hens at the house. They changed my place to the other table with the nicer people so I am completely happy now.

This morning we have not had a chance to do anything this morning yet so I have nothing to report.

Well dearest boy give my love to your family and keep all you want for yourself and don't be too lonesome for your girl. Be good to my boy and remember to look at the moon at night.

Dearest goodbye, with lots of love and kisses from your loving girl,
Lillie.

ഌഌഌ

Sept 12, 1916

Dearest Sweetheart:

Received your second letter and was delighted to hear that everything is coming along so nicely. Our only man went home yesterday, so his wife and the rest of us who teased him, the poor man, unmercifully felt slightly lonesome last night. It is decidedly chilly this morning though the sun is shining brightly and we are enjoying ourselves as much as ever. But lovey my feet were very cold when I awoke this morning as the mountain air is very cool at night.

Well lovey I am not lonesome yet but I think that I am getting a little homesick so I shall be very glad to get home Saturday. We are all going together on the 4:10 train which is supposed to reach the city about 6:30 in the evening. So if my boy does not mind journeying over to

Please excuse the little blots. The pen splattered.

Georgetown, I shall see him somewhere around that time. If you can't, why, call up Dad and tell him to come over. Yesterday we went down to visit an old mountain woman who lives in a little one-roomed hut on the side of the mountain. She looks like an old witch, very old and bent. Seemed to be very nice though. She had some chickens, seven dogs and a calf, a grandson, and a husband.

Well dearest I don't know what else to write about as we do so little up here except just having a good time. But it won't be long before I shall see my boy again and then we can talk it all over together. So lovey darling I shall say goodbye, with fondest love and lots of kisses from your devoted and loving girl.
Lillie

ഋഌഋ

Sept. 13, 1916

My dearest Boy:

There is a severe scarcity of news today I am sorry to say, but there may be more tomorrow as we expect to go to Harpers Ferry this afternoon if we can get enough to go. Four people went yesterday from here. They say it is a beautiful and very interesting trip.

We did not do very much of anything yesterday but sew and read and roam around. Last night we took our usual walk up to the gate and then when we came back we sat down in the living room. That is where we all congregate in the evening. Some of us read, usually another girl and myself. Effie sews, and the rest play cards. The people divide naturally up here: the jolly bunch and then the old hens. We nearly drive the sedate ones mad, I guess, but that never worries us very much. One of the girls knows lots of foolish songs and she was singing them last night, so we laughed from the time we sat down until we went to bed. The lights (I believe they are acetylene lights) would not work last night so we had to have lamps.

I am sorry to hear that Baby Ruth has been sick and hope she will be alright. I suppose Mary Lynch wants to go to the wedding, Dorothy's I mean, she is so very interested in all Dorothy and I do. I wonder if Will and Dorothy have found a tenant yet that hasn't any encumbrance. Just think, just about three weeks before they are married. Poor things. You see my sympathy is impartially distributed. Well we shan't want any sympathy when we take the broad leap will we?

Well, dearest, your letters have been very interesting and dear, and I have enjoyed them very much. Well love, how is my boy and how is he getting along? I shall be home in four days now, just think. I am beginning to wish for home now, though I am having a lovely time.

Well sweetheart goodbye with all the love of my heart and lots of loving kisses.

Lovingly.
Lillie

ᏅᏅᏅ

5405 Verilonesome Ave.,
Lonesome Park
Washington, D.C.

My Dear Little Girlie:

Received your sweet letter dated Sept. 12, and am glad to hear that you are still in good spirits and not so lonesome. I have not much to say as I seemed to have shot my bolt in my first couple letters, (excuse this expression) but will do my best.

Last night I took a nice long walk to the "Revere" and saw a very nice play called, "The Better Woman," which was a very interesting film. I also walked back, and of course during my journey to and from the theatre my only thoughts were of my little sweetheart in Bluemont, Va. and of course the walk did not seem long at all, in fact it was not long because I left my house at 7:25 and was home again at 9:45.

I notice in your last letter (Sept. 12) that you say you have received my second letter, I cannot understand this, as this will be the fifth letter that I have written to you.

I have only been around to your house twice as I wanted to give them a rest for a change so that they would not get tired of seeing me so often. Tonight I am not very presentable for I need a haircut and shave very bad, and have a couple very prominent bumps adorning my forehead, but I shouldn't worry as my little girlie is not here to see me.

After mailing this letter, I am going up stairs to take a much needed shave and then I will adorn my best old suit and take a little walk up to the basement of the church where they are going to hold a meeting, and try to organize a Holy Name Society.

My plans for Saturday are to try and get off at 12:30, take in a movie, then go to confession at 3:30 and get out of church at about 4:30 and be over in Georgetown in plenty time to meet my darling little sweetheart at 6:30 for whom I am very, very lonesome. Darling, I am sorry you can't stay longer, but I must admit that I am glad Saturday is near, so let's cheer up, for next year we can take our vacations together.

Lot of our old time love and sweet kisses so. goodnight

Yours as loving as ever
Your darling boy
Ferd

ଓଓଓ

Thurs. Sept. 14, 1916
Washington, D.C.

Dear Sweetheart:

Received your letter and pretty Post Card of yesterday and am glad you are still enjoying yourself, and hope you will feel the effects of your little vacation.

Dearie, as you are going to leave for Washington Saturday afternoon, I will make this my last letter as you will not receive this until Friday and Saturday morn you will be getting ready for home and Saturday evening I will have the pleasure of being in my little sweetheart's company once again.

I have not much to report anymore but will once more do my best.

Wednesday after mailing my letter to you I took a stroll up to the basement of the church and attended the meeting for the organization of a "Holy Name Society," we had a pretty good crowd for a starter including the honorable Charles Beck of 741 Longfellow St., Brightwood. We had a nice meeting which consisted chiefly of speeches by several prominent Holy Name Organizers, namely Mr. Michael Shafer and Mr. H. Doyle. The election of President was the only one which was not unanimous, and that was won by Mr. Donovan who won over Capt. Edwards by a vote of 24 to 22. Mr. Glover was elected Vice President, Mr. John King, Secretary, Mr. Robert Hunter, Treasurer and Capt. Edwards D.C.N.G., Marshall. After the meeting, cigars were passed around and of course to be sociable I took one, but for a change I lit it and smoked part of it and believe me I can taste that stogie yet. I walked down from the meeting with part of the Schrider family, Eddie Lynch and several other fellows. During the course of conversation Eddie Lynch said, "Ferdie, how is it you are off tonight?" Of course I replied that my girl had gone to Bluemont, Va., for a little vacation, then John Schrider spoke up and said, "Believe me that girl thinks a lot of you, because I am in a position to know."

There is a black cloud hovering over this town right now as the Negro Odd Fellows are holding a convention here. They are known as the "B.M.C" whatever that means, but anyhow one of the darkies down work came up to Mr. Yates and asked him what "B.M.C." stood for. Mr. Yates thought for a moment and replied, "The only thing I see it could stand for is "Big Mouth Coons," the colored fellow got peeved and said, "Just like you Irishmen."

Everyone in my family have all said, "I am glad it's you who have to write all those letters." I told them, "Well, I guess if I let my feelings get the best of me I could write her a good size book."

Well, honey, the boss has left me off for Saturday, and I will be at Georgetown waiting when the Bluemont Special arrives at 6:30.

Well, I hope that you continue to enjoy the remaining hours there and that you will have a pleasant ride home to your waiting sweetheart.

Your Loving & Affectionate Sweetheart
Ferd
P.S.
Do not expect any mail from me Saturday as we will see one another when the car pulls in at Georgetown at 6:30. LOVE & KISSES xxxxxXXXX

ᘐᘏ

They are on their normal Saturday afternoon walk through the neighborhood, but Ferd guides them on a different path than usual. The warm day and clear sky highlight the street of gardens, flowers, and tidy little row houses to best effect. It is lovely, and Lillie exclaims over the yards, each more engaging than the last; here is a street of gardeners. Ferd slows and finally stops in front of one of the row houses. Lillie presumes that something particular about it has caught his eye, and she stands to admire it as well. Cheery red shutters against pale yellow painted brick, white trim and front porch, and gingerbreading on the steep second-story gable. March has only just started, but here are camellias, already in bloom, and happy-faced jonquils. Fat buds cover the rhododendron, and the rose bushes are blushed red with their new spring growth. It looks like a picture from the storybooks she remembers Christine Hilfinger reading to her.

She sighs at the vision, and looks up at Ferd. He is smiling at her with a look of great anticipation. She can't help but smile back. "What? What is it?"

"What do you think of it?"

"It's like something out of a fairytale."

"It's yours."

There is a long pause while Lillie contemplates the house and then Ferd. She cocks her head at him, still smiling. "What do you mean?"

"I haven't signed the papers yet, because I wanted you to see it first, but everything is all lined up. Bill Knightly from work told me about it, and when I came to see it, I knew you would love it. I wasn't sure that I had saved enough money yet, but Mr. Johnson is willing to hold the paper and has already agreed to the payments I was able to offer." The words are tumbling out in his excitement, but he is starting to sense her hesitation. "I know it's small, but for the first few years there should be plenty of room for us...for babies..." His consternation grows as she continues to smile gently at him as he struggles at her silence.

Her confused look comes to mirror his own, but then she laughs and puts her hand on his arm. "Oh, Ferd, don't be silly! I could never leave my parents."

He fights to make sense of this. So far, nothing matches the scene he has repeatedly imagined in the many weeks leading up to this moment. "Lillie, we're getting married." He works to keep the question mark out of his voice.

Lillie's brow furrows. "Of course."

"Then I don't understand."

"Mother and Dad are getting older, Mother in particular; her arthritis has gotten so bad she's decided to retire. It won't be long before they won't be able to do for themselves. I can't leave them alone."

Ferd looks at the house again with a sinking feeling. "So you want them to move in with us?"

She laughs that light, tinkling laugh that opens the whole world for him. "Of course not, silly." Ferd's relieved sigh is caught in mid-exhale by her next words. "When we're married, you'll move in with us."

He feels physically sick, unable to breathe and looks desperately for a place to sit down. The only bench is in a yard down the street, and he has to will himself not to let his legs buckle under him.

"Ferd? What's wrong?"

He finds that he is incapable of speech, or of looking at Lillie for fear of openly weeping. He looks instead at the house, which is perhaps even worse. In the time that he has been negotiating the purchase, so proud of being able to keep the secret beyond conferring with Charley, his co-conspirator, he has constructed a detailed picture in his head of Lillie and himself in the little house: she, in the kitchen, the garden, making bright curtains for the windows; he, coming home from work, helping to arrange the furniture just so, pushing the wheelbarrow, planting fruit trees. That vision is draining away, and he cannot bear the concept of what replaces it.

"I cannot live as a guest in your parents' home."

Lillie's brow is now knitted firmly together in her increasing concern, but she is still sure this is just a minor misunderstanding. "But Ferd, you won't be a *guest*. You'll be my husband. You'll be family." When he still does not speak or look at her, she closes her eyes against tears and says quietly, "Grandma always lived with us."

"Yes, she lived with you and your parents. Your parents did not live with *her*."

Her voice is now a whisper. "Is there a difference? I don't see why it matters."

"Why it matters?" He forces himself to lower his voice and keep it even. "Do you not understand? You're asking me not to be the head of my own household."

At this point, neither one of them can look at the other. Instead, they both look at the house in silence, a physical gap between them. Ferd begins to grasp that, during all the time he had been building a picture of life in this tidy little house, she has been picturing their married life as simply a continuation of her normal existence. After all, 741 is the only home she's ever known. Perhaps she just doesn't understand yet that they need to forge their own identity as a couple, as a family, both for themselves and for their future children.

Conceding to himself that she needs to come to this realization on her own, with time, does not make it any easier to give up his vision. No evenings alone in the soft light, no lingering Saturday breakfasts...no privacy. What he says is, "I don't know how I'm going to tell Mr. Johnson."

There is silence. Finally he looks down at Lillie and sees the runnel of tears that she tries to hide as she catches them in her handkerchief. It destroys him to make her unhappy, here on a day that he thought would fill her with pride, excitement, possibilities. How could he have been so wrong?

He slides his arm around her waist and kisses the top of her head. "I'm sorry, sweetheart. I thought—I just thought this was something you wanted."

"And I just thought you understood."

As they walk home, he keeps his arm about her waist, and she sometimes rests her head against his chest, but there is a space between them.

Charley sees them coming up the street toward the house. He's been out in the yard since early morning, putting in the onion starts, checking the progress of the lettuce and asparagus, starting to construct this year's tomato scaffolding even though those plants don't go in for another two months. His hat is tipped back, his hand at his neck as he considers an expansion of the front flowerbed. He glances again, and immediately sees that something is wrong. Ferd is pale and deflated, and Lillie's eyes are red. They pause at the gate, awkward, which is noteworthy in itself. Normally, he would leave the two alone, discreetly moving in a different direction, but it occurs to him that they could use someone to intervene.

"Well, hello, hello! Back from the walk, eh? Lillie, you should see the lilies! They're coming up like a little marching army of green. We'll get some good pin money from them this year. Mr. Cammack will be up to his pits in lilies!" Lillie loves the lily-of-the-valley that Charley long ago planted in the shade of the apple trees, with their heady scent and delicate little bells. He looks at Ferd, trying to engage him. "Two bits from the florist for every bunch, enough to pay the winter coal bill!"

Ferd nods politely but remains stiff; Lillie's head is tilted down. "I guess I'll be going now," he says. "Have a good evening."

Lillie nods and opens the gate. Charley is truly stumped now. "Ferd, you won't be staying for supper? I'm sure Em has already set the place."

At the mention of Emma, Ferd winces. "Thanks very much for the invitation, but I should be getting home now."

Lillie brushes past Charley up the sidewalk to the porch swing. Her head is turned away from them.

As Ferd turns to go, Charley catches him by the sleeve. A look passes between them, Charley with a question and Ferd without an answer, miserable, bereft. He simply shakes his head and walks back down the street toward home.

Charley stands for a moment, considering things. He walks up to the porch and sits next to Lillie, and as she turns to him, he puts his arm around her. She buries her head into his shoulder, and sobs silently. He sees that her handkerchief is a sodden ball, and takes it from her, replacing it with his own. Charley knows how to wait; he's a patient man.

When she is finally able to speak, it's simply, "Oh, Daddy," as the tears begin to flow again. She hasn't called him that since ninth grade. "I've made such a mess of things. I didn't know. I was certain he understood. I never even imagined…but he was so proud of it, and now I've taken that away. But I didn't know."

He waits again, but when nothing else is forthcoming, he kisses the top of her head and gives her a comforting squeeze. "You'll have to give me more than that."

"He was planning to buy a house. He took me to see it today."

"I know. I helped him lay out the arrangements."

She pulls back and stares at him wide-eyed. "You knew? But you never said a single thing."

"A man needs to keep his word when he's sworn to secrecy."

She has her eyes squeezed shut and her forehead wrinkled against this unexpected turn. "Does Mother know?"

He can't suppress a chortle. "You can be sure she does not." He pushes gently against the floorboards to start the swing rocking, and she settles back into his arm. "So you didn't like the house? Ferd and I agreed that it was just the thing."

"It was beautiful."

Now it is Charley's turn to be stumped. "Well now. I can see that I'm missing the sad part of this sad story."

"But Ferd is to move in with us."

Given him a hundred guesses as to what was going on, and this would never have made it to the list. "Ferd surely did not know that."

"No. He does now." A fresh set of tears, though just a few this time, roll to her chin. "I would never mean to hurt his feelings, but

I can see that I have. And to know that you helped him, well, I don't understand that at all. It's as though you didn't know either."

Normally taciturn unless there's a punch line involved, Charley sees that the situation calls for something more. "Lillie, I have never loved anything in this world more than I love you. But a father raises a daughter knowing that someday he's going to have to concede her to another man. It's a painful thing for him, but also the right thing. You're going to be a married woman soon, and even if I were doing the choosing, I couldn't do better for you than Ferd. That man would die to make you happy. But I'm sorely disappointed that you would ask him to."

He can see that Lillie is appalled beyond speech, but he continues. "For him to be a proper husband, and for you to be a proper wife, you need to make your own way. Together." He is not making any headway. "You can see how it would be for him here." Still nothing. "If you insist on it, Ferd will marry you and move into this house. But you'll be killing a piece of him if you do."

She has long since pulled out of his embrace, and through the tumble of emotions that wrestle with each other across her face, the one that stands up and bellows is *Betrayal*. Propelled by sobs of outrage, she sweeps into the house. Charley sits for a moment, eyes closed, head tipped back, and sighs.

There is to be no supper tonight, the meal left in mid-preparation in order for the crisis to play out to its full extent. There is a flow of quiet voices, open sobbing, obvious comforting, all occurring outside of his immediate vicinity. Eventually, Charley fixes a cold plate for himself and goes back to reading the paper. When Emma finally appears in the kitchen to clean up the wreckage of the lost supper, he sits back and openly considers her. She moves in her normal efficient way, but he reads an unseemly air of satisfaction in her. "I surely hope that you've had no hand in this, Em." Her back remains to him, and he finally returns to his paper, resigned to what's to come.

ᘓᘐ

Mr. and Mrs. Charles J. Beck
request the honor of your presence at
the marriage of their daughter
Lillie May
to
Ferdinand J. Voith
on the morning of Wednesday the ninth of May
nineteen hundred and seventeen
at nine o'clock
at the Church of the Nativity
Brightwood, D. C.

Babies, Babies, Babies

1917-1932

It does seem odd, at first, to have Ferd there with them. Of course, he is practically a fixture at the house during their courtship, but until now there has always been a *good night* on the front porch. Now *good night* is an entirely different matter altogether. Now he is always there, throwing a hitch in the long-established rhythm of the household. Now she understands practical concerns like the awkwardness surrounding the bathroom. She feels hurt that Ferd is stiff and unnatural, and suddenly neither one of them can relax around the other. When she finds herself aggravated at him for not knowing how things work at 741, when she hears herself actually say, "Well, we're not *at* your mother's house, are we?" she knows it's time to do something. *I wonder if Mr. Johnson's house is still available. Would he even speak to us now, after all that?* She is almost at the point of saying something to Ferd when she realizes why she's been queasy and irritable. After that, she feels as though the decision has been made for her.

Lillie and Emma are so caught up in the pregnancy that it gives Ferd some breathing space, and he and Charley have plenty of time left on their own. In that space, Ferd gains more traction as a full participant in the family, helped significantly by Charley, who never even once considers saying to Lillie *I told you so*. Watching Emma fuss over Lillie as she grows ever larger, Charley observes to Ferd, "You'd think this was the first child ever born in the history of mankind."

But Lillie has also learned her lesson. She makes certain that she and Ferd spend time away from the house, going to the movies or theatre at least once a week, taking long walks in the evenings and on weekends, even in the later months as the weather grows colder and she feels as big and awkward as a freight wagon. She understands now that Ferd is the head of *her* household, and of the family that she hopes will grow far beyond this first little one. As she begins to act that way, Ferd slips naturally into the role and they regain the balance between them.

Emma won't hear of Dr. Cavanaugh's attending during such a *delicate* time ("Are you feeling delicate, Lillie?" "No, Dad, not particularly."), so he refers them to a Mrs. Dorfman, a highly regarded midwife who delivers the babies of some of the more well-to-do families in town. That's enough to sell Emma.

They are only a month shy of delivery at the turn of the year. Lillie manages to stay awake until midnight on New Year's Eve, and as pots and pans are banging on the front porches throughout the neighborhood, the baby joins in the celebration by kicking wildly. Ferd leans down to kiss her, and Lillie puts his hand on the spot where the little party is underway. They smile at each other as Lillie tells him, "I think that 1918 will be our best year ever."

Ferd and Lillie reside in Mary's old room, the only one that doesn't adjoin Emma and Charley's, but for her lying-in, she and Emma ready Lillie's old bedroom in the front. She is at the sewing machine putting the satin trim on a baby's blanket, and she's in fine rhythm on the foot pedal when her water breaks. She hops up and lets out a little shriek. At the moment, she's more irritated at the damp spot on the upholstered stool, and concerned that she might be dripping on the rug, but then Emma swoops in, bellowing for the laundry girl, Lydia, to come help her support Lillie to the bedroom.

"Mother, I'm capable of getting myself up the steps. I'm not collapsing."

"Nonsense. Take my arm and hold the bannister." Once in the bedroom, Emma tells Lydia, "Go fetch Mrs. Dorfman. Go!" Lydia flies down the steps but is soon back again. "What?" Emma demands.

"But Mrs. Beck, I don't know where Mrs. Dorfman is," she says meekly, eyes downcast.

"Of course you don't," Lillie comforts her over Emma's little huff of irritation. "It's fine. I'm fine."

"Stay with her," Emma orders the unfortunate Lydia, and then marches down to the hall. She grabs up the telephone and jiggles the hook, blatantly interrupting the daily Mrs. Garrett-to-Mrs. Price roundup of local scandal and innuendo, and demands that they relinquish the line to her for the emergency. "It's Emma Beck," she tells Mrs. Dorfman. "It's time." Of course, it is now mere seconds before the gossips light up the area with this latest news.

Mrs. Dorfman arrives soon after to offer her initial assessment. "First ones are rarely fast, you know," she tells them both. "The contractions have hardly started yet. Be prepared for this to take some time."

Lillie nods and turns to Emma. "Can you please call Ferd and let him know? The number is by the telephone."

"You heard Mrs. Dorfman. There's plenty of time."

"Yes, I know, but I promised I would, and his supervisor already gave him permission for us to call." Emma is busy fluffing the pillows and doesn't say anything. "Mother, if you don't phone him, I promise I will walk downstairs and do it myself."

Emma chuffs again, as though to herself, and goes back downstairs with Mrs. Dorfman, who promises to stop by again in a few hours. Emma picks up the receiver to hear the continuing Garrett-Price saga, shrugs her shoulders in resignation at an invisible observer, and hangs up again. She uses the same gesture when Lillie asks if she's talked to Ferd. "The line was tied up. I'll try again soon."

By Mrs. Dorfman's next visit, Lillie's contractions are consistent and intense. She can't imagine how anyone has ever survived this, being ripped apart from the inside. The pain is so excruciating that each time it subsides she thinks that her mind must have exaggerated it, until it rears up again. She finds herself fearing the result, imagining that only a beast could cause that much pain.

She is breathing hard, dreading the next onslaught, when she hears footsteps pounding up the staircase; from the sound, she knows they're being taken two at a time. The door crashes open though Emma tries to block it, and there is Ferd, his breathlessness matching hers. Emma's protests bounce off him without effect as he sits beside her on the bed and grabs up her hand in his own, and blots her forehead with the other. "Oh, Lillie, how is it? How are you? Are you badly?"

She tries to smile at him. "I'm better now that you're here."

"I thought you would have called. I asked the girls at the desk and they said there was nothing all day."

"But how...?"

"I saw Mrs. Dorfman's boy out front."

Lillie turns her red-eyed outrage at Emma, who puts up her hands to deflect the look and shrugs again. Just then, the Beast opens its jaws once more, continuing its one-sided battle to tear her open, and she bleats in pain as she crushes down on Ferd's hand. He nearly falls off the bed in alarm, and it is Mrs. Dorfman who grabs his arm from the other side and in one motion takes him to the door. "This is no place for you. We'll let you know when there's real news."

Ferd gives her one last desperate look before she closes the door on him, and he hears Lillie's anguished cries on the other side. He puts his palm and forehead against the door and closes his eyes for a moment, then pushes back and slumps downstairs. Charley is waiting for him in the kitchen and hands him a cup of coffee. "Probably going to be a long night, Ferd. You may as well get comfortable."

When it's all finally over—when Lillie sees that she has not been delivered of a monster after all, but instead a tiny red wrinkled squalling perfect sweet little girl, held up for her to see by Mrs. Dorfman—Lillie whispers, "Ferd should hold her first." This statement interrupts the handoff from Mrs. Dorfman to Emma in mid-reach, and both women look at her. Lillie looks straight back at Emma. Mrs. Dorfman pulls back and tells Emma, "We'll be all cleaned up by the time you come back. He won't have cause to pass out."

Emma's shock at the dismissal causes her journey down the steps to be slower than usual, but Ferd's speed back the other way more than makes up for it. He doesn't crash in this time, but he is even more breathless than before. Mrs. Dorfman waits a moment for him to calm down before expertly arranging him to hold the baby correctly. He gapes at the tiny bundle he's holding, and his mouth opens and closes over and over with no accompanying sounds. Lillie is smiling so hard her whole face hurts, though the sensation barely registers.

Finally, Ferd is able to ask, "What is her name?"

"Margaret Helen. Margaret Helen Voith."

"Well that's fine, fine!" Charley says from the doorway; Emma is still on the stairs. "Welcome to the family, little Margaret Helen Voith."

ཀྵ

Margaret Helen makes her appearance a scant ten months after the wedding. She is followed twenty-one months later by Eleanor Mary, and another twenty-seven months more by Frances Elizabeth. Each one is healthy, each one is perfect. By the time Lillie is preparing to deliver the fourth, she is followed everywhere by a trail of little girls, each one trying to copy whatever she does. Charley calls them *the ducklings*.

Francie has just turned a year old, and Lillie is about four months from having the next one when Ferd decides to try again. He is home from work a little later than normal one evening, and he gives her an extra little hug in greeting. She smiles back at him, and can tell something's afoot. "What?"

"Not 'til after dinner," he teases her. "Which better be extra good."

She has a feeling she knows what his news is, and, once they bundle themselves up for their evening walk, leaving the unhappy girls behind with Emma and Charley, she finds out that she's right. When Charley helps him to get the job at the Bureau of Engraving and Printing, Ferd starts as a laborer on the printing floor. He rotates through each of the jobs there: pressman, checker, separator, cutter, bundler. People he meets are fascinated at the concept, and always want to know *what's it like to be around all that money?* Ferd's answer: "It's just a lot of paper. And a lot of paper cuts." Except for the press operation, it's mind-numbing work, and Ferd looks for every opportunity to advance his position. His boss seems to like him and is impressed at his attention to detail and ability to spot printing flaws that most would overlook. After some hands-on tests of his drawing skill and manual dexterity, he is recommended for a position as an Apprentice Engraved Steel Plate Finisher. Though it means a move to the old Bureau building up the street, Ferd enjoys the quiet and orderly environment; it's more than he can imagine to be assigned his own stool and work stand. From there, he moves up into the full position, which eventually earns him a five-cent-an-hour raise. Again he quickly impresses his supervisors at a time when the Bureau is overworked and understaffed; nonetheless, because rules are rules, he has to work a total of four years between the two positions before he can make the next step up.

"Engraved steel die finisher," Ferd tells her proudly: that is the step up. In contrast to the rote tasks of the printing floor, which frown hard upon imagination or creativity, engraving work demands the highest order of skill and artistry. The engravers who work at the Bureau are some of the finest in the world, and the plates they produce for currency, securities, and stamps are painstakingly executed works of art. Standing between the engravers' artwork and its use in the printing process is the engraved steel die finisher. Ferd stops beneath a street lamp as he pulls out a sheet to read to her from the official job specification: "'...to prepare expertly, to alter, correct, and finish blank and intaglio engraved steel dies; deftly, exactly, and economically to remove blemishes from portraits, vignettes or other engraved matter, resulting from error or injury; skillfully and correctly to clean and prepare engraved dies in finality for perfect reproduction by steel plate transferring methods....' Let's see, what else? Oh, here, under Qualifications, '...noteworthy dexterity with tools and abrasive agents used in the work of steel die finishing; normal eyesight; exactness and mechanical aptitude; and appreciation of the art values of the work in hand.'" He ends with a flourish.

"*Appreciation of the art values*!" Lillie repeats in wonder. She wraps her arms around him as well as her situation allows. "Oh, dearest, I am so proud of you! How wonderful!" With a twinkle, she tells him, "I'm glad they recognize your dexterity and exactness."

"And my normal eyesight."

They laugh together as she squeezes his arm and they continue on their walk. Ferd feels it's time to press his advantage. "It's a substantial increase. Fifteen cents an hour." Lillie freezes in place and gapes at him. "I know! It's more than I thought." He starts them walking again; it's easier to do this when he isn't looking directly at her. "So, I was thinking, with all that, maybe—well, maybe now is a good time for us to look for a house."

He feels it: the second's hesitation in her next step, the movement of a deeper breath. "Oh, Ferd." So many unmistakable layers of meaning are held in these two words, and he feels his hopes draining away as surely as if she had pulled a plug.

He forces himself to keep his voice level and light. "Forget I mentioned it."

They finish their walk in silence, Lillie still holding his arm. Ferd curses himself for this fatal blunder. If he'd waited until the raise had time to show its value, for her to understand what it means to their circumstances, she may have been more receptive. But now he's used up his last best chance. On top of that, he's ruined his own good news, so that now neither one of them wants to talk about it.

When they return home, Charley is in the kitchen with the *Evening Star*. Ferd pours himself a cup of coffee and sits down across from him. Lillie takes a turn around the kitchen to make sure everything is tidy. "Has Mother taken the girls up, then?"

"A little bit ago. Most of the commotion has died down, so sounds like they might have finally settled in."

"I think I might go up too. This little one is growing heavier by the minute!" Only she and Charley smile at that. She stands by Ferd with her hand lightly on the nape of his neck. "Dad, did you hear Ferd's wonderful news?"

"I might have had an inkling."

"Well, I'm just glad they finally recognize your hard work,

dearest. I'm so proud." She leans down to kiss his cheek.

It's awkward for him to return the kiss from his seat, so he reaches for her hand instead. "I'll be up soon."

The two men sit in silence, broken occasionally when Charley chuckles to himself at the political news or the comics. Finally he closes up the paper and drains the last from his cup. Ferd is staring without seeing at a spot on the table; his eyes are visibly red. Charley continues to sit, waiting.

"Looks like we're here permanently."

Charley considers that, nodding thoughtfully. "Well, it'd be awfully quiet around here without you two and the ducklings. I'd sure miss it. And now we all get to see what's in store with this next little one." He stands up to start his nightly household patrol of turning down gas lamps and closing doors. At the threshold, Charley pauses. "This is your home too, Ferd. As much as anybody's."

ꕤ

With the ducklings, there are all the normal childhood illnesses that parents can only pray to get through with all souls unscathed. There's no whooping cough or—God forbid—polio, but all three girls get chicken pox at the same time, which keeps Lillie and Emma occupied full-time with cold compresses, calamine lotion, bed rest, and lots of attention. "Oh, Gramal," Eleanor tells Emma, "It feels so good when you rub my itchy feet with your scratchy hands." And beyond some scrapes and stings there are no major scares—well, except for the time Margaret tips head-first into the pond, or when she shadows Ferd out through the attic window and onto the roof but then shrieks bloody murder when he tries to take her down the ladder. He gives her a firm paddling for that episode. But all in all, they are sweet and attentive, and it's possible to get them to focus on a quiet activity all at the same time.

And then, well: boys are a revelation to her. Perhaps if she'd had a younger brother, she would already understand that boys are practically a separate species in their own right, completely baffling in their endless creativity toward chaos. Before having sons, she could never have imagined a creature that bears so much watching while being so completely impossible to keep an eye on. Dirt appears on them as though they hold a positive electrical charge. Charley Boy—Charles Joseph Voith—is from the start a quiet, introspective, studious boy, who is obviously influenced by the simultaneous cooing and bossiness of his older sisters; he nonetheless demonstrates that same thoroughly unsocialized fascination with bodily functions unique to boys, and invariably finds ways to make any stick or rock into an imaginary or real instrument of destruction.

And still, Charley Boy barely lays the groundwork for the outsized personality of the next one. (As she first holds him, with Ferd standing there beside the bed, Lillie gently suggests, "*John Ferdinand* would be easier for him, wouldn't it?" and Ferd agrees it would.) Johnny, her dervish of a boy, constantly in trouble, causing trouble, or seducing others into instigating trouble. But what a charmer! A mischievous grin, twinkling eyes, always a ready, impossible story to explain the latest catastrophe. He is forever dancing on the razor's edge of going too far; often enough, he falls off the edge.

And that is the other part about boys that is completely foreign to her, and to which she has a hard time adapting. In her entire life, no one has ever raised a hand to her. With the girls, a stern look or word from her is often all that's needed to maintain order and ensure obedience. It is a hard lesson for her that those words stay with a boy for about as long as it takes you to say them, and they often need a far stronger follow-up to make the words stick. Over time, her Charley Boy seems to appreciate the possible consequences of mischief, so that, left to his own devices, she can typically count on him to behave himself. When he is found in punishable circumstances, the instigator is almost surely Johnny, who just doesn't seem to care about outcomes. If she were to describe the difference between the two, she might say that Charley Boy does a mental calculation to weigh the joy of the misdeed against the possible result of getting caught, and the percentage chance that he can get away with it; Johnny just throws in, consequences be dashed. If he's forced to, he'll pick up the pieces later.

There is the day that she is outside working in the front garden while the girls play hopscotch on the front walk, Dorothy in the playpen, and she hears a commotion up the street. She stands up to see Mr. Phelps from a block over with a hand on the collar of each of the boys. Even at this distance, she can see which one is struggling to get away and which is slump-shouldered in disgrace. As the trio comes closer, she is better able to see Mr. Phelps' bug-eyed purple rage as he hauls her six- and seven-year-old sons up to her, both of whom are a muddy, sodden mess.

"Mr. Phelps?"

"Mrs. Voith, these two boys belong to you?"

Of course he knows that they do; he just wants her to own up to it. She dreads to know what happened, but it's coming soon enough. "Why, yes, Mr. Phelps, they do."

"Well, these two were hiding in the bushes and throwing mudballs at the cars driving by."

"Mudballs?" She keeps her eyes fixed on Mr. Phelps so that she does not have to look at her children yet.

"Yes, they were at that big puddle down the block, making mudballs. Probably with rocks in them!" His outrage is causing him to spit as he lays out the accusation. "Well, just look at them! Ask this one what they were up to!" He is, of course, shaking Charley Boy as he says it; even Mr. Phelps can tell that no one is getting anything out of Johnny.

She has to look at them finally. Charley Boy won't meet her gaze and Johnny's eyes are flashing in anger to be so man-handled, but collectively they are a disaster. She can absolutely picture it: they are drawn to the huge mud puddle near the road, which always forms after a good, hard rain and stands for three or four days afterwards. They start by standing a bit away from the soft edges and throwing ever-larger objects in to get the biggest splash, followed by poking around with sticks and making little canals to draw water this way or that. That progresses to the building of large mud earthen works, great dams to go with the canals—their own Holland in miniature—which requires the engineers at this point to be on their hands and knees. Realizing by now that there will be no hiding the wreck they have made of their clothes, they may as well go all in. Plus, it forestalls the inevitable moment when they will have to slink home. From there on, it is a steady progression of making mud pies to throw into the water, then into the street, then at the side of a nearby building. Perhaps that first car is an accident, causing them to look wide-eyed at each other, but when the car doesn't slow, she knows that it is Johnny who forms that first mudball with intent.

"Well?" Mr. Phelps is demanding.

"I'm sorry?"

"I don't want the apology from you, Mrs. Voith. I want it from them."

"Believe me, Mr. Phelps, I was not offering you an apology. Do I understand that your car was one that was hit?"

"No, I saw them from my window."

"Then I believe there are others to whom the boys owe an apology. I'll simply offer you my thanks for bringing them back home." Her gesture indicates that it is now time for him to release his grip and turn them over to her. He does so, reluctantly, but not without muttering, "Children running wild in the streets," and casting a dark look at her work smock, which doesn't hide her impending maternity. She is waiting for him to make an even more caustic remark about over-procreating when you obviously can't handle what you already have, but any thought he has in that direction dries up when he unwisely makes eye contact with her.

She takes custody of the two, placing a hand gently at the spot where Mr. Phelps grabbed their collars. As soon as he is under Lillie's hand, Johnny stops resisting. The three girls have been watching with great interest. "Margaret, go upstairs and bring me back some towels and a change of their clothes. Eleanor and Frances, take Dorothy and go inside." It isn't a suggestion. "Boys, you go out to the pump house and peel yourselves out of those clothes. I'll be there in a minute." Each child does as instructed; she waits a moment before going inside and taking Charley's razor strop from the back of the cellar door. As a girl, she loved to watch him sharpen his straight razor against the leather, and back then, that was its only use; now, taking it up makes her stomach hurt.

Margaret comes in through the hall with the towels and clothes. She sees the strop and hesitates. Lillie takes the things from her, tucks them in her arm, and touches Margaret on the cheek. "Thank you."

Lillie walks as slowly out to the pump house as the two have before her. Every time she has to do this, it makes her die a little inside, but she will not have her boys behave like savages. She knows Ferd will understand if she waits until he comes home to have him do it, but that feels cowardly to her, and she understands that it will drive a harder point home with the boys if she does it herself. She knows that both men in the house see the strop as a matter of course, having been boys themselves, raised by good parents in normal circumstances. What has been more surprising to Lillie in learning how to raise boys is to find that, as tender and loving as her mother was in raising her, Emma would have undertaken this chore without hesitation or compunction. Lillie has yet to find a way to be that pragmatic.

The boys are at the pump, stripped to their underwear, and have made the conciliatory gesture of hosing the mud off themselves under the frigid well water. They are shivering and miserable. She has come to understand that the anticipation of punishment is at times even worse than the punishment itself—in this case, for both parties. She braces Charley Boy against her left arm and lashes the leather strap across his legs five times. He bites his lip and gasps with each stroke, but does not cry out. Johnny, almost eighteen months younger, does the same.

She keeps them standing. "I'm ashamed of both of you. Charley, you're older, you should know better. Johnny, I truly don't know what I'm going to do with you. You were damaging other people's property, and you could have hurt someone or hurt yourselves. You're not to do anything remotely like this again. Do you understand?" They both mumble, staring at the ground. "Look at me and say you understand."

Once they do, she wraps each one in a towel and rubs them dry before helping them dress. She leaves them out at the pump house to fully recover before coming inside, but as she walks away, she hears

Johnny say in a too-loud whisper, "But that was an awful lot of fun, wasn't it?"

ꕥ

Time and events are measured in children. The horrifying riot between whites and coloreds that lasts days and kills so many is in the summer of 1919, when she is expecting Eleanor, even as they delight in Margaret's first adventures tottering around the big yard; and the 1925 Ku Klux Klan march on Washington is the same day that eighteen-month-old Johnny toddles right out of the yard, and she, panicked to the point of hysteria, finally finds him all the way down the hill on Kennedy Street. She holds Baby Francie the two nights they all stand outside to watch the Northern Lights, lit by a massive solar storm that knocks out telegraph service. The family attends the dedication of the breathtaking Lincoln Memorial a month before she delivers Charley, and all three girls manage to drop their ice cream cones, one right after the other, within minutes of getting them. The day that she brings home the new potty chair for Bernie and Dorothy—after Johnny manages to break the one all the others have used, so that these two have had to use an old pot—she can see their faces in the window watching for her, and Bernie is there as soon as she sets it on the porch, his pants already unbuttoned, and Dorothy so angry not to be the first. That same day, she gets the call from Sister Bernadette that their old friend Professor Dettweiller has died, and she finds herself weeping as she hasn't in many years. The unhappy surprise of the stock market crash, right after Charley starts school, seems to shock her out of her extended morning sickness with Jeanie, and the fires in the White House and the Capitol, one week apart over the holidays that same year, happen just as Dorothy turns five. The only event Lillie remembers for itself is 1924, the year that Ferd and Charley's beloved but hapless Nationals actually take the World Series in an extra-inning Game 7, saved by the great Walter Johnson. She remembers because Ferd proudly displays his programs and score cards from that magical season for years.

It takes the accretion of years and children for her to see patterns emerge. Every one of them has a distinct personality, which is visible from the moment that first beautiful, blessed shriek announces the arrival. She discovers that she can influence but never change who her children are, which by turns is a source of both comfort and concern, but teaches her a valuable lesson in human nature. The differences are evident in simple things, like each seven-year-old's approach to the first day of school at Nativity. Margaret is eager and shy in equal measures, and Lillie whispers to her at the threshold, "Button up your brave suit, sweetheart." Eleanor marches up to the schoolyard, looks around with hands on hips, and demands, "Why are they all crying?" Francie sees a tiny little girl weeping at her mother's side and walks over to put an arm around her shoulders. "It's my first day, too. Do you want to go in together? My name is Francie." Charley Boy is up early and has his notebook and pencil case at the ready, having spent several years working through the math and spelling homework the girls bring home. Johnny knows it's hopeless to resist, but churns in such a bad humor that he practically generates his own thundercloud. Over the years, the universally beloved Sister Fredericka greets every child with a kind word and a warm smile. When she says, "Well, hello, John Voith, we've been so looking forward to having you here," even Johnny is charmed.

She naturally thinks of them in groups—the girls, the boys, and the babies—and notices how language evolves from one group to the next. The youngest ones learn to speak sooner and practically in complete sentences, given the sea of voices that constantly washes over them. Emma is always *Gramal*, one word in the very first handful that Margaret forms, and which carries through the whole tribe. But Charley, forever *Granddaddy* to the girls, mysteriously becomes *Granner* to the boys and the name is passed seamlessly to the babies. Lillie herself starts out as *Mamma* to all of her children, since that is how she refers to herself with them, but that transforms into *Mother* when the girls start to echo her name for Emma.

After that, there's a point at which each child decides it's time to join the grown-up children, and *Mamma* becomes *Mother*. Ferd is always, always *Daddy*.

Pigeons

July 1932

Ferd stands in the loft of the barn, unconsciously stooping a bit to account for the low rafters. He is stroking the breast of one of his best pigeons, which, for its part, calmly grips Ferd's index finger, alternately stretching its neck and cooing with a slightly inquisitive inflection. There is a race in the morning down in Virginia that includes several clubs that form the area concourse, and Ferd is weighing his strategic options. Competition is always fierce, and not just within the concourse. Members constantly vie for best times within their own clubs, and each trainer is forever testing to achieve the personal best for his own loft. So: fierce, yes, but always friendly. The fellows bond naturally in their shared passion for an arcane sport.

As he stands in the window of the loft, considering the weather forecast for the morning, he admires the view across the Brightwood Park treetops; on a clear day, and with some strategic pruning, he would practically be able to see his parent's house on Illinois Avenue. Not for the first time, Ferd considers how different life would be if his father had not early on had the foresight and faith to move the young family from his hometown of Baltimore down south to Washington. The Voiths and Bollingers, Millers and Becks all have relatives in Baltimore, but visits to see them always leave Ferd unsettled. He feels guilty at his palpable relief in not being one of them. And now, with the economic disaster crushing so much of the country, the contrast between life in Baltimore and Washington is painful to contemplate.

ᢀ

As a young married man, August Voith works in a downtown haberdashery and lives in a tiny apartment with Dorathea and their children Sophie, Ferd, and baby Frank. A trained musician who has yet to find work as a musician, he worries about the future, and assesses his prospects for advancement for himself and his family as bleak. Along with many other German immigrant families, his has settled in Baltimore, where there is an established German community and work to be had.

Unfortunately, the work most readily available is manual labor, dirty and dangerous—the docks, the warehouses, the factories—though that work typically pays more than his safe job at the shop. He is still idealistic enough to trade less money against the risk of ruining his musician's hands, but when Doro tells him that she is expecting again, he begins to consider that idealism isn't going to feed the family.

Though it hasn't paid off for him yet, Gus is a great believer in education as the foundation for eventual advancement. Unfortunately, the local school system is substandard and dangerous. In just his first year of school, Ferd has his lunch taken from him often by the schoolyard toughs, more than once by force, which sends him home bloodied. Even Sophie has endured a roughing up from some older girls who take her neat appearance and attentiveness in class as provocation. Beyond that, the neighborhood, which is tidy enough when Gus and Doro move in as newlyweds, is now picking up speed in its descent into seediness. Gus needs to get his children out of the trenches and onto higher ground.

Expanding the number of music students he tutors is always a challenge. He needs a moneyed clientele who can pay to have him come to them, and to provide their own instruments to boot. He can neither afford a piano nor find an open square foot in the apartment to squeeze one into, and any of the wind and strings, particularly in the hands of a new student, creates more of a rumpus than even Gus's increasingly rough-and-tumble neighbors will put up with. In this regard, though, the shop proves a boon. Fitting a gentleman for a custom suit offers a particularly ripe opportunity: beyond in itself attesting to the client's means and station, the otherwise gaping silence of the fitting begs to be filled instead with a friendly, meandering chat. Gus becomes adept as a tour guide along any conversational path, leading to the subject of children, of raising them and educating them, and of ensuring they have the proper cultural skills, including—of course—musical training. He treads with care to keep anyone from complaining to Mr. Hogarth that he is soliciting. Gus leads them right up to the end of the path, but steps aside at the last possible moment so that it is the client who asks about the possibility of lessons.

The increase in his client base allows him to put more money into his small savings, but it keeps him away from home more than he likes, and the savings aren't growing as quickly as he needs them to. Plus, coming home at night after spending his evenings in the richly appointed homes of the well-to-do makes it that much harder to see his own sleeping children wedged into the corners of the only home he can afford. When Leo is born, he sits at night in the rocker by the window, cradling his infant son and considering what to do next.

It is an old friend from school who first plants the idea that Washington City should be his family's destination. He offers that the streets aren't paved in gold, necessarily—in fact most of them aren't paved at all, causing them to be a muddy swamp in the wet and a choking dust cloud in the hot—but the city is nevertheless a paradise of opportunity, upward mobility, and clean fingernails, all in the form of federal government jobs. Just a few years earlier, Oskar decamped to make his fortune in the growing capital city. He figured he would try his luck in the port of Georgetown, a place that gives Baltimore a run for its money as a grimy, brawling slough; the waterfront is a section of town where the nicer folk never venture. But the port had fallen onto economic hard times from the confluence of a bad flood, the railroad, and a motivated effort to divert business dollars into the new downtown, and Oskar was quick to pick up the scent of the far better opportunity available just up the road. In a blink, he finds himself working as a clerk in a cramped little basement office containing about four more fellows than can actually fit, but it's warm and dry, and he doesn't end each day by peeling himself out of filthy clothes before collapsing into bed, too tired even to eat his small supper. By the time he has Gus thinking about the possibilities, Oskar has gotten several small raises, a promotion to acting assistant senior clerk, and about eight inches more desk space. It is a little slice of heaven.

Buoyed by these reports, Gus makes his decision. Well before dawn one morning, he dresses in his best coat, collects his creased music portfolio now containing his papers—birth certificate, diploma, a summary of his skills and experience—and gives Doro a kiss, then another for extra luck. He boards the train that takes him from one Union Station to another, where Oskar collects him on his way to work. Gus feels like a country rube on his first trip to the big city, and Oskar navigates so confidently through the streets that Gus can't keep his bearings in his rush to keep up. Finally, they enter a building, walk up one flight and open a door into a large open room with wooden benches, a long counter, and lots of people. Oskar waits with him in the line at the counter, where the clerk eventually hands Gus a stack of forms and a number. Oskar has just enough time to walk him to an open spot on a bench and say he'll look back in at lunchtime to see how things are going.

The next several hours offer a glimpse into the grinding gears of bureaucracy at its best. The dizzying succession of forms each demands virtually identical information to the forms that came before. He attempts to hand the forms in at the counter and is curtly told to sit back down and wait until his number is called. He hasn't even made it back to the bench when he hears the number. Again, he tries to give this clerk the completed forms, and is told, "No, you keep those until after." Gus does not ask, "After what?" He is shuttled off to a smaller room, this one furnished with wooden classroom desks and populated with other dazed, glassy-eyed applicants. They sit in silence. No authoritative presence is in the room, but no one is willing to risk the possible repercussions of speaking. Every so often the door opens again to admit one or two more bodies.

Finally, after about forty-five more minutes, when all the desks are filled, a gray, rodent-eyed man comes in through a different door, carrying a stack of paper and a cupful of pencils. He walks through the aisles, slapping a pencil and a paper-clipped set of pages face down on each desk, making an irritated little huffing sound as he does so. Though not a person in the room makes the slightest movement toward the paper, the man keeps saying, "Do *not* turn the paper over until I tell you to begin." When he finishes his journey among the desks, he stands at the front of the room, and speaks as though he is waiting for someone to argue with him. "You will have one hour for the test. No additional time will be given for any reason. I will call ten minutes and five minutes before the hour. If you attempt to speak to anyone, look at anyone's paper, or allow anyone to look at your paper, you will be removed immediately and will not be allowed to return. You will not be allowed to leave the room during the test for any reason. You will..." As the proctor continues to recite his many rules, Gus takes comfort in knowing that there isn't another person in the room besides this man who has any more understanding of what is going on than he does. Therefore, whatever is coming, he has as much chance as anyone to muddle through it.

The litany finally ends. There is a long pause and the muscles in the room tighten, straining against the gate, anticipating the starting gun: "Begin." Papers flip over in unison, everyone desperate to understand what it is that they must complete in the hard inflexible space of one hour. Though he is anxious too, Gus takes the time to assess the scope of the task. He quickly reads through the questions as though he is looking at a musical score for the first time, in which he lets the music play in his head to get a feel for it. There are multiple choice, fill-in-the-blank, and short answer questions, math problems—both equations and word problems—and even an essay question. He starts with the math, wanting to get though the word problems first in case they demand extra time. The essay is three hundred words on a topic of the applicant's choice, which Gus decides to leave until last. He composes it in his head as he works through the other problems.

As he lays out his strategy, he can hear heavy breathing coming from the man to his left. They exchanged friendly nods earlier as Gus sat down. He estimates the man to be about his age, neatly dressed and with a fresh haircut; Gus may as well have been looking in a mirror. The heavy breathing is undoubtedly caused by test anxiety, something Gus is used to dealing with in his students, who, no matter how proficient, freeze like rabbits caught in the open at the start of every recital. But then he hears the snap, clear and crisp, of the pencil breaking under the pressure of the applicant's chokehold. In the silence that follows, as cold horror paralyzes the man, Gus forces himself to keep his eyes down and his natural sympathy in check; nothing will make him risk being removed from the room, never to be allowed to return. How little it takes to reduce a man to the level of a frightened schoolboy, Gus thinks, of both himself and his neighbor, as he resolves to hold his own pencil lightly. He can feel the man's desperation, eyes darting wildly to beg help from some quarter among his seatmates, precious seconds slipping away in his own striving for a future.

This eventuality is not covered in the earlier review of test protocol, so it is impossible to know what course of action is considered acceptable. After an eternity of minutes spent chewing through options with no clue of their possible outcomes, the man finally raises his hand, holding the pencil broken point up, in the hope that the proctor will understand. Gus hears the huff of disgust from the front of the room, the heavy standing up and walking down the aisle, the smack of a new pencil against the wooden desktop. "You should try being more careful," the man snaps, and Gus can't help but think, *You should try being more human.*

He finishes easily with almost fifteen minutes to spare. He spends the time reviewing his answers and rereading his essay, which he admires as spare but eloquent. It describes his first experience hearing Schumann's *Kinderszenen*, a set of deceptively simple piano compositions; to this day, hearing or playing his favorite movements makes him both happy and wistful at the same time. When he feels certain that the test is exactly as it should be, he turns it over, sits the pencil on top, and folds his hands on the desk. Though he keeps his eyes locked on a cobweb draping down from the ceiling near the front of the room, he perceives with sympathetic relief that his neighbor to the right has recaptured his composure and is confidently finishing up the last of his answers. As time draws down, though, Gus can tell that others in the room are not in nearly as tidy a state. At the warning of "Ten minutes," there is an uncomfortable shifting among the applicants, and the sound of paper rattling grows. By "Five minutes," the smell of sweat and panic is palpable, and then a collective groan as the proctor snaps, "*Time.* Pencils *down.* Turn your paper face down on the desk. There will be no talking until I collect all the tests. Hand me your application papers, but do not touch the test. *I* will pick up the test."

Gus sighs silently. Like the very worst schoolmasters, this petty man derives obvious satisfaction from his ability to exercise control and generate misery in the sixty minutes he has with each roomful of adults who are just looking for a job. As the proctor pauses at Gus's desk to snatch up his test and receive the application forms, Gus looks him squarely in the eye with steady and undisguised disdain. The man startles for the briefest second, then cools. With a dismissive sniff, he moves to the next desk.

Before he finishes his rounds, the door at the back of the room opens, and another man comes up to the proctor's desk and waits, hands in his pockets. The proctor wends his way slowly back up to the desk and makes a show of organizing and straightening the stacks of paper. Finally, after running out of paper to fuss over, the proctor leaves the stacks on the desk, and, without even glancing at his successor, walks out of the room.

"Good morning," the man says as the door closes sharply, then glances at his watch and smiles. "Actually, good afternoon. I'm Mr. Young. I know you've all been captive for a long time now, so you'll have about forty-five minutes to use the rest room and get some refreshment from the cafeteria. After that, we'll all come back to this room and then we'll take a few of you at a time to meet with a physician and have a personal interview. Are there any questions?" Stunned at the show of humanity and the first coherent information any of them have received all day, no one can think of what to ask, or they still fear retribution if they respond. "Okay, then. Miss Stevens will point you to the toilets and the cafeteria. Be back here by one o'clock. Don't worry, there are clocks everywhere." He chuckles as he says this, and pushes himself upright from leaning on the desk. The room takes this as permission to stand up, finally. Miss Stevens has appeared in the doorway at the back, crisp and efficient but not brutal.

Gus's first imperative, even before the toilet, is to look for Oskar. He fears—correctly, as it turns out—that Oskar's lunch break has been far ahead of his own, and he realizes that they've made no specific plans for a rendezvous point. It seems that there is no end of things that he has neglected to ask in preparing for this day, but having gotten this far, he feels sure now that he has the resources to survive it.

At five minutes to one, Gus makes his way back to the room. His earlier seatmate arrives almost at the same moment, and they take the opportunity to shake hands and quietly introduce themselves as they go back to their desks.

"Herman Olafssen."

"August Voith. Gus." As Gus suspects, their stories are similar. Herman, a few years younger, already lives in Washington City with his wife and two children, with a third on the way. He was in a comfortable position as a clerk in a law firm, until the firm's partners were arrested for embezzling their clients' money. The notoriety of this event within the legal community makes everyone else at the firm unemployable. He has since taken work in one of the city's new department stores, but he needs a better job soon or he'll be forced to move his family out of their current apartment.

Herman and Gus have been speaking quietly as the room fills in again. They are comfortable enough now in the presence of Mr. Young, who is chatting at the front with Miss Stevens, to continue their conversation. They don't notice Mr. Young approaching until he is coming down their aisle. Gus wills himself to stay calm; has he misjudged this man's affability? Mr. Young's open expression doesn't change, though, as he stands in front of the two men. He nods to Herman and then says quietly to Gus, "Mr. Voith? Yes? I want to let you know how much I enjoyed reading your essay." At Gus's obvious surprise, Mr. Young explains, "I use the break time to scan through the tests and applications to see what we have. It's rare that we get a musician applying for a government job."

Gus can't help himself, "And it's rare for a musician to get any kind of job at all, Mr. Young."

Mr. Young laughs out loud at that. Heads in the room snap to look over at them. "Well, I take your point there, Mr. Voith. At any rate, I'm going to have Miss Stevens bring you in for your interview now." As he turns to go, he catches the distress on Herman's face. "Don't worry, sir. I'm certain you did fine as well."

As Miss Stevens walks over to collect Gus, Herman whispers, "Good luck."

ꙮ

Gus reaches home just as darkness falls. He has already rescheduled his students to a different evening, not knowing how late he will be, so he has the uncommon treat of sitting down at a weekday supper with his family. He gives Doro an extra big kiss and hug when he comes in, but won't say anything about his day immediately. At dinner, he asks Sophie and Ferd about the school day while he helps Frank to control his knife and fork. Finally, after the dishes are washed and put away, he lights his pipe and sits in the big armchair, while Doro, in the rocking chair, nurses the baby, patiently waiting for Gus to tell her what happened. The novelty of having their father at home draws the children in, and eventually he has Frank in his lap and the two eldest on the floor by him. And so Gus tells the story of his day.

He does finally manage to catch up with Oskar, who stops by again on his way out of work. As they walk back to the train station comparing experiences, it becomes obvious that government processes have tightened up significantly just since Oskar came onboard. "Gus, if I'd known it was *that* kind of nightmare, trust me, I'd have let you in on the secret."

After a cursory physical exam in which he's checked for lice and asked questions he's already answered on the medical forms, Gus is sent to the room for his interview. He is surprised to see Mr. Young again, who sits with the examiner, a Mr. Chase. Gus recognizes his many application forms arrayed on the desk, with his exam peeking out from underneath them. Mr. Chase looks at his identification and other credentials, then sits back and considers Gus. "It looks here that you play a number of instruments, Mr. Voith. Tell me about that."

Gus is thoroughly stumped at their interest in his musical abilities, but decides to imagine that it is a good sign of something. "Piano is my favorite, of course, and that's what many of my students play. The violin is the next most popular. I don't have many students for the flute, but it's one of my favorites—even though Mr. Mozart would disagree with me there. He didn't have much use for the flute." He glances at Mr. Young to gauge whether he is on the right path with his narrative.

Mr. Young smiles and asks, "You listed some other wind instruments on your application?"

"Certainly. Clarinet, saxophone, trombone. Oboe. Tuba if I have to," he smiles.

"Have you ever played in a band, Mr. Voith? In some kind of larger musical ensemble?"

"Yes, in school we had a very well-respected band. I also play for the church choir. And we have a pretty good group that plays at the Knights of Columbus." To his own ears, this sounds weak; he wishes he had more compelling examples.

There is a silence as the two examiners glance at each other and consider him. He considers them back. Mr. Young finally breaks the silence. "Mr. Voith, did you know that the U.S. Government employs musicians?"

(At this point in Gus's narrative, Doro gasps in surprise, the sharp jolt finally dislodging a significant burp from Baby Leo, who is draped over his mother's shoulder along with a clean dishtowel to catch the spit-up.)

"I surely did not," Gus tells the two men.

Mr. Chase offers some more forms to him. "You'll need to fill these out before you leave. They'll contact you sometime in the next two weeks to let you know about the audition."

"Audition?" He looks at Mr. Young.

"I don't think you have anything to worry about, Mr. Voith. I'm guessing you'll be able to play whatever they hand you."

"But...audition for what?"

"The Soldiers' Home Band."

ꙮ

Ferd is only six years old at the time, but he remembers this night as the turning point for his entire family. None of them have ever heard of the Soldiers' Home before, an asylum for old and invalid military men established after the Mexican War. The grounds also house the summer retreat that has been used by several presidents, Lincoln, chief among them. But to imagine that it has its own United States band!

It is the key to their improved fortunes. Within a month, they have packed up all of their belongings and moved into a rented row home on K Street, a palace compared to their Montford Avenue apartment in Baltimore. Suddenly, Gus is a man with a future. Even then, Ferd can see that his father is different, happier, whistling as he strolls the new streets with his hands in his pockets, bringing home different instruments to practice and demonstrate for them all. With newborn Baby Dorothie over her shoulder, while Gus plays, Doro takes turns dancing with them, now that they have a parlor and several feet of open floor space. It takes time to re-establish a student base in the new city, but as Gus begins teaching again, the money is for savings rather than for making the rent.

In not too many years, Gus can afford to buy the row house on Illinois Avenue, which puts them into Brightwood Park and the Nativity parish, which is where Ferd meets Lillie May Beck, which is what truly changes his life for good and all.

Ferd turns from his contemplation to find Dorothy and Johnny up in the loft with him. They each have a pigeon out of the coop and are handling them just as Ferd is, quietly, gently stroking them.

They know that they are allowed to do this, but only in this way and only while he is here. Even Johnny behaves himself in the loft. "Can we go with you tomorrow, Daddy?" Dorothy wants to know.

Ferd smiles at her. "I don't see why not. You can be my assistants."

From just below them, Ferd hears a shriek followed by wailing, which kicks up a ruckus in the flock of geese. "What's going on down there?"

Charley Boy calls back up. "It's Jeanie. She's afraid of the feathers from the pigeon coop. She doesn't want them to fall on her."

Ferd sighs and chuckles at the same time as they all tuck the pigeons back in their coops and climb down to rescue Jeanie from the attacking feathers. As he scoops her up and swings her around to make her laugh, he considers again how grateful he is to his father for making his own future this one, for he can imagine none better.

Tuesday, 18 April 1933

For the second day in a row, Ferd awakes with a disoriented jolt, and it truly takes him several seconds to process that he's in the hall, and another one or two to resolve that the ghostly shape in front of him is not the last vestige of a dream but rather Charley Beck, in his white work shirt, holding the newspapers and the day's bottle of milk. As he moves to stand up, Ferd discovers what it means to have slept all night in the chair, and groans audibly. With an effort, he unfolds himself completely and pushes upright.

"What time is it?"

"A little after five. Been there all night?"

Ferd stretches and flexes his back until he's able to make it crack. "Yup." The word communicates volumes, including chapters on one-upmanship and jockeying for position, and a whole book on the origin of strained familial relations.

"Let me buy you a cup of coffee. It's already on the stove." Ferd follows him into the kitchen and Charley pours. "Good?" and Ferd nods as he takes a first slurpy sip. "Good. Come with me." Cups in hand, the two head back through the hall and up the steps.

Meantime, on the second floor, Emma awakens with much the same jolt that shakes Ferd; even so, she remains slumped in her chair, the permanent curve of her back naturally pushing her forward. For a panicked second, it seems to her that she can't move, until she realizes that she can, but that unlocking the seized machinery of bones demands a liberal lubrication of pain. Arthritis is burrowed deeply into every nook. She hears Lillie's ragged breathing before she can lift her head enough to see her, reminding Emma of why she has spent the night hunched by the bed.

By the time Charley opens the door, though, Emma is up and tidying the room, wringing out the cloth, dabbing at Lillie's forehead, checking for heat with the back of a hand against a cheek. Lillie remains immobile. Ferd pushes past Charley to sit on the other side of the bed. He resists the desire to grab Lillie's hand, which rests on top of the coverlet, but he reaches out to stroke her fingertips. Charley watches from the door, and, just as Emma is drawing herself up to protest, he says, "All right then, Mrs. Beck, time for us to go make breakfast." The look she shoots at him bounces off with no effect. "Ferd's here to take the second watch. In the meantime, we're about to be trampled by the trotters shoving to the trough."

"If she wakes up…"

"Ferd can handle it. Doc Cavanaugh'll be here to check in before we're done anyway." She stays where she is, eyes on Lillie. "Emma." It is a tone he rarely uses.

Finally, she moves in front of him through the door, and he closes it behind them. He watches her on the stairs, which are ever more of a chore for her; walking downstairs demands close attention and a firm grip on the banister. Once in the kitchen, though, her movement seems almost fluid. Together they've performed this dance of meal preparation enough that it's practically a ballet. Without breaking rhythm, Charley says, "I expect you to sleep in our bed tonight."

She appears not to hear, as she fills the kettle at the sink and goes to light the burner under the big skillet. As she turns to step back into the kitchen, Charley blocks her path. "You'll not bar the man from his own room."

"She's my baby."

"And his wife." There is a standoff. "It does neither of you any good, you or Lillie, for you to cripple yourself up more just so that you can sit by her bed. Ferd's younger, he'll do it."

Finally, she meets his eyes. This is a rare enough exchange—Charley virtually never commands or demands—that she knows he is serious. What's more, she knows somewhere down in her ragged bones that another night in that chair will wreck her. She is saved the insult of an actual concession, however, by a timely knock at the back door.

"Ahoy the house," Dr. Cavanaugh pokes his head into the kitchen. "I presumed you'd be up and about already. How's our patient?"

Forestalling Emma's huff of complaint at not being allowed to know, Charley tells him, "Not awake yet. Ferd's up with her. Her breathing's still ragged but seems she had a quiet night."

"Well, I'll just go take a quick look in on them. I promise I won't wake the household."

He has barely turned to go into the hall when Emma tells him, "I'll come with you," almost overtaking him at the threshold.

Charley knows that he is on his own to make breakfast for the mob.

ཨཎ

Lillie is the third person today to wake with a jolt, eyes big, startling up from the pillow. It makes Ferd leap up from his chair as she drags in air to propel a barking wet cough. She waves him still with one hand while the other grabs up the dishtowel at her side to catch the product. This is one nighttime transformation he hasn't noticed: the delicate cotton handkerchief replaced by a rough substantial towel that can stand up to the onslaught.

Her face is an alarming red, and he fears that she is suffocating in a losing battle for air. Her head tips back, but he can't tell if that is cause or effect as the fit subsides. Her hand flutters out toward the side table and he leaps again to pour water, which she sips cautiously. She smiles a little at him and he can see that her lips are chapped. She sees him notice and says, "Vaseline," then reaches out to take the jar from him and dab the jelly on her lips. She hands it back to him. "Menthol?"

He has no idea what she's asking for. He scans the bedside as she gestures, and then starts moving things aside. He puts his hand on an unlabeled jar and sees that she nods at that. He unscrews the top and is smacked by the unmistakable medicinal smell, finally realizing that this is the tang that pervades the room. He leans in to hand it to her just as she tips her chin up. "Can you—?"

He fumbles for a moment, finally sitting the jar back down as he carefully unbuttons the first few buttons of her nightgown. She puts a finger farther down, indicating how many he needs to open to get the job done. He drapes the fabric back, and starts to dab the grease onto her chest. "Rub," she tells him. She draws again with a finger to indicate a wide area that includes her neck and all the way up to her shoulder blades.

The smell floods his nostrils, causing an involuntary deep breath that opens up all of his breathing passages. Lillie is also breathing more easily and evenly as he re-buttons the nightgown, her head back and eyes closed. He gazes at her, her face composed again into the soft, sweet expression he's used to seeing when she sleeps. That is three times, three in a row, where he doesn't anticipate what she needs or, worse, has no clue. He doesn't remember Dr. Cavanaugh mentioning the menthol rub, but then realizes why not: with ten children between them, Lillie and Emma hardly need coaching. Why does he? Has he been so inattentive all these years to the demands of the sickroom? All this time he thinks himself a participant and now he's proven merely an observer. Whatever else might have evolved if they had struck out on their own all those years ago, he's now undeniably dependent in making sure Lillie gets through this.

She's not asleep. "Darling, can you help me to the bathroom?" Her voice is low and thick. Getting out of bed, out of the bedroom, and down the hall is a slow procession, with several stops to rest, but he brightens that she is up and moving. At the threshold, she tells him, "Just give me a moment. I'll open the door when I need help." He waits, listening as he does for the telltale sound of stirring children, which Ferd is sure is only moments away by now. The toilet flushes, water runs in the basin, and the door opens. "No blood," she tells him with a little nod. She is wetting a cloth, and when Ferd closes the door she turns her back to him and drops out of her nightgown. "How does it look?"

He gasps to see the swaths of bruises puddling in ugly, uneven patches across her shoulder blades, hips, and thighs, leaching out in muddy rivulets of browns, greens, purples, and blacks.

"It's probably even worse than yesterday. I can feel it more. The bump on my head even has its own pulse."

Ferd is horrified at himself that he has practically forgotten what's behind all of this: Lillie's fall on the steps. Already that seems like eons ago, when, in fact, it's only forty-eight hours. His failures continue to mount. "I'm not sure how you can even walk," he tells her.

She is starting to wilt and needs to hold onto the basin while he helps her to wash up and put on a fresh gown. "I guess I won't be getting dressed again today. Father Bischoff will scold me for sloth."

He knows she's joking with him, but he hears himself say, more forcefully than he means to, "I'd like to see him try."

It is another slow progress back down the hall and they are almost at their room when the boys' bedroom door opens and Jeanie scoots out. "Mamma!" she shrieks, then in response to Ferd's instant gesture of reproach, she repeats in an elaborate stage whisper, "Mamma!" as she launches herself at Lillie.

Lillie braces for impact, but Ferd inserts himself between them and absorbs the blow. "Your mother isn't feeling well, Jeanie. You need to be quiet."

Jeanie blinks at them, unconsciously putting a hand up to her ear.

"Go get cleaned up for breakfast, sweetie bug." Lillie's voice is becoming thick and throaty. "And tell Gramal to wash your ear with the big red squeezy."

"I doan wanna," she pouts, wrapping her arms around herself.

"Well, I guess I'll tell her, then," Ferd warns her, and even Jeanie is old enough to know that if an adult ends up having to do something that a child is told to do, punishment for that child comes quickly afterwards. She mumbles and kicks at the hallway runner as she drags herself toward the bathroom.

Lillie is breathing hard and starting to rasp by the time he's able to get her back into bed. He grabs up the towel and holds it for her through another coughing fit, and then helps to hold the water glass while she sips. "More menthol? No? I think you need some hot tea, then."

She smiles and says in a ragged whisper, "I think you're right."

Out in the hallway, almost as though someone rings a bell, there is a sudden blast of activity: doors opening and slamming, voices calling, complaining, laughing, yelling. Finally, Margaret's voice cuts through the clamor in a harsh whisper, "Be quiet! Mother's still asleep." They hear a tiny voice protesting, but can't hear the words. "Well, then, she's trying to sleep. Keep it down."

Francie is saying in surprise, "Hi, Dr. Cavanaugh!" and Ferd can hear Emma's heavy footsteps on the stair.

"Maybe your mother is bringing the tea." He opens the door and steps into the hallway. "I want everyone downstairs in five minutes, and I don't want to hear another sound from any of you, starting now."

Even as he's saying the words, Jeanie is yelling, "Gramal, you need to wash my ear with the squeezy!" and Francie is grabbing her arm and hissing "Be quiet!" and Jeanie is protesting loudly, "But Mamma and Daddy said so!"

Order is restored as Emma finally arrives at the top landing, and children start heading downstairs. She precedes Dr. Cavanaugh to the room and Ferd looks back to Lillie just before they arrive. "No tea."

Meanwhile, left on his own, Charley is not having a good day with breakfast. In the flurry of activity yesterday, no one has gone to the market. He finds that they have exactly three eggs. There isn't enough time to make oatmeal. He considers cold cereal, but the wheat biscuits in the cupboard are stale, and the weevils have gotten to them. Finally, he mixes up a batter for corn cakes, warms some applesauce in a pan, and cuts up the very last of the sausage links in order to give everyone a few pieces.

It's also clear that there isn't enough bread for the lunch sandwiches. The bakery delivers bread every day directly to their kitchen counter, but today is Tuesday, and Charley silently curses the delivery boy. Rufus, never the shiniest penny—"That boy is out of his depth in a puddle"—has nonetheless taken a shine to the laundry girl down at the Johnsons who comes Tuesdays and Fridays. His mooning over her at the Johnsons' back door means that bread delivery is now predictably late on those days. If Rufus doesn't get here during breakfast, Charley's going to have to come up with something inventive for the lunch sacks to feed the horde.

Which is descending on him even now, though more quietly than is natural. The silence is broken by the gathering cry of an unhappy infant above them, which increases in volume as though the radio knob has been transferred to his belly button. In the kitchen, the ruckus kicks up when Charley, instead of serving individually, puts all the food on platters in the middle of the table, which generates an uncivilized free-for-all. The youngest two fare badly until Francie snags them each a corn cake.

"Charles, what's that on your shirt?"

"A bobby pin."

"Any reason why?"

"The button came off." Charley continues to look at him expectantly. "Gramal wasn't here to sew it back on."

"Are your fingers broken?"

Charley Boy looks around the table for some backup, hoping someone knows the answer to the riddle.

Charley's gaze follows his around the table. "Tell me no one here knows how to sew a button on." The girls slump down a little, hoping they aren't asked to demonstrate now; they still have to do their hair. "You kids need to start learning how to do things for yourself. Your ma and gramma weren't put on Earth to do your bidding."

Charley is so rarely out of humor that the kids are wide-eyed and silent, though the house is still pervaded by the piercing wail from above them. "Go change your shirt."

Charley Boy is almost afraid to say anything now, and flinches a little. "The other one's in the wash."

There's a long pause until Charley shakes his head. "Well, maybe your tie will cover it up. But don't complain to me if the nuns call you out for it." He looks around the table. "Finish your breakfast. Same drill as yesterday: clean your plates off and gear up the lunch line." He fixes the five eldest with a look. "Time to learn how to do the wash. Starting when you get home from school today."

As he goes back to the pantry stove, there's a general grumble. "Thanks a lot, Charley," Johnny tells him. "Get us all in trouble."

"It was just a button!" Charley Boy protests.

Margaret looks at the kitchen clock and puts a hand up to her hair. "Okay, hurry up." The kids shovel in the last of the food and crash their plates into a stack at the sink.

Eleanor organizes the assembly line, but the problem is immediately obvious. "Granddaddy, there isn't enough bread!" Charley comes out of the pantry with the tea on a breakfast tray, along with a cardboard carton that he plunks down on the counter next to Eleanor. "Graham crackers?"

"Never had a graham cracker sandwich? Just slather 'em with peanut butter and jelly and give everyone a few extra. If Rufus comes while I'm gone…" He doesn't finish the thought, shaking his head as he walks out with the tray. "That boy doesn't have the good sense that God gave dirt."

He carries the tray up the steps and meets Ferd in the hallway carrying Tommy, who is finally freshly diapered but still unfed, so that his unhappiness continues. Wordlessly, Ferd indicates a trade.

Charley sits the tray down to take the baby. "Did the Lord make you out of lead, Thomas? You better start learning to walk soon, 'cause you're way too big to carry." Ferd has the tray, and Charley tips his chin toward the closed door. "How are things?"

"She was well enough to walk to the bathroom and clean up a little this morning, but now she's having trouble breathing again, and Dr. Cavanaugh says her lungs sound more congested. I was just coming down to make tea, so thanks."

Charley looks down at Tommy, who is red-faced and gathering himself to wail. "Ferd, I got to get to work."

Ferd visibly slumps but knows it's true. "Can you get him started with breakfast and I'll be down soon?"

He nods. "When I get in, I'll talk to them about taking a day or two, at least until she's back on her feet."

Charley lugs the unhappy baby back downstairs, passing several children running back the other way, and plops Tommy into his highchair. To quiet the squalling, Charley puts a chunk of zwieback in his fist. Lunch preparation is over, though there's still a mess on the counter and table. He can hear the girls giggling and gossiping while they fluff at themselves in the dining room mirror. It's his turn to glance at the kitchen clock, even though he knows that no miracle is going to get him to work on time now. In a small bowl, he mushes together some remains of corn cake and applesauce, stirs in a splash of milk and pulls up a chair next to Tommy, who is gnawing on his hard tack. Charley uses the spoon to sidle the hand away in order to get some mush in. Tommy turns his open mouth to the spoon while he keeps his eyes on his fist. Even before he completely swallows the spoonful, the zwieback returns. Charley looks around him. "Well, this is a turn of events, wouldn't you say, Master Thomas?"

It is just occurring to him that he hasn't seen the two little ones lately when there is a crash and a yowl from the spring porch, and a miniature Emma voice scolding, "I tole you not to!"

Charley knows better than to leap up and leave the baby alone. If a child needs to be sacrificed, better that it's the one foolish enough to do whatever it is that Bernie's just done. "Are you still alive, boy?" Charley calls out to them.

"Yeah."

"Can you walk?"

"Yeah."

"Well, then walk yourself in here and let me see what mess you've made of yourself."

Tommy is talking to Charley in that earnest, insistent way of babies just starting to fiddle with the keys to language, and is grabbing at the spoon that has stopped delivering its payload. Bernie comes back into the kitchen, bearing his skinned and bloodied forearm before him like a battered scepter.

"I tole him no! I tole him not to climb up the shelfs."

"I appreciate the update, Miss Jeanie. Well, at least you're not dripping. Bring me the dish towel."

Tommy makes a grab for the bowl but Charley lifts it out of reach as he takes the towel from Bernie and wipes through the hopscotch patches of blood, skin, dirt, and tiny flecks of paint. "What else? Does everything still move? Show me." Bernie does a little dance of bending and twisting to prove that nothing's broken, then Charley holds him still to wipe down the knee scrape and calf scratch that have already started to harden over.

"What'd you break?" As Bernie goes into the dance again, Charley snorts. "On the porch, boy. What got broken on the porch?"

"I dunno. Stuff."

Tommy pounds his palms down on the tray, sending up a splatter of drooled cracker, and demands, "Bah!"

The boys wander back into the kitchen with Dorothy, Charley Boy careful to hold his school tie over the offending bobby pin, and they rifle through the lunch sacks to find theirs. They check the contents and exchange a look of disappointment, but after the breakfast unpleasantness neither one says a word.

"Dorothy, go tell your sisters that if they don't quit fooling with their hair and get themselves off to school, I'm going to drag them out of the house myself." Dorothy runs into the dining room and loudly repeats the threat word for word. The girls file back into the kitchen, quieter but still giggling among themselves, and pick up their lunches. Charley is back to spooning mush into Tommy's avid baby-bird's mouth, and gestures at the counter with his elbow. "I guess you all figure that mess is going to clean itself up, too." His eyes narrow as they just look back at him anxiously.

"But Granddaddy, we have to get to school!"

"Oh, *now* you're in a hurry to get to school. Now that you're done wearing all the reflection out of the dining room mirror, *now* you need to get. Well, then, I guess you better get." There is an uncertain pause, but then Charley feints at getting up from his chair, and the children scatter like kitchen roaches when the light turns on.

Bernie is heading back out to the spring porch with Jeanie right behind him. "Both of you, get back here, now. Sit yourselves down and don't move until I tell you. And why do you keep tugging at your ear? What's wrong with it?"

Jeanie hunkers down, looking guilty, and puts a protective hand over her ear. "Nothing."

Charley's in a mood all right, and even he doesn't know where it's coming from. Mr. Greenley will have his unders in a twist when Charley shows up late, but Charley's got no problem telling him to go pound sand. Has he never been left on his own to deal with all of the offspring? Probably not all nine, but there's a tipping point where the actual number doesn't really matter anymore. He feels as though someone has snuck itching powder under his shirt. And then there are creeping footsteps on the spring porch, a trip over some of Bernie's mess, and "Dang it!" followed by a sucking-in noise of someone suddenly remembering that he's trying to be quiet.

When Rufus peeks around the door, hoping to sneak in and out without anyone noticing, he is met by Charley's angry glare, and blinks at the sense of having sprung a trap. He gingerly lays two loaves of bread on the counter and begins to back away as Charley slams his hand down on the table. "An oath on it, Rufus Boyle! If you don't hurry up and marry that girl so I can finally get my bread on time, I swear I'll flay the skin off that bony back of yours, and don't think I won't! Moon at her on your own time!" Charley starts up from his chair again, this time all the way, and Rufus makes a squeaking noise as he backpedals onto the porch and promptly trips down the steps with a metallic crash; he is up and out the back door like a spooked deer.

Still standing, Charley looks up at the ceiling, "Dammit, what is going on up there?"

Even Tommy gapes at him, big-eyed, in stunned silence. A noise starts to bleed into the stillness, like the low-pitched buzz of a June bug against the window screen, until Charley realizes that it's the rising sound of Jeanie starting to cry. Tommy is mere seconds behind her. Bernie never cries, but even he puts his head down into his unscraped arm on the table. Charley closes his eyes and deflates in a sigh. "All right. It's all right." He lifts Tommy out of the high chair and continues around the table to first tousle Bernie's hair and then press Jeanie's head against him in a half hug.

They are still posed like this when Chloe picks her way through the spring porch wreckage and steps into the kitchen. "Mr. Charley?" She's again more than two hours early today, certain that she'll be needed, but finding Charley Beck still at home at this late hour makes her suddenly fearful.

He sees it in her eyes, but has no idea what news there is to give her. "Mrs. Beck and Mr. Ferd are upstairs with Dr. Cavanaugh and Miss Lillie. They've been up there and I've been down here a long time. Long enough to make everyone breakfast." He gives her a tired smile.

"Long enough for someone to make mischief on the back porch too, I see," as she looks at Bernie's fresh scabby patches and takes Tommy. Her voice drops. "Mr. Charley, are you going to work today?"

"I've been trying for a while now."

"Well, then, you go ahead and go. I'm here." She puts her forehead against Tommy's conspiratorially. "All of us going to clean up the mess on the porch, aren't we?"

Charley takes a pencil and scrap of paper from his shirt pocket and scribbles a phone number, hands it to her. "Call if you need to."

"I surely will, Mr. Charley, though I'm saying a prayer I don't need to."

"You and me both." He picks up his own lunch bucket before walking out the back door. "I thank you, Chloe."

She nods at him. "Don't you worry, Mr. Charley. We'll all be fine."

Charley's discussion with Mr. Greenley does not go well. There are raised voices and even some veiled threats of lowered performance evaluations and charges of insubordination. Charley does not actually use the words *go pound sand*, but the effect is similar. Mr. Greenley's secretary Madge secretly cheers Charley on as she listens from her desk, not even needing to strain given the volume. But she knows to seem concerned when Mr. Stillwell comes out of his office and stands by her desk. He looks at her with an obvious question. "Mr. Beck's daughter has taken badly and he was delayed to the office this morning." Mr. Stillwell looks at his watch in surprise. "Oh, no, sir! He's been here for several hours; it's Mr. Greenley who's only just gotten back to his office."

Mr. Stillwell raps on the door as he opens it. Mr. Greenley stands behind his desk, fists pressed against the blotter. Red splotches pulse on his cheeks. Charley's face is composed, but his body seems to be tightening. Mr. Stillwell's presence eases the tension on Charley's springs, while making Mr. Greenley sputter in guilty explanation. It has always been Charley's bad luck to draw direct supervisors who are mean, stupid, or just dithering: Mr. Greenley is only a rung or two removed from Old Grimsley, who disappears for good the day he finally goes barking mad. Charley is, however, sometimes fortunate in the next layer up in his management chain, and Mr. Stillwell is one of those happy accidents. He listens for about thirty seconds to Mr. Greenley's incoherent defense before he turns to Charley. "Madge tells me that Lillie's ill." Charley nods once. "Well, it must be bad, since you're never late for work otherwise," he says straight at Mr. Greenley. "Maybe you need to be at home today more than you need to be here. We'll manage somehow." Mr. Greenley's words evaporate, the red splotches now merged at his forehead and chin. "I'll walk out with you."

He walks with Charley as far as his own office, shakes his hand. "Give Lillie my best; I'm sure she'll be back up in no time. But call me directly if you need to."

And this is why Charley is back on Longfellow by noon, carrying his still-packed lunch pail. He sees Dr. Cavanaugh emerge onto the front porch, stand for a moment, then actually sit down on one of the porch steps and rub his face. Charley draws in a hard breath at this, but doesn't want to startle the doctor who obviously thinks he's alone and unobserved. But then he looks up and sees Charley and starts to stand up; Charley waves him back down and joins him on the step. "Is it that bad, then?" he asks quietly.

"She was doing well. She drank most of the tea, and asked if she could nurse the baby, but I didn't think it was a good idea."

Charley nods. "I guess that little one's getting weaned all in one go."

"Then she had Chloe bring the other two upstairs to sit on the bed with her. Jeanie told her a story about Mr. and Mrs. Squirrel and their squirrel children who steal eggs from the Easter Bunny and bury them to grow egg trees." He smiles to himself and gazes into the middle distance.

"Doc?"

"I had to give her an injection of morphine. She was caught up in a coughing fit so bad that she truly couldn't breathe." He looks down and away. "It was a bad moment for everyone. Chloe was able to take the children out of the room before the worst of it, though."

"And now?"

"She'll be asleep for a few hours. But I need to find a better way to ease her breathing. That's where I'm going now. I'll be back as soon as I can."

"Going to see your expert again?"

Dr. Cavanaugh slumps a little. "He really is the specialist in respiratory complications. But he'll never set foot in the house again, you have my word on that."

"Doc, you've been looking out for this family for almost twenty years. You're the one we listen to, and you haven't steered us wrong yet."

"I appreciate it, Charley. I'll be back as soon as I can."

Charley watches him to his car, until the doctor pulls away and disappears in the direction of Illinois Avenue, then pushes up with a sigh and goes inside.

ꕥ

Chloe's morning has been less chaotic than Charley's, but still off balance. The normal rhythm of the weekday household is knocked off time, and missing two of three people, and it takes rushing to catch back up again. Cleaning the mess up from the porch takes longer with four little hands helping, but it's important that they participate. Tommy is on her hip most of the morning, unless she is right there with him. This one has done everything extra early—rolling over, scooting, crawling, jabbering—probably from a deep instinct of self-preservation, and she can see him trying to puzzle out the trick of pulling himself up by the furniture. So the two of them are on a trip into the cellar to see what's on the canning shelves when she realizes that there is still laundry hanging up from

Sunday. That will need to wait until she's able to put Tommy down for a nap. Then she takes the children upstairs for a visit, which is lovely and comforting until the coughing fit starts, and she knows to hustle the children out. To take Jeanie's mind off that upset, she replaces it with another, having put two and two together between seeing the rubber syringe on the counter and Jeanie's tugging at her ear. Then she's finally able to clean up from breakfast and lunch-making, which prompts her to take a full inventory of the ice box and pantry. Supplies are low. She could collect everyone up for a trip to the market, but that will take too much time and is sometimes problematic anyway. The D.G.S. is convenient, though small, but depending on who's at the counter, she is often left to cool her heels while the clerk waits on the neighborhood residents. The folks at the Hilltop Market know all the local help and treat them fine, but some of the other customers can get huffy. Besides, the household runs a tab at the Market, and they deliver, so she calls in her list of groceries and they promise the boy will be there by mid-afternoon. But since Rufus at least dropped the bread and ran, she can make the little ones their normal peanut butter and jelly sandwiches for lunch. For Tommy, she mashes together asparagus and a little bit of ham from Sunday dinner. He is an avid eater with no need for coaxing; she can tell he's building up reserves for another growth spurt. She thinks his build will be somewhere in between the two older boys, who are tall and slender like Ferd, and Bernie, who is solid and lower to the ground.

Chloe has her own large brood that combines with her sister Camille's to make a full and frenetic household. William, her youngest, is almost two now and it seems he'll be her last, after Zephraim's lower half was crushed when the lorry he was unloading hopped its chock. A determined man, he uses upper body strength and grit to work the line at a canning factory, but he won't be fathering any more children. She couldn't love him any harder if he were Samson, King Solomon, and Hector all rolled into one.

Her schedule at the Beck/Voith's varies to accommodate Camille's work schedule with a family just north of Walter Reed. They are both blessed and grateful to work for even-handed households. Chloe knows firsthand the misery a bad family can inflict. It's odd how this works: in South Carolina, where most of her cousins still live, the moneyed families openly mourn the loss of the plantation economy but are unfailingly polite to the household staff. Northerners, perhaps over-congratulating themselves for being geographically on the right side of the War, feel they've earned the right to treat the help with rude disdain. The ugliest part is when even the youngest children echo the attitude, and she knows there's no one to knock them back onto the better path. This household is a joy; she'll be here for as long as she's needed.

And right now she's needed to do laundry. After putting the baby in a clean diaper and down for a nap, she consigns Jeanie to the girls' room and Bernie to the boys' for their own afternoon quiet time. Someone is in the bathroom and the door to the Voith bedroom is closed. It is eerily silent.

Which makes her doubly surprised when she comes through the kitchen again, on her way to the cellar, and finds Charley Beck sitting at the table. The contents of his lunch pail are strewn amidst today's *Herald*, which has been waiting for him since before the morning milk arrived. "Mr. Charley! I didn't hear you come in!"

"The breeze blew me in like a feather, since I hadn't eaten my lunch. I was hungry as a new-dug grave."

"You're home then?"

"Tossed out on my ear." He smiles at her.

"Not so! They'd never do that!"

"Well, it was nip and tuck there, and a bit more nip than tuck." He tilts his head up, indicating the upstairs. "I saw the doc outside and he told me about the coughing fit. Are the charges okay?"

"I think so. They're down for naps while I get laundry started."

Without discussing it, he joins her. They pull the sheets from the lines downstairs and air them over the lines in the backyard. Chloe is a practiced hand at wrestling the Easy Wash into the kitchen, so Charley goes to collect up the dirty clothes. Some are in the hamper built into the bathroom linen closet, but he also goes bedroom to bedroom. Both children are asleep, though it takes him a minute to find Bernie, who, oddly, is curled up underneath Charley Boy's bed. He listens at the door to Lillie's room before opening it up, and stands gawping: Emma is in her rocking chair, which someone has pulled into the room, and Ferd is in the bedside easy chair, and they, along with Lillie, are fast asleep.

Chloe sets up the ironing board while Charley starts the first load in the washer. Over the course of the afternoon, Tommy is picked up, cleaned up, given some milk, and set down to scootch himself around the hall under Chloe's watch; Jeanie and Bernie are given the all-clear to come back downstairs and have cookies and milk before running outside; and Ferd appears bleary-eyed in the kitchen to see whether there is anything to be had in the ice box, and sits at the kitchen table staring at the remains of the morning paper before climbing the stairs again.

The big bed sheets are hard to manage on the ironing board, but Chloe has years of practice. Which is not to say it goes quickly, but the stack of pressed and folded sheets is impressive by the time the children are back from school, and Charley is hanging another batch of clothes on the line, when they swarm into the kitchen to raid for gingersnaps and milk. The noise of the churning Easy Wash and comforting sight of Chloe ironing sheets in the hall signal that this morning's threat is forgotten. But then Charley walks back into the kitchen with an empty basket under his arm and an unsettling smile.

"The grocery boy hasn't shown up yet, so don't worry that there are any cookies for you. I gave the last ones to Bernie and Jeanie. But you're just in time to take care of your own laundry. I've made sure to save it for you."

Which proves to be unhappily true; their clothes are piled in several baskets by the washer. Charley wants to hear the girls explain how the process works: load the clothes in just so—no cramming—measure out the soap powder, add the hot water from the kitchen faucet through the hose to fill the tub, agitate, rinse, and wring. It turns out that the girls haven't exactly been paying attention all this time either, and everyone needs Charley's remedial instruction. In the midst of this home economics lesson, Chloe puts her head in from the hall. "The doctor called and says he's on his way, and he'll need some help setting up."

Charley gives final instructions that everyone is a full participant, and they're either running the machine or hanging clothes until it's all done, and then they're to put the machine away. And no dinner until then.

Upstairs again, he finds both Ferd and Emma awake, in their chairs on either side of the bed, staring at the sleeping Lillie. The sound of her breathing is ragged and painful. "Ferd, Chloe says Doc is coming and will need a hand. You want to come down with me?"

Dr. Cavanaugh pulls up almost as Charley and Ferd step onto the porch. They join him at the car to help him unload; Ferd takes two bulky parcels wrapped in butcher paper, while Charley carefully hefts a large steel cylinder. Dr. Cavanaugh lugs a wooden crate.

"Is she still asleep? How's her breathing?"

"Ragged," Charley says, as Ferd says, "Labored."

"Well, I think this will help."

"And exactly what is this?"

"An oxygen tent."

Charley taps on the bedroom door and waits a beat before peeking his head into the room and then opening it. "Em, we have some equipment to set up here. Doc, you just tell us what you need done."

Dr. Cavanaugh slips out of his coat and begins to roll up his sleeves. The men unpack the parcels and lay out all the components, and consult a hand-written set of instructions. It's a bit of a puzzle, and Charley stands playing at the back of his neck for a moment, considering, before he says, "Oh, I've got you. Here, Ferd, you hold this. Doc, if you'll go around the other side, I'll hand you this end."

Charley moves Emma's rocker for her so that there is room to work. Lillie lies motionless in the middle of the bed, her slow breaths making the creaking sounds of a hinge that needs oiling. Working around and over her, the men are focused and efficient, and there is something happy in the activity, an optimistic feeling that they are finally doing something useful.

Once they have the frame set up, they wrestle a little with the isinglass, light gauge but stiff in its newness and with a tendency to stick to itself. This property is used to hold the flaps closed and keep the oxygen inside the tent. They keep the flaps open while they work through the tubing and connections for the oxygen, and Dr. Cavanaugh carefully explains the cautions and safety measures to use in handling the cylinder, managing the air flow, working around the tent, and generally being aware of the dangers of the gas. "No open flames. No smoking in the room."

"My pipe stays outside the house, Doc. Mrs. Beck doesn't like the smell of tobacco."

"Good. Just make sure that anyone who's in this room knows all these things too."

Together, they puzzle through the setup of a crude air conditioning system that will keep the inside of the tent cool and dry. Charley has a homemade ice box out in the barn where he stores ice blocks harvested from the rain barrel in winter. Packed thick in sawdust, the supply often lasts him through the summer, depending on how often he goes fishing. He retrieves a small block to tote back upstairs, and is the subject of several baleful looks from children on his way through the kitchen.

Next, they review the advice about proper gauge readings to ensure that everything is working as it should. Finally, there is a chart that Dr. Cavanaugh has created on which he's recording Lillie's vital statistics each time he takes them. "Lordy, Doc, it's just like we're in a hospital!" Charley tells him.

"Well, this tent is the only other thing a hospital could do that we weren't doing here. And far better for her to be among family."

Finally, the entire structure is complete and connected. The fan that blows over the ice isn't as noisy as they'd feared, but Charley can only imagine how much electricity it draws. Dr. Cavanaugh carefully cracks open the valve on the oxygen cylinder, opens it all the way, and then gives it half a turn back. He waits a moment for the air to start flowing, then closes the flap on the tent. He shows them how to check that there aren't gaps in the skirt where air can escape, and illustrates how much caregiving can be done just from sliding hands and forearms under the tent, without having to stop the flow and open the flaps.

"At any rate, her breathing should start to ease soon."

It's an odd tableau: Ferd standing on one side of the bed with Dr. Cavanaugh, Charley and Emma on the other, all of them frozen in identical attitudes, staring ardently, hopefully, at the obscure figure in the center. Pilgrims at the shrine, supplicants awaiting a blessing.

It takes close listening to peel back the hum of the fan and low hiss of oxygen to uncover the moist sound of breathing, but they each suss it out. The change is gradual over untimed minutes, but eventually unmistakable. The creaking subsides. Their suspension persists.

Until, from below them, two voices yell out at the same time, followed by a stupendous crash, and then the pandemonium of many children shouting all at once. Charley moves instinctively for the door, and soon realizes that no one is behind him. Lillie has their complete attention. *At least we've got a doctor in the house if someone's severed a limb.* Chloe has put Tommy down for a nap at some point, because he's kicking up a ruckus from his crib. *Well, it's just a houseful of hollering now.*

It takes him mere seconds to get into the kitchen, which is completely empty because everyone is crowded onto the spring porch. His appearance clamps the mouths shut like he clicked off the radio. He presses through the crowd, knowing that if it's a dead body, someone will have said something by now. And he sees that at least it's not the body of any of them. Like a turtle that's been flipped on its back, the Easy Wash lies helpless and inert at the bottom of the porch steps, leaking the last of its soapy water. It's obvious: piloted by amateurs, the machine gathers too much speed on the slope, one of the casters slips into the void, and the downhill momentum propels the whole thing "ass over tin cups," he says darkly. It's a testament to the gravity of the situation that there is no cacophony of voices all protesting innocence on the various impending charges. "No one's lying under there, are they?"

"No, Granddaddy."

"It fell." This helpful bit is from Dorothy, so he lets it pass.

Chloe, eyes wide, stands at the open door at the bottom of the porch, a garden basket under her arm, Jeanie and Bernie on either side of her. Almost in wonder, Bernie says, "I didn't do it."

"Charles, help me to set it back up." The two Charleys stand on opposite sides of the downed machine, and Charley Beck calls the count to three. They muscle past its top-heavy desire to lie back down, and stand it upright on its casters. The side is staved in and the roller's askew; this will take some time with the ballpeen, and that's just for the cosmetic work. He'll have to open it up to find the true extent of the damage.

As he's doing the repair calculation in his head, he hears his stomach growling, notices the softening light, and recognizes the warm aroma of something tasty on the inside stove. "Chloe?"

"Mr. Charley?"

"Whatever you're cooking smells extra fine." He is back upstairs, turning the corner into the pantry.

She is stirring the chopped vegetables into the big soup pot. "I'm making chicken broth for when Miss Lillie wakes up. She'll need something easy."

"It's long past time for you to head home, isn't it?"

"I can stay if you need me to. I just need to call to the house—"

"No, but just, can you come early again tomorrow?"

"I can, Mr. Charley. Camille's people were grateful when Miss Lillie let me help out when their daughter was so sick, and they said they hope to return the favor." In fact, the Weavers came to the house with a basket of pie and preserves to introduce themselves to Lillie and say thank you. Camille will simply explain that Lillie is sick and the Weavers will grant all the flexibility needed for the two women to manage the crisis and still keep all three households running.

Charley rubs at the back of his neck and mutters, "Now I just need to feed the rest of the hellions."

In response, Chloe ticks off a list as she pins her hat on: the boy was late with the groceries, so there wasn't time to put the roast in, but there's the chicken meat stripped from the carcass that's currently forming the broth on the stove; there's the potatoes that are with the groceries, plus the last of the gravy, and some more asparagus fresh in from the garden; for Miss Lillie, the broth just needs to simmer another hour or so, and Mrs. Beck will want to strain it through cheesecloth before spooning it up.

Charley sees her to the back door to make sure there aren't any random machine parts on the steps that she might trip over. "You're a lifesaver, Chloe. As always." And for Charley, this is a literal truth.

Back up the steps into the kitchen. "You heard her. Let's get to it. I have a baby to fetch. Try not to break anything else while I'm gone."

This time Charley is empty-handed when he meets Ferd on the landing with the now-dry baby. "She's definitely breathing much easier, and her color is so much better. Cavanaugh says the oxygen will probably help her come out from the morphine soon."

"Well, Chloe's got broth on the stove to be ready for her. Anyone up here planning to eat dinner?"

Ferd glances back at the bedroom door. "I doubt it." Handoff complete, Ferd slips back into the room and closes the door behind him.

Charley stands at the top landing for a moment, he and Tommy considering each other. "Well, Thomas, here we are again."

Dinner is a silent affair, interrupted only by Tommy's babbling and occasional banging on the tray with his little wooden spoon. The potatoes are underdone and mealy, the asparagus overdone mush, and the chicken and gravy manage to get burned in the reheating. Even Charley Beck picks at his before muttering around the table, "This is the only dinner any of us are getting. Might as well figure out how to eat it."

"Is Mamma still resting, Granner?"

"Yes, Jeanie."

"Where's Daddy?"

"He's with your mamma."

"And Gramal too?"

"Yes, Jeanie."

She stares at her plate and blinks, sensitive to the telltale sound of aggravation in an adult voice. "I wish she could be all better."

Charley looks around the table at the glum faces. It's been a bad day for everyone. "You're not the only one, Jeanie."

He's putting Tommy down for the last time today—early, but he's hopeful it will take—and decides to finally allow himself a visit. He taps on the door before entering and finds Dr. Cavanaugh pacing and Ferd and Emma sitting in their chairs on either side of the bed; Emma is fingering her rosary beads as her lips move silently. They hardly acknowledge his arrival.

And then: Emma is a wing-beat faster than Ferd at seeing the eyelid flutter, and it is stunning to see her move so quickly, picking up a glass of water from the bedside and throwing back the tent flap. Charley is the first to the tank to turn off the oxygen flow. Lillie sips the water Emma holds for her, but doesn't start to cough. She lies back against the pillows and closes her eyes, but they flutter open again and she spends a moment looking at each of them and at her surroundings. When she speaks, her voice is gravelly but clear enough. "Well. This is new."

Near Misses

August 1932

A Washington summer is a physical being: a shaggy, slobbering beast; relentless, inescapable, forever panting its heavy, humid breath into the face of each citizen and pushing its weight against the wilting populace, demanding attention—a constant, unwelcome companion.

Inexplicably, the nation's capital is built on a swamp. George Washington chose it because he wanted the capital built from the ground up—a new, shining city to represent a new, shining nation—instead of repurposing an existing city like Philadelphia, which would come with its own history and significant baggage. To Washington's thinking, the area is perfect, a blank slate, virtually untouched by development. Little wonder, since most people have had the good sense to stay away. Granted, the choice of a southern city is the quid for the votes Hamilton needs to fund the new country's debt, but still: a man who spends his early years as a land surveyor might know better. The swamp is drained bit by bit, often poorly, as the city pushes past its boundaries and more land is needed. Entire bodies of tidal water are rerouted and contained in concrete culverts, Tiber Creek forced out of existence by engineers who bury it under Internal Revenue. The city's malarial climate proves unconquerable, however, prompting Teddy Roosevelt, famously and unfavorably, to compare D.C. to equatorial Africa. Though a Washington spring can sometimes be ephemerally sublime, each summer oozes in on a glistening slime trail to suck initiative and industry from the inhabitants like a vast, enveloping leech.

In an especially cruel summer, sleep might be traded as a commodity on the exchange floor, to make a killing for the man who divines how to package and sell it. The closest anyone comes is in the invention of the electric fan. Electric being dear, most homes have only one, trained jealously each night onto the family's breadwinner. There, in its flow of heavy, damp air, he might find fitful sleep and be able to slog, hollow-eyed and drained but still functional, back to work the next day.

As a dual-earner household, the Beck-Voiths own two fans. This affords Emma and Lillie a bit of relief, since each enjoy some spillover of air movement in bed at night, but it helps the kids not a whit. Inevitably then, some variation of the same conversation conducts itself multiple times each summer, as though from a script passed child to child over the course of years:

Child #1: "How come Daddy and Granner get the fans?"

Lillie, cleaning up from dinner: "Because they have to go to work in the morning, so they need to get a good night's sleep."

Child #2: "Why can't we have a fan, too?"

Lillie: "You don't need a fan."

Child #1, flopping in emphasis: "But it's so *hot*. We're going to *die*."

Lillie: "You're not going to die."

Charley, looking out from behind his newspaper: "Back before the 'lectric, it was a common thing for little children just to burst into flames, walking down the street."

Child #3, always the youngest: "Really?"

Lillie: "Dad, you're not helping."

Charley: "No, it's true. People had to carry around buckets of water with them, just in case."

Skeptical silence.

Child #2: But why can't we…"

Ferd, passing through from the parlor: "Stop pestering your mother."

Child #1: "But…"

Ferd: "Not another word!"

Silent assessment of available gambits.

Emma, not even looking up from the mending: "You know, when *I* was your age…"

Collective groans; a slouching away in defeat.

Charley, going back behind his newspaper: "Works every time."

In truth, of course, summer is the very best season: no school, long days, and relaxed bedtimes. There is the twink of fireflies in hedges and fists and jars, the games of hide-and-seek in the shadows of twilight, the forays to the creeks for crawdads and bullfrogs. It's the call from the huckster, the side of his truck open to show fruits and vegetables as it rolls slowly by, singing out things like, "Peaches, cantaloupe! Watermelon! Ripe to the rind!" The umbrella man only pushes a cart, but he has a song, too: "Um-ber-ellas! Um-ber-ellas! *To* fix, to *day*?" The adults enjoy the season too, with its inherent permission to unpin and pull up a chair. Of an afternoon, Charley's cronies collect in the back to pitch horseshoes, drink home brew, and tell tall tales, while the children chase each other shrieking through the sprinkler. Interspersed with the repeated clanks of the shoes are eruptions of deep-throated laughter and Charley's voice rising above with "Hot hominy! Hot hominy!" or some such nonsense.

When the swelter is unbearable for even the heartiest among them, the pump house is the final dependable retreat. The coolest spot on the property, the open-sided pump house is shady, damp, and mossy-smelling. The family and their friends tend to collect there, sitting on the perimeter benches to let the sweat evaporate; a body might even catch a shiver from the change in temperature. But the centerpiece of the pump house is the well itself, which contains the sweetest, purest water, so cold straight from the pump that it makes a person's teeth hurt.

That well, thirty feet deep, is still a point of pride at 741. Emma likes to show it off to new neighbors or visitors from church. The garbage men, collecting from the alley behind the houses, have tacit permission to come in through the back gate and drink from the pump, letting it splash over their dripping faces and necks as they drink. It is satisfying to pump the substantial hickory handle, counting to see how many times it takes for water to start flowing.

The strongest among them can do it in three titanic down-strokes.

Early one August morning, the garbage men come walking into the yard, laughing among themselves as each mops his brow or neck with a pocket kerchief. Three Italian brothers who hail from Baltimore but have discovered that work in D.C. is both more plentiful and better-paying, Sondy, Yoc, and Jiggs collect garbage for the city in the morning and offer themselves out as handymen in the afternoon. They help Charley out on the rare occasion that he needs some extra muscle or another set or two of hands. This morning they find him standing over the open well hatch, looking down, as he rubs the back of his neck in thought.

"Mr. Beck?" Sondy ventures. "Everything okay?"

Chloe is just outside the pump house, digging new potatoes from the garden. She looks up as the men walk past, and Yoc touches his cap to her; she nods back and returns to digging.

"Hmmm? Oh, fine, fine, boys. Just going to do a little maintenance work. Go ahead and get yourselves a drink; I still need to set up the block and tackle."

"Something we can help you with?" Yoc asks as Jiggs starts to pump.

"Don't you boys have to finish your route? And I know Miss Quigley always has a fresh pitcher of lemonade for you at the end, eh, Jiggs?" He winks at Yoc. Etta Quigley is perhaps sixty years old, but giggles like a schoolgirl as she pours lemonade for the three strapping men with their matching heads of thick, dark hair and impressively wide noses. She is particularly taken with Jiggs, whose broad shoulders pull his work shirt taut.

Yoc laughs. "No, sir, we're done for the day."

Sondy adds, "And we hear Miss Quigley is visiting with relatives this week, so Jiggs missed his usual refreshment." Jiggs, red-faced already from the sun and heat, just rolls his eyes.

"All right, then. I could probably use a hand."

Yoc and Jiggs go to retrieve the block and tackle from the barn, while Charley and Sondy discuss the plan. Chloe walks through once or twice on her way from the garden to the house and back, pausing each time to breathe in the cool, green air. By now the children are tumbling from the spring porch into the yard. They are immediately drawn by the knot of people in the pump house and run over to investigate. From behind them comes Emma's imperious voice, "You children stay away from there! I don't need any of you falling into the well! Margaret and Eleanor, bring them back over here!"

Margaret, thirteen to Miss Quigley's sixty, is mooning at Jigg's broad shoulders, too. As he turns, he catches her staring at him, and looks back at her openly, offering a disconcerting smile. Her eyes drop immediately, as her face turns red. "Margaret!" Emma calls sharply, "Now!"

As the girls herd the younger children away from disaster, Margaret sighs. "Isn't he dreamy?"

Eleanor shakes her head. "Don't be silly. You can't marry a garbage man."

In place of playing around the well, the children gravitate to the huge concrete birdbath that Charley constructed years before. It is eighteen inches high and four feet across, with a one-inch copper pipe coming up through the center that burbles an invitingly thick stream of water. In the early hot weather, the children share it with countless tadpoles, whose numbers dwindle as they suck in their tails to squirt out their legs and eventually hop away. Dorothy, Johnny, and Bernie are already in the bath, and Johnny is strategically putting his thumb over the pipe to see how far he can squirt the water.

"Francie, please keep your baby sister from climbing into that monstrosity," Lillie sighs as she sits heavily on the garden bench. She is just two weeks from her due date and the heat is a trial.

Francie coaxes Jeanie away from the inviting pool. "Jeanie! Jeanie, look at the witch doctor! See it?" They both crouch to look at the iridescent dragonfly, resting on a coneflower as its huge buggy eyes scan the area.

Lillie sighs again, her hand rubbing the spot where the baby's foot, or elbow, or hand, or all three at once, are poking at her. "Whatever got into Dad to build that thing? It's hideous." Lillie continues to rub her belly and tries not to think about the heat. "Margaret, do you remember when you fell into the lily pond by the arbor?"

Margaret is standing to one side, gazing ardently at the figure of Jiggs stringing a set of ropes from the pump house rafters. The sound of her name snaps her from her reverie. "What? Oh. No, I don't. I fell into the pond?"

"Indeed you did. You were about five, and you told us later that you were trying to catch one of the goldfish. You tipped right in, headfirst. If it weren't for Mr. Reddy, who was helping Dad with some yard work that day, well...he heard the splash and ran over to scoop you out." Lillie gazes at her daughter who is still staring into the pump house. "And thank heavens he did, or we wouldn't have you here to get all moony over the workmen." Margaret blushes and retreats to the swings, where there is a better view anyway.

Emma straightens up from pulling some crabgrass and considers the activity in the pump house. "Whatever is it that Mr. Beck is doing over there?"

"I can't even guess. You know the trouble Dad gets into whenever he takes his two weeks off." At breakfast this morning, the start of his annual vacation, Charley ticks off a list of the things he is planning, and this activity with the well isn't even among them: spreading manure on the fallow bed at the back; laying new asphalt shingle on the garages he rents out; stump-pulling, gravel-digging, and maybe even a good brush fire out at the farm; and, of course, painting the side of the house that is up in rotation for a fresh coat. The first few years after he built the house, he put on a full new coat every year, until the paint thoroughly soaked into the wood. Since then, he paints one side of the house each year, so that each side gets a new coat every four years. If Charley ever runs out of things to do on his vacation, he makes things up; the *Monstrosity*, in which the children now play, is ample proof of that. At this point, Lillie hopes that he never retires, because that much free time in Charley Beck's hands will surely kill him.

Chloe comes down from the porch with a bushel basket and heads back toward the vegetable garden. "Chloe, what are they up to at the well?"

"I don't rightly know, Miss Lillie, but they sure are making a big enough fuss about it."

Lillie watches for a moment longer, then heaves herself up. "I guess I'll go take a look. It's cooler in there anyway." Margaret stands up from the swings, hoping to follow. "Oh, no you don't, missy. You stay right where you are."

Chloe is ahead of her as she walks across the yard, and it looks like the party is finally breaking up; two of the hired men are standing to the side, assessing their handiwork, while the third is wiping his neck with his kerchief and scanning the yard until he spots Margaret. *We'll need to put a stop to that.* Charley is standing over the open well, looking down and holding the pulley in his hand. He pushes it out of the way, and turns to say something to one of the men, when Lillie sees the tackle swing around and hit Charley squarely in the back. His arms start to pinwheel in an effort to regain balance, but his weight carries him forward. The other three men are frozen where they stand, and Lillie feels a shriek rise inside of her. And then Charley is yanked back, hard enough that he almost topples the other way. Chloe, walking by at just that moment, has thrown the basket down, grabbed two handfuls of Charley's waistband, and heaved.

There is a stunned, gut-punched silence while everyone considers what has just nearly happened. Finally, Chloe says, "Lord above, Mr. Charley, we nearly lost you there!"

He grasps Chloe's hand and bows over it like a gallant, but then looks up with a grin. "Well, at least we already have the tackle set up so you could haul out whatever was left!"

Lillie still has her hands clapped over her mouth when Emma comes up to stand next to her. "Well, that was the first near-miss of this vacation. Shall we guess how many more?"

ᘓᘐ

While Charley Beck is always an easy source of pocket change, during the summer, there is an awkward imbalance in demand over supply. Most days, while the children are at home and faced with urgent needs for movies and ice cream, the C.J. Beck Savings and

Loan is typically at work. Hence, there is a constant pressure to scout for fresh sources of revenue. When he is unavailable and the situation is desperate, Charley's favorite chair is almost as reliable as the man himself, provided it hasn't been mined for a few days. Failing that, the boys stalk the streets, heads down, scanning for change.

Less predictable but always cause for excitement is a visit from Miss Bessie. An aged widow who lives in one of the row houses across the street, Miss Bessie lacks a telephone. On the occasions she needs to make a call, she simply visits the Beck/Voith household. Without a word or a knock, Miss Bessie lets herself in through the front door to the hall, where the telephone stands on its little table in the corner. News of her arrival sweeps through the ranks of the Voith children as a sort of chemical transmission; anyone who sees her arrive wants to keep it a secret, but the rest all find out anyway.

Emma has decreed that no one is to go into the hall while Miss Bessie is in the house, to allow her some privacy. This creates an oddly silent shoving match within the youthful mob crowded in the kitchen and parlor doorways. If Emma comes upon them like this, she shoos them away, though it's possible to sneak back around through various routes. More drastically, their eager anticipation is sometimes deflated by the arrival of Charley himself, who observes them in amusement before pushing through the crowd and into the hall to say hello.

But as often as not, they are successful in stalking Miss Bessie to the very end of her phone call. On hanging up, she carefully places a nickel on the phone table to cover the cost of the service, and then, as quietly, leaves. At the barest click of the front door, the crush of bodies explodes toward the table. It is an even match among the five eldest: the girls are lithe and long-legged, while the boys carry more weight and muscle. The younger ones, of course, have no chance, but give it their best anyway. Intentional tripping of others is fair game, but tends to slow the perpetrator down. The victor will march off, holding the nickel aloft in triumph.

Through unlikely happenstance, one day Jeanie finds herself alone in the hall when Miss Bessie arrives. She is whispering intently to her doll Sally when the door opens. "Hello, child," Miss Bessie says to her. Jeanie still doesn't understand who Miss Bessie is, or why there is a game associated with her. She and Sally watch as Miss Bessie dials the phone, and wander over to take a closer look. She rests her chin and fingertips on the edge of the table while she stares, Sally peeking over from the crook of Jeanie's arm. Miss Bessie has several long white hairs sprouting from her chin and the top of her nose, and her eyes are kind of white too. Jeanie wonders if she is a witch; she looks like one. Scottie Jameson once taunts Jeanie, "You're grandma is a witch—a hunched-up warty old witch!" and Jeanie tells him, "No, she's not. She's just Gramal." But maybe Miss Bessie is a witch.

Miss Bessie doesn't say anything to the phone, but then jiggles the silver hanger and dials again. Still nothing. Bored, Jeanie is about to take Sally outside to the swings when Miss Bessie hangs up again, and takes out a coin purse. Jeanie sees coin purses like that produced every Sunday when the money basket is handed around in the church. People always put money into the basket, but no one ever takes any out, except for that man once who does it after looking around. So Jeanie stays to watch as Miss Bessie puts a nickel on top of the table, but then picks it up again and hands it to Jeanie. "You make sure your granddaddy gets this, for letting me use his phone."

"'Kay." She isn't really listening because she has a picture in her head of the candy jars at the store and of herself standing in front of them with that nickel.

Jeanie follows as Miss Bessie walks out through the front door, but stops at the top step. On the sidewalk, Miss Bessie turns and waves. "Goodbye, child." Jeanie waves back, glad that the witch lady is leaving. She sits on the porch swing and makes Sally dance in her lap while she sings a song.

A stampede explodes from around the corner, Eleanor in the lead but Charley Boy and Johnny about to overtake on the stairs, and barrels into the house. Only a moment later, the kids wander back out, joined by Francie, who has raced in from the backyard.

"But, but she always leaves a nickel."

"And Granner's not even home."

They turn and look at Jeanie, who pauses in her song and looks back. "No sense asking her." The boys shrug at each other and Francie shakes her head as they all drift off, and Jeanie starts her song again. It sounds like *candy candy candy candy.*

ꕥ

Ferd comes into the house through the spring porch, and Lillie automatically tilts her cheek toward him for a kiss. The roiling steam from the canning pot has turned her red and slippery, and the kerchief tied around her hair is soaked. "How was the farm?"

"Hot. And your father tried to kill us again."

Charley's voice calls out from the kitchen, "Oh, Ferd, are you still complaining? Don't be such an old woman." He walks out to the porch and surveys the stove. "What is it today?"

"Peaches."

"Ah, so it is." Charley dips a spoon into the cook pot of peach compote that is ready for canning and gives it a taste. "That's fine. Fine."

"So what happened this time?"

"What do you mean, *this* time? Was there a *last* time?"

"And there will be a *next* time, too," Ferd tells him. "You're a rotten driver."

"Nonsense; there's nothing wrong with my driving."

"What about when you backed the T off the road at the farm and it slid all the way down into the ditch and they had to bring in a tractor to pull you out?"

Charley nods at the memory. "It was an adventure."

Ferd's voice has an edge to it. "With the boys in the backseat?"

"Makes a great story."

"So. What happened this time?" Lillie asks again.

"You know that hill coming up from the farm where it hits Route 1, where you have to creep out until you can see the traffic coming up on the left?" She nods. "Well, your father, the racecar driver here, gunned it up the hill and took that right turn on two wheels. Never even glanced at the oncoming traffic."

"And yet here you are, telling the story."

"Only because God looks out for the feeble-minded."

"Ferd!"

"Here I am, hanging on to the dashboard, still waiting for the impact, and cool as a May breeze he turns to me and says, 'You know, Ferd, Charles and John are turning into two fine young men.'"

"And so they are."

"You are a menace."

Charley dips the spoon in and takes another lick as he walks back into the kitchen. "Oh, Ferd, stop being such an old woman."

Lillie keeps her head down to hide her smile as she fills the jars, but he can see it. "Oh, so I *am* an old woman."

She turns, cradling the big wooden spoon to offer him a taste. "Ferd, when was the last time you saw me get into the T with Dad at the wheel?"

"Mmmmm, very good. Well, he can fix them like nobody's business, but he sure can't drive them."

It's true. Charley had been working on cars since before the Model A, and he loves his T like a second child, but the nuanced understanding that he brings to their care does not translate into an ability to operate them. On this point, he is either unaware or unconcerned. Ferd is pretty certain it's the latter.

Lillie leans against the doorjamb and wipes her brow, pressing her other hand against her belly. Ferd is sweating just from standing on the porch. "This is awfully hot work. Where is your mother?"

"She's getting the last of the peaches and the zucchini that we're doing tomorrow." She smiles ruefully at him. "Always a bumper crop of zucchini. Anyway, at least I can stand in one spot to do the canning; she's doing all the climbing and bending. What's coming in at the farm?"

"We got some nice corn today, and a couple watermelon. Do you want to sit down for a few minutes?"

She waves at the canning jars, up to their shoulders in a cauldron of boiling water. "No, I need to get these filled." She looks down as she rubs her belly again and sighs. "Just think, by the time the apples and grapes are in and done, this little one will be almost two months old."

Ferd puts his hand over hers and smiles. The quiet moment is shattered by a loud call from two rooms away: "Granner! Daddy! Mother?" They share a last smile and eye-roll as Lillie turns back to the stove and Ferd goes in through the kitchen to look to this latest crisis.

He finds Dorothy, in her wet bathing suit, coming through the parlor and preparing to bellow for them again. She is trailed by Mr. Elliott from next door. "Hush, Dorothy, I'm right here. Go back outside."

He shakes hands with Mr. Elliott, a retired D.C. police officer formerly in the mounted division, who used to keep his horse in the yard behind his house. "I'm actually looking for Mr. Beck," he explains. "About the gunfire."

Ferd has to stop himself from groaning out loud. Charley sometimes forgets that he is no longer living out in the rural countryside, surrounded only by woods and wildlife. Over the forty years since he built the house, civilization has encroached on all sides, and the neighbors don't appreciate Charley's using his .22 to deal with the squirrels that steal walnuts from his trees, or to keep down the local population of feral cats.

Without any idea where Charley is at this moment, he leads Mr. Elliott out into the kitchen and they meet Charley coming up from the cellar, wiping his hands on a rag. "Well, howdy do, sir."

"Mr. Beck. I came over because, well, as you know, my wife recently fell and broke her hip…"

"Yes, I was very sorry to hear; how is she feeling?"

"Well, she's recuperating, and the doctor feels strongly that she needs to rest. She needs quiet. He was fairly emphatic on this point."

"Certainly, certainly. Wise advice."

"And, so, Mr. Beck, I felt certain we had an understanding about the rifle."

"The rifle?"

"Yes. You agreed that you wouldn't fire it in the yard anymore. For the squirrels."

"Oh, is that it?" He laughs. "No, sir, I took your concerns to heart. I promise I haven't shot at the squirrels in quite some time. Plus, the .22 has started to misfire pretty often, so I can't depend on it anymore."

"But we're hearing a gun being shot in your yard."

Surprised, Ferd asks, "What? Right now?"

"Yes, now. This afternoon. You can understand my wife is quite upset by it."

Charley rubs at the back of his neck. "I see your point. It's not the squirrels so much as it is the gunshots."

"Yes, Mr. Beck, that's it exactly."

Ferd is glaring at Charley, who shrugs. "It's the boys. We set up a target for them out back."

The two men follow Charley outside, to the far corner of the yard. As promised, the two eldest boys are taking turns firing at a row of tin cans set up on a rock in front of a stand of trees. They're standing with their backs to the Elliott's yard, and the acoustics neatly reflect the report in that direction.

Charley looks on with admiration. He's taught them how to handle the gun with respect and care, and he can see they have taken the lessons to heart. When the gun misfires on Johnny's turn, he watches as the boy makes sure to eject the bullet before resetting the firing pin.

"Like I said, it's taken to misfiring, so I gave it to Charles to use for target practice. They're both very responsible with it." While Johnny is still working on the rifle, Charley calls to them. "Boys, we need to put the gun away now. Next time, we'll have to go out to the farm for target practice."

There is an indistinct grumbling sound, but Charley Boy collects the rifle and ammunition, and he and Johnny head to the barn to put them away. With quiet restored, Charley walks with Mr. Elliott back toward his house and Ferd hears him saying, "And how are those two lovely girls of yours, Alice and Eva? I see them out in the garden all the time. For the life of me, I can't understand why the boys haven't snapped them up already."

Ferd feels heavy as he walks back in through the spring porch, back to Lillie, still working in the steam of the canning pots, still red and dripping, still two weeks from delivering their next child, the ninth. He leans against the kitchen doorway and closes his eyes.

"Dearest, what is it?"

"Oh, it's nothing." He shakes his head and laughs. "It's just that sometimes I wish that I could pretend for a minute that I have the smallest bit of control over my own family."

ဢဢ

Charley stands and considers the left side of the house, rubbing at his neck under his old fedora, his other arm akimbo. The left side is the easiest of the four in the quadrennial rotation, but that doesn't mean it is quick or effortless. It has five windows, plus the attic dormer and all the shutters. At the moment, he is surrounded by ladders, tarps, and buckets full of tools: hammers, screwdrivers, saws, chisels, pry bars, a torch, a three-foot level, a plumb bob, a chalk line, and every size and shape scraper imaginable. Over many, many years of house painting, Charley has learned that this is the basic set of tools he needs just to start the job, and at that there are probably a few he is still missing. When he discovers what they are—invariably, one at a time—he will have to stop what he is doing, climb down from wherever he is hanging, and go in search of the missing item. No one ever helps Charley with the painting. Ferd has offered to help pay someone else to do it, and there is no incentive great enough to coax the boys to participate. It is just as well; anyone else would do a half-hearted job, which is worse than not doing it at all.

"Granner, why you gots a hole in your neck?" pipes Jeanie's little voice behind him.

"That's where the boa constrictor bit him and started to suck out the juices," Dorothy states authoritatively.

"Nuh uh," Bernie tells her. "It's where he keeps his pocket lint."

"You ninny. Why would anyone keep pocket lint?"

"To stuff his pillow with! He said so!"

"You're both wrong," Charley tells them, and he bends down to Jeanie with his hands on his knees. "That's where they plug me in at night so I can recharge for the next day."

"No!" That from Dorothy; Jeanie just blinks at him.

"Yessiree. They have a special 'lectric cord and they pop it right in there and plug me into the wall. Next day, I'm right as rain." With big eyes, Jeanie feels at the back of her own neck. "No, no, you're not going to have one yet. You need to be as old as me before they fit you with the socket."

"Does Gramal have one?" Dorothy demands to know.

Charley whistles. "Oh, girlie, your Gramal doesn't ever need any plugging in, believe you me."

Dorothy says to Bernie, "I still think it was the boa constrictor."

While the kids continue to debate behind him, Charley sets up the short ladder. He always starts low on the scraping, so when he figures out what else he needs, he doesn't have to go as far.

"Hey, Granner," Johnny calls as Charley is about to start up the ladder. "Are we doing the fire today?"

He stops, tool bucket in hand, and looks pointedly around him at the ladders, tarps, and various implements before looking back at Johnny in time to see Charley Boy give him a sharp elbow in the side. "He's scraping the house, dummy."

Charley laughs as he looks around again. "Hmm, what was your first hint?"

Charley Boy shrugs, "You said so at breakfast this morning."

Charley considers these two—the two grandchildren he's with most often, who help while he works on cars and other mechanical devices, showing true curiosity and asking intelligent questions—and wonders where he has gone wrong. "If you boys are going to stand there being soft-headed, I've got scrapers and ladders enough to go around."

The threat is enough to disperse the crowd and ensure that Charley is left entirely alone through the painting project. He starts up the ladder.

Charley is deaf enough now that even Jeanie, still a toddler, knows to speak up when trying to talk to him. And yet he finds when he is up on the ladder, he can hear all sorts of things: the fights, taunts, and general clatter of the children in the backyard, Chloe singing as she beats out the rugs on the other side of the house, an exchange at the front gate:

"Hello, Jeanie. Do you remember me? I'm your Aunt Dorothie."

Silence.

"And this is your cousin, Dorothie June. Say hello."

A little girl's voice, "Hello."

Long pause. "My big sister is Dorothy."

"That's right. We have lots of Dorothys in the family! Is your mother home?"

"Uh huh."

The gate unlatches. "Well, I'll come in and visit with her for a bit. Why don't you and June go play together?"

The girls obviously start to walk away, because Jeanie's voice is fainter. "This is Sally. She's my doll."

"I have a doll too. Her name…" That is as much as he can hear.

Charley is about to climb down the ladder to say hello and make sure that Dorothie isn't just left standing there, when he hears footsteps coming down the walk from the house.

"Dorothie. What are you doing here?" It is Emma, and her tone is not welcoming. Charley stays where he is.

"June and I were out for a walk, and I thought I'd come see Lillie."

"Well, we're very busy with the canning today, so it's not a good time. Perhaps you should collect up Dorothie June and finish your walk."

There is a long pause. The front door opens. "Dorothie! Hello! I didn't hear you out here!" Charley can hear the slow, heavy steps down the porch stair to the front walk. "I'm coming!" she laughs. "It just takes me longer right now!" He pictures Lillie giving Dorothie a hug, made awkward by her large belly. "Let's go around back, where it's cooler. We should still have some lemonade if the kids haven't finished it off completely!"

"Dorothie can't stay. She just stopped in for a minute."

"What? But you just got here!"

"Your mother said you're very busy with canning, so I won't keep you. If you call June from the yard, we'll be on our way." Charley can hear the effort she puts into keeping her voice level; her face is probably red, but it is certain she is not going to allow herself to cry in front of Emma. *Good girl.*

Just now the girls come shrieking back around past Charley's ladder and into the front yard. Jeanie has obviously gotten over her earlier reticence, and they are each holding onto one of Sally's arms as they run. Sally's arm seams are straining under the rough use.

"Sweetheart, we're leaving. Say goodbye to Jeanie."

The whining starts immediately, but is cut off; Lillie knows by now that Dorothie needs to leave quickly in order to save face. She walks Dorothie to the gate; another hug in the silence and then a low exchange that Charley can't parse. The gate closes and Charley looks to catch Dorothie's eye in hello, but she has her head down as she hurries by, June's hand clamped firmly in her own.

"Jeanie, take Sally in the backyard and ask Francie to get you some lemonade."

"'Kay."

There is a long pause as the two women obviously wait until Jeanie is out of earshot.

"Can you please explain to me what just happened?"

"I will not have that woman anywhere on my property."

"*That woman*? *That woman* is my sister-in-law! *That woman* is Dorothy's godmother!"

"Well, I can't help that, but she comes marching in here bold as brass—well, I can certainly stop her from coming into the house. Margaret, Eleanor, and Francie are practically young women now; what kind of example do you want to set for them? And to have her daughter playing with yours!"

"Dorothie is a lovely person, on top of being Ferd's little sister, and I won't have you treating her like some, some…" Lillie can't bring herself to say like what.

"Lovely? Divorced! I'm a Christian woman…"

"You're certainly not acting very Christian right now! Christ wouldn't act like this!"

"Christ didn't have daughters!" There is a steely silence. "Father Bischoff might still let her into church, but that doesn't mean I have to let her into my home."

"I thought it was my home, too." Charley hears the hard footsteps back up the walk, up the steps, and into the house, with the door shutting firmly behind. It is rare that Emma does not get the last word, but here it is Emma who is left standing on the front walk. Charley goes back to scraping.

Apparently, though, the last word needs some underlining and an exclamation point, as everyone discovers the next day.

"Dorothy!" Lillie calls into the kitchen from her stool at the sewing machine. "Come see whether this fits!"

All eyes turn to her as Dorothy scrambles down from her chair at the breakfast table. In the hall, she peels down without prompting to her underwear. Lillie is letting out the Easter dress she made for Dorothy last spring. They tried it on last night and Lillie marked the points for alteration. Now she has basted in the changes and is giving it a test-fitting. "Here, turn around. Arms up." She maneuvers the dress carefully over Dorothy's head so as not to pull out the temporary stitches, and buttons the back. "Let me see. Can you move your arms okay?" Dorothy demonstrates. "Turn around once." Lillie automatically rubs her taut round belly as she appraises with a critical eye. "It doesn't look like it's pulling anywhere. Does it feel tight? No? Okay, I'll sew it in, then."

Dorothy pulls her shorts and shirt back on and returns to her seat at the kitchen table. Summer breakfasts are later and unhurried, much different from those during the school year. The rest of the children are still there, Emma at the sink, Charley Beck behind the morning paper.

"What's Mother doing?" Eleanor asks her.

"She's fixing my Easter dress."

"Why?"

"We're going to downtown. On the cars!"

Emma turns sharply from the sink. "What, today?"

"Yup. After breakfast."

Charley's paper comes down. "What for?"

"Visit Aunt Dorothie. She works at a store."

The entire assemblage is quiet for a moment, taking in this information. "Just you?" Charley Boy asks.

Dorothy nods, basking in the attention.

"Why you?" Bernie wants to know.

"Well, now, Master Bernard, Dorothie is aunt to all of you, but she's godmother to your sister here." Charley Beck is beginning to suss out Lillie's intent.

"Why do you get to ride the cars?" Bernie persists.

"Just you," Johnny repeats in wonderment.

Time alone with their mother is the Holy Grail among the Voith children, constantly sought and jealously guarded. Voith children pray to be individually struck down by the mumps or chickenpox for the joy of having Lillie nurse them, slowly if their luck holds, back to health. That Dorothy is to spend hours—hours!—taking a trip downtown with her, standing at the car stop, sitting together on the bench seat, holding hands on the street, maybe even eating at a lunch counter! It is enough to make even the oldest ones feel the sting, as though they are suffering material loss.

"Okay!" Lillie calls again. This time Dorothy eases out of the chair so that they might gawp at her longer, understanding now that she has taken the prize.

Normally, the table would be down to the last straggler or two, the rest already dispersed out into the summer day. Now no one is moving. The children have to see with their own eyes the truth of this travesty, but each also fosters the tiniest hope that if they are here, within view, Lillie might tap another to join the small party. Even Charley, whose paintbrush is nagging at him to pick it back up, is drawn to see how this will play out.

Emma is scraping plates loudly, smacking silverware onto the counter. "She is doing this to spite me." She turns accusingly to Charley, as though he is culpable. "Don't think I don't know what's going on."

"You might run the house, Em, but you don't run the world. She'll go if she wants to."

Dorothy dances back in, dressed in her yellow Easter dress with pink and blue flowers, rickrack at the hem and sleeves. She plans to take a spin or two to show it off to best effect, but it only takes a second to see that envy and awe has turned to resentment, and she quietly retakes her seat.

And here in the doorway, wearing her Sunday maternity dress and pinning on her hat, is Lillie. She snaps open her pocketbook to check that everything is in order.

"When will you be back?" Emma asks, her voice flat.

"Sometime this afternoon, I suppose. We're having lunch with Dorothie at Hecht's."

There is a collective miserable exhalation, felt rather than heard. *Afternoon. Lunch.* And not just at a counter, either: at a fancy department store. Their wretchedness is complete.

"Ready?" she says to Dorothy, and holds out her hand. Any care for her siblings' bitterness evaporates as Dorothy takes Lillie's hand.

"That child might come at any time," Emma tells her blackly.

Lillie looks squarely back. "And so he might. In the meantime, we're going to visit my sister-in-law, Dorothy's godmother."

Charley has gotten up, meaning to see them on their way. So too has Jeanie, who plants herself on the other side of Lillie and takes her hand. "Me, too."

"No, sweetie bug, you need to stay here. Francie will turn on the sprinkler for you."

Jeanie's forehead wrinkles in concern. Perhaps she has not made herself clear. "I wanna go."

"I know, Jeanie, but not today." She looks around at the glum faces. "Okay, we'll be back later. Don't miss us too much."

Charley follows them through the hall and out to the front step. They hear him bidding goodbye as the door closes.

Standing alone in the middle of the kitchen, Jeanie's face begins to melt like warm candle wax, and she puddles onto the floor in a wail of disbelief and abandonment. The rest of the children look on, feeling as though they would like to join her there.

ꙮ

Ferd often jokes, "No one better ever say anything bad to me about John L. Lewis," that labor boss who is loved and despised in equal measures. "Without him, I wouldn't have a job!" His appreciation is so great that he serves as secretary of the newly formed American Federation of Government Employees, as soon as a local is established and available to the Bureau of Engraving. The security of a federal government job, coupled with the additional protections offered by the union, provide dependable employment in a dark time, for which a father of nine might give sincere thanks on a nightly basis.

Even so, federal government employees are subject to regular furloughs in the teeth of the Depression. Multi-day furloughs are not uncommon, and Ferd has learned to budget for them. And while he never comes to enjoy them—his nervous stomach won't settle down enough for that—he learns how to fill them with meaningful activity.

His brood, on the other hand, seems to see these midweek days of having Ferd at home as something akin to Christmas and 4th of July rolled up in a package and tied with a bow. When it happens during summer vacation, their excitement propels them through the house like popcorn.

So when a one-day furlough coincides with Charley's house painting, the round-the-clock back porch canning juggernaut, the final weeks of Lillie's pregnancy, and yet another suffocating August day, Ferd decides it is time to get the children out of everyone's hair and take them off to the beach. Emma and Lillie pack lunch while the children stampede into putting on bathing suits and finding towels. They stuff themselves into Ferd's big '29 Hupmobile—boys in the back, girls in the middle, and little ones sprinkled where there is room—and start the hour-long journey to Beverly Beach.

An hour alone in a car with eight overly excited children: it takes Ferd only a few miles to realize that this is the first time he's tried this excursion solo. Lillie has never stayed behind until today. Ferd is thankful that he doesn't usually have to do this by himself, and considers now that this will probably be both the first and last time. He reminds himself that the drive out is nothing compared to what he can look forward to on the drive back: another hour, this time with eight hot, tired, cranky, damp, sandy, sunburned children stuffed in the car.

"Do you think the water's still cold?"

"Are we there yet?"

"No, by now it should be pretty warm. It always is by August."

"Johnny always dives under all at once, even when it's still cold."

"It's better to get it all over and done with."

"Are we there yet?"

"The sand will be hot, though. I hate burning my feet."

"But no jellyfish!"

"They're not jellyfish. They're sea nettles."

"It doesn't matter, 'cause there won't be any."

"Are we there yet?"

"I *hate* sea nettles."

Unique in the area, Beverly Beach is a paradise for swimming because it has a sea nettle net. The kids are unpleasantly familiar with the beaches where there isn't one. In the dry summers, when there has been scant rain for a month or more, the sea nettles are so thick they look like stepping stones, able to support a walk clear across the Chesapeake Bay. Then, because there is no possibility of swimming without getting stung—the long, gelatinous tentacles wrapping around arms and legs, draping themselves across backs and necks, leaving big red welts—the only entertainment becomes finding sticks or boards to drag them out of the water, poke at them, and egg each other on to pick them up by their harmless bells. They are dragged onto a board or rock out in the hot sun to see how short a time it takes for them to dry out into a shrinking wet spot, the whole nasty thing eventually vanishing into a single salty ring.

"I want to go on the swings."

"Can we go to the arcade, Daddy?"

"Oh! Can we?"

"We'll see, but everyone has to stay together. Do you hear me? No running off. There's only one of me, so I can't have you all going in different directions."

"Gosh, Daddy, this is the first time you've ever taken us to the beach, just you."

"I know, Francie; I was just thinking the same thing."

Margaret gasps quietly, her eyes big.

"What is it?" Eleanor asks, but follows Margaret's lead and keeps her voice down.

"I forgot. Mother's not with us. What about the sign?"

"What sign?"

"The sign at the entrance gate. The one that says, 'Gentiles only.'"

"So? We're Catholic; that means we're Gentiles."

"But…but Daddy's nose is so big. What if they think he's a Jew? And Mother's not here to make sure they know. If they think he's a Jew, how would we prove he's not?"

Margaret is afraid that Eleanor will laugh at her for being silly, but now Eleanor looks worried too. "I don't know."

"What do you think they would do?"

Eleanor gives her a look of alarm. "I, I don't know."

"What's going on back there?" Ferd glances at them over his shoulder, though his view is partially blocked by Bernie ("Are we there yet?") standing on the hump with his arms thrown over the front seat. "Sit down, Bernie. What are you girls whispering about?"

"Nothing, Daddy!"

"Nothing, hmm? It better not have anything to do with boys."

Margaret and Eleanor say nothing the rest of the trip, queasy with uncertainty, desperate in the hope that they will not be detained, questioned, and expelled from the beach on suspicion of being Jews.

ꕥ

It is close to the end of Charley Beck's vacation: painting finished, farm squared away, the bulk of the chore list accomplished. "Hello! I'm home!" Charley bellows as he stomps up the steps of the spring porch and thumps down a bushel basket. "What is that stench? Tell me that's not something we're supposed to eat later."

"You know perfectly well what that is, Dad. Mother's making soap."

"Ah, the semi-annual making of the soap. Hog rendering doesn't stink this bad."

"Well, it *is* hog fat. And the lye probably doesn't help."

Emma comes up from the cellar and out to the porch carrying heavy cardboard boxes that she has already cut down to about six inches high. "Oh, you're back." She sits one next to the stove, gives the kettle a stir to check consistency, and begins to ladle it out into the box. She stops after a minute and sniffs the air. "What is that smell?"

Lillie and Charley look at each other, and Charley rubs under his hat. "I expect it's the stench of lard and lye cooking on the stove there. That you're slopping into that box."

"No, that's not it." She eyes the bushel basket that's leaking onto the floor. "What sort of dead fish did you drag into the house?"

"I don't know what you think you're smelling, Mrs. Beck, because it's not fish and it's not dead."

"You mean to tell me that you went gallivanting out of here at three o'clock this morning to go fishing with your cronies and you didn't bring back any fish? It certainly smells like fish to me. And what do you mean it's not dead?

With the toe of her shoe, Lillie pops the woven lid from the basket handle, then pushes the lid off. She hops back and lets out a little shriek, clapping her hand to her mouth. "What in heaven's name--?"

They all look down at the basketful of mossy green, scrabbling, clawing, bubble-spitting creatures, all maneuvering to gain purchase up the slatted sides. Every so often there is a loud snap or crunch as one of the bigger ones catches hold of another with a heavy-jawed claw and clamps down.

"We weren't getting any bites, so the fellows decided we should go crabbing. Fred Schultz brought his trotline, so we spent a few hours and brought up tons. It was a hoot, and the boys tell me these make some good eating."

"What do you do with them?"

"Steam 'em up in a big old cook pot." Charley hooks the lid back on, and hefts the basket.

Emma has gone back to ladling; if the contents of the box don't cool uniformly, the soap breaks apart when it's cut into bars. "And where do you propose to do that?"

"Well, I had been proposing to do it out here, but that was before the soap factory geared up. I'll be doing these on the kitchen stove."

"Dad, I don't think—"

"Charles Beck, you'll do nothing of the kind!" But Emma is talking to his back, as he carries the dripping basket into the kitchen.

In the pantry, he has just gotten the large soup pot from under the cupboard and sat it on the stove when the first child discovers the basket. The swarm descends almost as though a nickel is involved.

"Do *not* put your fingers in there! Keep your hands out!" Lillie commands.

"What are they?"

"Do they bite?"

"Granner, what are you going to do with them?"

"Oooh, look—it's white on the bottom!"

"They're ugly."

"Can we keep them?"

"How many legs do they have? They look like big spiders!"

"This one almost don't got any legs at all. Where did they go?"

"I think that big one ate 'em all."

"They got orange claws!"

Charley has pulled on his heavy canvas gloves, and he toes a few of the kids aside so that he can slide the basket next to him in the pantry. He grabs up the first big crab from behind and lifts, but several others are hanging on like a daisy chain and aren't letting go. He drops them back into the basket, and decides to set the soup pot on the floor next to them instead. Lillie is as fascinated as the kids to watch all this, and even Emma is glancing into the pantry from near the sink. "But, Dad, they're still alive. How do you kill them?"

"No, no, you put them in the pot live and steam 'em 'til they're bright red."

"Bright red? But they're green now!"

"And white and orange!"

"How do they turn red?"

"Why do they turn red?"

"Cause they're mad you cooked 'em!"

"Yeah, they're *steamed*!"

Lillie's voice breaks through the chatter. "But what about cleaning them?"

"Nope. Just as is."

He reaches into the basket again, with his eye on the children, and lets one of the big crabs clamp onto empty canvas at the tip of one of the gloves. He yanks his hand back with a roar, crab flailing from the glove, and the children scoot back in horror, shrieking. Charley throws his head back and whoops at the prank, then pulls the crab from his glove and drops it in the pot.

"Dad, that was mean! Look, you made Jeanie cry." Lillie, unable to bend over and pick her up at this stage of pregnancy, instead presses Jeanie against her and rubs her head to soothe her. "Tell Granner he's mean."

"Mean, Granner."

"That's right."

When the kids realize they've been duped, they slide back in again for a better look. He grabs up a few more, again daisy-chained, and puts the whole string of them in. After a minute's consideration, he lifts the basket, tips it up, and begins to shake them into the pot. The first few slide in, but then a tangled knot of crabs tumbles out, skips over the edge of the pot, breaks apart, and hits the ground running.

There is perhaps a single second in which the entire company tries to puzzle out how this is another of Charley's tricks, when they realize in unison it is not. The kitchen explodes in shrieks and yelps, and a chorus of dancing feet desperate to avoid the claws of skittering crabs.

Arriving home from work, Ferd parks his car and crosses the yard toward the back porch. He hears yelling, shrieks, and wailing coming from the house, and breaks into a run. He bursts through the porch and into the kitchen, just in time to hear Charley say, "No, that's it. I think I got them all." Ferd looks around the kitchen at Lillie, Emma, and children pressed against the walls or standing on the kitchen chairs. Jeanie is the one wailing and pressed against Lillie on one side; Dorothy, red-eyed and clutching her mother's skirt, is on the other. "It's safe to come out now."

"Jesus, Mary, and Joseph, what is going on in here?"

"Oh, hey Ferd. I'm just cooking up some crabs. A couple hopped out of the basket and we had some excitement. But I got them all corralled again," he re-emphasizes around the room.

"Some excitement, indeed. You nearly had us all drop dead of a coronary, Charles Beck."

"Come take a look."

Ferd whistles his admiration. "Those are some nice looking hardshells. You'll enjoy those."

"We're having them for dinner."

"Well, I won't be. Anymore, they make me break out in hives. Too bad, too, because I love hard crabs. I can give you a hand cooking them, though."

Ferd rolls up his sleeves and joins Charley in the pantry. While they work, he tells Charley about summers growing up in Baltimore where boys crab all along the wharves and sell their catch for a nickel a dozen to the dock workers; how Sunday afternoons his father would buy some of the good crabs, brought up from the clean water out in the Bay, steam them, then lay out the last week's newspaper on the table outside their apartment building, and pick and eat them until all the Voiths and several of their neighbors were stuffed full of crab; and finally how, once the family moves to D.C., his father would still go down to the Maine Street wharf a few times each summer and bring back a bushel for the family.

The boys and a couple of the girls rediscover their courage enough to collect near the pantry door. When Ferd takes the lid off the pot to check progress, the steam smells of seaweed and saltwater. While he works, he gives the children instructions to collect Emma's discarded cardboard, Charley's old newspapers, and some butcher paper to lay out on the kitchen table, then some paring knives and the nutcrackers. Lillie and Emma just watch the preparation in stunned silence. "What sort of supper is this supposed to be?" Lillie wants to know.

"I thought only poor people ate crabs," Emma announces.

When the table is set for the feast, Charley Beck holds the soup-pot while Ferd tongs the crabs out onto the middle of the table in a large pile. "They're...orange," Francie says.

Ferd nods. "They're beauties. Get them while they're hot," he encourages.

"No one is going to make me eat one of those things," Margaret announces and promptly leaves the kitchen. Francie hurries behind her.

Johnny and Charley are at the table, but even they hesitate as they look at the alien creatures, which stare back with beady black eyes. "Are you sure they're dead?" Bernie wants to know.

Gingerly, Charley Boy slides one in front of him, and with two fingers turns it over and back again. "What are you supposed to do with it?"

Charley pulls up a chair, and grabs from the pile. "Okay, then, walk us through it, Ferd. How hard could this be?"

Pulling up the apron, ripping off the back shell, cutting off the eye stalks, scraping out the mustard, and snapping off the big claws, all before digging the meat out—that's how hard it could be. When Ferd mucks out the yellow-green mustard with his thumbnail and scrapes it off on the back of the discarded shell, the groans of disgust chorus around him. Even the boys are just watching, unwilling even to peel back the apron. Bernie plays with one of the dismembered claws that slides from the pile, until he finds that even a dead crab's claw can bite your finger.

"Okay, that's enough of this," Lillie announces. "I have a houseful of children to feed, and now no dinner."

"We can do something with the cold ham in the ice box, I suppose," Emma muses out loud.

"Well, Ferd, I guess I had no idea what a production this was. Fred Schultz said it was the easiest thing in the world."

Ferd looks around at his now-tiny audience, deflated. "But taste the meat! Look at that! A big chunk of backfin coming out whole, that's what makes it worth it." Ferd is tempted to eat it himself, and damn the hives.

Charley pops the nugget of backfin into his mouth and considers it. "I'm with you there, Ferd; this is mighty tasty. But I fear a body could starve in the time it takes to strip one."

"I just went slow so you could see. My mother can pick a crab clean in under a minute. Lillie? Won't you just try it?"

Lillie turns from the sink, drumming her fingers on the counter top. "Hmm, let me see: a big hard spider that you boil alive without cleaning it, that changes color from green to orange, and that you have to gut like a deer carcass with your fingers in order to eat? Oh, I think I'll pass on that. Boys, put those back. Dad, clean that mess off the table."

With a sympathetic look at Ferd, Charley begins to wrap the crabs in the butcher paper. Ferd pleads, "You *can't* just throw those away."

"I don't rightly know what I would do with them. Who would want them?"

Well, my parents for one, but Ferd can hardly bring them the rejects from his own dinner table. He can't keep the bitterness out of his voice. "Someone else from Baltimore, apparently."

The next morning, at the end of their garbage route, Sondy, Yoc, and Jiggs head into the Beck pump house for a long, cool drink of water. Jiggs is the first to spot the large paper sack on the bench, and the scrawled note, *For the Trash Boys—enjoy*. He opens the sack and breathes in. "Oh, Sondy, lookee what we got here."

Movie Night

August 1932

The girls love to watch their mother get ready to go out. When they are younger, they sit or lie on their stomachs on the big bed, or stand inside the doorway of the bedroom, while she sits at her dressing table. She tidies her hair and fixes in the ivory combs, pins the lovely pale blue and ivory cameo from Ferd at her collar, and puts the slightest bit of rouge on her cheeks. If the weather is cool, she puts a fitted jacket on over her best blouse or good dress. They keep up a running stream of words the whole time: "Oh, Mother, you look so pretty," "Which movie are you going to see tonight?" "Will you stop for an ice cream after?" "Owww! Stop kicking me!" "Well, then stop hogging the whole bed!" At some point, Lillie turns and gives them the look, and they quiet down. Soon after, Ferd—relegated to the bathroom to ready himself for his weekly date with his wife—comes back into the bedroom, hair slicked down, and the girls are herded out of the room.

Now that they are older, their favorite part of movie night is at the end. After Lillie and Ferd return home, talking and laughing to each other in low tones, Lillie stops in to the girls' room to sit on one of the beds and tell them all about the evening, and to hear about their day. It is her chance to be alone with them, to talk to them as budding women, and allow the girls to ask questions they can't raise in front of the rest of the family. Listening to her daughters gossip about how hard certain classes are, which teachers grade best, which girls are insufferably stuck up, and, most often now, which boys they like, she realizes how soon they will be grown and starting their own families. Each one now is closer to adulthood than to childhood. How quickly that has happened, almost without her noticing. She wonders whether she has done a good enough job to prepare them for real life.

She has no concerns for Eleanor. Athletic, confident, and practical, Eleanor has held her own practically from the time that she pulls herself up using Lillie's skirts. Tennis is her sport, and she regularly beats the local boys in the matches they play, to the point where many won't face her anymore. She has a knack for clever practical jokes, typically executed against Johnny and Charley, but is also a natural leader with a sense of responsibility. Lillie finds herself relying on Eleanor for many things, one of which is as an unsuspecting sounding board. That is why, early in Lillie's pregnancy with Jeanie, she uses a rare opportunity of being alone with Eleanor to practice discussing some of the facts of life.

They are walking home from church, and Lillie knows that if she thinks too long about it she will chicken out. So she just plunges in. "You're going to have a new brother or sister soon. Did you know that?"

"Really? Oh, that's so neat!" She takes Lillie's arm and hugs it to her, then continues to hold her hand as they walk. "What do you think it will be?"

"I don't know. What do you think?"

Eleanor considers. "A boy. We need a boy to make it even."

"That's very generous of you. Most girls would just want the unfair advantage." They smile at each other and continue walking. "Eleanor, do you know where babies come from?"

She answers without hesitation. "From God."

"Well, that's true, but they don't come directly from God."

"Oh, you mean from the angels."

"No, not from the angels. It doesn't just happen like that."

"It did for Mary."

Long ago, Lillie promised herself that she will arm her daughters with the knowledge that they need before menarche, so they won't suffer the confusion, panic, and humiliation that she did when her own time arrived. Emma, perhaps hoping to forestall the day's arrival, never prepared her for it, and that ignorance left Lillie with a painful memory. Even with her resolve, though, Lillie knows she is running out of time to have this conversation with her eldest, but also understands that Margaret requires a delicate delivery for this kind of information. Hence this early practice discussion with Eleanor, whom she feels certain will take it in stride if Lillie makes a mess of the attempt, which seems to be the direction this is headed.

"That's how we know Mary is so special, and that she is the Mother of God, because it doesn't happen that way for anyone else." She waits during a long pause.

"Then how *does* it happen?"

Lillie takes a deep breath. "First, you have to be old enough. And the way that you know you're old enough is that one day you'll feel something like a stomach ache, only lower down than your stomach, and then you'll see blood in your underpants, or in the toilet. But it's nothing to be afraid of; that's the way it's supposed to happen. That's when you go from being a girl to being a woman."

It takes a long time for Eleanor to sort through this information. "How old will I be?"

"I don't know. It's different for everyone. I was twelve and a half."

"So after that you have a baby?"

"No. It's just how you know you can. It takes a man and a woman to make a baby, and I didn't marry Daddy until I was almost twenty-two."

Lillie waits with dread for the next obvious question. She has never quite worked out in her head what she will say, and she is afraid her words and courage will desert her when she tries to describe *that* process. To her relief, Eleanor is concerned with other things. "You bleed?"

"Yes, usually for several days, and then every month after that for several days."

"Every *month*?" Lillie nods, but Eleanor is incredulous. "Well, what are you supposed to…"

"Just come to me when it first happens, and I'll help you."

They continue walking, almost at the house by now, as Eleanor puzzles over this new concept. Finally, she stops and puts her hands on her non-existent hips. "Well, it all just sounds messy to me."

Lillie laughs out loud, relieved that she has made it through her first awkward attempt at this conversation. She can now envision a path through the entire explanation with all three of them on the next movie night. "Oh, I agree with you there, sweetheart. But do me a favor, and please don't talk to anyone else about this yet. I want to be the one to explain it to the other girls."

In her best ten-going-on-twenty-three impression, she rolls her eyes and lets out a little huff. "You needn't worry; I have no idea what I would even *say*."

Lillie laughs again as she puts her arm around Eleanor and squeezes. Under her breath, she murmurs, "Amen to that."

ജ്ഞ

Francie, the beautiful child, is the musician in the family, more accomplished at the piano than Lillie ever becomes. The one blonde in a completely dark-haired family, her delicate features have always drawn comment and admiring looks. But rather than becoming vain and entitled as so many attractive girls do, Francie remains generous and levelheaded, even steely when circumstances demand.

One day, Lillie steps out on the porch in time to see several larger boys begin to taunt Dorothy and Bernie, who are playing on the sidewalk just outside the front gate. One has blocked their escape route into the yard, and another has just shoved Bernie. Not yet five but sturdy and pugnacious, Bernie is willing to go down swinging against one, but here he knows he is overmatched. Terrified, Dorothy is in tears. Before Lillie even makes it from the porch, she sees Francie storm from the side yard to the gate, burst through, and grab one boy by the ear and another by the arm. She stops the third from running by piercing him with a murderous look.

"What do you think you're doing? Does that make you feel big and important, ganging up on two little children? What a bunch of snotty-nosed cowards you are! How dare you?" They are all at least as tall as she, and heavier, but she has the ear of the biggest one, the instigator, and she twists it hard. "I know where you live, Edwin Livermore. What do you suppose your father will do to you once my father pays him a visit? Hmmm? No worse than I'll do if I catch you picking on little children again." She waits one more long beat before she lets go of the two, and all three run.

Edwin waits until he is far enough away before turning to yell, "I'm not afraid of you!"

Francie yells back, "Ha! Tough guy! You practically wet your pants, Edwin!"

She kneels to comfort her little brother and sister, wiping Dorothy's tears away with her sleeve, then takes them each by the hand and walks them to the house. Lillie, who has been watching from the porch in case she is needed, steps aside to let Francie take her charges into the house. She catches Francie's eye to smile her approval and says, "I think perhaps it's time for cookies and milk."

ꕥ

Margaret is the dreamy, artistic one, sweet-natured but with a romantic and, Lillie fears, unrealistic concept of life. Sometimes Lillie wonders whether Margaret's artist's eye bathes everything in a warm, gauzy light that makes it hard for her to see things as they really are. There is one movie night when Lillie sits on Francie's bed, recounting whichever movie she and Ferd have seen that evening, whatever is popular at the time, full of boys wanting, getting, losing, and getting their girls again, all tied up neatly with weddings at the end.

"Is that how it happened with you and Daddy?" Francie wants to know.

"Well, when I first knew your father, I thought he was a big nuisance. He kept hanging around and getting in the way."

"Getting in the way?"

"Oh, yes! Another boy was attempting to court me, and I was very interested in having him court me, at least in the beginning." She smiles at the memory. "I know I've told you that story before, about Daddy and Jack McGraw."

"But what happened? What changed?"

"Your father was very persistent. He wore me down." Eleanor and Francie laugh with her. Margaret lays stretched out across her bed, apparently only half listening. More seriously, Lillie says, "I came to realize how much he meant to me, and how I could always be completely myself with him. After that, there wasn't any question anymore." She shakes her finger at them with mock sternness. "Not that there weren't bumps along the way, mind you. Just because you find the right person doesn't mean it's all smooth sailing."

Eleanor asks, "Is that how you know you've found the right one? Because you can be yourself..."

"Because you marry him," Margaret answers from across the room. All three turn to look at her, as she gazes up at the ceiling.

"What do you mean, sweetheart?" Lillie asked.

"Every story ends that way," she shrugs, as she rolls over and props her cheek on her hand. "All the books and movies. They get married and live happily ever after. That's how it works." She rolls back down on the bed to gaze at the ceiling again, and exhales in a dreamy sigh. "I can't wait to get married so I can be happy just like you and Daddy."

Even the girls are struggling to follow her logic. "So, just being married makes you happy?" Lillie asks.

"Of course."

Eleanor snorts. "Well, if *that* isn't the silliest thing I've ever heard."

Margaret sits up on her bed. "It's not silly. It's true! Isn't it, Mother?"

Lillie is alarmed that this is the conclusion Margaret has drawn from living longest within the embrace of happy parents. "Don't you suppose that it matters which boy you marry?"

Margaret struggles to make her point. "But you marry him. That's how you know. That's how you know he's the right one."

Lillie moves over to sit down on Margaret's bed, and puts an arm around her. "Sweetheart, Jack McGraw was handsome and charming, and rich, too. From the outside, I guess he looked like every girl's dream. It would have been easy for me to be swept up in that completely, and be foolish enough not to notice your father, who wasn't flashy at all. I could easily have married Jack McGraw, but it wouldn't have made him the right choice. And I promise you, Margaret, that I would *not* have been happy." She looks at all of them. "You're all growing up so fast, and soon, well, there will be plenty of boys to choose from. You need to choose wisely." She squeezes Margaret in close to her and kisses her head. "Now, do I need to confiscate all those romance novels you're always reading?

ഇൽ

Movie night is a sacred ritual for the Voiths, which precious few things are allowed to disrupt. Only a true crisis or a new baby prevent Ferd and Lillie from enjoying their weekly night out together. In fact, one movie night is interrupted, already in progress, by Tommy's precipitous arrival. This particular night, the phone at 741 rings late in the evening, and Charley happens by to answer it. The whole house can hear his side of the conversation, since he is deafer on the phone than anywhere else.

"Hey, Ferd! What are…? What's that now? You…right in the middle of the movie, you say? Hope you got your money back, heh! So now you're where?" Emma has made it from her rocker in the bedroom to the bottom of the stairs in record time, and is trying to take the phone from Charley. Charley is holding her off with a stop-sign hand while he tries to concentrate on the conversation. "St. Ann's? Now, which hospital is that? … Oh, the infant asylum! Well, I'll be. That's an odd spot. How…?" Charley listens for an extended time, nodding and making significant noises. At this point, Emma is on the verge of an aneurysm, and is clawing for the phone, but Charley just turns his back, and she can gain no purchase. There are several children collected at the bottom of the steps by now, eager for the news. "Well, if that isn't a story to be told! Lillie okay? And the child? Uh huh, uh huh. Has she figured on a name yet?...Oh, that's fine, fine! Well, give them both a kiss for me, and go have a cigar for yourself. When will we see you?" Charley looks at his watch and nods. "Right-o. And Ferd? You stay away from all those loose women in there, you hear me? Okay then. Bye now."

As he hangs up, Emma lets out a yelp of insult and thumps him on the back. Charley holds up his hands as he turns around. "What's this, then? Oh, did you want to have a word, too? Well, why didn't you say so?" He winks at the children as Emma sputters in her fury. "Well, Voiths, it seems you all have a baby brother." A mixture of whoops and groans greets the news. "Your mamma's decided to call him Thomas Philip. And there you have it."

"That's not *it*! What else?" Emma demands, practically stamping her foot.

Charley's hand goes up to the back of his neck. "Else? Hmmm. Oh, well, everyone's fine."

"What time was he born? How long is he? How much does he weigh??"

Charley squints into the middle distance. "Ferd didn't say there was anything peculiar, so I presume within the normal tolerances."

Emma actually shrieks. "Charles Beck, I'm going to wring your neck." She interrupts him before he can remark on the rhyme. "And what are they doing at the infant asylum? To think of my child in that, that *place*! How could she possibly give birth there?"

"Didn't have a choice. Master Thomas demanded to make an immediate appearance, and Ferd had to improvise. It's not like they don't have the facilities, you know."

"Facilities that any street strumpet can use at her convenience! What will people say?"

Charley raises an eyebrow at her. "Maybe they'll say that your daughter has a fine new son, helped into this world by the good-hearted nuns of the Daughters of Charity." He turns to the whole collection of children now assembled on the steps, Bernie and Jeanie joining late and still rubbing their eyes. "Well, now, I say this calls for a celebration. I'm sure I saw some gingersnaps in the cookie jar!" He leads the cheering procession into the kitchen, leaving Emma to stew in her own juices.

ꙮ

Of course, most movie nights don't feature so much excitement. The household develops its own routine around the weekly event. While Lillie and Ferd finish dressing, the older children sprawl in the parlor with Charley to listen to the big floor console radio, which is turned up loud so he can hear. They are old enough to understand most of Eddie Cantor or Ed Wynn's routines, but everyone including Charley likes Joe Penner the best; his humor is so broad it's like being hit with a barn door. Emma keeps the younger children with her in the kitchen, distracting them with an early dinner; this way, they don't get upset to see their mother leaving, and Lillie is saved from having grubby hands and drippy noses wiped against her nice dress. Ferd and she come down the steps into the empty hall; he, opening the door for her with a flourish, and they, arm in arm, disappear from the house without a word to anyone.

Then, everyone is fed, Charley at some point telling the table, "Your Honor, he sopped his bread in my gravy, and I hit him!" Dinner is followed by homework, reading, or more radio, then time for bed, youngest to oldest. The girls, of course, have the latest bedtime, but on movie nights they often choose to head upstairs anyway to wait for Lillie's post-movie visit and news of the evening. The two boys are afforded some leeway to read in bed with flashlights, as long as they don't keep Dorothy awake past her bedtime, tucked in her little nook in the former closet. But especially on movie night, all three take advantage of the door cut into Dorothy's sleeping nook, the one that connects to Emma and Charley's room. They ease the door open and slide through quietly, while Emma is still deep in her prayer book, rosary beads in hand. If they disturb her before she's finished, she sends them packing back through the door and no reading for anyone. But they know they are safe and she is close to finishing when she begins to read aloud.

"Hail! holy Queen, Mother of mercy, our life, our sweetness, and our hope; to thee do we cry, poor banished sons of Eve; to thee do we send up our sighs, mourning and weeping, in this valley of tears..."

Soon, she closes the book and closes her eyes. Many times she doesn't even need prompting to start a story, which is sometimes from Lillie's childhood, sometimes from her own. This night, Dorothy says, "Tell a story about when you were my age! I love those stories. They change all the time!"

Emma considers her. "When I was your age, my papa kept two horses in the stable around the corner from where we lived, and paid the stable owner to take care of them. My papa taught me how to ride, and the stable man, Mr. Gustafson, taught me how to do everything else."

"Ride? A horse?" Charley Boy asks when he first hears this story. It is impossible to picture Emma, stern, serious, and crippled with arthritis, on top of a horse.

"Why, yes, I rode a horse for many years, right up until I met Charles Beck." The kids would be less amazed if she were to say she used to grow wings and fly to Persia. "I would go every day after school and as much as I could on Saturday and Sunday. I learned what to feed them, and the proper way to cool them down and groom them after riding. I took care of the tack, and Mr. Gustafson showed me how to check a horse's age by its teeth and to tell whether it's well-shod. Well, one of Papa's mares foaled…"

"What's a *maresfold*?" Dorothy wants to know.

"One of the horses had a baby. And I helped to take care of her, so she knew me, and she'd wait at the door of her stall for me every day. Papa let me name her, so I called her Blaze for the white mark on her forehead. I helped to train her to walk on a lead and take a bridle. Well, one Saturday, Mr. Gustafson was out and left one of the little stable boys in charge, so I decided to take Blaze out for a ride."

"Without asking? Oh, Gramal, that's naughty!"

"Yes, Dorothy, it certainly is."

"I did something naughty to a horse that time, 'member? The horse with the cart that was behind the house? Johnny and Charley told me to throw that corncob at it, and I did. But then Mother found out and gave me a spanking. But it wasn't my fault! They made me!" Dorothy has reminded herself of the injustice of the incident, and her eyes blaze in accusation at her wicked brothers.

"And what did your mother tell you when you said that to her?"

Dorothy slumps. "She said I threw the corncob, so I was

'sponsible, and that I can't do something bad just 'cause someone tells me too. And then she said that Johnny was the devil."

Even Johnny is surprised by this report. Emma gives Dorothy a stern look. "She did not say that Johnny is the devil. She said that the devil tempts us all in many ways, but it is up to each of us to resist him."

"Well, it was Johnny tempted me, so he's the devil."

"I believe that the devil just got to Johnny first." She casts the same stern gaze on the boys, who are busy looking elsewhere. "Now, do you want to hear the rest of the story, or not?"

"Yes!" Dorothy appears to have moved beyond her outrage. "What happened? Was it bad?"

"I'll tell you. I rode bareback, since she wasn't saddle-broken yet, and we went for a long ride, way out into the country. Finally, we stopped in a field that was full of wildflowers, and they were so beautiful, I decided to pick a big bunch to bring home for Mama. So I slid off of Blaze and started to pick the prettiest ones, and when I turned around again, what do you suppose I saw?" The children look at each other and shrug, stumped. "The tail end of my horse, galloping off in the direction we just came from, getting smaller and smaller every second."

Dorothy gasped. "Then what?"

"I yelled after her and started to run, but I saw it was hopeless. She had already disappeared. It took me over two hours to walk back home."

"Did you cry?"

"Oh, indeed I did, almost the whole way. I was afraid that Blaze had run away for good."

"*I* would have run away for good," Johnny says to Charley Boy.

"I considered that, too. That's one reason it took me so long to walk home; I was dragging my feet. But I was also thinking that Mr. Gustafson might not be back yet, and I could pretend not to know what happened to Blaze." Dorothy gasps again to imagine that Emma would consider fibbing. "Eventually I forced myself to walk back to the stable."

"What happened? What happened?" Dorothy bounces up and

down to know the ending.

"Well, the first thing I saw was Blaze, back in her stall, being groomed by the stable boy. The second thing I saw was Papa and Mr. Gustafson, staring at me with their arms folded over their chests, looking very cross. Mr. Gustafson said, 'You're not hurt?' I said, 'No, sir.' Papa said, 'You didn't fall?' I said, 'No, sir. I, I got off and forgot to tie the lead.'" Emma is taking each of the roles as she relates the story, looking stern or penitent by turns, and changing her voice to match. "Papa said, 'Miss, do you know that we were just about to go riding out to look for you? That we had imagined the very worst, when this little filly came galloping up to the stable door minus the thieving rider who had stolen her away without leave?' I had my head down in shame and was crying like anything. And then he took me in his arms and hugged me tight, and said, 'Oh, my sweet, what should I have done if you'd been hurt?'"

Dorothy gives a little shriek and claps her hands. She is always a fan of happy endings. Maybe they went to get ice cream after.

The boys, on the other hand, are mystified. "You didn't get the strop?" Charley Boy asks.

"We would've," Johnny observes.

"Right that minute," Charley Boy agrees.

"Oh, Papa never used the whip on me," Emma tells them, matter-of-factly, "just on my sister, your Aunt Mary." Lillie would undoubtedly be horrified to know that Emma is relating this information to the children. "He had a horsewhip he kept inside the house, since he never used it on the horses. Just on Mary."

"What did she do? Was she wicked?" In old stories, there is always a wicked stepsister, though Dorothy still isn't sure why a step is involved in being wicked.

"No, she wasn't wicked. She was sick, but he thought she was pretending, so he used the whip to get her to stop."

"Is that why she's crazy?"

"Who said she was crazy?"

Behind Emma's back, Johnny goggles his eyes and lolls his tongue at Charley Boy, who snorts back a laugh. "They do," Dorothy waves her hand at the boys, "and the girls too. They call her Crazy

Aunt Mary."

"I see you making faces, John Ferdinand, and don't think I don't." She turns back to Dorothy. "*Crazy* is an ugly word, so don't you start using it too. Mary wasn't pretending. She has a condition called epilepsy."

"Oh, where you fall down and roll around on the ground and swallow your tongue," Johnny demonstrates for them. "Granner and me saw somebody do that right on Georgia Avenue that time."

She points at him to sit up. "Not that kind. Her kind makes her go into a trance, right in the middle of whatever she's doing, even talking or eating. Just like someone pressed a button, and then they would press it again and she would pick up right where she left off. So it looked to Papa like she could just stop it if she wanted to. He thought if the whip didn't make her stop, it would at least teach her a lesson. So between the trances and the whippings, and then being afraid of both, she started to be different. Different from most other people."

There is a pause as the children consider this. Finally Charley Boy ventures, "But he was a doctor. You said so."

"Yes, he was. He was a surgeon." She can see that Dorothy is confused. "A surgeon is a certain kind of doctor; he can…"

"Cut you open with a knife and scrape out the bad stuff!" Johnny finishes for her.

Emma glares at him. "Is it time for you to go to bed, then?" He sits up straight and makes a show of closing his mouth as the nuns make them do, with his finger pressed against his lips. She turns to Dorothy again. "He specialized in cupping and leeching, which is a way of drawing impurities out of the body."

Charley Boy tries again. "Didn't he know she was sick? Couldn't he have made her better?"

"Even these days, no one knows how to cure epilepsy."

Dorothy says to Charley Boy, almost as though Emma isn't there, "Maybe he was just a bad doctor."

"Oh, but he was a very good doctor. I told your mother that she wouldn't have worried half so much when Charley Boy went in for mastoid surgery, if only Papa had been there to do it."

Johnny and Dorothy both look at Charley Boy in surprise. He looks a little suspect himself. "I don't remember it. Just that Mother told me I was a baby, and that's why I have a scar behind my ear."

"That's right. You were very sick, and you were only eight months old. You kept getting bad ear infections and they spread and took hold in your mastoid. Lots of children die from that, but you were very lucky." Now all the children are looking at her in alarm. "But with Papa it wouldn't have been luck. It would have been skill."

Dorothy pats Charley Boy's arm in assurance and sympathy.

Emma continues. "Papa told me lots of stories about all the people he helped."

"Like what?"

"It's getting late, and your mother will be home soon, wondering why you're not long ago in bed."

"Just one story, Gramal, please?"

She sighs and sits back in the rocking chair, thinking. "Well, after he came back from the war and then his service in Alabama…"

"The Great War?" Charley Boy interrupts.

"The Civil War."

Johnny sits back in surprise. "That was, like, a hundred years ago!"

"Not so much as that. I was alive during the Civil War, you know. Well, he went out to the Dakota Territory to be a doctor for the troops who were protecting people from the Indians."

"Were there cowboys too?"

"No, just soldiers and settlers. It was very dangerous, with just a tall fence and the soldiers to keep the Indians from overrunning them all. Sometimes they let a few of the friendly Indians in, and the captain who could talk to them said they called Papa *the big fat medicine man*. Anyway, Papa said that there was still society at the fort, and they had parties, and the ladies all dressed up. Well, there was a band that played for the soldiers and at the fancy parties, but the bandmaster, Mr. Clark, the one who stands in front with the baton, his eyes were diseased and he couldn't see anymore. And the doctor who was at the fort before Papa said there was nothing to be done for him; he was just going to have to be blind. Well, this doctor, Dr. Knickerbocker, always looked down his nose at Papa, and thought himself the better surgeon. 'So!' Papa said to his friends there, 'the great Dr. Knickerbocker finds himself stumped, does he? Says it's hopeless? Perhaps he is merely unequal to the task. Perhaps I shall call on Mr. Clark and invite him to know what a real surgeon can do!' And that's exactly what happened. Papa treated Mr. Clark and restored his vision to what it should have been. And when Mr. Clark, a particular friend of the Post General, told of the great success and started to lead the band again, why, everyone but the Irish flocked to Papa as their own doctor!"

Dorothy laughs with Emma, delighted at another happy ending, though she is still sorry about the whipped little girl with the trances.

And then at about this time, they hear it: the front door opening into the hall and indistinct but recognizable voices. They all hunker down a little, as though that will keep them from being found out. A moment goes by, and then Lillie's voice floats up the stairs: "Mother, I'm certain I don't hear the voices of any of my children up and awake who should have been in bed and asleep hours ago!"

By the time she is finished speaking, the kids have scrambled back through the door and dived back into bed. They can still expect a visit from Lillie to give them each a kiss goodnight, even though she is supposed to be kissing sleeping children. In the push through the closet door this night, Dorothy says to Charley Boy, "How close to a hundred do you think Gramal is?"

Charley Boy jumps into his bed. "I don't know. Pretty close, I think."

Wednesday, 19 April 1933

On Wednesday, the food starts to arrive, and the women with it. The change in routine at 741 is instantly parseable by the neighborhood tribe, as clear as smoke signals, summoning them to the aid of one of their own. Francie is still in her nightgown when she answers the day's first knock, believing that it might be Dr. Cavanaugh. Instead, it is Mrs. Morris from down the street with a covered dish. "Hello, dear. I know it's early, but I wanted to drop this off in case you all needed something for breakfast."

Even Francie, with her innate grace, isn't sure what's called for here. "Oh! Well. It smells very good. Thank you." There's an awkward pause while Francie considers whether she is supposed to invite Mrs. Morris into the topsy-turvy household. There is a line of children queued up in the hall, just out of immediate view of the doorway, waiting anxiously for Chloe to iron their clean but wrinkled school clothes, since no one thought to bring them in off the line last night and wouldn't have known what to do with them if they had. After the fresh delivery of groceries last night, and an on-time drop-off from the bakery this morning, Charley has had more luck with breakfast today than yesterday, but the lunch prep isn't complete and Tommy is still upstairs, shrieking as though he is being boiled down by the savages.

Dr. Cavanaugh rescues Francie by coming up the walk just behind Mrs. Morris and saying, "That's very thoughtful of you, ma'am. Francie, why don't you take that in to the kitchen?"

"How is Mrs. Voith, Doctor?"

"I know she's grateful for the kindness and prayers of good neighbors like you."

Of course he knows nothing of the kind, though he presumes it could be true. What he does know is that after Lillie wakes up last night, Emma feeds her almost an entire bowl of broth thickened with mushed up soda crackers, before Lillie falls back into the pillows, exhausted. He knows that Charley rigs up an ingenious system to allow Lillie to drink whenever she needs to without having to open the tent. All she does now is turn her head to grasp the rubber tube in her mouth and drink as though through a soda straw. He knows also that before he leaves for the night, she says to the room in general, as she's drifting off, "Leave the bedroom door open. This is scary, but not knowing is worse." If she has been awake since then, he doesn't know about it. He also can't know that when Charley makes good on his insistence that Emma sleep in their own bed, she complies without complaint, or that Ferd spends his third night in a chair, but in a spot from which he can feel Lillie's out-flung hand pressed against the isinglass.

"We'll be sure to tell her you stopped by. I know the family will enjoy the delicious dish you made for them." His soothing tone and smile send her on her way before she realizes she knows nothing more about Lillie's condition than she did when she was chopping potatoes and onions more than an hour ago.

Dr. Cavanaugh finally steps into the hall, where Chloe is just closing up the ironing board and several pajamaed children, grasping school clothes, hurry by him and up the stairs. "How are things this morning?" he asks her.

"Don't know yet, Doctor, sir. Mr. Charley says Miss Lillie and Mr. Ferd were both asleep when he looked in at five, and Mrs. Beck was about to go in to them. I'm just going up to get the little one now. Poor thing has been kicking up a fuss for the longest time."

But just as Chloe puts a hand on the banister and a foot on the step, there is another knock on the door. She and Dr. Cavanaugh exchange a look, as he continues up the stairs and Chloe turns back to answer. She groans inwardly when she sees that it's Mrs. Gardner, casserole dish wrapped in a tea towel, who arches an eyebrow before stepping past her into the house. "To see Mrs. Beck."

"She's indisposed just now, ma'am. I can take that for her…"

Mrs. Gardner sweeps through the hall, continuing toward the kitchen as Chloe tries to get ahead of her so she can at least give Charley fair warning of the approaching storm. Mrs. Gardner, though, forms a cold front that pushes the head winds before her, blowing open the kitchen door. Chloe can see the look that passes through him before that door closes and there is yet another knock on the front door. She hears Mrs. Gardner saying, "Well, the cyclone certainly has hit here, hasn't it, Mr. Beck," and Charley's honeyed response: "Well, it certainly has now, Mrs. Gardner."

Children trudge down the steps behind her as she opens the door. This time it is Alice and Eva Elliott from next door, Alice carrying pound cake still warm from the oven. "How is everyone, Chloe? Is Lillie doing better?"

Chloe is gesturing for them to come in, knowing they are welcome visitors, and opening her mouth to speak, just as she hears a sharp call from upstairs, "Chloe!"

Unnecessarily, Eva says, "Don't wait on us," as Chloe dashes up the steps.

Ferd is a little abashed as she gets to the top. "I'm sorry, I thought you were in the kitchen. Can you heat up some of the broth from last night, and maybe some tea also?"

She nods but says, "Tommy?"

"I'll get him."

Just then Dr. Cavanaugh looks out from the bedroom. "Ferd?" and Ferd immediately ducks back into the sickroom.

Chloe takes two seconds to put her head into the other bedroom to make sure that Tommy is still in one piece despite the blood-curdling screams, but knows that dealing with him now will take too long when she's already been given instructions.

Alice meets her at the bottom of the stairs. "What can we do?"

It's a sincere question, and Chloe only hesitates a beat before saying, "The baby needs to be changed and brought down for his breakfast. Just follow the hollering."

She takes a deep breath before pushing into the kitchen. Charley isn't immediately visible, but Mrs. Gardner has captured the school-bound children—finally in clean, ironed clothes, with all buttons properly in place—and pressed them into a work detail. As a unit, they look at Chloe, wild-eyed, pleading, trapped. "Mrs. Gardner, these children need to be getting to school."

"Dorothy, I still see crumbs on that board. And John, I don't know who ever taught you to sweep the floor." There is a muffled sound coming from the kitchen table; Jeanie has a fist half in her mouth to try to keep the crying in. "I told you to stop sniveling, Jean Louise. It's high time you learn to sit properly in a chair."

Chloe gives Jeanie a discreet stroke on the back of her head as she moves to the pantry to put the kettle on. Eleanor is there already, scrubbing the counter, her mouth set in a tight line. Then, as she retrieves the broth from the icebox, Chloe glimpses Bernie, tucked out of sight beneath the table. Perhaps Mrs. Gardner lost count of how many there are, and it's clear that Bernie is calculating when to make a break for the back door.

Once she has the broth on the stove, Chloe steps back into the kitchen. "Just as soon as I run breakfast up to Miss Lillie, I'll get this kitchen scrubbed up spic and span. But there'll be no explaining to the nuns if these children aren't in school on time. I'm sure you understand, missus."

There is a deadly silence as Mrs. Gardner turns herself squarely to Chloe, who doesn't flinch. All movement stops as the older children exchange worried glances. "It's obvious there's no discipline in this household, so I can't say I'm surprised. Children and servants don't speak unless they're spoken to."

Charley emerges from the cellar, wiping a refurbished piece of washing machine with a rag. He doesn't need to have heard the words that have been said. "Well, I'll be. I appreciate the help with the kitchen cleanup, Voiths, but you'll have to run to get to school before they sic the dogs on you." The broom hasn't even finished clattering to the floor before the children clear the threshold; Charley takes the opportunity to give the two younger ones the sign to high-tail it into the backyard. Chloe has already moved back into the pantry. "Now, Mrs. Gardner, we surely appreciate your visit and the fine dish you've brought for us. I'll be certain to drop the plate back off to you once the family's finished gobbling it up."

His attempts to sweep her in front of him out to the hall aren't working. She's holding her ground. "Mr. Beck, when one of my neighbors is taken ill, I know it's my job as a Christian woman to help out however I can. And I know you'll thank me to take this bedlam in hand and…"

"Now, Mrs. Gardner, I'm already thankful for the dish. You can't ask me to be thankful for much more; it's a hard burden to bear."

"Mr. Beck…"

"Mrs. Gardner, maybe you and some of the other Christian women can say a prayer for our Little Bedlam here, and we'll call it even. Thanks for stopping by." He is already holding the door open to the hall, and invites her with a sweeping gesture to precede him.

There are a few seconds of stand-off, but it's clear Charley isn't planning to move before she does. She huffs her way to the front door. (Charley would later say, "She left in a huff, with a tiff and a snit trailing close behind.") "Well, Mr. Beck, it's clear to me you have the family you deserve."

"I thank you, Mrs. Gardner, for giving me some of the credit."

Chloe comes through with a tray just as the door closes, and Charley almost puts his head against it, but he has a twinkle in his eye when he turns to Chloe. "My pa used to tell me that trials like that are discounts on your time in Purgatory. I sure hope that took a big chunk."

"My folks believe either you get to Heaven directly or you never make it at all."

"I wonder where Mrs. Gardner…" He cuts himself off. "Better not to speculate."

Chloe starts up the steps with broth, tea, and two plates of Mrs. Morris's breakfast casserole and the Elliott's pound cake for Ferd and Emma, just as the sisters start down the steps, Eva holding a freshly washed and diapered Tommy on her hip. He grips her free hand and chews her ring finger like an ear of corn. "I declare, Miss Eva, you're a natural."

At the bottom of the steps, Eva extracts her finger and hand from Tommy, who is unwilling to relinquish either, and passes him to Alice. "I need to get to work, but Alice can stay."

"Ah, that's right. You're over at Treasury, too. Be sure to tell them hello from me."

He gives her a little bow as he opens the door, and surprises Mrs. Labofish, caught with her knuckles inches away from the first knock. She carries a small picnic basket, and wide-eyed little Louise peeps from behind her. "Mr. Beck, I understand that Mrs. Voith isn't feeling well. I want to…"

Perhaps she's not certain what she wants. Charley is certain he wants a little less foot traffic. But as he so often says himself, people in Hell want ice water. Alice is already in the kitchen with Tommy in the big high chair, when Charley escorts in Louise and Mrs. Labofish and puts the kettle back on the stove. It's barely two minutes later that Chloe shows in the latest visitors, young Mrs. Tappan and Mrs. Monroe, trailed by her own Sarah. The two girls, both Jeanie's age, are sent into the yard to find her and Bernie. The next to join is Mrs. Clayton, who brings a freshly roasted chicken in anticipation of lunch and dinner needs.

In the pantry, Chloe finishes making tea and Charley pulls the nicer cups and plates from the cupboard. "Mr. Charley, I need to go see about the folks upstairs. I told them I'd be back up directly."

"And I need to rebuild the washing machine, or this family will never have clean clothes again." He rubs the back of his neck. "Go on up, I'll take care of the hen party."

It's a good thing that everyone brings food, since all the food is needed to feed the people who bring it. Charley emerges with the tea, plates, silverware, and napkins, and the women swarm him to take over even as they pepper him with questions: *How is Lillie feeling? What's ailing her? Where is Mrs. Beck? Are you and Ferd both home from work? Does that mean it's awfully serious? Is the doctor with her now? Do you think she'd like visitors?* Finally, it ends with the frightening statement, *Don't you worry now, Mr. Beck. We're here to help take care of everything.* He exchanges a look with Alice, who is obviously sympathetic. She has already been relieved of Tommy by one of the women, who says, as though Alice isn't in the room,

"What is the only unmarried woman here doing caring for a baby?"

Once the group of women closes back in on itself, Charley mouths to Alice *Run!* and slips out onto the spring porch and the far more understandable language of a non-working mechanical contraption. Just as he starts to dig a bit deeper into the innards, the porch door bangs open and three little girls—red-faced, wailing, and each one holding a different spot on her head—storm through, followed behind by Bernie, who says simply, "I didn't do it." Behind him, Charley sees that it's started to rain, steady and soaking, which means that there will be no getting these four back outside now. He looks plaintively at the Easy Wash. "Lord save us. It's going to be a long day."

Chloe returns to the sick room with her tray to clear the dishes. Lillie lies in her tent, propped up by her pillow mountain, eyes closed, but has eaten almost the entire bowl of broth and finished the tea. The plates for Emma and Ferd are dishcloth-clean; she should have brought more.

"What's going on down there, Chloe? It sounds like we're having a convention."

"Miss Lillie has a kitchen full of well-wishers, Doctor, sir. They'd surely like to come up and say hello."

"No," Emma and Ferd say together, and Dr. Cavanaugh agrees. "She needs to save her energy. Having all those people here would be too much."

The slamming door and penetrating shrieks of three-year-old girls make Lillie stir and open her eyes. From behind the isinglass, her voice has a fuzzy echo, as though she is speaking from a distance through cotton. "The broth is delicious, Chloe. Thank you for making it for me."

"It warms me to see you eating, Miss Lillie. That will push you right out of that bed. And when you feel like trying solids, we have a kitchen full of food just waiting for you." She looks to the other three. "Can I get you all some more of what the ladies have brought? It's been stacking up all morning. Doctor, sir, have you eaten?"

"I'll come down with you, Chloe. I have a few more patients to get to this morning." He tells Ferd and Emma, "I'll be back in a few hours. Remember, we're trying to go without the laudanum, but if she starts having trouble, you can give her a normal dose."

Ferd nods and says to Chloe, even as his stomach rumbles, "I'll take some of whatever you have."

"There's a fine roast chicken that's still warm from the oven. And I'm almost certain there's biscuits and corn bread."

Again the slow, far-away voice: "Go downstairs, eat at the table, Ferd. Civilized."

"Oh, Miss Lillie, he won't be able to eat a bite. Those women will swarm around, pester him so he can't get in a forkful. Better let me bring up a plate."

Dr. Cavanaugh follows Chloe into the kitchen, where women wash dishes from their impromptu tea. A sniffling child occupies the lap of both Mrs. Monroe and Mrs. Labofish, though the slabs of chocolate cake each clutches, and now partially wears, help to make things better. With all those legs, Bernie can't hide under the table, but he manages to swipe a few cookies and hunker in a corner of the spring porch, steps away from Charley and the Easy Wash.

Chloe scans the room. "Now, where's Jeanie got to?"

The women glance around and at each other and shrug. "She was just here a minute ago."

Chloe immediately walks out through the dining room to the parlor as Dr. Cavanaugh goes into the hall. She hears him say, "Chloe," and she joins him there. Against the back wall, Jeanie has her head down in her folded arms, on top of her drawn-up knees. Chloe stoops down and touches her gently on the head. "What's wrong, child?"

Jeanie lifts her head, her face red and tear-stained. "I want my mamma."

"Oh, baby—"

"It's not fair. They all got their mamma and I don't got mine." Which is true. After they form a huddle around the groundhog burrow at the back of the yard to poke at it with sticks, the burrow collapses under their feet, propelling three little inclined heads inward to bonk against each other, sending three little girls weeping into the house, but only two of the girls find a familiar and comforting place to curl up, where they are cooed and cossetted back into better spirits. And fed chocolate cake, too.

Jeanie puts her head back down and presses her palm against her ear. Dr. Cavanaugh says, "Her ear is bothering her again?"

"All week now. It's not so bad yet, but I think soon."

"You've flushed it with the syringe?"

"Yes, sir, but...well, Doctor, sir, I'm only here during the day." Hearing them talk about her, Jeanie huddles down even farther, muffling the sobs that make her shoulders shake. "Could I maybe take her up to see Miss Lillie, just for a few minutes? You see how hard it is."

Dr. Cavanaugh chews his lip. "She was drifting off to sleep when we came down. Let's wait until she wakes back up again and see how she's feeling, yes? I'll be back in just a couple of hours." Bag in hand, he collects his coat from the rack and lets himself out.

Chloe strokes the top of Jeanie's head. "Do you want some cake, child?"

Jeanie hasn't moved, muffling her reply. "I want my mamma."

Chloe knows full well how dangerous it is to say *maybe* to any child, but she feels it's necessary right now. "The doctor says that maybe we can go up and visit with her later. After she's had a nap and you've had a nap, too. Now, do you want some chocolate cake?"

Grudgingly, Jeanie looks up and nods. Chloe helps her to stand and then wipes her face with the hem of her apron. "Blow," she says, holding the apron to Jeanie's nose and then wiping again.

When Chloe pushes open the door to the kitchen and Jeanie spies the girls still where they were, she backs back into the hall. "All right then," Chloe sighs and takes her around the other way to sit at her place in the dining room. "Don't you move while I'm gone."

She passes through the kitchen and the women making plans among themselves, Tommy being bounced absently in a lap. It only takes her a minute to find Bernie's hiding spot, and she tells him quietly, "I've got cake for you if you behave yourself in the dining room. Go sit next to Jeanie and I'll be in directly."

Bernie sits himself as instructed. Cake is always worth behaving for, unless it's coconut cake, which isn't worth anything. He and

Jeanie are silent while they wait. Finally, Chloe comes back in with a big tray. She lays out an old bath towel on the table; glasses, only a third filled with milk, which is still courting disaster; and finally, two big slices of cake, each with a spoon. She ties dishtowel bibs on them both. "No crumbs, no spills, no noise, understand? I'll be back in no time."

Chloe takes her tray back into the kitchen as Bernie fists his spoon to gouge out a big chunk and shovel it in. He has only just started to chew when he sees that Jeanie is still just sitting, "S'matter?"

"Those people need to go 'way. I don't like 'em."

Bernie has the next big spoonful at the ready, hovering just outside his mouth, waiting for him to finishing swallowing. "I like this part."

ജ ☙

One of the problems of having a house full of well-intentioned, seasoned homemakers determined to be of help is that each one runs her own household just so, and does it without ten other homemakers involved. Every one of the women has at least a drop or two of Mrs. Gardner in her. Without a strong organizing force—Emma, for example—the women set out in all directions, each deciding for herself what needs to be done, and how. The result is that some things get done and redone and others don't get done at all.

When Chloe comes back out of the sick room, leaving Ferd digging into his chicken and corn bread at the card table, a covered plate waiting for Emma in case she wants something, and Lillie sleeping inside her bubble like some enchanted princess, she is horrified to find Mrs. Monroe scrubbing the bathroom tile, and Mrs. Clayton and Mrs. Tappan stripping the sheets from the girls' beds. Sheets are done on the weekends. "Sheets are done on the weekends," she hears herself say out loud, and belatedly adds, "Missus."

Mrs. Tappan, young, pretty, and just starting to show, begins to apologize, while Mrs. Clayton just looks at her. "We'll take care of this. No need to concern yourself."

Chloe puts her head back into the sickroom. "Just warning you, some of the housekeepers have found their way upstairs. I'll go ahead and pull the door closed."

Everywhere she turns, it seems, there are women who've taken over, sure that they are doing what needs to be done. She is shooed and dismissed, and she can't track what-all the women are fooling with so that she can go behind them to set things right again. She finds Bernie and Jeanie scrubbed down and in the parlor, Bernie on the floor playing cars and Jeanie clutching Sally tight against her and glaring at the other two girls, who sit stranded on the sofa with nothing at all to do. Pre-empted from any of the chores she has on her mental checklist, Chloe finds her way to Charley, still at the bottom of the spring porch.

He smiles in relief when he sees that it's her. "Hot hominy, a friendly face! I've been overrun by an army of women. Relentless. Unstoppable."

"Did you get to eat?"

"I'm thankful they didn't tie me down and force it into me."

She sighs and shakes her head. "They mean well."

"Thank the Good Lord for that. If they didn't, no one would survive. Well, least not a man and a colored woman; we don't get a protest."

"How's the machine?"

"I think I've got it all back in one piece. I was going to go get Ferd to help me wrestle it back up the steps so I can try it out."

Chloe puts a hand on her hip and looks at him from under her eyebrows. "These womenfolk been putting me aside all day, Mr. Charley. Not you too."

"Oh, so they mean well, do they?"

Chloe matches Charley step for step in moving the heavy machine back up the stairs and into the kitchen, which for the moment is blessedly empty. The area is spotless, with the baked goods covered on the counter and the perishables already tucked into the icebox, but Chloe sees immediately that things have been put away in the wrong place. *Lord, tell me they didn't rearrange the cupboards, too.*

Charley is hooking the washer up to the kitchen sink when Mrs. Clayton appears in the kitchen, trailed by Mrs. Tappan. "Where is the wash kettle?"

"The wash kettle?" Charley echoes. Mrs. Clayton still launders her sheets and other bulky items by setting up a large copper cauldron in the backyard over a low fire and agitating with a giant-sized wooden paddle. It often takes a full day to fill the kettle, heat the water, churn the sheets, and rinse them a few at a time in the rinse bucket before hanging them up. "Did it stop raining, then?" he says almost to himself as he peers out the window.

Mrs. Clayton rolls her eyes as though she is dealing with an imbecile, and turns to Chloe.

"Missus, Miss Lillie put the wash kettle away in the cellar once she got the machine." It's true that it takes the Easy Wash several cycles to match the volume of Emma's big old kettle, but it's useable in any weather and eliminates at least one time-killing and back-breaking step in the endless laundry cycle.

Mrs. Clayton squints from them to the machine and back again. She can only press a hand to her brow and shake her head as she brushes past Mrs. Tappan and leaves the room.

Mrs. Tappan stays behind, and looks at them both with a shy smile. "It seems we've fully crossed the line from helpful to burdensome. I just can't find a gracious way of excusing myself."

Charley winks at her. "It's like trying to stand firm against a whirlwind. We're having no luck either. Let me walk you to the door." Mrs. Labofish is dusting furniture in the hall as they walk through, and she arches an eyebrow. Charley says for her benefit, "Make sure you rest, now, Mrs. Tappan, and take care of that little one," then says low, "You come back anytime, my dear."

Once again, the timing is impeccable as Dr. Cavanaugh just now steps onto the front porch. He and Mrs. Tappan smile and nod to each other as they pass. To Charley: "How's the patient?"

"I haven't made it upstairs lately. Today we have all these industrious women who've helped us shake up our routine." He turns to smile sweetly at Mrs. Labofish, and finds she has somehow transformed into Mrs. Morris, who must have snuck back in to join the work crew. She carefully dusts the exact furniture that Mrs. Labofish attended mere seconds ago.

A few minutes later Dr. Cavanaugh joins Charley and Chloe in the kitchen, where Charley is making some additional adjustments to a gear mechanism. Above them, Tommy starts to cry, still just a low sound, and Charley vaguely wonders which one of the women has been mothering him. "Chloe, if you still want to take the children up, Lillie says she'd like to see them."

In the parlor, Mrs. Clayton has found the carpet sweeper and is attacking the carpet as though it has offended her. The two visiting girls are asleep on the sofa, heads at either end to avoid another collision. In the corner, Bernie has built a road of blocks and makes engine noises as he races two cars hurtling at each other into a head-on crash. Jeanie and Sally are tucked into Charley Beck's favorite easy chair. Jeanie sings a song while Sally dances; it sounds like *Bunny, bunny, Easter bunny. Bunny, bunny, Easter bunny.*

"Jeanie, Bernie, your mamma wants to see you."

Jeanie immediately scrambles up and starts to run toward the hall, but Chloe catches her. Bernie looks concerned. "I didn't *do* it."

Chloe almost laughs. "She wants to say hello. She misses you."

"Oh." That's obviously different, then.

She takes them both by the hand and gives them instructions as they climb the steps. "Your mamma's in bed and resting, so you talk in a soft voice and keep yourselves still, or I'll march you right back out again. She's behind a see-through curtain, but that's just to help her breathe easier, so you pay it no mind."

Charley comes up behind them on the stairs. "I'd like to put my head in, too. Make sure everyone's behaving theirself."

At the top of the landing, they see Mrs. Monroe still cleaning the bathroom. "It's a wonder the tiles aren't scrubbed off the walls," Chloe marvels under her breath, and Charley snickers.

Jeanie forgets herself as she gets to Lillie's bedroom and runs in, but stops when she sees the tent, even taking a half step backward in surprise. Lillie is giving them a drowsy smile through the isinglass.

"It's okay, sweetie bug. Don't be afraid. Come on up here with me."

Ferd is standing next to the bed and Emma is in her chair on the other side. When Jeanie starts to pull herself onto the big bed by grabbing the covers, Ferd lifts her up and sits her next to the tent, then lifts Bernie too. "Both of you, behave," he tells them; Lillie has invited them in over his objections. Chloe stands discreetly in a corner, in case she's needed to whisk them away.

"Hi, honey. What have you been up to?" Lillie's voice is croupy and low, unfamiliar, and so a little frightening.

"Playing cars."

Jeanie reaches tentatively and pats Lillie's hand, which has snuck out below the tent skirt. "Are you resting, Mamma?"

"Yes. Dr. Cavanaugh says I have to."

"Do you feel bad?"

"A little."

"When will you be better?"

Lillie waves off three adults who are just about to scold her for asking questions. "I don't know, Jeanie. I hope soon."

"Please be better soon."

"Oh, sweetie bug, I'm trying as hard as I can." Jeanie puts two fingers into her mouth and furrows her brow. "I'm going to close my eyes a little. Why don't you tell me a story while I'm resting?"

Jeanie thinks for minute. "Once on a time, there's a beautiful fairy princess that lives in a big white castle. With a yellow roof and pink shutters. She gots beautiful party dresses every day, and a sparkly crown. And she eats cake and cookies whenever she wants, and all her brothers and sisters have to do everything she says."

Lillie smiles, her eyes still closed. "That sounds wonderful. What's the princess's name?"

"Jeanie."

"Who didn't see that coming?"

"Hush, Dad. What else, sweetie bug?"

"So, umm, so then a mean old witch flew into the castle and yelled at the princess to sit still and eat her vegetables."

In an aside to the group, Charley elaborates, "We're all still smarting from Mrs. Gardner's visit this morning."

"And she put a bad spell on the princess's beautiful mamma, the queen, who went to sleep and woke up in a bubble that she couldn't get out of, no matter what. So she told the princess to go find Big Jesus, 'cause he knew what to do. So the princess went to look for Big Jesus all over. He was hiding behind a rock but no one said which one, and there were lots of rocks. Then he came out from behind the rock, and went with the princess to see the queen in the bubble, and Big Jesus said *You can come out in three days.* 'Cause that's how long he was behind the rock, so he knew how long it took. And so then the queen got out of the bubble and took the princess and they went to the castle and the queen got the big broom out of the closet and shooed the mean witch out and shut the door. And Big Jesus was there and said *Amen.*"

The adults blink at each other, a little stunned. Lillie's eyes glisten, and she and Ferd exchange a long look. "Amen," he whispers to her.

"Big Jesus?" Charley wants to know.

Lillie's eyes are closed again, but she smiles. "Christmas is Baby Jesus. Easter is Big Jesus." She reaches out to grasp Jeanie's hand. "Sweetie bug, that's the very best story I've ever heard. Thank you for telling it to me."

Tommy has been crying on and off for a while now, though the sound isn't coming from his crib across the hall as they might expect. With the spell from the story broken, they realize he's launched full-bore into an impressive wail.

"I'd cry, too, if I had all those women passing me back and forth all day long, never a minute's peace."

The wailing increases in volume and pitch as it approaches the open door, but the sound is wrong, as though it's coming from the floorboards. The baby—apparently pulled from his crib, set down on the floor and then somehow forgotten—propels himself lizard-like down the hallway, his too-full diaper leaving a slimy trail behind him. Everyone turns to look as he appears in the doorway, sits down in his own puddle, and continues his purple-faced cry. Lillie's face moves beyond pale to translucent, and her breath catches. She can hardly get out the words. "Who left the baby alone?"

Chloe scoops him up from the floor and wraps her apron under him to catch the spillage. "Bernie, Jeanie, you come with me, but watch you don't step in the wet." While they scootch down from the bed, Chloe says under her breath to Charley, "Those women need to get, now."

"Emma, it's time you get the big broom from the closet and shoo all those women out and shut the door. And Big Jesus and me'll both say *Amen!*" He hands her up from the rocker and follows her slow progress from the room.

"Lillie, we're going to let you rest now," Dr. Cavanaugh says as he finishes making notes on his chart.

Impulsively, Ferd reaches for her hand and presses it against his lips. "My beautiful queen."

She tries to smile but it crumbles from her face. "Oh, Ferd. I'm so sorry." Her breath is catching again, her voice raspy.

"No. Just please be better soon."

"I'm trying, dearest. As hard as I can."

ꕥ

Emma makes short work of the neighbor infestation, and Tommy, clean and dry once again, eats as though he's just been rescued from a year in the dungeon. In one pass through the house, Emma sees a hundred things that are out of place or just flat wrong. Once Charley runs the Easy Wash through a test cycle, Chloe takes the opportunity to start the sheets that have been pulled off the beds prematurely. Even though no one makes them and they fight the urge, Jeanie and Bernie both fall asleep in the parlor. At some point, Voith children start to trickle in from Nativity, and Chloe puts out some of the snickerdoodles and oatmeal raisin cookies from Mrs. Tappan. Normally, such a treat provokes grabbing and a bit of shoving, but the children are uncharacteristically quiet today.

"Why the long faces?" Charley asks as he snags a cookie.

There's silence as a look goes around. Finally it's Eleanor who says, "We were late to school. She made us late to school."

"Sister Fredericka scolded me. She said she was *disappointed*."

Dorothy's eyes, red already, well up once again at the thought. "It's not fair."

Francie pats Dorothy's arm, looking miserable too.

"Granddaddy, is Mother feeling any better?"

Charley rubs at the back of his head. "Well, she's sleeping right now."

"When can we go see her?" Johnny wants to know.

"We'll see what Doc Cavanaugh says when he gets back. Jeanie and Bernie were able to have a good visit earlier," he tells them brightly.

It is exactly the wrong thing to say to children who have endured a day of hardship and injustice. It is bad enough that they are shipped out of the house while everyone else stays at home, but that Bernie and Jeanie enjoy precious time with Lillie, while they are reprimanded and rebuked, is a bitter pill. It's already been three days without a bedtime visit, which looks now as though it will extend into four. They have all seen the isinglass tent, both last night and this morning, but have had no invitation to come in, no reassuring smile, no word of encouragement. Jeanie senses the darkening mood pointed in her direction and slides down low in her chair, a cookie gripped tightly in one hand.

Margaret, in the ninth grade at Paul Junior High School, appears in the kitchen red-faced, and drops her belongings on the table with a thump. It is the only time Charley has ever looked at Margaret and thought *furious*.

"Detention! They gave me *detention*! I was late for first bell, and they made me sit in a room for an hour with the likes of Jimmy Jameson, who broke some boy's nose during recess!" She throws herself down in the chair, and her rage dissolves into wrenching sobs.

Eleanor and Francie both pull up chairs to her and murmur comfort; even Charley Boy offers his handkerchief. Chloe brings over a glass of milk and stands behind her. As the sobbing subsides, Charley asks the assembled, "Didn't any of you just tell your teacher what happened this morning?"

Every child turns to stare at him in disbelief, and with such force that Charley rears back a little. Charley Boy finally says, "Granner, we're just kids. Grown-ups don't ever listen to kids."

Charley considers this and sees the truth of it. In any dispute between a child and an adult, everyone presumes the child is at fault. Attempt at a defense is seen as further proof of guilt and, even worse, a lack of remorse.

It is at this moment that there is yet another knock on the front door, and Charley groans out loud. "No. No!"

When he doesn't move toward the hall, Chloe does, but he stops her with a look. She gives him one back. "Mr. Charley, today's been a trial, but as far as I know, we don't leave visitors standing on the front porch."

Charley rolls his eyes and harrumphs, but goes to the door even so. He'd be less surprised if he found himself greeting a uniformed ringmaster leading an elephant. Instead, it is a pack of nuns.

It's impossible for him to cover his look of shock, but perhaps that's to be expected. "How do you do, sir. I'm Sister Floricinda, principal at Nativity School. The sisters and I wanted to pay our respects; we understand that Mrs. Voith has taken ill?"

"Ahh, come in, come in. I'm Charles Beck, Mrs. Voith's father." Even Charley is diffident in the face of all this virtue.

"These are Sisters Fredericka, Donald Ignatius, Grace, and Marcellus Xavier. They are some of the Voith children's teachers."

They nod to him in turn, and he nearly falls over when he takes in the face of Sister Donald, whose wimple and penguin-bibbed habit can't hide her movie star looks. "How *is* Mrs. Voith?" Sister Floricinda is asking.

"Ahh, she's resting right now."

"Are the children here?" Sister Fredericka suggests.

"Ahh, let me get them." Charley is having trouble regaining his natural equanimity. As he turns to the kitchen, he sees that Chloe has come into the hall behind him and she helps to fill in the gaps.

"Sisters, please sit down. Can I get you some tea?"

He puts his head into the kitchen. "Voiths, you have visitors. Make sure you're cleaned off when you come in."

On second thought, he steps into the kitchen to lift Tommy from the high chair and wipe him down before carrying him out to company also. The kids are still exchanging looks and moving hesitantly. "Well, come on then. Don't keep the sisters waiting."

"The sisters?"

"Which ones?"

"Well, all of them, I think." Johnny is backing away as though he plans to break for the spring porch. "There's nothing for it now, John. They're in the door, so you'll have to go say your howdy-dos."

A line forms, marching as to the gallows. Charley Boy mutters, "This is so not fair."

Bernie and Jeanie have no particular idea of what's going on, but it doesn't seem as though they are the ones in trouble, so there's no harm in following.

The nuns are still standing when Charley herds the children into the hall. Not one of the older children is willing to make eye contact, but Dorothy looks pleadingly at Sister Fredericka, who walks right over and puts her arm around Dorothy. The tiny nun is not quite a foot taller than her first-grade student.

Charley says, "Well, you know all of these Voiths. Here are the three that you'll be getting eventually. Bernard, Jean, and this one is little Thomas."

Chloe comes back down the steps with Ferd behind her, his brow furrowed. "Sisters?"

Sister Floricinda steps forward. "Mr. Voith, we just wanted to offer our prayers for Mrs. Voith. We didn't realize that she was ill. And we wanted to visit the children."

At Ferd's deeper look of confusion, Sister Marcellus smiles and offers, "Each of us had a late Voith child this morning. It took some time for us to realize that all the children were late, and then to understand why."

Ferd throws a look at Charley, who tells him, "Like I said, we're all smarting from Mrs. Gardner's visit."

Chloe says again, "Won't you let me fix you some tea?"

Sister Floricinda has moved to Johnny, her favorite, and puts a hand lightly on his arm as she says, "Oh, thank you, no. What we'd like to do is have you all join us in a prayer for Mrs. Voith."

As Chloe takes Tommy, Charley whispers, "Ask Mrs. Beck to

come down. She'll want you to stay with Lillie." He meets Emma on her slow progress down the stairs to join them in the hall.

There is a nun per Nativity student as they all kneel. Charley helps Emma to her knees on the rug. Bernie retreats to stand near the kitchen door. Jeanie has sidled over to Sister Donald Ignatius, openly staring, transfixed, and stands close beside her as the nun kneels to pray. Sister Grace, who taught Margaret last year and has Eleanor now, puts Margaret next to her. Even that kindness can't erase the thought that Margaret remains the one Voith to receive no absolution for today, an ugly blot now on what has been a spotless record.

"Dear Lord, we pray for our sister, Lillie Voith, and ask that You bless her with the gift of health, and return her soon to the heart of her loving family. We pray for her family, that they remain strong in their faith through this difficult time, and find comfort in Your merciful love. In Jesus' name, we pray."

The chorus joins in. "Amen." Francie wipes tears from her cheeks.

It takes more effort for Charley to help Emma back up from her knees, and she leans heavily against him. Above them, Chloe and Tommy appear at the banister overlooking the hall. "Mrs. Beck, Mr. Ferd. Miss Lillie is awake now." Emma is the first to the steps.

The sisters excuse themselves soon after Chloe's announcement, but with assurances of their own and God's interest in a positive outcome. The vigil remains in the hall, the children deciding this is their best hope for getting in to see Lillie and no one willing to risk being left behind if the invitation finally comes. The wait is nearly unbearable for them, particularly as they watch Emma and Ferd disappear upstairs, Chloe come and go with trays, and, finally, Dr. Cavanaugh stride through with his black bag and just a single nod to all of them.

Charley comes into the hall with Tommy, who is droopy in his need for a nap. There is an expectant clench in the children. "Did anyone say you can't go upstairs?" he wants to know. "If they did, I'm not sure how you'll use the bathroom or go to bed."

It is a shared but unexplainable certainty: if they go upstairs, it will be irresistible to try to go into the room, but if they are rebuffed, it will be more than they can reasonably bear.

"Granddaddy, can't you please ask if we can see Mother now?"

"Yes, Eleanor, I can." He and Tommy make the trip up the steps; moments later, he comes back down alone. "Your mother says she wants to see you all, and as soon as you can get up there. Your father and Gramal say be quiet about it."

It is the fastest scramble with the least amount of sound the Voith children have ever executed. At the door to the bedroom, though, they pull up, unsure. The oxygen tent looks as though it has swallowed Lillie, and she is growing small and distant as it digests her. She pats the bed on both sides of her. "There's room."

Emma makes a harrumphing noise and Ferd says, "Lillie."

The words her brain forms but her lungs cannot support are, "Stop it, both of you. What possible harm do you think this will do? My children want to see me and I want to see them. At least let me have that." What comes out is: "Stop. What do you think?"

The children stop midstride, misapprehending her words. She smiles encouragingly at them and pats the bed again. They climb up carefully, attempting to forestall the next reproach, from whichever quarter it might come.

She gestures at the enclosure. "Don't mind." She tries to take them all in, look at each one in turn, push herself out to them.

They are silent, with no idea where to begin. Of all of them, it is finally Johnny who is able to say, "How are you, Mother?"

She beams at him. "Tired. Behaving?"

He blushes and looks down, "Yes."

She looks around. "What else?"

They know without discussing it that *what else* will only be happy things from the last few days: Francie's selection for the recital, Charley Boy's receipt of the lone perfect score on the big math test, Margaret's completed painting. Dorothy's news cuts close when she says, "And Sister Fredericka came to see us and gave me a hug!"

Lillie looks up at the adults. "The fine Sisters of the Third Order of Franciscans called on us this afternoon to see how you were feeling," Charley explains. "Led us all in prayer."

"Mmmm," Lillie responds and her eyes flutter closed. Her hand slips out under the tent and casts about among the blankets until it touches another. She opens her eyes to see that she has caught Francie's hand, and says, "Hail Mary."

It takes Francie only seconds to realize what Lillie is saying; once she starts, others join in, and Lillie's lips move to form the words: "Hail Mary, full of grace, the Lord is with Thee. Blessed art Thou among women, and blessed is the fruit of Thy womb, Jesus. Holy Mary, Mother of God, pray for us sinners, now and at the hour of our death. Amen."

Lillie squeezes Francie's hand but doesn't open her eyes. Dr. Cavanaugh says gently, "Time to say goodnight, I think."

Lillie pushes her eyes open and says, "Kisses first. Can open the tent?"

Emma and Ferd again make protest noises, but Dr. Cavanaugh speaks over them. "It should be fine for a little bit."

What an odd turn this is, when it is always Lillie who visits each of them every night, bed by bed, hearing prayers, tucking in, answering questions, ruffling hair, kissing cheeks, sending each child off to sleep wrapped in the glowing certainty of her love. This backwards procession is better than one more bedtime with no goodnights, but Lillie's normal comforting scent is cloaked in menthol, and the tent, even just ducking inside for a few seconds, even with the flaps open, feels like a threat. It's not just the girls who are red-eyed as they drag themselves from the room.

ꙮ

The pigeons aren't having a very good week either. Tucked out of sight, up in the barn, they are no one's primary concern. Charley makes it into the loft a few times to top off water and toss in feed, but these pigeons have been raised in a thoroughly German household where *clean* is the starting point and *immaculate* is the expected outcome. Birds are never the tidiest of creatures, but as the pigeons thrust their heads about and coo, they sound a querulous note, as though alarmed now to find themselves up to their tail feathers in down and droppings.

It isn't even five o'clock when the children kiss Lillie goodnight, emerging from her room in no better spirits than before. Charley decides to *take their mind off a toothache by putting a thumbtack in each shoe*. To that end, he sends the boys out before dinner, armed with trowels and buckets, and with strict orders to leave the pigeon coops in the state Ferd would, if only he were available to do it himself. There is inevitable groaning, until Charley tells them, "If you make me pick something else, I promise it will be worse."

Chloe offers again to stay beyond her normal time, and again Charley declines. Dinner will be easy with all the food in the icebox, but he has to find a suitably distasteful activity for the girls, too. As she pins her hat on, Chloe gives him the answer. "Silver polishing. The ladies never got that far today."

"Genius!"

That is not the word the girls use when he describes the assignment, and he considers their position. "Well, the boys are cleaning the pigeon coops. Just say the word and you can start scraping too."

Hiking back from having checked that the boys really are scraping, he finds the smallest ones poking at the little cast iron stove in the yard. "No, I'm not going to light it for you. You'll yammer at me for bread crusts and water."

"I just want to burn sticks," Bernie promises.

He's considering that Dorothy is old enough to be doing something productive, like helping him cut asparagus, when he sees Ferd's older sister Sophie. She's by the Elliott's front gate, visiting with Mrs. Elliott and her daughters. Charley makes his way out through the front yard to join the ladies, and he tips his hat all around. "Why, Sophie Price!"

"Why, Charley Beck!" They share a warm smile, but then Sophie grows serious and puts a hand on his arm. "How is our Lillie doing?"

"She's still on liquids, but the kids just went up to see her and they had a fine visit." He can hear the hollowness in his voice. "Did Ferd call you?"

"Oh, he didn't have to; you know how word travels. Miss Alice was just telling us about this morning, so I promise not to intrude. But you know Mom, Dorothie, and I are all right here, and I expect you to call if you need anything. Anything."

"I think it would do Ferd good to see you. Why don't you come on in?" He winks at her. "He's been spending far too much time with my lovely bride the last few days." He tips his hat again to the Elliott women. "And just to clarify, you ladies are never an intrusion. You stop by anytime."

Charley offers and Sophie takes his arm. They rarely see each other but share a quiet affection. Charley reminds her of an older version of her husband Elgie, and she's just the kind of no-nonsense woman that has always appealed to him. He opens the front door for them, and they are met by the sound of Tommy wailing from above. Charley looks heavenward in mute appeal. "I guess I'll get them both, then," he tells her.

"I'll start some tea."

He heaves Tommy up from the crib. This time he's wet but not stinky, and Charley does a quick and expert diaper change that includes constant coverage to prevent an unwelcome squirt in the eye. With the baby slung under his arm, he puts his head into the sick room. Dr. Cavanaugh is already gone, promising to be back near normal bedtime. "Ferd, your big sister's in the kitchen. Why don't you go down and say hello." He see's the hesitation. "Tommy and me'll keep your chair warm for a few minutes."

Charley dandles the baby on his knee, while Tommy chews on his fist and makes a low noise in his throat, which becomes a buzz with the vibration from the jiggling. He thinks at first that Emma is sitting perfectly still in her rocking chair, staring vacantly at the tent, but then he realizes that her lips are moving silently while her finger traces down the text in her open prayer book. It looks for all the world as though she is a blind woman, sussing out words by touch.

"Em," he starts to say, then decides to leave her be.

"Baby," comes the raspy voice from deep inside the tent, and he nearly drops Tommy in his haste to go to her side. Emma snaps into focus at the word, but allows him to step in.

"Lillie? What do you need, sweetheart?"

"Baby," she says again, and makes a feeble gesture at Tommy, who's squirming and starting to fuss.

"Here he is! We're about to go find him some supper."

"Kiss."

Her gesture toward herself is swallowed in the bedclothes, and Charley cannot fathom what she means. Finally, he gives Tommy a kiss on the head and looks to see if this is her intent. He laughs out loud to be hit full force with an Aggravated Lillie expression—narrowed eyes, compressed mouth, cocked head—so characteristic, so *normal* that he actually feels a sting behind his eyes. "I guess you're saying that's not it, then."

Finally, she's able to lift her hands high enough for him to clearly see them signal *give me the baby.*

Charley weighs the alternatives. He knows that if Ferd were here, he would never allow this. Emma will almost certainly protest when she sees what he intends. It's even money what Dr. Cavanaugh might say. But it's Lillie there, distorted behind the isinglass, but it's still Lillie, and she has a right to demand, to have a say in what goes on here, in her own room, in her own house, with her own children.

With Tommy held in one arm, he turns the oxygen down, waits a moment, then peels open a flap of the tent.

"What is it? What's wrong?" Emma says from behind him. He can hear that she is struggling to get up from her chair; she's been sitting too long.

"I'm going to put him in your lap and lean him against you. Can you make a crook with your arm?" Lillie nods once as she does it, her soft gaze on Tommy.

He leans in to arrange the baby and is almost knocked off balance when Emma hits him in the back. "What are you doing?" she demands. "What do you think you're doing?"

Charley straightens up but stays ready to reach for the baby if he starts to tumble. "Emma, be still. Let her have her moment."

Tommy stops fussing as soon as he presses into Lillie. She puts her head down into his sleep-tousled hair, unable to inhale his reassuring baby scent, but he turns his face up to hers and reaches out. His open hand lands against her cheek and rests there as though in benediction, and they gaze at each other. *Sweet little baby, my little baby, who will you be? It doesn't matter who I am, I know you love me. Sweet little baby, my little baby, where will you roam? It doesn't matter where I go, I know you're my home. Sweet little baby, my little baby, will you be true? It doesn't matter who I love, I'll always love you.* She sings it to him in her head while her mouth forms the words, and now his hand presses against her lips, fascinated by their movement. She hopes he can catch the words before they disappear, and she kisses his hand to help seal them in.

Tommy starts to slide, and Lillie is too limp to hold on; Charley scoops him up. Lillie's head is already back against the pillows, her eyes closed. Just before he lowers the flap again, he is almost certain he hears her say, "I'm ready now."

Thank You for Another Fine Year

Fall-Winter 1932

"Next!" Charley calls as he unties the knot at the back of Johnny's neck and shakes hair out of the sheet onto the grass. Johnny runs his hand over the stiff bristles of his fresh razor cut. Charley Boy, already shorn, is doing the same thing. It's irresistible, like wiggling a loose tooth or picking at a scab.

"Okay, Miss Dorothy, let's set you up here." Charley stacks some big books on the stool and helps her to climb up and sit. With a practiced flick of the wrist, he whisks the sheet around her and ties it at the nape of her neck. The sheet covers the stool, the books, and all of Dorothy save her head. After a stroke or two of the comb, he claps onto her head a shallow metal bowl that is almost identical to the helmets once worn by the doughboys. Charley has trouble restraining a guffaw, but it won't do to laugh; the young ones are skittish enough already, and a laugh at their expense will start the waterworks.

"But I don't want the bowl. I want the razor too."

"Well, now, the razor is for the boys. You'd look awfully funny going to your first day of school with a bristle head, wouldn't you?" Dorothy slumps on the stool and Charley pokes at her. "Sit up straight and still now, so I get the cut right. You don't want me to miss."

Back-to-school haircuts are usually Emma's job, but today she is busy with the first of the apples and the early grapes, and Charley is the substitute barber. He presses the bowl against the nape of Dorothy's neck and clips hair to the edge of the bottom lip. He walks around to the front, slides the bowl forward a touch, and snips off the bottom of the bangs that protrude. He removes the bowl with a flourish, runs a comb through to find any stragglers and makes a few final adjustments. The cut is exactly two lengths: one for the bangs, and one for the rest, which ends one inch below her ear. Charley has this down to under five minutes. The boys get done in four or five strokes that take little more than thirty seconds.

He peels off the sheet. "Off you go then. Margaret? Francie? The chair is open."

The girls, sprawled on a blanket in the yard, look up from the magazine they are sharing and laugh. "No thanks, Granddaddy. We'll do our own."

"Are you saying that my hair-cutting skills aren't what they ought to be?"

"Oh, no, Granddaddy. I would *love* a bowl cut!" Margaret declares dramatically, and they both collapse into hysterics.

Emma comes down from the spring porch with a basket of laundry for the line. Dorothy is kicking at a dirt patch, still miffed about the haircut. "Why do boys get to do everything they want, and girls never get to?"

Charley is dismantling his barber chair. "Like what, now?"

"I don't know." Kick. "Like setting off firecrackers, and dropping water balloons on you from the trees." Kick. "They light fires in the woods and then pee on them. It's not fair." Stomp. "Why can't girls pee like that?"

Emma looks over from the laundry at this, her mouth set. "And exactly who has been doing this in front of you?"

All eyes turn to where the shorn boys have been lounging. As if by magic, they have melted away.

ꕥ

After dinner, Emma claps her hands at the bottom of the stairs and yells, "Shoes!" There is a great crashing about as the children stampede down into the hall, carrying last year's school shoes. Ferd follows behind with several shoeboxes. Lillie sits on the hall sofa holding week-old Tommy, with Jeanie sidling in next to her, and assesses the possibilities for swaps.

Knowing the answer, Ferd asks over the ruckus, "Do anyone's shoes still fit?"

No. As usual, then, Margaret's go to Eleanor, Eleanor's to Francie, and Charley Boy's to Johnny. "I can't get my feet in," Johnny says, sitting on the floor with one foot halfway into one of Charley Boy's old shoes.

Ferd kneels down on the floor in front of him. "Stand up. Let me see. No, point your toe to slide your foot in." He holds the shoe as Johnny steadies himself with a hand on Ferd's shoulder and tries to work his foot into the shoe. It's hopeless. "Well, so much for that," Ferd sighs.

"Well, the boy has shot up like a beanstalk this summer," Charley observes. "He's as tall as Charles now."

As for Dorothy, Francie's shoes are far too big for her, even stuffed with newspaper. "Oh, Ferd, she'll trip on the stairs," Lillie tells him as Dorothy clomps back and forth as she has been directed. "Where are the other shoes you brought down? Mother, see what you can find there." Over the years, Lillie has saved shoes that still have good wear left in them for just this eventuality. Emma picks out a pair, and Ferd helps Dorothy put them on and tie the laces. "Oh, now there you are. Those will do nicely! Do they feel all right? They don't pinch? Good. So we're down to just needing three pair."

Bernie has been sitting among the scattered shoes, trying them on and attempting to tie a bow as Francie has shown him over and over. He stands up triumphantly. "Did it!"

"Well, look at that! You certainly did!"

"You put them on the wrong feet."

"Those are girls' shoes."

Ignoring his brothers, he asks Lillie, "Do I get to go to school now?"

She shifts the sleeping baby over to her other shoulder and

reaches out to him. "No, honey, it's Dorothy's turn to start school this time. You have another year before you go to school. You still get to stay home with me and Jeanie, and the baby."

Beside her, Jeanie is tugging at her sleeve. She is sitting with her legs stuck straight out in front of her, and her toes don't even reach to the edge of the sofa. She is barefoot. "I don't got shoes."

"I know, sweetie bug, but these are school shoes. You don't need school shoes yet. Thank goodness."

"I'm not a baby," Bernie insists, looking at Jeanie. "I'm big enough to go to school."

"Why do you want to?" Johnny wonders.

"I'm not a baby neither," Jeanie insists back.

"Charley and Margaret always get the new shoes," sighs Francie, whose school shoes are invariably two years old.

"Should have been born first," Margaret flounces at her.

"Okay, that's enough of that," Ferd tells them. "Everyone, shoes put back away upstairs, now. Margaret, you get to collect these up and put them back in their boxes. Take them up to your mother's wardrobe." Francie shoots Margaret a look back.

As the children troop toward the stairs, Lillie says, "Well, it looks like we'll be going to Ida's tomorrow." There is a chorus of whooping that propels them all upstairs, as though they have been told to get ready to go right now.

Ida's Uptown Department Store is a shopping nirvana, filled with untold riches of merchandise that cost nothing to behold: things long desired, things unknown to exist until this moment but now instantly coveted, things with no discernable purpose but still, somehow, crucial. But the thing that Ida's has above all else, that makes shopping for shoes as popular as a trip to Beverly Beach, is the x-ray machine.

The x-ray machine in Ida's shoe department is a tangible demonstration of what happens when modern technology intersects with American ingenuity. No longer does the shoe salesmen have to guess at how well a pair of shoes fits his customer, pushing in on the toes or feeling around at the heel. No, he just puts Mister or Missus, Junior or Janie, in a pair of shoes, stands them on the platform and pushes the button. There in the viewing porthole, displayed in fine black and white contrast, are the foot bones, wrapped in a fuzzy shadow of toes and heels, and finally overlaid by an outline of the shoes. The best part is, it's free and Ida's lets the clientele try it as often as they like. The kids like to try it pretty often.

The Voith children know the rules about these outings, and the older ones strictly enforce the rules on the younger ones, since misbehavior tends to paint with a broad brush that besmirches even the most innocent. Hands in your pockets, center of the aisle, inside voices, and no asking for anything. Every child has been left at home at least once for rules infringement on a previous trip.

It's Saturday morning: Emma is still canning, and Ferd has a half-day shift, so Charley has agreed to come along. This is Lillie's first expedition with Baby Thomas, so the extra supervision comes in handy. As the troop makes its way inside, Charley and Lillie are greeted warmly by the manager, Mr. Thompson, who fully appreciates the revenue stream generated by a now thirteen-person household living mere blocks away. "What can we help you with today, Mrs. Voith? Mr. Beck?"

"Time for shoes."

"Of course, of course. Probably some new school clothes as well?" he suggests hopefully.

The kids have already made for the back of the store where the shoes are sold. Since it's the Saturday before school starts, the department is busy, and the Voith children aren't the only ones with the idea to give the x-ray machine a workout. Because every kid there has had similar coaching about the consequences of bad behavior, a line forms with no prompting, each child waiting a turn. It's a more orderly line even than the one for the diving board at the pool, where shoving or cutting gets you thrown out for the whole day. Here, when one of the less socialized kids neglects to observe protocol to stand down when a salesman approaches with a customer, one of the other kids will pull him away by the arm and hiss in his ear to follow the rules. The x-ray machine at Ida's breeds a self-policing community.

Dorothy whispers proudly to someone beside her, "That's my

brother," as Charley Boy steps up to the machine, the salesman beside him to assess fit. Both Charleys are less interested in the resulting image than in how the machine works, and they each ask probing questions of the salesman, who is delighted to seem as though he knows all about it, and whose answers become increasingly suspect.

Francie has Jeanie's hand as they reach their turn, and helps her stand in the right spot. The machine makes a metallic buzzing sound and a distant *chunk* as the picture shows up in the viewing portal that Jeanie has to crane her whole body to see. "Look, Jeanie," Francie points out to her. "That's what your toes look like under your skin. Let's see what mine look like." Francie x-rays her own foot. "See, mine are just bigger than yours."

Jeanie doesn't even know the words to form the questions she wants to ask, but it is the most amazing thing she has ever seen. But, oh, the countless hours of fascination and entertainment this machine will offer in coming years!

ꕥ

The boys pile out of the T almost before it comes to a stop. The day is cold for early November, and they have on their work coats and watch caps. Charley takes his time getting out of the car, and surveys the lot to assess what needs to be done. "Get the tools out of the back, and we'll split up some firewood before we light the rubbish pile." He knows that Charley Boy's and Johnny's interest is in the annual bonfire, and he uses that incentive to get some enthusiastic exertion from them.

They pull out axes, the crosscut saw, some shovels and heavy rakes, blankets and brooms, the gas can and torches. Johnny eyes the lunch pails, wondering how early he might be able to open his up. Charley sees him looking. "Better not, boy, or you won't make it to suppertime." As a simple lesson in resource management, Charley has taken to letting Johnny go hungry if he empties his pail too soon, rather than sharing anything from his own lunch.

He sets the boys up with the crosscut saw at one of the huge felled chestnut trees. Since Johnny's latest growth spurt, he and Charley Boy are well-matched on opposite sides of the saw, and Charley watches for a minute to see that they set a rhythm before he picks up an ax and starts to split logs into manageable lengths of firewood. It's not long before coats and hats are lying off to one side, and sweat is beading. "All right," he says when he judges they've all made good progress, "go get the lunch pails." They each pick a log or stump to sit on out in the sunshine, enjoying the break and the extra sandwiches tucked into their pails by thoughtful women. Then they are back at it, the rhythm of the saw blade punctuated by the regular crack of the ax making a kind of soothing music. Charley pauses to swipe his handkerchief across his forehead and open the canteen, which he passes to the boys. Another car pulls up next to the T, and Mr. DeMarr and Mr. Downs climb out. Charley screws down the canteen cap as he ambles over toward the men, but says over his shoulder, "You're still working."

Charley Boy and Johnny pick up the rhythm again, though they steal glances every so often. It won't be long now. Clyde DeMarr, a barrel of a man with a stub of unlit cigar permanently clamped in his teeth, uses the corner of a fence post to pop the top off a bottle of his freshly made homebrew, which he hands to Charley. Cecil Downs has a long head and a laugh like a braying donkey, and right now he is thoughtfully picking his teeth with his pocketknife. The two men lease the adjoining plots of farmland, and they've also come by to enjoy the year-end, brush-clearing bonfire.

"Heard I missed a good one while I was away, Chalkey," Mr. Downs observes, wiping the knife on his sleeve. "Clubber says you nearly set the whole countryside afire. That spot yonder does look awful crunchy."

A quick scan of the surrounding tree line reveals scorched bark and an absence of undergrowth. Charley, a firm believer in the value of a well-contained forest fire to clear debris, nods amiably. "It was nip and tuck there for a few minutes, but me and the boys kept it under control."

"C's just afraid you're gonna roast his pigs one day," says Mr. DeMarr.

Charley considers it, nodding. "Be a hell of a barbecue."

Mr. Downs brays out a laugh, unconcerned that they are making fun of him and his prize hogs next door. "That it would be, Chalkey. I know you'd be first in line with vinegar and a fork."

The three men lounge against Mr. DeMarr's car, drinking beer and watching Charley Boy and Johnny work the crosscut saw.

"Now, that right there is a thing of beauty," observes Mr. Downs.

"Those boys know what they're about. They run that saw like old hands."

"They're good boys," Charley agrees.

The boys can feel that they are being watched, assessed, and they try not to bind the saw under the pressure of observation. They don't want to embarrass themselves or Charley in front of his friends. Finally, there's a definitive crack as the cross-section of trunk they've been working gives way to gravity. Two more passes with the saw and the section drops completely free; Charley Boy, anticipating the direction of roll, steps out of the way before it crushes over him.

"I think that's enough for today, then," Charley calls. "Come over and say hello." He has taught them not to slouch and mumble as so many boys do, but to make eye contact and offer a firm handshake. For their part, shaking hands with Charley's friends makes them feel grown up, as though they are part of the men's peer group. Only without the beer.

"All right, boys, let's light 'er up." The torches have been standing in a bucket with just enough gasoline at the bottom to draw up into the rags. The boys press them against the side to wring out the excess—everyone has learned the lesson from that one time—and hold them out over the edge of the debris pile. Charley Beck strikes a wooden match on his thumbnail, and lights the extended torches, and the boys split apart in opposite directions, lighting up the edges until they meet again at the back. They keep watch for the escaping creatures that have made a home inside the shelter. A big rat snake materializes by Johnny's feet, leaving an endless S in the dirt as it breaks for a safer spot.

It's been a dry year, and the pile lights up fast, starting with a satisfying crackle that's soon overtaken by the low roar of a large, hot fire. The men sit back, knowing that they will need to move again as the heat intensifies. Charley Boy and Johnny circle the blaze at a distance, shovels at the ready and blankets in hand, vigilant for escaping embers. They've already cleared a wide firebreak around the pile, but fire demands respect and no one has any true desire to roast Cecil Down's pigs prematurely.

"How do those boys do in school?" Mr. DeMarr wants to know.

"Well, Charles is the scholar of the family. He likes to puzzle out the math problems, understand the why of things. John's the complete opposite. He doesn't take well to the lecturing and sitting still." All three nod together in their understanding of that. "Lillie tells me that the principal has taken a shine to him, though. Helps smooth some of the other rough patches." It's true. Sister Floricinda is captivated by Johnny, so like her little brother Willis, who died of consumption years ago. She's been known to intercede on Johnny's behalf when his tendency toward chaos generates yet another rough patch.

Charley chuckles. "This summer, they built model boats. Good size, you know, that they could race in the Tidal Basin or wherever. Charles started first, sketching out a plan, so John decided he wanted to build one too. So here's Charles, drawing out blueprints, running his calculations, and there's John with a hammer, saw, and glue. Both boats were beauties in the end. They just got there two different ways."

"Two sides of the same coin," agrees Mr. Downs.

"Well, plus the one learned that you can't figure everything out on paper, and the other found out that a little bit of planning ahead saves a lot of rework and raw materials."

Soon the men move farther back from the fire, their fronts still getting roasted in the heat while their backs feel the chill of the late afternoon. The boys' faces are red and crisp, and new holes are singeing into their charred old barn coats. Mr. DeMarr passes beers from the tub they've hauled over from the car.

Charley rubs at the back of his neck. "It's getting to be time for you to pick me out a fat hog, Cecil."

"Oh, so now my pigs are good enough for you, are they?" He

snorts out his donkey laugh. "When?"

"I'm thinking before Thanksgiving. You have time next Saturday?"

"Sure. I'm doing a few other hogs that day, I could use some extra hands. You in, Clubber?

"Wouldn't miss it."

"You figure on bringing the boys this year, Chalkey?"

"I'm not sure what their mother will have to say about that." Hog butchering isn't for the faint of heart or the uninitiated. Even when he and Emma raised pigs at the house when Lillie was a girl, he wouldn't do it there in the yard; he trucked them out to a friend's farm for the autumn slaughter.

"How many pigs you figure you done by the time you was their age, C?"

Mr. Downs thinks on that. "No counting. But it's different times now, Clubber. We all came from a farm, but these boys were raised in the city. Can't expect them to have rendered many hogs."

Mr. DeMarr nods, conceding the point. "But they do know how to coax music from a cross-cut saw."

The fire has died back considerably, so that it doesn't bear so much watching, but they will let it burn down some more before working to get it completely out. "Charles, go get the .22. We'll get in some target practice." To his companions he rolls his eyes. "Talk about being in the city. This summer, the neighbors complained about the boys using the gun in the yard, so that was that. When I built that house, it was out in God's country. Now it's hemmed in on all sides. No room to stretch."

"Can't use a gun, but then they complain about the rabbits eating the kitchen garden and the stray cats yowling all night under the windows," Mr. Downs observes.

The boys take turns aiming at chunks of wood that the ax has scattered. When the gun misfires for the third time in a row, the men collect around to see whether anything might be adjusted. The dying fire picks this moment to cough up a flaming bolus of pine tar that lands in an unstacked pile of firewood. Everything else is dropped as the entire party grabs up a shovel or blanket to douse the flame.

"I guess that's the hint it's time to kill the fire," Charley tells them. With help from Mr. DeMarr and Mr. Downs, they use the rakes and shovels to break up the fire and smother it.

"Found another turtle," Johnny says, poking at it with the rake. "Nothing left but the shell."

"How many does that make?"

"Four."

"If we could just get to 'em soon enough, we could make some turtle soup," Mr. DeMarr suggests.

"Oh, that's some good eating right there, is turtle soup, Clubber," Mr. Downs agrees.

On the ground it is now almost full dark, though the sky still holds the fading light. All of them sweep the area to make sure they're leaving nothing behind. The T is now repacked, hands are shaken all around, plans confirmed for the slaughter of a hog the following weekend, the boys' attendance to be affirmed or vetoed by their mother. A thoroughly successful day.

The boys are tired and sore and drifting toward sleep by the time Charley pulls up to the barn, and they haphazardly empty the T. The hand tools, brooms, and .22 are all stacked together in a corner. They drop their barn coats on the floor of the spring porch and join Charley in the kitchen, hoping for some kind of supper.

"Dear Lord, did you boys actually stand *in* the fire?" Lillie wants to know. "You're wearing enough charcoal to be in the church minstrel show. Look at you!"

Unable to look at themselves, they look at each other. Under the soot, their faces are roasted red, and the tips of their ears and noses are actually crunchy from the heat of the fire. They grin at each other.

"Mr. DeMarr and Mr. Downs hadn't seen the boys since the spring. They were both impressed. Said you had two fine young men here."

Compliments about her children always make Lillie soften. She cups each one under the chin. "Yes. You are my good boys, aren't you? My good boys. Now take yourselves up to the bathroom, peel out of those smelly clothes, and clean up if you want any of the roast from dinner. Hurry up, tomorrow's a school day."

On the rounds of her nightly tucking in, she can still smell the smoke wafting from the boys. She squeezes into Dorothy's closet to sit on her bed and ruffle her hair. "Did you say your prayers?" Dorothy nods. "Are you going to have a good day in school tomorrow?"

"Uh huh. Sister Fredericka says that any day being together is a good day."

"You like Sister Fredericka very much, don't you?"

"Oh, yes!"

"You know, all your sisters and brothers had her in first grade, too, and they all liked her just as much." Eventually, Sister Fredericka will teach first grade to every Voith child. Tiny, sweet-faced, and innately patient, she is able to maintain order among seventy squirming, uncivilized first-graders with kind words and a smile. Lillie is long used to hearing, "Sister Fredericka says…" at least twice a day when she has a child in first grade.

"Well, you be good and pay attention." Lillie leans over and kisses Dorothy. "Goodnight, sleep tight, don't let the bedbugs bite."

"'Kay. G'night."

Lillie ruffles Dorothy's hair again. The bedbugs will bite, of course, as soon as each of them is asleep. There's no avoiding it. It's lice that she dreads. The one bad episode they had a few years ago was a nightmare that she does not want to repeat. Once schools starts, she is vigilant about checking heads every day.

Rigid routines on school mornings prevent bedlam. Outfits are laid out the night before, down to underwear and socks. In the morning, Charley is first up, retrieving the *Herald* and the *Post* from the walk and the day's milk from the galvanized container on the front porch; Chevy Chase Dairy delivers dependably by five each morning. He wants time in a quiet kitchen to drink coffee and read the morning papers, leaving the time after dinner to devote to the *Evening Star*. Emma and Lillie come down next, while Ferd uses his one small slice of uninterrupted time in the bathroom. Emma starts breakfast while Lillie packs lunches. The peanut butter is store-bought but the jelly is put up from the fat black grapes that Charley grows in the arbor, enough for a school year's worth of lunches. The boys each get an extra sandwich, and Lillie sometimes wonders as they continue to shoot up whether she ought to give them three.

The school-age children are expected to get themselves up or risk being rolled out of bed by the bottom sheet, courtesy of Emma or Ferd. In contrast, the younger ones are told to stay in bed until one of the girls comes for them; otherwise, they will be up with Charley and underfoot all morning. The girls love to torment the boys by hogging the bathroom beyond their allotted time, to the point that the boys sometimes have to resort to using Emma's chamber pot, often still unemptied from the night before. Lillie has been known to break up the conspiracy by unceremoniously opening the bathroom door. Even after all that time in the bathroom, the girls still use the big dining room mirror to finish their hair and, when they're old enough, to put on makeup.

This morning, Margaret is downstairs first. This year has been fraught for her, as she is the first Voith to make the transition from parochial Nativity School to public Paul Junior High School, and the culture shock is still palpable. After eight years of quiet, orderly hallway processions and hands clasped on desktops at the start of class, to walk into, well, pandemonium, not to put too fine a point on it, leaves a mark. That first awful day, the Nativity girls huddled together; the boys put on a slightly better front but formed a similar self-protective group. Even Celeste Maybridge, beautiful, conceited, and envied through eight grades, shared the girls' wide-eyed panic and was welcomed into their lifeboat. Of course, it couldn't have been more obvious that these were the new Catholic kids than if a cross were branded onto each forehead. Two of the girls, unsure of what to wear when no instruction had been given, wore last year's uniforms; the ugly, long-sleeved blue serge dresses were a misery to wear in any weather and were now so tight that one girl had already ripped a seam of the underarm.

By November, days have settled into some level of predictability. It is an unlovable school, stalked by gangs of toughs who find the end of the day a good time to draw fresh blood and easy money. The teachers are pale and ineffectual. Margaret finds herself wistful for iron-fisted Sister Mary Joseph, who would have taken the whole place in hand in the space of an afternoon, with time left over to do Stations before dinner. Like many of the Nativity girls, Margaret learns to stay quiet and keep her head down, focusing on her studies. Others revel in the untasted freedoms of public school to the point where they outcompete the natives. Celeste Maybridge's lipstick and pin-up-girl sweaters, hidden in her locker, beyond a mother's scrutiny, are proof enough of that.

Lillie gives Margaret an encouraging squeeze as she sets a plate of eggs and sausage in front of her. "Eat up now. You need your strength to tackle the day." They share a smile of understanding. Lillie has consoled Margaret that this is just for one year and then she heads to a good high school, McKinley Tech, where she will be on equal footing with all the other students in her class. Lillie has not yet found a way to console herself that every one of her children will have to endure Paul Junior High School also, a year alone without one other Voith to share the burden.

More children trample into the kitchen, including Bernie and Jeanie, who have been released from their beds by Eleanor. Emma has gone up and gotten the baby, and Lillie sits down to nurse him. Charley and Ferd get up from the table at the same time. Ferd drives sometimes, but today they are taking the streetcar. He leans down to kiss Lillie. "Have a wonderful day, dearest," she tells Ferd, then smiles at Charley. "You too, Dad." Margaret jumps up too, preferring to arrive at school early and slip in ahead of the mob. She kisses Lillie, who gives her one last squeeze of encouragement before she goes.

The boys finally make it into the kitchen, dressed and combed now that the girls have relinquished the bathroom. Finally everyone is being fed. Lillie looks around the table. "Hmm, I seem to remember that someone here has a birthday this week."

"It's me! Is it me?"

"No, Bernie, you had yours over the summer."

"I wanna birfday," says Jeanie, who has only celebrated two so far, and carries only confused recollections of the last one.

"Yours is very special, sweetie bug. It's the first day of spring, which we all look forward to very much. But we have to have Thanksgiving and Christmas first."

Jeanie doesn't clearly remember Christmas either, but she has heard the stories. That is good enough for her.

Lillie looks down the table at Eleanor, who is uncharacteristically blushing. "Thirteen, that's a big number! Have you thought about what you want for your dinner?"

In the beginning, Lillie tries to replicate the parties that Emma used to throw for her, with thirty children, Chinese lanterns in the garden, and a lavish menu of sweets. Ferd is horrified and Lillie quickly realizes it's an unsustainable model when more than one child is in the mix. The celebrations became smaller and smaller until they are simply family dinners in which the celebrant is allowed, within reason, to set the menu. There are some interesting dinners over the years.

"Gramal's potato salad, roast beef and gravy, and corn. Chocolate cake with ice cream and peach pie."

"Sounds like someone has thought about it a lot," Emma says, but adds, "I'm glad you like my potato salad."

Lillie glances up at the clock. "Okay, time to go! Plates on the counter. Make sure you take the right lunch. Does everyone have a coat? Francie, make sure Dorothy has her mittens, please. It's cold this morning. Hold hands crossing the street!" A herd of children presses in for kisses. She tells Johnny and Charley Boy, "If you can't get rid of that smoke smell by tonight, you're both taking a bath."

They gape at her in horror. "But we just had one on Friday!" Johnny protests.

She cocks her head at them. "Tonight."

They slouch off, taking their lunch sacks from Emma in dejection.

Quiet at last. Jeanie is fashioning a hat for Sally from a napkin, and Bernie as usual is seeing what he can construct from his breakfast leftovers. Emma stands at the sink, scraping plates, and Lillie puts Tommy on a clean diaper over her shoulder to burp him. She sighs. "If it's Eleanor's birthday already, then it's time for Thanksgiving, and then Christmas, and then four more birthdays right in a row. I swear that it comes around faster every year."

"It does," Emma tells her. "Every year goes faster than the one before, until it's a complete blur."

"Can I go outside?" Bernie asks, sliding down from his chair.

"Me, too." Sally gets bonked on the head as she is dragged first from the table then from the chair.

"Faces and hands first," Emma tells them. Bernie clamps his eyes shut and screws up his face to prepare for the onslaught of a rough, wet dishtowel to wipe off the remains of breakfast. He maintains that grimace even as Emma scrubs his hands. She finally whacks him on the leg with the towel to dismiss him, and Jeanie steps up, hands outstretched. Emma licks her thumb to scrape at a crusty scab of grape jelly on Jeanie's cheek.

"Gramal, why you got sandpaper on your hands?"

Emma stops in surprise, and Lillie can't suppress a laugh. Hands on her hips, Emma tells Jeanie, "Child, that's not sandpaper, that's hard work."

"You gots hard work on your hands?"

Emma and Lillie share a smile over Jeanie's head. "Every minute of every day. Now go get your coat and bring me your shoes and socks."

The days at home have a rhythm too. Chloe comes mid-morning except Wednesday and Saturday, when she's there at seven. She does the general cleaning and ironing. Emma cans and bakes, and takes care of mending. Lillie does most of the marketing and sewing, and of course the parenting. Everyone does laundry. After Lillie feeds and burps Tommy, he goes down for his mid-morning nap. If the weather is nice, she puts him in the pram and takes Bernie and Jeanie for a long walk, usually to the market and possibly the park. After that, it's time for lunch, followed by naptime for all three children, Jeanie and Bernie in separate rooms to encourage quiet, with strict orders to stay where they are until called. Not long after, the Nativity gang storms in for graham crackers and milk, then back outside in dry weather. Margaret comes in later, having stayed after class to work on her latest art project, the one bright spot in her year so far. Time to start dinner while the kids are outside or, in bad weather, up in the attic. Finally, the men are home and it's dinner, homework, bedtime.

Outside, the afternoons have their own timetable. The Elliott sisters are in their garden, either planting bulbs or digging them, depending on the season. The same kids from the neighborhood public schools pass by every day. Betty Giller, who lives in a row house down the block and who, in not many years hence, will be known as Mrs. Charles J. Voith, looks on wistfully as she walks by the yard, thinking, *They're so lucky. They have swings.* In the remains of the Beck barnyard, though much reduced over the years, there are still a few chickens and a small harem of geese lorded over by a mean old gander whose amorous adventures play out with such punctuality that the local schoolboys collect at the side fence every afternoon at three o'clock to snicker and point.

This afternoon after everyone is home from school, the kids bundle up to go outside. The sun is bright but the air is cold. Winter is on its way. Charley Boy is throwing a baseball high in the air and catching it when he sees Bernie over by the barn, dragging something behind him that looks like a fat stick. With a shock, Charley Boy realizes it's the .22, which he left standing among the other tools last night in his rush to get inside to supper. He has been made wholly responsible for that gun, and Charley has made clear what irresponsibility will mean.

"Bernie!" he yells as he drops his glove and breaks into a run, "put that down now!" Bernie turns and looks at him, not understanding. Charley Boy grabs the rifle from him. His adrenalin is pumping and he's angry because he knows he's at fault for leaving the gun out. "Don't you know how dangerous that is? You *never* play with a gun! It's not a toy! What if someone held this gun up to your chest and pulled the trigger?" And to drive home the point, he does just that.

For the fourth time in a row, the gun misfires.

Unfazed by the lecture and unaware that he has just missed being shot pointblank with a rifle, Bernie shrugs. "'Kay," he agrees, and wanders off to the swings.

Charley Boy's legs turn to rubber. What was he thinking? He

wasn't thinking. He aimed and squeezed the trigger without any thought at all, a reflex almost. But in the second that he squeezed, as he grasped what a bone-headed thing this was, he remembered that he had never cleared the rifle after dropping it to douse the fire, then picking everything up in the dark, and then leaving it out for Bernie to find. And now he has just nearly killed him.

Charley Boy unloads the rifle, checks and rechecks it, cleans and oils it, gets out the ladder, puts the gun up on its rack far out of reach, puts the ladder back, and closes the barn door, all the while shaking as though he has palsy. He picks up his ball and glove and puts them in the garage, exactly where they belong, then, until he is called for dinner, he sits in his bedroom on the edge of his bed and tries to stop shaking.

ꙮ

Emma has the still-warm bird on the low countertop in the pantry. "See, you need to hold firm so he doesn't slide while you're plucking. Here, I'll hold him and you try. Feel how the feathers pull free? Just a small handful at a time or you'll leave some here and there, and that takes more time to clean." Margaret comes away with a handful of feathers, leaving a clean spot on the big turkey. "Just right. Francie?"

Francie takes a handful and says, "Oh!" in surprise as the feathers pull away.

"If this were a chicken, I'd just tuck it under my arm. That's easier. But this bird is every bit of 20 pounds, so he's too big to handle like that." She takes over, efficiently denuding the bird as a cluster of children gape.

"Did Granner kill the turkey?" Dorothy wants to know.

"No, the people at the farm did that, long before you were awake this morning." Charley knows better than to bring a live turkey home to a yard full of children and think he'll be allowed to take its head off and serve the carcass for dinner.

With a heavy cloth, Emma takes a flat bladed spatula that has been heating on the stove and begins to singe the skin. "'S'at?" asks

Jeanie, fingers over the counter edge to help her see better.

"Gets rid of the down and the feather nubbins."

Jeanie puts two fingers in her mouth and wanders away, unenlightened. This flurry of preparation over the last several days is without precedent in her memory. Margaret and Charley Boy have each tried to explain it, but it's all a jumble of Indians, boats, and somebody named Pilgrims. Dorothy makes a funny paper hat in school and wears it around the house, pretending to be Pilgrims. Jeanie finally understands that the people were happy because someone gave them food, but that still doesn't make sense. "Why din they go to the store?"

Lillie enlists the girls' help starting the week before, polishing silver, taking down all the good serving dishes and plates, airing out the table linens. The little ones are sent outside to collect fallen leaves and acorns to make a wreath and a centerpiece for the table. Lillie keeps a list of what is needed, to cut down on the number of trips to the market. Baking starts several days ahead, and Emma is glad to see the girls finally taking an interest in learning how to make a piecrust. They watch and listen as she explains, and they each try their hand at mixing the dough with the pastry blender and rolling it out. Transferring it into the pie plate is the hardest part, but she shows them how to mend the dough with a little dab of water and a patch from the remainders.

The men are pressed into service to do the heavy lifting as well as to keep the little ones and themselves out from underfoot. With Lillie and Emma so busy, the rest take turns entertaining Tommy by playing peek-a-boo or blowing on his bare tummy or dancing him on their laps. At one point, Lillie comes across Charley in his easy chair, Tommy tucked in the crook of his arm; both are fast asleep. Lillie gently lifts Tommy up without waking either one. Later, Charley snorts himself awake, feeling the absence, and checks around his chair to see whether he has dropped something.

Before dawn on Thursday, Charley takes himself out in the T to get the turkey, tagged for him at the farm two weeks ago. Emma and Lillie are deep into the day's work before he even walks out the door. Breakfast today is oatmeal, self-serve. Emma is willing to put up with the children flocking around her while she plucks the bird, but then anyone not helping with dinner is ordered into their coats out into the chilly gray day. Later, when it starts to drizzle, they are let back in to stay in the parlor with Ferd, Charley, and the radio until dinner is ready.

And then it is. Emma issues the ten-minute warning in which everyone is to wash hands and be back downstairs and seated in assigned chairs. Today, there is a scuffle to get to the table, but they all stutter a little at the threshold when they see the enormous spread in the dining room. Jeanie wasn't aware that there is that much food in the whole world. Once they're in their seats, Emma makes a sweeping entrance with the huge white platter and the beautiful, brown, crispy bird. She sets it at the head of the table where Ferd waits with the carving knife. Charley has long since ceded the role to him. Instead of carving the turkey, Charley says grace for the family. "Lord, we're gathered once again at your table. We'd like to thank you for another fine year, and for the addition of another healthy baby, to make sure we don't sleep overly much. We thank you for the bounty of food laid here before us, put together by all the exceptional cooks among us at 741. Mostly, we thank you for watching over us all and keeping us safe, so that we can be here together today as a family. In your name. Amen."

There is a chorus of *Amens* and many signs of the cross. Ferd begins to carve, while plates are passed and filled and passed back. To prevent whining or tears on this special day, Lillie is careful to give the littlest ones only food they are familiar with, clearly separated into little piles on the plate. Once everyone is served, Lillie sighs happily and announces, "Okay, we're going to take turns saying what we're thankful for, from A to Z. I'll start. I'm thankful for *all* of you!"

"That's cheating, Mother!" Francie laughs. "It's supposed to be one word!"

"But she says it every year," Eleanor says.

"Because it's always true," Lillie says. "Besides, they're my rules."

Ferd chimes in, "Apple of my eye," and he and Lillie exchange a broad smile.

"Now everyone's cheating!" Dorothy protests.

"Okay, okay. No more cheating. What else, beginning with A?"

Answers are called out, becoming increasingly ridiculous as the participants run out of ideas. "Artichokes!" "Alligators!" When Charley Boy offers, "Arithmetic!" Johnny nearly chokes on his stuffing.

Jeanie keeps turning in her seat, looking around the room. "Jeanie, you need to sit still," Lillie tells her.

"But Mamma—"

"What is it, sweetie bug?"

"Where the Pilgrims?"

"The Pilgrims?"

"They're sad cause they're hungry. The food is for them." Jeanie sees that the grown-ups are laughing. "An't it?"

"Oh, sweetie. Today we're *remembering* the Pilgrims, and all the things that make us happy and thankful.

"And we are happy and thankful," Charley says, holding up a speared green bean, "that this food is for *us*!"

ꕥ

"I need you to hold still, Charley, or it's going to be lopsided. We can't have Joseph show up at the manger badly dressed."

The long robe Lillie is pinning announces the many times it's been used as a costume, with new strips of fabric extending sleeves and hem as needed each year. Lillie decides she likes the effect, the different fabrics in successive shades of brown, much like a muted coat of many colors. Standing next to Charley Boy as Joseph, Dorothy is trapped in an angel's costume of bleached muslin, which has been starched so many times it stands up with or without an occupant. Until it's shortened, she practically has to stand on her tiptoes to keep the unflinching collar from strangling her.

While Lillie is marking the alterations, Ferd and Charley come in, fresh from their evening walk from the streetcar. "Well, well, what have we here?" Ferd asks after he leans down to kiss Lillie.

"I'm an angel!" Dorothy announces over the edge of her robe.

"Yes, you certainly are," Ferd agrees. "I see it's time for the big

Christmas pageant again. Who's running it this year?"

Lillie helps the children to wrestle out of the robes. To them: "Tell Johnny it's his turn next." To Ferd: "Sister Donald Ignatius."

Charley snorts. "No. Even if she's eighty-five and rides a broomstick, no one deserves to be stuck with a name like that."

"You know perfectly well nuns choose their own names when they take their vows, Dad. And she's lovely."

Unconvinced, Charley glances over at Ferd, who nods with an arched eyebrow and mouths, "Gorgeous."

"Ferdinand John Voith, as though I didn't see that. You men. You all gossip about how a young woman as attractive as that becomes a nun."

"I think I've heard the women speculating about it, too."

"Awful suspicious. She's probably hiding from the law."

"Dad, stop."

Johnny comes into the hall and stands where Lillie points, and she pulls a tunic over his head. She pins a strip of brown fabric along the short hemline, pulling pins from the corner of her mouth where she holds them at the ready, and then marks the final hem.

"And what are you supposed to be?" Charley asks him.

"Shepherd boy."

"Do you get to say any lines? Well, let's hear them, then," Ferd suggests.

Johnny takes a deep breath, throws his arms out, and bellows, "Behold!"

Ferd and Charley wait. Finally, Charley says, "Guess you need to study your part some more."

"No, that's all."

"One word?"

"Sister said one was enough."

The door to the kitchen opens and Emma stands in the threshold; the inviting aroma of baking wafts in behind her. "Whatever you have cooking in there smells mighty good, Em."

"Thank you, Mr. Beck. Too bad for you that you won't be eating any of it."

Charley pulls a face at Ferd. "Well, I guess I've been told."

To Johnny, Emma says, "Wash up for dinner." To Lillie, she says, "I've pulled the cranberry bread out of the oven; do you want me to put in the pies?"

The holiday baking industry at 741 starts up just as the grape and apple harvest ends, and it is now in high hum. Even before Thanksgiving, Emma begins the long process of making her locally famous fruitcakes, to give them enough time to soak in their brandy bath. She only makes a few each year, and they are widely and hotly anticipated. At the church's Christmas fair, the highlight is a baked goods auction, and Emma's fruitcake always commands top dollar. Some of the other women in the parish have tried to replicate it, but there's no mistaking an Emma Beck fruitcake.

There is plenty of company for the fruitcake, though, from divinity and meringues to sugared walnuts and Russian teacakes. In between Thanksgiving and Christmas, if something isn't in the oven, it's being prepped to go in, and there's typically a line of treats waiting their turn.

Filling in any open chinks between cooking times are the many other Christmas-themed activities. After all, the bakers are also the cleaners, the decorators, the list-makers, the card-writers, the grocery-shoppers, the crafts-planners, the supervisors, the gift-makers, the gift-buyers, the gift-wrappers, the gift-hiders. Lillie loves every moment of it.

Ferd and Charley provide the muscle, like wrestling all those decorations down from the attic, as well as help with anything that involves electricity or mechanical parts. Every year brings the tedious search for the one burned-out bulb in the light string that causes the entire set to remain dark, and heaven help them if there are ever two at once.

The kids, of course, are giddy in anticipation, bouncing around the house as though collectively gripped by an urgent need to pee. Even the ones who are beyond the Santa years—but sworn to secrecy on the matter—are swept up in the excitement and even nostalgia for the perfect Christmas. And unlike Thanksgiving, when no one really bothers to explain things to Jeanie, Christmas brings a torrent of breathless information tumbling out randomly.

"It's Baby Jesus's birthday!"

"But we get the presents!"

"Well, only if you're good, or Santa knows not to bring you anything."

"And we always have a really big Christmas tree that Granner cuts down and brings home and puts up in the parlor."

"And we decorate it on Christmas Eve, and Santa finishes it when he brings all the presents! And we hang our stockings in the kitchen and he fills them up!"

"You get to go downstairs first, Jeanie, 'member? Cause you're the youngest."

"I wonder what I'm getting this year."

"What are you gonna ask Santa Claus to bring you?"

"Just remember not to go near Mother and Daddy's room, or you won't get any presents at all!"

As the discussion swirls around her, Jeanie looks to Sally to help sort things out. Despite having been delivered in an earlier Clausian visit, Sally remains mute and unhelpful on the subject.

It doesn't really matter whether it makes any sense, though, when she is wearing a tea towel as an apron and covered in flour, gleefully punching out little gingerbread girls with the cookie cutter she's been handed. When Charley and the boys come stomping into the kitchen one Saturday, dragging a huge pine tree behind them, and proceed to stand it up in the parlor, Jeanie's fuzzy vision of the large elm tree in the front yard somehow making its way into the house begins to fade. Then Lillie sits the three little ones at the kitchen table with crayons and paper to write their letters to Santa. Dorothy is furiously scrawling out her list while Bernie makes big blue loops on his paper. Jeanie watches for a moment. "I want the red crown," she says, reaching, and Lillie hands her the crayon. Jeanie holds it in her fist to draw a house—two windows, a door, a chimney with smoke curling up, and two big flowers. It is her favorite picture to draw.

"Dorothy, you're going to have to pick one thing from your list."

"Really, just one?"

"Really, just one. Bernie, what does yours say?"

"I want a slingshot."

"Hmm. We might need to talk to Santa about that one. What about yours, Jeanie? What are you asking Santa for?"

"Asking Santa?"

"Yes, you need to tell him what you want for Christmas." Jeanie is perplexed, and Lillie thinks for a bit. "Do you know how you like to push Tommy in his pram? Well, maybe you'd like your own pram for Sally. Do you think you would?"

"'Kay."

"You need to write it down. See how Bernie did?"

Jeanie scratches some lines and circles on her paper, then leans back to show to Lillie. "That's not writing," Dorothy protests, showing off her cursive, which covers the front of the paper. "You and Bernie can't write yet. You haven't been to school."

"Dorothy, you peck in your own barnyard. I don't see that you've chosen your one thing yet." To the other two, Lillie says, "It's okay. Santa knows what you wrote."

She walks them out into the parlor where there is a fire in the fireplace. "Now we send them to Santa. Bernie, do you want to go first? Here, let me do it." She takes the paper from him and slides it onto the logs, and they watch the corners curl and blacken before the flames pop out of the center and eat the paper from the middle to the edges. "Okay, Jeanie, let's send yours. Dorothy, what did you pick?"

Dorothy sighs heavily. "I guess the roller skates."

"That's a good choice. Here we go." The last list crumbles into the glowing ashes. "Now, if you all keep being extra, extra good, then Santa might bring you what you've asked for."

Extra, extra good means picking up after themselves without being asked, and brushing teeth and getting into bed with no fussing, and a whole host of other unlikely activities. It's all because Santa is watching, and maybe Baby Jesus too, and they apparently talk to each other to make sure no slip-up goes unnoticed. It's nerve-racking.

After what seems eons, it is Christmas Eve. There is a light supper, since no one is willing to sit still long enough for a full meal.

Charley Beck and Ferd have successfully strung the tree with lights, and Lillie has unpacked the years' worth of ornaments; she says a quiet prayer for minimal breakage this year. Francie plays Christmas carols on the piano while the little children hang ornaments haphazardly within the short range of their reach. Lillie, Margaret, and Eleanor discreetly move ornaments out of the crowded greenery below to create a more balanced overall effect. Ferd and the boys are pressed into service to reach the higher or more awkward spots. Emma, holding Tommy, and Charley stand back to gauge the overall effect, offering direction and advice. When they are done, the tree is still lacking its glittery dressing of garland and tinsel, which will be applied after all the children are in bed. Finally, Lillie claps her hands, and announces, "Okay, stockings and then bed!"

There is almost no room left on the kitchen mantel for any more of the colorful stockings embroidered with each child's name. There's a new hook and a new stocking this year for Tommy, which will hold his first Christmas silver spoon. With him tucked on her hip, Lillie coos at him while she hangs his stocking for him. Jeanie is next and manages to hold up under all of the coaching she receives. Margaret is last.

"I'll be up in ten minutes to tuck everyone in. Remember, everyone stays in their own bed, and no getting up in the morning until Daddy or I come to get you. It's not too late for Santa to change his mind."

"But isn't his sleigh already packed by now?"

Charley chuckles. "Well, you know he carries extra coal with him just in case there's a last minute change in behavior."

The night is long and restless, with more than the normal number of trips to the bathroom or chamber pot. Emma and Lillie slip downstairs at five a. m. to start dinner preparations, since it will need to be ready right after church. Charley is already there with his coffee and newspaper. It's still full dark when Ferd and Lillie, in their robes, open bedroom doors to let children out. At the top of the steps, Lillie lines them up by age; they would be stair steps if the boys hadn't shot up in height to be nearly even with Eleanor.

"What made you start doing this, Mother?" Francie asks.

"It's what they used to do in your granddaddy's family, since there were so many children. I always wanted to do it too, but there was only me so it was hard to form a line!"

"We just did it so we wouldn't misplace anyone," says Charley at the bottom of the stairs, holding his coffee.

"Okay, Jeanie, start us down the steps. Dad, make sure she goes right into the kitchen. No peeking in the parlor!"

Lillie and Ferd bring up the rear of the procession that goes down the steps, through the hall, and into the kitchen, where the stockings now bulge with Santa's largesse. The kids sit at their places at the table and marvel over the delights they find inside: candy canes and tiny Whitman's Sampler boxes, die-cast cars for the boys, hair combs or necklaces for the girls, the tiniest set of cups and saucers for Dorothy to use in the big dollhouse Charley built years ago, a palm-sized baby doll with a pacifier and bottle for Jeanie. And in the toe of each stocking, the rare treat of an orange. The treasures are tucked back inside, the stockings rehung for later. Finally, *finally*! Lillie leads the procession back through the hall and into the parlor.

There is a collective gasp as the children take in the scene. The tree's multi-colored lights seem to twinkle against the tinsel that reflects like a thousand tiny mirrors in the darkened room. The big Lionel train set circles the tree, which is surrounded by an impossible number of packages. Santa Claus has most surely been here. "Oh, Mother," sighs Margaret, "it's the most beautiful tree ever."

Lillie and Ferd settle into the couch, Lillie with the baby in her lap, Ferd's arm around her shoulders. Lillie glows as she watches the scene unfold, kept from erupting into complete chaos by Emma's policing, and Ferd watches Lillie. Her happiness in all this is what he loves most about it. She catches him watching her and slides in closer to him. "Oh, Ferd. When I was a little girl, this is exactly the Christmas I always pictured in my head. Thank you for giving me all my perfect Christmases."

"Well, then, Merry Christmas, Mrs. Voith."

Most of the wrapped presents are the practical things that growing children need—socks and sweaters, scarves and mittens—but also books and puzzles and other little toys. Jeanie unwraps a set of Lillie-made dresses and bloomers for Sally, and sits dressing and undressing her as the frenzy circles them.

The presents from Santa arrive unwrapped, but remain partially hidden behind furniture and under the tree. Charley sits in for Saint Nick, serving up the big present to each child. Margaret gets an easel and pastels; there's a new tennis racquet for Eleanor, and a tabletop zither and sheet music for Francie. The boys get a shared gift of both a large Erector set and a bow and arrows. The latter is a calculated tradeoff against a chemistry set, which Ferd feels sure would cause more widespread damage. Dorothy and Bernie each get their requested gifts, though Lillie has extracted a promise from Charley to spend significant time with Bernie to teach him all the rules of slingshot use. He also gets the boys' old sled, which Charley refurbishes with new paint, varnish, and wax, making it look brand new.

Finally, from behind the sofa where Ferd and Lillie sit, Charley wheels out a doll-sized wicker pram, with a wrought iron push bar and metal wheels, complete with a sun-hood and a pillow and blankets. Charley wheels it over to Jeanie. "Well, now, lookee what we have here. Isn't this just the thing?"

"Dad, show her how the handle works."

"See, you can shift the handle. You can push from behind so your little baby can look out at the big world, or from in front, so you and your baby can look at each other."

Jeanie stands looking at it. "It's...it's for me?"

"Yes, sweetie bug. Santa brought it for you, just like you asked."

She touches the handle, then the hood, and the blue-ticked canvas lining, the pillow and blanket. She doesn't know the words to say that this is the most wondrous thing she has ever seen. She looks at Lillie, who is smiling at her, but Jeanie is so thoroughly overcome that she bursts into tears.

It only takes a moment to confirm that they are tears of joy, and to wipe them away so everyone can admire the pram and the other delights that Santa has brought for them all. Lillie has collected around her all the felted, glittered, sculpted, and painted objects that the children have made for her under the direction of the nuns or older siblings. The children also helped to pick out an apron for Emma, a set of handkerchiefs for Charley, and some wool gloves for Ferd. Lillie and he have exchanged a custom-engraved money clip and a gold crucifix, which Lillie keeps reaching up to touch.

"My heavens, look at the time," Emma says. "If we don't get ready now, we're going to be late for Mass."

The church is extra full today, with extended families swelling the normal ranks of the congregation, greetings thick with hearty cheer and admiration for each other's holiday finery. There's a warm sense of anticipation as Father Bischoff leads the procession to the altar. Today's Mass is an extended celebration, though, and there's no hiding the swell of squirming, rustling, and whining from the always-restive younger set. They are not alone today, as the press of extra people in the pews, among heavy coats and scarves, leads to a general sense of overheating, possibly even claustrophobia, as the protracted Mass plods forward. Still, the congregants take up the recessional hymn with gusto, their rendering of *Joy to the World* vibrating with a commanding bass that propels them all out of the church and into the glittering cold day.

By the time they arrive home, the earlier excitement is exhausted, and the children discover they are starving to the point of collapse. The turkey has been roasting since before stockings are opened, so it is not long before Christmas dinner is laid on. Once again, the dining room is a shining vision of silver, linens, candles, and china. Emma calls the children in from playing with their new toys, and at the threshold Jeanie looks from the table to Francie. "Pilgrims again?"

After the feast, there is time for belt loosening and napping on the sofa or playing jacks and marbles under the big tree, before it's time for the next Voith holiday tradition: the annual family visit to Illinois Avenue. When Ferd goes over to visit by himself, he easily covers the distance on foot in a bit over five minutes. In the cold, damp, and early darkness, with the whole family, piling into the big car is a necessity. Charley sees them off at the door, saying to Ferd, "Wish your folks a merry Christmas from us. Hope everyone's well." Emma remains in the parlor, darning socks.

Ferd pulls up at the tidy row house with candles burning in the windows and a lighted Christmas tree visible in the front room. Before he has even helped Lillie, holding the baby, from the car, Gus is standing in the open doorway, hailing the visitors. "Hello, hello! Come in out of the weather! Hello, my dear, how are you? And here's the newest little one!" as he accepts Lillie's kiss on his cheek, and peeks down at Tommy under his blanket. "Mother, they're here!"

The children crowd into the house, all but the oldest feeling shy and uncertain in the small space and unfamiliar company. They have been counseled to be on their best behavior, but, in these circumstances, they aren't even sure what behavior is allowable.

Doro emerges from the kitchen, carrying trays of cookies and other treats, followed by Sophie and Dorothie with coffee and hot chocolate. Sophie's husband Elgie, never without a beer in one hand and a cigar in the other, now holds them both in one hand to free the other for greetings. June is with him in the parlor too, working on a beginner's cross-stitch that Santa brought. The adults exchange embraces, handshakes, and Merry Christmases. There is much exclaiming over the surprising growth and increasing age of the children. Dorothie and Dorothy exchange a familiar hug, since they have lunched together with Lillie as recently as August.

"Mom, where's Feeny?" Ferd asks.

"He'll be along soon, dear. Gus, just a tiny bit of bourbon in the eggnog! We don't want anyone falling down the steps!"

"Ferd, Dad's produced another fine batch of the homebrew," Elgie indicates with the bottle he's holding. "Make sure you try some."

Doro herds the children to the table for hot chocolate and cookies, knowing that's the fastest way to warm them to the company. She puts out bottles of the excellent root beer that Gus also produces. Like many Germans during the long, dry years of Prohibition, he has quite the little brewery set up down in the cellar. Gus doesn't distill his own spirits, though, which is another reason to dole out the bourbon carefully.

Jeanie and June are surprised when they find each other at the far end of the table. "You came to my house," Jeanie tells her.

"And we played with your doll," June says, pointing to Sally in her new outfit. "This is my doll. Her name is Annie."

As they fall into close conversation, the two girls and their dolls squish together on the same seat and help themselves to the snickerdoodles.

Tommy is passed among the women, who coo at him in that tone invariably used on infants, while he gurgles back at them and flails his fists and feet. Elgie stands with Ferd as they look on. "How do you suppose you ended up with such a passel of children, Ferd?"

Ferd smiles at him. "Just lucky, I guess." The front door swings wide, letting in a gust of cold air, and Ferd turns. "There he is!"

"Feeney, what's kept you, boy?" Elgie goes to shake his hand and close the front door behind him.

"Leo, dear!" Doro bustles over to get a kiss. "Where's Mattie?"

"Hello, mum! Merry Christmas! She's over to her folks tonight. I'm batching it!" The twinkle in Leo's eye and flush in his cheeks say that he's gotten into someone else's bourbon eggnog already. He makes his way around the room, kissing and shaking hands. He stops at the dining table and sweeps Margaret's hand up to offer a gallant kiss. "How do you do, Mrs. Godmother?"

She simultaneously giggles and blushes. "Enchanted, Mr. Godfather."

When he gets to Lillie, he grabs her by the waist, lifts her up, and spins once with her before setting her back down. "How's my best girl?" he asks her.

Playfully, she smacks him on the arm. "Feeney, you are a mess!" she tells him.

At the table, Johnny leans over to Margaret. "Is Uncle Feeney's name Feeney or Leo?"

Margaret whispers back, "It's Leo. No one will ever say why they call him Feeney."

Elgie overhears the exchange and calls out, "Hey, Feeney, the kids want to know why they call you that."

Leo pulls himself away from Lillie and slides back over to the table. "Well, I'll tell you. When I was little," he looks around for a candidate and points at Bernie, "younger than this fellow here…"

Lillie breaks in. "Don't you dare tell that story to the children!"

Leo continues as though he hasn't heard. "I used to pick up cigarettes in the street, the ones that were still lit, and smoke them." There is a gasp from Dorothy. "The lady who lived next door saw me do it a few times and said I was a fiend." The children exchange skeptical glances. If it were Charley telling this story, they'd be pretty certain he was pulling their leg. "No, it's true! Ask your father. So Frank, your Uncle Frank, thought that was pretty funny and started calling me Fiendy. Ended up being Feeney."

"Hardly an appropriate tale for a Christmas Day," Doro admonishes him as she passes eggnog to the adults, and makes a show of holding his back. "And to think you were named after the *pope*!"

Leo leans in to kiss her as he deftly lifts the eggnog from her. "Well, there you go. The holy Leo was already taken. What could I do?"

A shriek pierces the room as two little girls hurtle around the corner from the back bedroom. June is pulling a wheeled horse that Sally and Annie are riding, until the force of the turn flings them both off as the horse swings wide and upends, wheels spinning. Jeanie claps her hands and squeals, a sound that only little girls of a certain age are capable of producing.

Both Lillie and Dorothie step forward on the brink of a reprimand when Doro puts a hand on Lillie's arm to still them both. "Let them be. June has few enough playmates. I'm happy to see them enjoy themselves."

Still, Lillie says to Jeanie, "You need to quiet down," and Dorothie gives June a stern look.

The girls are momentarily silent until they turn back to the wreckage of the riding accident and collapse again into giggles.

Dorothie slips her arm through Lillie's and leans in. "She's right you know. June spends all her time with fusty old us. It's a shame..."

She leaves the thought uncompleted, but Lillie understands. Jeanie is too young to be of much interest to her older brothers and sisters; Bernie cleaves to the boys when they allow it, and Dorothy now has school friends. June, though almost two years older, is closest to Jeanie's age, and they seem well matched. So. *It's a shame they can't be playmates.*

Leo comes from behind them and throws an arm over each woman's shoulder, thrusting his head in between theirs. "What are you girls up to? Sophie says it's time for presents!"

Everyone presses into the parlor so that Sophie can hand out the presents she has bought for each of her nieces and nephews. "Poor Sophie," Leo observes to Gus. "She started the tradition when there weren't nearly so many of them. Now there's no backing out of it!"

Still, Sophie enjoys buying the children gifts, even as their numbers swell. She likes the challenge of finding things she thinks match each child, enjoys the ritual of wrapping them, picking out a bow, and attaching a name card. But mainly she loves watching them open the presents. When Margaret opens hers, a beautiful hand-painted silk scarf that makes everyone *ooooh* and *ahhhh*, Leo slides over to tie it for her at her throat. "Why, you are every bit the vision, Mrs. Godmother!" he tells her.

"You're so very kind, Mr. Godfather!" she giggles.

Bernie's eyes narrow at her. "Are you married?" he demands, which makes all the adults laugh.

"No, silly," she tells him.

"Then why does he keep saying Missus? No one says Missus unless they're married."

"Boy has a point there," Gus observes.

"They're just teasing, honey," Lillie explains. "Uncle Feeney and Margaret are Jeanie's godfather and godmother."

At her name, Jeanie looks up in surprise. This concept of godparents is vague, and she stares at these two—one a stranger, the other her biggest sister. No matter what, no one is going to make her call Margaret *mother*.

Doro brings over her present to the family. Lillie passes Tommy to Ferd as she accepts the familiar box. Every year, Doro buys the Ferd Voith family a large box of chocolates; Lillie unwraps it and holds it out. The children are permitted to select one chocolate from the big gold foil box; with no pre-poking or give-backs allowed, the kids hope they choose well. "Say thank you," she prompts them.

For her namesake and godchild, Dorothie also puts a gift under the tree. When Dorothy unwraps this present, a beautiful set of paper dolls that are actually made of cardboard and cloth, along with a collection of fabric outfits for them, all the women exclaim over them and point out the detailing, as Dorothy glows. Jeanie notices the disparity in both the attention and the number of gifts. She gives Lillie a querulous look, but Lillie frowns and shakes her head.

Doro sees the exchange. "Well, Jeanie, your Aunt Dorothie is also your sister's godmother. That deserves an extra…" She stops herself, realizing that she's just about to make things worse.

There's that word again, and Jeanie looks back up at Margaret and Leo with a mix of suspicion and expectation. They look back at her, and grasp that they've been caught short. Until this moment, it has never occurred to Margaret that she might be expected to produce a gift for Jeanie based on her special role as godmother. Leo is the baby of his family; outside of a gift or two he's bought Mattie, Leo's never gotten anything for anybody.

"Ahh, I see," he nods. "All eyes on me. The need to rise to the occasion."

Leo folds himself down on the floor in front of Jeanie so that they are eye-to-eye. "Feeney, what are you up to now?" Elgie wants to know.

"Say, what are you hiding back here?" Leo asks Jeanie as he sweeps his hand behind her ear and pulls out a nickel.

Her forehead wrinkles at it as he puts it in her palm. Well, this is not much different than the game with the witch lady who comes to use the telephone.

Leo purses his lips, considering. "There must be something bigger than that in the coin bank you're keeping in there. Oh, I see something now." Leo makes a pantomime of bracing himself against Jeanie's shoulder and pulling hard from the direction of her ear, as though something is stuck. Finally, he makes a *pop!* as he dislodges and flourishes a huge, shiny silver dollar, holding it out in front of her. "Now *that* was worth going in for!"

Jeanie's eyes widen and she is surrounded by laughter and

exclamations of surprise ("Oh, Feeney, that's too much!" "No, Feeney. That's *too much*!" "Managed to redeem yourself there, didn't you, boy?"). Something like a squeak escapes from Johnny at the thought of Jeanie's stumbling into such a windfall. The pounds of candy that money will buy!

Jeanie didn't know there was money in the world that big or heavy; it covers the whole of her palm and then some. "Let me keep that for you, so you don't lose it," Ferd tells her.

She walks over and hands it to him, but, feeling all the eyes on her, she hides her face in his pant leg, suddenly shy. He swoops her up and sits her on his arm, whispering something to her. She turns her head to the magician. "Thank you, Uncle Feeney."

There's time for some more cookies and root beer—Charley Boy, Johnny, and Bernie huddle in a corner and practice belching at each other in undertones, until Bernie produces one at full volume—and a beer or two among the men. Gus brings out his saxophone, accompanied by Sophie and Francie on the piano, and there are some unserious attempts at dancing. And all the while, Jeanie keeps tugging at her ear and shaking her head, attempting to dispense the coins that remain behind.

ꙮ

It's New Year's Eve, the tail end of the holiday break, and things are feeling ragged, as though the vacation has gone just that much too long. Lillie has decreed that everyone under the age of eleven put on a coat and get out into the unseasonably mild day. Dorothy, Bernie, and Jeanie play with the little cast iron stove that Ferd retrieves for them from the barn earlier in the week. Bernie builds up the fire with the sticks they have all collected, while Jeanie boils water in the little saucepan and Dorothy uses the child-sized skillet to toast the bread heels Emma gives them. The stove is one of Santa's gifts brought several years ago to a young Francie. At the back of the yard, Charley Boy and Johnny practice with the bow and arrows brought this year by Santa, taking turns aiming at a target they have painted on a tree, and possibly now and then at a squirrel bounding unwisely across the lawn.

In the Voith family, the date is less about being the last day of the year as it is about being Dorothy's birthday. Lillie and Emma are in the kitchen putting together her selected menu of roast chicken and potatoes, candied yams with extra brown sugar, and a hefty apple pie. Because it's New Year's Eve, though, they also make the traditional Berliners, doughnuts filled with jam and sprinkled with sugar. Emma fries the sweet dough and Lillie uses the big pastry syringe to pump this year's cherry preserves inside the cooled doughnuts.

Lillie has been making lists in her head and sighs. "Next week is Johnny's birthday, then Francie and Margaret a month after that, and then Jeanie a month after that." She sighs again. "Well, at least then it will be spring."

"Just consider, darling, that you still have four months with no birthdays in them."

Lillie thinks about that. "You're right! We still have April, May, September, and October open!"

"With just a little planning…" Emma smiles mischievously.

Lillie laughs. "You know, I've needed a New Year's resolution. This could be just the thing."

"If you start now, you'd be able to tick September off the list. Or certainly October." Emma is laughing now, too.

"Oh, my, that would be starting the year off right!" Lillie is laughing now to the point that she ends up squirting jam on herself with an indelicate blurt from the syringe, which makes them both laugh harder. Lillie tries to lick the jam off her fingers, but ends up smearing it across one cheek.

Charley stands in the doorway holding his lunch box, still in his hat and coat. "Jesus, Mary, and Joseph, what are you two hens cackling about?"

Ferd comes in behind Charley. "What the…?"

At the sight of Ferd, both women become hopeless. Lillie gasps for air, while Emma tries unsuccessfully to wipe the tears off her cheeks, even as she produces more. Charley shakes his head sadly. "They've lost their marbles, Ferd. Dropped them all over the floor.

I'm going back outside where it's quiet. I recommend you come, too." Over his shoulder, he adds, "I sure hope this doesn't mean we don't get supper."

Charley has no cause for worry. The women recover sufficiently to present a beautiful birthday dinner for Dorothy, who turns seven today. The family sings a blaring rendition of *For She's a Jolly Good Fellow*, and, with Francie at the piano, shifts almost smoothly into *Auld Lang Syne*. It's still hours until midnight, but this has become the family tradition.

In the parlor as the evening wears away, Lillie and the girls work on a large and intricate jigsaw puzzle on one of the card tables they've set up, while the two Charleys and Ferd take turns playing knock rummy. Johnny is engrossed in building a crane with the erector set, and the little ones, already in their pajamas, make up nonsensical games out of tiddlywinks, jacks, pick-up sticks, and dominoes. The radio plays in the background; Lillie refuses to turn it up for Charley until very close to midnight. As though it were any other night, Emma does mending in the lamplight, every so often reaching with the poker next to her chair to stoke the fireplace.

Eventually, there are children curled up asleep on sofas and chairs, but they rouse themselves as Charley is finally allowed to raise the volume on the console radio. He settles into his chair and tunes in to Rudy Vallee and the Connecticut Yankees, who are airing a special New Year's Eve broadcast. At the start of one song, Ferd takes Lillie's hand and draws her to the center of the room to dance, which makes the girls swoon theatrically. It's getting close to midnight. The program cuts over to the folks in Times Square in New York, who are narrating the festivities there, as the crowd waits for the famous ball to drop into the new year.

Charley raids the kitchen and hands out pots, pans, spoons, and spatulas to all the children, then opens the front door in readiness. On the radio, the countdown starts, and everyone at 741 joins in. "...five, four, three, two, one, Happy New Year!"

Charley and the children stand in the cold of the front porch, banging like crazy people on their pots and pans and shouting, joined on all sides by their neighbors, who are doing the same thing.

The radio is now playing its own rendition of *Auld Lang Syne*, and Lillie finds herself dabbing at her eyes. She feels Ferd's arm around her waist, and he puts his head down to kiss her. "Happy New Year, sweetheart."

They stand for a moment looking out at the chaos on the porch. "Do you know why Mother and I were laughing so hard this afternoon? We decided we need more children around here."

They look at each other and burst out laughing. "I see what you mean."

She turns fully to him, her arms around his neck. "Happy 1933, darling. I feel as though this will be our best year ever."

Thursday, 20 April 1933

By now, a new sort of routine has established itself at 741. Any visitor familiar with the normal workings of the household would notice the difference immediately, the most startling being the quiet. The only one who doesn't understand the new rules is Tommy, whose wailing seems to get louder, possibly in contrast to the silence, possibly because it prevents his being ignored or forgotten.

With the intrusion of the new reality comes a wordless détente between Emma and Ferd, a level of accommodation and even cooperation that has never blossomed in sixteen years. Both are worn down, spent, and their last reserves are saved for Lillie. There's no energy to spare on personal conflict.

Emma continues to spend nights in her own bed, Charley beside her *snoring to rattle the cotter pins*, as Joe used to say. Ferd grows used to the bedside chair, to being awake the entire night, except that he startles up each morning at five a.m., just minutes before Emma arrives for the day. They use the bathroom in shifts, and sometimes fall asleep in their opposing chairs. It even comes to the point that Emma might retire to her bed during the day for an hour or two of sleep; Ferd uses the boys' room for the same purpose. With no discussion, they agree that Lillie is never left alone.

Most telling is that they participate equally in Lillie's care. There is a lone exception to this parity: when it becomes obvious on Tuesday night that Lillie cannot get up to manage her own toilet, a bedpan becomes necessary. Ferd produces a likely vessel and begins to peel back the bedsheets. Lillie's hand reaches under the tent to touch his and she shakes her head. "No, dearest, not you. Not that. Mother will do it."

Still, after the tent goes up on Tuesday, there's a charge of excitement in the room, as though they all know the ordeal is drawing to a close and it's just a matter of a little more time. Wednesday, everyone watches for the expected upticks: small bites of toast or applesauce, a stronger voice, unencumbered breath. Instead, it's as though the day teeters on a ledge, with no definitive movement in either direction.

Right now, on Thursday, there is a grim and silent council convened around Lillie's bed. Dr. Cavanaugh is finishing his standard morning checkup of the patient: listening closely to heart and lungs, counting pulse, checking temperature and blood pressure. He's taking longer than normal and Ferd suspects that he is simply stalling, trying to delay the inevitable need to say something. Whatever it is, it's not going to be good news.

It's well past nine o'clock. This morning's bowl of broth and pot of tea already stand cold on the little card table. There's been no laudanum administered since Dr. Cavanaugh's decision to see how Lillie does without it. Each one has tried to coax her eyes open this morning and been unsuccessful. Lillie isn't waking up and no one knows why.

"Doc?"

The prompt starts him from his contemplation. "I thought, yesterday, that her lungs were starting to clear." The unspoken point is that they are not. "Her fever has spiked a little bit."

"But why won't she wake up?"

He squints in thought, and says almost to himself, "I don't know." They watch as he goes to his medical bag and sorts through items, finally pulling out a small leather case from which he takes a scalpel. With one hand, he peels back the bedclothes from the lower part of the bed and uncovers her foot. Emma sees him bring the scalpel up and jumps from her chair, almost shrieking, "What are you doing?"

Ferd is up too, and even Charley is concerned. "Doc?"

Dr. Cavanaugh realizes how alarming this must look. "I'm just checking for a response." He scrapes the back, blunt edge of the scalpel against the soft instep of her foot, and her leg draws back in a reflexive flinch.

"That's a good sign, then?"

He nods, but is obviously distracted in his thoughts. "I need to use the telephone."

"Of course." Charley catches a look from him and says, "I'll walk down with you." At the telephone table, he says, "I'll go make some more coffee. Come on back when you're done."

The pot on the pantry stove percolates and Charley glances at the Tuesday *Star*. Dr. Cavanaugh comes in and sits down heavily. His face is drawn and his eyes look almost sunken. There's a cup of coffee in front of him, milk and sugar within reach, before he finally speaks.

"Her lungs are filling up, and I worry that her heart is affected too. I thought surely by now…." His voice trails off.

"And home is still the best place for her?"

"Charley, if there were any better place, I'd take her there myself." He pinches the bridge of his nose with two fingers. "There isn't…I don't have anything else to try."

"Leo. This isn't on you. No matter what happens."

A sad smile. "I'm usually the one comforting the family, not the other way around."

"Is that it, then?"

He rubs a hand over his face. "It's possible she'll recover, but if she does, it's not through any of my doing."

The two men sit in silence as the coffee grows cold. "Doc, you've got other patients you need to see. If there's any kind of change, we'll call you."

Dr. Cavanaugh pushes himself up. "Maybe you should ask the sisters to visit again."

"I feel certain we won't have to ask."

After the parade of visitors yesterday, though, today seems eerily quiet. There have been a few knocks at the door, which Chloe handles; consequently, a fresh batch of sweets and savories line the counter. By now, there's an embarrassment of food in the house, and yet even the boys pick at whatever is put before them, uninterested. This morning's breakfast is a silent, sullen affair. Any vague hope the children might have of being allowed to stay home with everyone else is crushed when Charley says, "Better get going. Don't want to be late two days in a row."

There is a long list of chores that Charley could be taking care of now. This is the first time in his entire working life that he's been home during the day outside of his annual leave and the few holidays. In other circumstances, this is a rare gift of time. If nothing else, he has the opportunity to soak up the two days of newspapers stacked in front of him on the table. Instead, he sits, silent and still for once, doing, thinking, nothing.

ꙮ

Miss Bessie, she of the change purse of nickels, is actually Mrs. Elizabeth Clayton, widowed wife of Andrew Clayton, mother to William Clayton, and mother-in-law to Matilda Clayton, one of yesterday's visitors to 741 whose splendid roast chicken provided dinner to the household last night and therefore went unenjoyed. Miss Bessie lives across the street from 741 and just a few houses up the block from Will and Tilly. Proximity is but one reason Miss Bessie uses Charley's phone instead of Will's.

As an aged widow living now with her even more aged brother in an old house, she needs regular help to maintain her home and yard. That help comes in the form of the dependable neighborhood garbage- and handymen, Sondy, Yoc, and Jiggs. Today, they are working in the front yard, raking, clipping, digging; and on the porch, scraping, patching, painting. After yesterday's rain, it's perhaps a little too wet to be stomping on the grass or turning a bed, but Miss Bessie is eager to get her annuals into the ground, now that the weather has turned so nice. Yoc is taking a moment with his handkerchief when he hears what sounds like sharp clapping, perhaps someone calling his dog to come, and he glances around idly to find the source. Unsuccessful, he tucks the refolded handkerchief into his back pocket and turns to pick up the shovel when he hears it again. Curious now, he does a more thorough scan of the area and realizes it's coming from across the street. It takes a moment for him to make sense of what he's seeing, though, and he squints to be sure. It is Emma, leaning out of an upstairs window, and now that she has his attention, she is clearly beckoning to him.

"Sondy, what do you make of this?" he says over his shoulder, and both Jiggs and Sondy look up.

"No idea."

Emma's gesture becomes more urgent though, and Yoc breaks into a jog as possible reasons begin to occur to him. "I'll see," he calls to the other two.

He stops on the front sidewalk and looks up to her. She looks haggard but not panicked, so he presumes that no one is hurt. Now she puts a finger up to her lips to caution quiet, and says in a stage whisper, "Come upstairs." Yoc is confounded, but starts to walk around to the back of the house. "No!" comes the sharp whisper, "the front door. Come upstairs."

This is fully outside the boundaries of his experience to date. No one ever invites the trash men to come in the front door. At 741, he has been in the kitchen and cellar, and always accompanied by Charley Beck. He hesitates and looks up at her again; she is clearly aggravated by the delay and makes an indefinite gesture that seems to signal him to hurry up. He mounts the porch stairs, but realizes that his work boots are a muddy mess. He can't possibly go into the house wearing them. Miserably, he bends to unlace and pull them off. When he's met by the sight of his two fully exposed big toes poking through his socks, he silently curses that he didn't just pick the shovel back up and keep working.

Yoc opens the front door as silently as possible and cranes his neck inside to look around. "Hello?" he asks cautiously.

"Up here." And, in fact, Emma is standing at the banister that looks down over the hall, but immediately disappears from view.

Yoc makes one last attempt to cover his toes before climbing the stairs. At the top, he finds Emma standing in the bedroom doorway. She points at the steel ladder that's bolted into the wall in the hallway. "I need you to get something from the attic." She adds, "My daughter is sick, and her husband is asleep in another room. I need something from the attic."

"Why sure, Mrs. Beck. Just tell me what I'm looking for." The wooden box is exactly where she describes, though larger than he anticipates. It's the ladder with its slick rungs, bolted so close to the wall, and he in his stockinged feet that make this such a tricky maneuver. It's really a two-person job, but no force on Earth will make him climb down empty-handed to walk all the way back out of the house to whistle for the other two. If he leaves, he's not coming back.

He heaves the crate across his back and shoulder, holding on by the sturdy rope on its end. He'll need to stay hunched to keep it in place, while letting himself down one-handed and keeping his feet pressed into the sides of the ladder, as he finds each successive rung. The pain in his feet surprises him, as though someone is digging into the soft instep with a blunt instrument, and it's magnified by the weight he carries. Relief floods through him when his foot finally touches the solid floor.

He carries the crate into the room, trying not to gape at the tent or at Lillie's indistinct figure inside. Emma points to the card table, which is now empty except for a kerosene lantern with its chimney removed. He stands to one side, trying to hide his toes, as she frees the hasp and begins to unpack. None of the items are familiar to him: a stack of tiny glass cups like shot glasses, though much smaller and with rounded bottoms, a pair of tongs that he sees are sized just right to fit the cups, oddly shaped cutting instruments. "Do you need anything else, Mrs. Beck?"

It's almost as though she doesn't hear him; she's fingering a ceramic bowl with two half moons carved out of opposite sides of the rim. "No, that's all," she finally says, and then, belatedly, "What does Mr. Beck give you?"

"Oh, no, ma'am. I'm happy to help. I sure hope Mrs. Voith is feeling better soon." She is fully absorbed in the contents of the box, and he backs away quietly until he is beyond the threshold before almost breaking into a sprint down the steps.

Back on the porch, the door safely closed again, he shoves his feet back into his boots and stuffs the laces down inside without even tying them. Sondy and Jiggs are standing outside the front gate, silently demanding to know what's going on. Yoc is almost to the gate when Charley saunters around from the side yard, followed by Chloe with the garden basket and Bernie and Jeanie each carrying a little bucket. Charley joins the cluster at the fence.

"Hello, boys. I saw you over at Miss Bessie's earlier. What brings you across the street?" He's clearly trying to puzzle out what Yoc is doing inside the gate while the other two have been gesticulating broadly at him from the sidewalk.

"Oh, Mr. Beck, I didn't think you were here today."

"Didn't think I was here?"

"Since Mrs. Beck called to me to come get the box. She said Mr. Voith was asleep, so I just figured you weren't at home for her to ask."

"Box? What box?"

"She asked me to bring a wooden trunk down from the attic and put it in the…in the bedroom. I sure am sorry your daughter's sick, Mr. Beck."

"What did it look like?"

Yoc illustrates the size with his hands. "About yea wide, so tall. I think it had medical tools in it, but nothing I've ever seen a doctor use."

Charley's mouth falls open. "Holy Mother of God," he breathes as he breaks into a run, and bellows "Emma!" as he slams through the front door.

ᘓᘐ

Ferd dreams that he wakes up into black, realizing in panic that he is flat on his back inside of a box not much bigger than he. There isn't space enough for him to lift his arms more than an inch or two above his thighs or to turn more than his head. Something is hitting on the outside of the box, like rain only heavier, followed by a weighty thump. *Clatter, clatter, thump, clatter, thump*. He knows what it is, in the way a dreamer know things in dreams: it is dirt being thrown on the lid of a coffin. Then something hits the lid with a heavy thud, so that Ferd can feel the top of the box flex inward. The gravedigger has jumped into the hole and stands on top of the coffin, pulling more dirt in around him with a shovel, which occasionally scrapes against the lid. Ferd's movement is so constrained that his fists and feet can only make feeble bumps against the box, and there is only a hoarse gasping sound when he tries to shout. Whatever noise he makes is swallowed by the falling earth.

Now Ferd wakes into light, the sun of midafternoon, disoriented, his heart pounding so hard in the back of his throat that he can taste it. He thinks he must still be buried in a nightmare, because he still can't move his arms or legs, until he realizes that he's tangled in the bedcovers, but even then he seems unable to wrestle out of them. By the time he frees himself, he is completely winded. He lies still, concentrating to quiet his breathing and slow his pulse. Finally, he's able to sit up in Johnny's bed and then stand. He feels as though his head is filled with sludge, trapping his brain in a slow-motion struggle to escape, and preventing his thoughts from connecting together in any meaningful way. It's unclear how much longer he can survive on anguish and insomnia.

He can't shake the feeling of oppression and dread that the nightmare leaves behind, though in the bathroom he scrubs hard with a cloth over and over to try to erase the images. Giving up, he wanders back down the hall to what used to be his and Lillie's bedroom. As he steps to the threshold, he hears the front door slam open below as though someone has kicked it in, and he wonders again whether he has slipped back into a nightmare, as he attempts to make sense of what he's seeing. The oxygen tent is open, a set of implements arrayed on the card table. The collar of Lillie's nightgown is unbuttoned and pulled back as it was for him to rub in the menthol. The room is dark, but at the bedside, the hunched figure of Emma is thrown as a shadow by the light of an open kerosene lamp, and she's holding a pair of tongs in the flame. The dream is so real that he can smell the burning kerosene. He hears words coming out of him, even though they don't form in his brain and he can't feel his lips move: "What in God's name…?"

There's a sound of hard, running footsteps behind him and he is slammed into the doorjamb. Suddenly, Charley is in front of him in the room, bellowing as he closes the distance. "Emma! No!" In one motion, Charley grabs the tongs and turns the wick down on the lamp to douse the flame. The tiny glass cup falls from the tongs and leaves a little trail of burned wool as it rolls along the rug.

Charley's fingers dig into her arms as he shakes her. "Have you completely lost your mind, woman? What the hell are you thinking? Are you *trying* to blow us all up?"

Ferd struggles desperately to force his brain to focus. "You were going to, to use those? On Lillie?" He hears his voice break.

"What are any of you doing? Nothing! Nothing! My baby is dying and you just stand there, stupid and useless! Do something! Why don't you do something?" She pounds on Charley's chest with her fists, her shouts dissolving into wracking sobs as he wraps his arms around her and she collapses against him. He whispers soothing sounds to her as he guides her from the room, and she weeps like a child into his chest.

Ferd still stands where he was pushed into the doorway, and he remains there until some faraway sense recognizes that the tent is still open. The automaton that operates his body checks the valve on the oxygen cylinder—at least Emma's vestigial sanity knew to shut off the flow—and turns it back on. He leans over the bed to close the tent again and feels his legs giving way. He ends up on his knees, clawing through the bedclothes until he clutches Lillie's porcelain-cold hand and presses it with both of his own against his face. Unlike Emma, he weeps silently, but there is no one here to comfort him.

His head is bowed and eyes closed, so he does not see that Lillie's eyes flutter open once, twice. Instead, he feels the briefest squeeze from the hand he holds. His head shoots up, and he presses hard back, waiting to feel it again. "Lillie? Lillie?" There is nothing, though; no movement, no sign of any kind. Now he's trapped in the anguish that he is fully imagining things, but afraid to move or blink or look away, in case he misses another sign.

Bunnies and Chocolate

Friday, 14 April 1933

"Oh, no."

"What is it?"

"Jeanie keeps touching her ear." Lillie groans. "That's always the first sign." She's watching from the kitchen window while Bernie and Jeanie play in the yard. After recent coaching from Johnny, Bernie is working to perfect his finger-snapping technique, and Jeanie has been trying all morning to copy him.

"She takes after Charley Boy, with all his ear infections."

"Oh, Mother, don't say that. I don't think I could live through that again."

But it's true that Dr. Cavanaugh has suggested that Jeanie's tendency toward both earaches and toothaches might be symptoms of a single problem, possibly mastoid-related like Charley Boy's. Or it could simply be that she's susceptible to ear infections and tooth problems. The worst part for Lillie is that there's so little she can do. For the toothaches, Dr. Cavanaugh has her make a paste of ground aspirin and water that she puts directly on the gum. That helps to ease the pain, but also eats away at the gum, which takes a long time to heal. At bedtime, not long ago, Lillie asked Jeanie what she has prayed for. "I ast Jesus please to make my tooth stop hurting." It almost makes Lillie cry.

She calls the two in for lunch. "Come over and wash your hands. Don't step on the baby." Tommy is crawling on the kitchen floor, and she's attempting to keep an eye on what he tries to put in his mouth each time he stops to sit. She stands next to their chairs at the sink to make sure they are washing, and she sees the smudges on Jeanie's ear where she's been rubbing. Lillie takes the damp dishrag and gently wipes the dirt off. Jeanie brings her soapy hand up protectively, but doesn't whine.

At the table, Emma is snapping the woody bottoms from asparagus stalks she's brought in from the garden this morning; it looks to be a bumper crop this year. Lillie slides Tommy into the old wooden high chair and sits down next to him. He still has trouble getting food from his fist into his mouth, and between the two he makes a mushy mess of his zwieback. She keeps an eye on Jeanie, who is chewing her peanut butter and jelly sandwich on only one side of her mouth, opposite the sore ear.

Once Tommy is wiped off, nursed, changed, and put down for his nap, Lillie sits Jeanie in her lap in the light of the front window and looks into her ear; she can't see any inflammation yet. "How much does it hurt?" Jeanie shrugs. "Here, lie down in my lap." Jeanie snuggles down, happy to be invited. Emma comes in with the hot water bottle wrapped in a towel, and Lillie rests it gently against the offending ear. Sometimes, when she catches it right in the beginning, the water bottle combined with frequent flushing with warm salt water staves off or lessens the severity of the oncoming infection. Even so, by Lillie's calculation, with Passion Sunday just two days off, Jeanie will likely have a full-blown ear infection right in the middle of Passiontide, probably just as Holy Week arrives.

This has been a challenging winter. There were a few really good snows, enough to get the kids out of the house for a few hours at a time, though packing them into their snowsuits seems to take several hours by itself. They make snow forts and have great snowball battles: boys against girls, bigs against littles, though with a ringer thrown in on the littles' side to even things out. While the snow lasts, the spring porch stays filled with damp mittens and snowsuits. But mostly the weather is just drizzly and cold in a way that makes everyone hunker down indoors. That much pent-up energy puts the devil into them all. She catches the boys using Bernie's new slingshot to shoot BBs out their open bedroom window at a flock of starlings. Bernie gets into Margaret's pastels and scribbles on the wallpaper in the hall. The girls manage to break a vase while playing an impromptu game of keep-away in the parlor.

Even Jeanie is seduced into bad behavior, as usual from a familiar source. It was not more than two weeks ago, with everyone seated at the dinner table, that Lillie notices a small whispered commotion, and sees Johnny motioning down toward the other end of the table. Then Jeanie pops up. She is standing on her chair, a clearly forbidden act. Giggling, she nonetheless recites in a clear voice:

Listen, listen! The cat's pissin'.
Where, where? Under the chair.
Hurry, hurry! Get the gun!
Oh, don't worry. He's all done.

A split second of stunned silence precedes the eruption. They all know the culprit.

Pop-eyed, Emma gasps, "John Ferdinand!"

Ferd's face goes from pale to red to purple, and Lillie chokes into her napkin, but that's to cover up the fact that she almost laughs out loud. Who else but Johnny would have the utter audacity to teach his baby sister such a horrifying rhyme, and then coach her to stand up and recite it at dinner? And Jeanie, a natural mimic, has the tone, inflection, gestures, and facial expressions spot-on. The littlest actress.

Some of the other children snort as they try to suppress the giggles that will get them in trouble, too. Charley doesn't feel the need to cover up his amusement; he smacks the table with his hand and hoots. "That boy is full of piss and vinegar!"

Ferd's chair is pushed back, and he glares at Charley before pointing an accusing finger at Johnny. "*You* taught her that! She is barely three years old, and *you* taught her to say that!"

As Ferd stalks to Johnny's side of the table to take him by the arm, Charley looks at Jeanie, who is sitting again and sucking on two fingers in bewilderment, and says, "That was a mighty impressive recitation, missy. How long did he have you practice that?"

Ferd marches Johnny in front of him, takes the razor strop from behind the kitchen door, and keeps going.

That is the last of the winter's major transgressions, though, and everyone makes it through in one piece. Finally, and none too soon, the weather turns; cold and rainy right up to the end of March, now it's trending markedly to sun and warmth. The garden has burst forth in lettuce, rhubarb, broccoli, and the first of the asparagus that Emma's been harvesting today. The irises, those strumpets of the spring garden, flaunt their come-hither flags without shame, and there are fat buds already on the peonies, which will be open just in time for the May altar. The whole neighborhood enjoys the beautiful show of narcissus and tulips that the Elliott sisters put in annually. The moveable feast of Easter is late this year, following as it does in the footsteps of the first full moon of spring, which means that green and blooms swaddle them all. Especially after this winter, Lillie has been looking forward to the Easter season, one of her favorite times of the year. The sense of renewal, of rebirth—not just in the obvious Christian way, but in an almost-physical bursting forth—feels like a gift.

Of course, she has her own gift now, sown and sprouting just like the fuzzy heads of the carrots or first tendrils of the sweet peas in the garden, and she smiles at the silly thought. By now, she knows innately when the seed is planted, understands the speed of germination, feels the tiny roots taking hold, limbs reaching upward, all still hidden. She waits a week for certainty, then delivers the news.

She sits at her dressing table in her nightgown, brushing out her hair. Bernie in his trundle and Jeanie in her crib are already asleep, and Ferd is changing into his pajamas. She watches him in the mirror and smiles as he hangs his clothes neatly on the back of the bedside chair. He catches her reflection and smiles back. "What?"

"Just thinking."

"About?"

"I wonder if it makes sense to have Dad put up a room in the attic. For the boys."

Ferd sits on the bed. "You mean as a bedroom?"

She smiles at her reflection. "It's a shame we couldn't switch the order of Dorothy and Bernie. That way we could have put him in with the boys and had more time to figure out a permanent place for

Dorothy and Jeanie. But with Dorothy getting older, I feel like we need to do some reshuffling."

Ferd considers the concept of the attic. "Well, it would be hot as blazes in summer. Not so bad in winter, and there's good light up there. I just wonder whether we'd all survive them being left alone so much." He rolls his eyes at the thought.

She sits her brush on the table and turns around. "Well, we're going to have to do something, because soon we'll be completely out of space."

Their eyes lock, his surprised, hers laughing, and they both stand up at the same time, meeting in the middle. "Oh, Lillie!" he says loudly enough that Bernie stirs and mumbles. He lowers his voice. "To think you weren't sure there would be any more."

She laughs quietly. "Hardy German stock."

He lifts her up and spins once around before setting her back down again. She, in turn, wraps her arms around his neck for a kiss. "Congratulations, Mr. Voith. An even ten."

"And to you, Mrs. Voith." They smile at each other, and kiss once more. "So, I guess that means I'll be visiting the attic myself!"

From her seat on the sofa, she gazes at the memory box sitting once again in its traditional spot next to the secretary, already open to the treasures inside. She absently strokes Jeanie's hair. "Does that feel better?"

"Uh huh." She reaches out. "Sally."

Lillie is able to scoop the ragdoll from the floor, and tucks her into Jeanie's arm. "Sally's your favorite baby, isn't she?"

"Uh huh. She listens good."

Of all the girls, Jeanie reminds her the most of herself. Age, gender, and birth order isolate her in ways the rest of the children never are, making Sally her closest playmate. The isolation worries Lillie because it does remind her of herself at that age. But Jeanie seems resilient, and all that time alone cultivates her imagination: she makes up songs and little dances, and performs them for herself, for Sally, for whomever happens to be there at the moment. She is a perfect mimic, innocently matching note-for-note the tone, facial expression, and gestures of whichever adult the situation most calls for. When she puffs up, puts a hand on her hip, and wags her finger, it is Emma's voice that will issue forth. If she tips her head to the side, presses her lips into a line, and casts a steely look, it's going to be Lillie, who tries hard not to laugh. Lillie doesn't want to encourage her, knowing that what's adorable in a two- or three-year-old is unattractive not long beyond that.

"You know, when I was a little girl, I had a doll just like Sally, and she was my favorite too."

"You was a little girl?"

"Yes, I was. A long time ago."

Jeanie considers this unlikely scenario as she sucks on two fingers. This is a self-comforting gesture left over from toddlerhood that Lillie still allows when Jeanie is sick or recovering from punishment. She pulls them out to ask, "Did you got lots of brothers and sisters?"

"Well, no, I didn't have any. It was just me and Gramal and Granner living alone in this big old house."

"They're your Gramal and Granner too?"

Lillie laughs, knowing how hard it always is for children to understand relationships at this age. "No, they are my mamma and daddy, just like I'm your mamma and Daddy is your daddy. But do you know what I wanted more than anything back then?" Jeanie shakes her head. "I wanted a little girl just like you."

The single painful sense she carries from early childhood is of an abiding loneliness, one that even her parents' unbounded love cannot fill. Or perhaps the feeling is something more like isolation, a separateness. Once she starts school, she begins to grasp more completely all the ways in which her life is different from that of everyone she knows: Her mother leaves the house for the office every day but Sunday. No one else's mother goes out every day for *anything*, except perhaps for the marketing. Until she is older, a series of nurses lives with them and cares for Lillie during the day. Miss Hilfinger—Christine—is her very favorite, but even Christine and her wonderful stories and games can't stop Lillie from wishing that her mother were there instead. She is stunned when she realizes that a nurse is not a standard household fixture, and that she is unique among her schoolmates in having one. Then there is the issue of parental age. While it takes her longer to grasp that husbands are typically older than their wives, she sees immediately that her mother is older—in many cases, far older—than any of the other mothers. The only one who is nearly as old as Emma is Sarah's mother, but Sarah is the youngest of twelve.

Even now, Lillie can clearly summon the ache of longing for a baby sister, not understanding at the time how utterly improbable it is that she is even here herself. How many years does she ask Santa Claus for this single present? In the end, she even concedes to Santa that she is willing to take a little brother, if only he will grant her wish.

There in the box beside the secretary, Emma's journal, dipped into so often in the wait for a new child, gives Lillie an understanding of her own loneliness, along with Emma's sadness at having to leave Lillie at home every day. More surprising is Emma's unhappiness at watching Lillie grow up; it's clear that Emma wants her baby to remain her baby always, to the point that the diary she keeps for twelve long years ends abruptly with the start of Lillie's first period and Emma's comment "the dread time has arrived," as though there is nothing left to say.

During their courtship, Lillie makes sure that Ferd knows she wants a big family; it is the one thing that she truly feels strongly about. After they are married, though, it doesn't take long to see there are no worries about a tiny family. Once she understands that she is reliably fertile, it falls to that most effective of all family planning tools, abstinence, to manage the spacing of the children. It's not the happiest of strategies from Ferd's perspective, but she hates the expression *Irish twins*, with its implied judgment of a lack of restraint. More importantly, she wants time alone with each new baby, and she wants to allow him or her to settle into the family before introducing the next child. By the time this baby is born, Tommy will be sixteen months old, which is just about right, from Lillie's thinking. She has time, then: time enough to plumb the memory box, to introduce the growing life to all that came before, to whisper, "Little baby, you are the sum of all our joy." Time enough to prepare herself and her family to welcome the next new member.

As though on cue, Tommy's wailing kicks up from the room above them. She sets the now-tepid water bottle aside, and helps Jeanie sit up. "Do you feel good enough for a ginger snap? Okay, go ask Gramal, and make sure Bernie gets one, too." As Jeanie dashes for the kitchen, Lillie calls behind her, "Remember, please and thank you!"

Tonight is this week's movie night, a rare occurrence, since Fridays are typically reserved for bath night. Before she starts dressing, Lillie fills the bulb-like rubber syringe and has Emma hold a bowl under Jeanie's ear while she irrigates. Jeanie squirms and whines, not because it hurts now, but because she associates the bulb with pain. If the infection should blossom, she will shriek at the sight of it.

"Jeanie, you need to hold still. You told me before this just tickles."

"I doan wanna."

"Well, you'll just have to." She sighs to Emma, "I hate it when the kids are sick on holidays. It ruins the whole thing for them. I don't want Jeanie to miss out; this will be the first Easter that she really remembers."

This is certainly a year for first memories for Jeanie, starting with Hallowe'en in the fall, when she is dressed in a shiny blue tunic and a wide cardboard cone with a scarf draping from the top for a hat, and told she is a princess. The overlapping and conflicting guidance offered by the others leads her to stand in the hall and look from the bowl of paper-wrapped taffy by the door to her tin bucket and back again. Finally she takes a piece of taffy, puts it in her bucket, and walks back toward the parlor before Ferd turns her around and heads her out the front door. After that, it's Thanksgiving, Christmas, New Year's Day, Saint Valentine's Day, Saint Patrick's Day, and, absolutely best of all, her birthday. Except for Bernie and Charley Boy, everyone else has already had their birthday, so she thinks maybe she is too little to get one. She's always too little for something, it seems. But then everyone starts telling her about the wonders of her upcoming birthday in that breathless, big-eyed way that signals she is about to become very confused.

"Aren't you ex*cited*, Jeanie? It's going to be your *birth*day!"

"And you get a cake."

"And you get to blow out the candles!"

"And you get all the presents, and no one else does, and no one gets to even help open them, neither," says Bernie, who's birthday is all the way in July and feels like it will never get here. Tommy's birthday is in August, but he doesn't count yet because he's just a baby.

As it turns out, her birthday is the least confusing of all the new things so far, since it doesn't involve pilgrims or reindeer or scary leprechauns. It's just overwhelming to finally be the center of attention. The weight of it becomes oppressive over the course of the day, so that when they all gather around her and sing *For She's a Jolly Good Fellow*, she erupts into tears. That makes everybody laugh and pat at her, but then they show her the presents, and it's just like Bernie says: they are all for her, just her. She now understands birthdays very well.

Bernie and Jeanie are old enough to eat dinner with the rest of the family on movie night, and stay up in the parlor for a little longer before bed. Lately, Emma has taken to making Charley turn off his blaring radio after dinner so she can read to all the children from the Bible or her prayer book. Emma isn't explaining the change in routine, but Charley suspects that Emma feels the oldest girls are becoming more interested in boys than in church, and she means to fix that.

Tonight she's having trouble getting them to settle down and listen. It seems the postponed bath night has made the children as giddy as though it were a holiday. She skips to the story of the Passion, since the suspense and brutality are likely to keep their attention. As always, Dorothy has the most questions. "Why were they so mean to Jesus? He never did anything bad."

"That was the way it was supposed to happen. God fore-ordained it; it was written in the Scriptures."

"Why didn't God make them stop?"

"Because He sent his only begotten Son to redeem mankind by

dying on the cross."

Francie and Eleanor share an eyeroll out of Emma's line of sight, while the three little ones just stare in gap-mouthed bewilderment.

"He had to die so that He could rise again." Nothing. Finally, she huffs in frustration. "If he hadn't done that, then we would never have Easter."

Dorothy gasps. "No Easter? Then we wouldn't have any Easter baskets! Or candy!"

Emma fixes her with a look. "That's not the important thing about Easter."

Bernie nods firmly in agreement. "Easter bunny and Easter egg hunt," he reminds Dorothy.

Charley Boy turns to Charley. "Granner, remember that time the egg was way up in the knot hole of the walnut tree? I saw it from across the yard, and I had to go get the ladder to get it back down."

"Yep, and everyone thought you were crazy when they saw you lugging the ladder out from the barn. But you got the last egg!"

Jeanie whispers to Bernie, "Eggs in the tree?"

But Dorothy hears her. "Oh, oh, Jeanie doesn't know about Easter!" Which unleashes a flood from all directions. Baskets with jelly beans, marshmallow eggs, and chocolate bunnies, and a real bunny rabbit that dyes real eggs and then hides them and makes everyone find them, and fancy new clothes, and a long time in church, and Jesus hanging up in a tree and then being dead and then coming out from behind a big rock.

Jeanie lets out a little bleat. First it was Jesus and Santa Claus, now it's Jesus and the Easter Bunny. It never makes any sense.

Emma has reached her limit. "Since no one plans to listen or learn, I guess it's bedtime for everyone. And I don't expect any visitors tonight, either! Straight to bed!"

The house is fully quiet when Lillie and Ferd return home; she listens at the steps as Ferd helps her with her wrap and hears no voices. They visit the kitchen to find Charley in his normal spot, but already draining his coffee in preparation for his nightly rounds.

"It's an early night tonight, Dad. I'm guessing my children were not particularly cooperative this evening."

"Not to your mother's liking, no. They were getting rambunctious in telling the ins and outs of Easter to Jeanie, and drowning out Emma's message of salvation. She sent them all packing." Charley folds the paper and pushes back with a chuckle. "Poor little Jeanie. Easter makes no sense all by itself ("Dad!"), without seven mixed-up voices yelling at you about it. I think she was having trouble holding up."

She shakes her head at him even as she kisses his cheek. "It's a wonder Mother didn't send *you* packing."

"Oh, Lillie, she tried that years ago. It never took."

Lillie makes her bedtime rounds, tonight only stopping to give each of the girls a kiss. "I hear you haven't behaved yourselves particularly well while we've been out. You can use tonight to consider how to do better next time." The girls slump in disappointment at missing the movie night recap. The boys pretend to be asleep, but Dorothy and Bernie actually are. When she leans over the side of Jeanie's crib, Lillie finds that she's fully awake, sucking on two fingers. Lillie gently pulls them away as she kisses Jeanie's forehead in a discreet check for temperature.

"Why are you still awake, sweetie bug? You should be asleep by now."

"Mamma, I thought chickens have eggs."

"That's right. They do."

"But why does the bunny have eggs? Did he steal them from the chickens?"

"No, sweetie bug. I think the chickens give them to him."

"Why does he hide them?"

"It's just a game. It's just like playing hide-and-go-seek, only the eggs stay right where they are until you find them."

Jeanie starts to put her fingers back in her mouth but Lillie stops her. "Is Jesus playing hide-and-go-seek?"

That's a surprise question. "What do you mean?"

"Jesus hides in the cave and then comes out again and surprises everyone. Is that like with the bunny and the eggs?"

Lillie concedes in her head to Charley that this is confusing, at least for a little girl, and considers how to explain it. "Jeanie, the

Easter bunny is just a fun thing. Easter is really for Jesus."

"Baby Jesus?"

"No, Christmas is for Baby Jesus. Easter is for Big Jesus." *Big Jesus*—that's certainly a new way to explain this. She imagines the circumstance that will prompt Jeanie to relate this explanation to the larger household, as she inevitably will. "God sent Jesus from Heaven to show us how much he loved us, and to show us that if we love Him back, we will never really die. Not permanently. Just like Jesus; he died, but then he came back to life again. And that's why we celebrate Easter."

"Died like Mittens?"

Mittens, one of the neighborhood cats, meets his end under the wheels of a delivery van trundling down Longfellow. That he is surprisingly intact means the adults can let the children hold a proper burial service for him. "Yes, but then Jesus came back to life."

"And pushed the rock away all by himself?"

"That's right, sweetie bug."

She lets out a sad little sigh. "I don't get it."

"Well, you don't have to get it right this minute; you'll understand soon. This Sunday is Passion Sunday, then it's Palm Sunday, and after that it's Easter Sunday." She strokes Jeanie's head. "Easter's my very favorite, sweetie bug. I hope you love it just like I do. Now you need to go to sleep."

"'Kay."

"Goodnight, sleep tight, don't let the bed bugs bite." Lillie leans down to kiss her again, and touches Jeanie's cheek right by her ear; Jeanie doesn't flinch.

When Lillie is finally able to climb into bed next to Ferd, he rouses a little. "What was that all about?"

"Jeanie's trying to understand about Easter, and apparently I'm rusty at explaining it." Even half asleep, Ferd shares in the joke. "But I think Jeanie's ear may have cleared up, thank heavens. Maybe we've dodged a bullet there."

"Mmmm," Ferd acknowledges, already on his way back to sleep.

Lillie snuggles down, her head finding its normal spot against his chest, where the steady sound of his breathing forms her own private lullaby, and joins him.

Friday, 21 April 1933

Gogarty the iceman has no first name as far as anyone is aware. He is simply Gogarty, and he has delivered ice to 741 since the day Charley brought his second-hand icebox into the still-unfinished house. He's since replaced his horse with a truck, but the old ice wagon persists, its undercarriage removed, bolted into the truck's flat bed. Beyond that, it may as well be 1894, for Gogarty looks exactly the same now as he did then.

With that as competition, Sven Gundarssen is a relative newcomer with only twenty years of delivering coal to the neighborhood. He and Gogarty often run their deliveries in tandem; they enjoy the companionship, while their customers enjoy the delivery of two of life's necessities with only one household interruption. Sven always travels behind Gogarty to keep from blackening the ice, and when the wind is blowing hard and erratically, they make their runs separately. Neither can begin to count the number of guffaws they've heard about a Swede delivering coal while an Irishman delivers ice. The naturally pale skin of Sven's face, ears, and neck—the only areas of him that are exposed during his deliveries—is permanently tattooed with twenty years of coal dust.

It's still early Friday morning when Sven and Gogarty pull up in the alley behind 741. Each man unloads his cart. Gogarty has a flatbed, two-wheeled barrow on which he can stack four blocks of ice at a time if needed; the Beck's only need one per delivery. Sven's coal cart is homemade, with a long scooped nose and hinged front axle that allows him to tip the cart all the way up to send the whole load down the coal scuttle on the side of the house. He makes sure to let folks know when he's about to make a delivery, since anyone in the cellar will otherwise be engulfed in a billowing, choking cloud of dust.

While they're loading up, Gogarty remarks, "Saw Rufus's truck down at Johnson's when we went by. I guess no one up this way is getting bread this morning."

"Guess coal and ice will have to do then."

Gogarty wheels his cart to the bottom of the spring porch steps; Sven, after giving a mighty push to get his cart moving, lands it right outside the coal scuttle on the far side of the house, then comes around to hold the door for Gogarty. It's unnecessary but part of the routine they've developed over many years. For his part, Gogarty takes a big bite into the sides of the ice block with his iron tongs, and hefts it expertly up and over his shoulder, which is covered by a thick leather pad. They both step into the kitchen, which is oddly deserted, as though somehow abandoned. There is only a low murmuring sound that seems to vibrate from the floor joists. Sven clatters down the cellar steps to check for occupants, while Gogarty opens the bottom box that holds the ice. Only a thin slab remains of the original block, and he fishes it out while balancing the new one by using a massive forearm thrown over the tong handles. There's only a little meltwater at the bottom, since the box drains through a pipe that empties into the back flowerbed, constantly watering a marsh mallow that enjoys the moisture.

As Sven comes back into the kitchen, saying, "No one below," Gogarty opens the food compartment to test for cold and whistles. "That's a lot of food, even for the Becks." Now he notices the counter, which is covered tip to toe with even more.

Sven follows his gaze. "That's a wedding or a funeral."

"No one in this house old enough for a wedding."

The low murmuring invades the stillness as they consider the ugly implication, and Gogarty finally understands what he's hearing. Someone, no, several people, from the sound of it, are praying the rosary. Ice in the box, tongs on the porch, he stands at the door to the hall and listens; the leader announces the second sorrowful mystery, The Scourging at the Pillar, and the group launches into the Lord's Prayer, which will be followed, he knows, by a decade of Hail Marys. Without considering, he pushes the door open just a sliver and looks out over a sea of heads; people are kneeling, each one fingering a rosary as the congregation tracks progress through the beads.

Charley stands just to one side of the kitchen doorjamb, and he startles Gogarty by pulling the door open enough to slip through, and it looks for a second as though Charley is leading in a little tango into the kitchen. Gogarty is embarrassed at the thought that he is snooping on a family in distress. Before he can even say anything, Charley tells them, "I didn't get a chance to go to the bank yet, boys. I hope I can settle the bill next time."

Gogarty is doubly embarrassed now. "Yes, certainly. I…"

"And can you put another two blocks into the ice house in the barn? I've used what I had."

This just confirms it for him. "Of course I will. I'm sorry for your troubles, Mr. Beck. It's Mrs. Beck, then, is it?"

"No. It's Lillie."

Gogarty actually stumbles at this, and there's a sharp intake from Sven. Gogarty has known Lillie all her life: he delivers ice to the house three days after she is born. She coos and kicks her feet at him, toddles unsteadily over to him, curtsies and says good day, poses for him in her cotillion finery, waves at him in the middle of her backyard wedding party, introduces him to each child in turn. It can't be true.

"She's very ill," Charley explains, which snaps Gogarty back into focus. "Her mother asked me to have the people from church come and say some prayers."

"Saints be praised, she's still with us, then. We feared the worst."

Charley looks at him for a long moment without really seeing, then puts a hand on Gogarty's shoulder as he moves back to the hall. "Well. Now you can hope for the best."

When yesterday's cupping incident unfolded, Chloe rang for Dr. Cavanaugh and asked Mrs. Cavanaugh to please send him just as soon as possible. Of course he arrives thinking that he's there to see Lillie, and it rocks him back a little when Chloe tells him that it's Emma.

"Mrs. Beck? Not Miss Lillie?"

"No, sir, Doctor, sir. Mrs. Beck had an episode. She's up in her room right now with Mr. Charley."

"An episode?"

"Mr. Charley can tell you."

The tableau in their bedroom is telling enough, as Charley sits on the edge of the bed holding Emma's hand and speaking in low tones to her. Emma's face is colorless to the point of translucence, but her red eyes are almost swollen shut. To Dr. Cavanaugh, he says, "The strain has gotten to her, Doc. Maybe you can give her something to ease her mind?"

"Well, the same tincture we've been giving Lillie will help. She needs uninterrupted sleep."

She won't take it from Dr. Cavanaugh, but allows Charley to coax her into opening wide and accepting the spoon, as though she is Jeanie finally taking her cough syrup. He strokes her hair back from her forehead as she starts to drift, but her eyes open again and she grasps his hand. "Tell them to come."

"Tell who?"

"Church. Tell them to come and pray. We need them all to pray."

"I will, Em. I'll tell them all to come."

Once again the signals go out, this time urgently and with purpose. Charley's lone call is to Henrietta Buckwedder, one of Emma's greatest friends and Lillie's godmother. Henrietta takes care of the rest, and the first wave of congregants rolls silently in through the front door before five in the morning.

After Jeanie, who retreats with a whimper, Francie and Charley Boy are the first of the children to be startled by the scene of this new development, and Francie races back upstairs to dress more completely. "Do you think something happened? Overnight?"

Margaret speculates, pale.

Eleanor's mouth tightens. "And do you think anyone would tell us?"

"But maybe today they'll let us stay home. Won't they have to?" Francie's voice cracks.

The answers are no, no, and, of course, no. Lillie's condition is unchanged, no one thinks to offer the children any sort of information, and Chloe is sent to muster them out for school, which removes any possible recourse of negotiation. Instead, the children collect in the boys' bedroom to discuss options. Jeanie has climbed back into her crib, clutching her ear and whimpering softly. Bernie is on Johnny's bed with his knees pulled up to his chest, and the others huddle to strategize.

"Maybe if we just stay up here, no one will notice we haven't left yet until it's too late for us to go."

"But you said the nuns were downstairs. They're not having school if the sisters are here."

"No, it's the convent nuns. None of the teachers are down there."

"We need to know what's happening."

"If we ask Granner, he'll tell us."

"While he's pushing us out the door."

"Make the people go 'way."

"Dorothy, you sneak down and listen to what people are saying."

"It can't be Dorothy. If anyone sees her, that'll be it for all of us."

They all turn to look at Bernie, who looks darkly back at them and pulls his knees in tighter.

"No one would pay any attention to him."

"He's too little to know what's going on."

"Am not."

"Are so."

"Not."

"Prove it, then. Go find out what they're saying."

Bernie would never back down from a dare. Still, he takes his time pushing down from the bed and through the group, but at last he pries open the bedroom door. As though captured in a photograph, Emma is perfectly framed in the doorway as she advances down the hall. She is fully dressed, every hair in place, face pale but composed, dry-eyed. She slows imperceptibly at the sea of children still in their pajamas— "Get dressed. You'll be late for school."—and continues forward. There is a collective, simultaneous deflation of defeat.

Emma's slow progress down the steps, chin up, makes her seem regal rather than arthritic. The recitation begins to drop off as people notice her, but she nods at them to continue. Henrietta is there as she steps into the hall, leaning in to say a quiet word, and offering her arm. Others reach up to provide support as she kneels stiffly. "...the Lord is with Thee. Blessed art Thou among women..." As familiar to her as her own name, the words of the prayer demand nothing from her, and she allows them to wash over her in a numbing, repetitive stream. "...Mother of God, pray for us sinners now and at the hour of our death. Amen. Hail, Mary, full of grace..."

ഋര

Early, before the first of the prayer circle arrives, Charley finds Ferd sprawled face-first, half on the bed and half on the floor, where he finally collapses from his vigil sometime in the dark hours of the very early morning. Charley starts to tap him awake, but thinks the better of it. He can't imagine how stiff Ferd will be when he finally tries to stand up, but considers it more urgent that he get some small amount of sleep. Charley allowed himself perhaps an hour as he watched protectively over a sleeping Emma. Now, he walks to the other side of Lillie's bed to lean in and listen; the sound is a faint wheeze and rattle. He pulls his watch to calculate how long it might be before Dr. Cavanaugh arrives and the chance that Chloe will be here earlier or later than that. He makes his way down the steps to the hall and the telephone. In the silent house, for once he keeps his voice low. "Sophie? It's Charley Beck. Sorry about the time. No, it's not that. It's just...can you come? I can't do this by myself."

It all materializes quickly enough: Sophie, Chloe, arriving

to help with the heavy lifting of the household; Dr. Cavanaugh coming to check on Emma and Lillie; the prayer circle forming and starting its low, monotonous rosary chant; Gogarty and Sven stumbling onto the scene and imagining the very worst; Emma making her regal progress into the hall; and finally, the children, miserable, unenlightened, ignored, dragging themselves downstairs to stand and gawp at what has taken over their house, even as the door quietly opens and more people stream in to kneel and join the prayers. Charley, against the far wall, is the only other person standing, and he gives them a small nod. It is Eleanor who attempts a silent negotiation for them, gesturing first to her group and then out to the kneeling assembly. Charley responds with the barest shake of his head, and with his chin indicates the door. He is mildly surprised to see several angry glares shoot back at him, but supposes he would feel the same way in their place. He knows, though, it will be far worse to let them stay, where the empty hours of waiting will breed an unhelpful stir-craziness that no one can afford right now. He meets the looks and holds them, until the heads drop and there is a collective shuffle out the front door.

It is Sophie who wakes Ferd and helps to pull him to his feet. She isn't able to convince him to find a bed and get some real sleep, but his relief at having someone else with him is so sharp that he has to wipe his eyes quickly when she turns away for a moment. He surrenders to her as she arranges him in his normal chair and uses her solid frame to block the view as she checks the bedclothes for dampness. He marvels that she knows without asking how to maneuver her forearms under the tent skirt, and at her crisp efficiency in testing for temperature, sponging off forehead and cheeks, dabbing Vaseline onto cracked lips.

He hears himself saying, "I thought she woke up last night; I felt her press my hand once, but that was all." He can't tell whether she's heard him, except then she leans in and takes up Lillie's hand in hers. "Lillie? Lillie, can you hear me? It's Sophie. Time to wake up, dear." She pats Lillie's hand, and then her cheek. "Come on now. You've got people here who need you." There is a long quiet moment before Sophie releases Lillie's hand, slides her arms out from underneath, and arranges the tent against air leaks.

They don't leave him alone anymore, understanding that he's beyond being capable of helping. Sophie, Charley, Chloe, or Dr. Cavanaugh: someone else is always there, treating him almost as a secondary patient. Though he has no sense of sleeping, he recognizes that his consciousness is patchy, because the people in the room sometimes change in the space of one eye-blink. Once he finds a blanket tucked around him in his chair, and another time the card table is pulled up next to him offering a sandwich and coffee. But no one beats him to the bedside when there is a sudden, rough gasp, and it is Ferd who sees Lillie's eyes rear open as her body coils for a coughing fit. Dr. Cavanaugh is only a step behind, and firmly moves him to one side in order to assess Lillie's condition. The cough makes a sound like old sheets being ripped into bandages. It seems as though Dr. Cavanaugh is a single river of motion as he holds a cloth for her, slides the drinking tube between her lips, holds the back of his hand against her forehead, and presses a stethoscope against her chest; the entire time, Lillie's eyes remain on Ferd's. It is what the two of them do sometimes, in the midst of household chaos or silliness, children shrieking and running, or even just when they are across the room or yard from each other: over a sea of heads, their gazes connect and hold for a moment. The look communicates without fear of interruption or eavesdropping, and what it says is *I love you*. Message delivered, Lillie's eyes droop and she slumps back into the pillows.

Ferd feels a stab of disappointment when Charley guides Emma into the room, knowing that he has lost his place at the bedside again; they will all defer to her now.

As Charley settles Emma into her chair, he tells Sophie, "I think the good news has given the congregation its second wind. They're going at that rosary in double-time now."

In fact, the sound resonating up from the hall below is louder now, grown from a murmur to detectible words. Emma leans toward the bed. "Do you hear that, darling? They're here for you. The church, everyone is here."

Lillie's eyes are just visible under the lids, and a little smile plays at her lips. She has to try several times for the words, "I hear them," to finally issue from her as a kind of creaking noise. The effort is clearly exhausting.

"Don't try to talk, Lillie," Dr. Cavanaugh tells her. "But I need you to try to eat some broth, yes? Let's take your temperature first."

The day progresses thus, with Lillie in and out, closely monitored, the clear monotone song of the congregation below welling up through the floorboards, propelling the swirling tide of caregivers, Ferd and Emma in their chairs on either side of the bed awash in the ebb and flow of sound, bobbing like buoys in the current.

Charley and Dr. Cavanaugh have developed their own silent form of communication, certainly not as nuanced as that of Ferd and Lillie, since it's had only days to develop, but sufficient to the moment. Charley can read the concern over the numbers Dr. Cavanaugh shakes out of the thermometer, the sounds that come to him through his stethoscope, and the analytic result of numbers and sounds that issue from the pumping of the blood pressure cuff. Over the other heads in the room, the two men exchange a look, and what that looks says is: *They need to pray harder.*

Saturday, 22 April 1933

The Voith children are loosely collected in the yard. Bernie, as usual, lies on his stomach across one of the swings, pushing himself forward and back with the toe of his shoe, and Johnny sits on the other, poking at the remains of a mud puddle caught in the low spot just beneath it. Risking splinters, Jeanie clutches onto the cross-piece of the swing's A-frame and lifts up her feet every so often to hang there until her arms get tired. Eleanor has lugged Tommy outside and put him in the grass by the bench where she sits with Margaret and Dorothy. Charley Boy is tossing a baseball up into the air and catching it, and Francie idly toys with a drooping pansy she's picked from the flowerbed. It's late afternoon, and they have all been banished from the house.

"How long do we have to be out here?"

"It's been forever. Maybe they forgot about us."

"We're staying out here until Granddaddy says it's okay to come back in. And we've only been out here a little while."

"I need to pee."

"Go behind the bushes then."

"I'm hungry."

"What if they forget and leave us out here and it gets dark?"

"Scaredy cat."

"Am not!"

"Are so!"

"Not!"

"Both of you, be quiet!"

There is momentary peace. With another push of his toe, Bernie asks of no one, "What's extra munction?"

Johnny snorts in derision. "You made that up."

"I didn't make it up. Gramal said it. She said Father Bishop was coming to give Mother extra munction."

"You're still a dumbhead."

Bernie shrugs, unconcerned.

Eleanor sighs heavily. "Johnny, just stop. This is exactly why they send us outside. Bernie, his name is Father Bischoff, and it's *extreme unction*, not *extra munction*."

Both Bernie and Johnny look at her. "That's still made up," Johnny complains.

Francie throws her flower down. "Do the nuns know how little you pay attention?"

"But what *is* it?" Bernie still wants to know.

Charley Boy snatches his ball out of the air and snaps, "It's last rites." As he says it, a racking sob comes from Margaret, and that makes even Johnny freeze. She buries her face in her hands and runs to the front yard.

In the ensuing silence, even Bernie is unwilling to ask the next obvious question. Finally, Eleanor explains, "It's just something they do when a grown-up is sick."

"*Just* nothing," Charley Boy snaps again.

"You don't know. It could…"

"You don't know either, so stop pretending you do!" He hurls the ball across the yard, slamming it into the side of the garage with a crash, and stalks off.

Charley Boy's anger, so uncharacteristic of him, is even more unsettling than Margaret's weeping. Francie and Eleanor both recognize the unmistakable sound of Jeanie starting to cry, which she has been doing almost constantly today, now that her ear is leaking fluid, and that seems to be just the nudge that Tommy needs to start wailing. Eleanor lifts Tommy to her shoulder and rubs his back, as Dorothy presses in against her, and Francie, red-eyed, pulls Jeanie up onto her lap. Bernie and Johnny, too masculine to seek comfort, push back and forth on their swings.

ꙮ

Charley greets Father Bischoff at the door and leads him into the hall, where many of his parishioners kneel in a circle and pray the rosary. The old priest, long the pastor of Nativity, wears his black cassock and carries a bag similar to Dr. Cavanaugh's. "Do you need anything before we head up, Father?" Charley asks him quietly.

"No, thank you, Mr. Beck. Let's go see your daughter."

Father Bischoff has known Lillie since the day he arrived at the parish when she was twelve years old. He presided over Lillie's marriage to Ferd and has baptized each one of the Voith children. He watches with a sense of fatherly pride as she shepherds her ever-expanding brood through Mass each Sunday with her manner of the gentle general. He's heard from parishioners and the sisters that Lillie has taken ill, and would have looked in on the family before now except that Passiontide is such a busy time and he hasn't found the opportunity.

When Charley Beck called the rectory to summon him, Father Bischoff felt certain that the request for extreme unction was made from an abundance of caution and the need to comfort Emma, rather than from urgent spiritual necessity. Because he is so sure of this assessment, his first sight of Lillie freezes him on the threshold of the sickroom.

He feels Charley's hand at his shoulder, the slight pressure helping him through the doorway, silently reminding him that he is the authority figure in the room, and that his flock, here in the form of Emma and Ferd, is looking to him for comfort and guidance. He steps to the side of the bed and busies himself with his preparations, unwilling yet to confront this reality. He takes his stole from his bag—one that is embroidered with Easter lilies in honor of the season and the sacrament's recipient—kisses it, and arranges it over his shoulders and down the front of his cassock. He opens the bottle of oil, blessed by the bishop, and sets it on the bedside table cluttered with the miscellany of the sick. Finally, he has to look at the bed, at Lillie, and he freezes.

Charley steps close to him and says quietly, "Can you bless the baby also?"

Father Bischoff is stunned. "She's with child?"

"We don't know anymore. She was."

The priest breathes in deeply to find his resolve. "Of course I can. May I open the tent?"

Charley turns down the flow of oxygen from the canister at the foot of the bed and comes around to lift the tent flap and fold it back over the top. "This should be fine for about ten minutes," he says and steps back.

More alarming than her gray pallor or the fact that she looks somehow shrunken is the ugly rasp of each inhale and rattle of each exhale. Though her eyelids flutter occasionally, he can't tell whether she is conscious. He touches her hand, but she does not respond.

He stoppers the bottle with his thumb and turns it over briefly, and starts with her eyes, reciting in Latin, "Through this holy unction and His own most tender mercy, may the Lord pardon thee whatever sins or faults thou hast committed by sight." He anoints her eyelids with the oil as he says this, making the sign of the cross with his thumb. He moves on to her ears. "Through this holy unction and His own most tender mercy, may the Lord pardon thee whatever sins or faults thou hast committed by hearing." And so the unctions progress to her nose, lips, hands, and feet. He tries to hurry, aware that he has only ten minutes before they need to close the tent again. He turns to put the oil away and when he looks back, her eyes are open. It's clear that she recognizes him, and her eyes give him the barest smile. A positive sign; perhaps the prayers have helped? Again, he looks up at Charley; it's hard to look at the others. "She's awake. Can she speak?"

"It's too exhausting for her to try."

He looks down at Lillie. "May I say your Act of Contrition for you, while you say it silently?"

She closes her eyes briefly in silent assent.

"O my God, I am heartily sorry for having offended Thee, and I detest all my sins because I dread the loss of Heaven and the pains of Hell; but most of all because they offend Thee, my God, Who art all-good and deserving of all my love. I firmly resolve, with the help of Thy grace, to confess my sins, to do penance, and to amend my life. Amen." He sees her lips moving just barely along with his words, but notices that her breathing is noisier now. Charley moves in, even as Father Bischoff is finishing the prayer, sliding the tent flap down again. Before it closes, Lillie's hand catches Father Bischoff's and squeezes, with surprising pressure. When she lets go, her arm slides once more protectively across her belly. He looks up at her through the tent, but her eyes are closed again.

The sacrament is unfinished. He knows she cannot receive communion; many needing this sacrament are unable to accept the host, but he has hoped to put the chalice against her lips to wet them with wine, even if she can't drink. Instead, he places his hand on the tent, closes his eyes, and murmurs a prayer for the unborn.

Unsure what to do next, Father Bischoff finally steals a look at Ferd and Emma. He is stunned to find Ferd glaring hard at him, his eyes blazing and his face red. Still, his voice is strangely even. "Offended? When has Lillie ever offended anyone in her entire life? Is this somehow supposed to be her fault?"

Before he's even finished, Charley is saying "Ferd, you know those are the words. We all say them every week. They don't change just because it's Lillie." But then they are all silenced as the sound of Emma's voice washes over them, words that become their own sort of incantation as she hovers at the bedside. "My darling, my sweet baby, my own Lillie. Lillie, Lillie. I was your age when I carried you, my own darling. My sweet Lillie."

The words continue to flow in their own rhythm as Ferd pulls his arm from Charley's grip and turns away.

Without comment, Charley hands Father Bischoff his bag and guides him from the room, and down the steps into the hall. "I'm sure you'd like to lead the folks in a prayer or two," Charley suggests with a gesture at the circle. "They've been hard at it for two days."

"Yes. Yes, of course." Charley heads toward the kitchen. "You'll not join us?"

Charley looks at him with something like pity. "You all are welcome to say as many prayers as makes you feel better. I find that

God decides for Himself what he wants to do, with or without any of us." He continues into the kitchen, leaving Father Bischoff with his flock.

Palm Sunday, 23 April 1933

"What is your earliest memory, Grandma?" Sitting by the bed as the inevitable marches toward them all, upright and intent.

"Kittens. I remember kittens."

For her, it's the flickering candles on a Christmas tree, the slight updraft causing a little Chinese baby ornament, hung by its neck with a silken red tassel, to spin slowly, hypnotically.

Violets collected from the dell where the fairies dance, snow scooped from the sill with chilled fingers, graham crackers shared with Tom the cat. Long walks tucked under a cape or resting against a shoulder. Warmth, safety. Love. These are her memories.

༺༻

There has never been a Sunday without church. And Palm Sunday is even one of the services that pique the children's interest, with the priest walking among his flock flinging holy water this way and that with his pestle, and the deacons handing out palm branches to even the youngest ones as the congregation recesses. Dire words of consequence for any sacrilege against the blessed fronds don't always prevent swordplay, or general whacking. That leads to swats on the behind, confiscation, and sometimes tears, but the anticipation breaks up the wretched monotony of the church service.

Without Mass, though, today doesn't feel like Palm Sunday or any Sunday. In fact, it doesn't feel like any day at all: every routine is upended, every rhythm disrupted. The time of day is told only by the quality of light in the windows. But there are people praying in the hall. They have been here constantly since Friday morning, working in shifts, sending a constant wave of prayer washing through the house, keeping vigil through the night, unlike Jesus's apostles who could not even keep Him company in the dark before His crucifixion. God will not catch these supplicants napping; He can search their hearts and find their intentions pure and their resolve unflagging. They hope that He does, that He judges their faith worthy, and rewards them all with His intervention on behalf of Lillie May Cecelia Beck Voith.

By now the children have learned to navigate their way through the prayer circle when necessary, but it's still hard for them not to feel invaded, as though, on top of everything, it isn't even their own house anymore. But at five-thirty in the morning, Jeanie is hungry enough, despite her inflamed and crusty ear, to wander down through the hall and into the deserted kitchen. She pulls a chair up to the counter and clambers up, dragging ever-loyal Sally with her. Sally sits on the counter as Jeanie peels back wax paper and tea towels to find what's available. The first thing she tries is cranberry bread, and immediately spits it out. Then she finds slices of jellyroll, which are much more to her liking. She has discovered brownies by the time Bernie pushes into the kitchen and wordlessly pulls up another chair to join her. Jeanie begins to whimper as she eats, but continues to chew.

Bernie considers her from the other side of a doughnut. "S'matter?"

"It hurts," she tells him, and puts her fingers up just below her ear. The slight pressure squirts liquid in a little fountain that splatters onto the floor, startling them both to the point that Jeanie nearly stumbles off her chair.

Bernie's mouth gapes in amazement. "Do that again."

She tentatively presses the spot, but only a few last drips roll down to her chin, and she wipes them off against her shoulder. "I can't."

"S'it hurt?"

Jeanie shrugs. "Not now," and reaches for a gingersnap.

ᘓᘐ

"Well, now, aren't you a vision."

"Do you like it, then?"

"The dress is fine. It's the girl in it that's special."

"Oh, Daddy…"

"What's all this, then?"

"Just nerves, I guess."

"Here, use my handkerchief. Can't have puffy eyes at your own wedding. Time to button up your brave suit."

"No, I don't need a brave suit. I have Ferd."

"And he's a man worth having. He'll be a fine husband to you and father to your children. Have you mentioned that there will be fifty?"

"Oh, he's been warned."

"Well, then, let's get this show on the road! No time to waste!"

"I love you, Dad."

"Love doesn't even start to touch how I feel about you, Lillie."

ᘓᘐ

Sophie has been an almost-constant presence since Charley's call on Friday morning, helping out where she can, trying to maintain a level of order, taking time here and there to join the ranks of the prayerful. The congregation swells as the news spreads of the planned extreme unction, and Doro, Gus, and Dorothie take the opportunity to participate also, assured that Emma is engaged upstairs. It is Sophie who ensures that Tommy is full and clean, and makes tea and coffee to accompany the food she lays out to sustain the prayer groups. She wants to offer comfort to the hollow-eyed children, but her presence simply reminds them that none of their own family is available to them anymore. Even Charley has faded away somehow, choosing to haunt the barn or garage or pigeon loft if he is not with the vigil in the sickroom. But when Sophie finally sits down in the empty parlor for some quiet moments to herself, she soon finds Dorothy and Jeanie on either side of her, and even Bernie has his back against the sofa as he pushes his truck back and forth on the floor. The others drift in, wordless. Francie aimlessly lets her fingers wander over the piano keys, then slides onto the bench and begins to play softly, something slow and melancholy.

ഇ

Crisp October. Children running or toddling; another on the way. The old copper laundry kettle steaming on its bricks. Hands and arms red, raw, and soapy as she scrubs at a stain. The delighted shrieks of Daddy! Daddy! foil his attempt to sneak up on her, but he slips his arms around her from behind as she presses a soapy hand up to her forehead, attempting to corral a wayward strand of hair.

"That's a very fashionable kerchief you're done up in, Mrs. Voith."

"Why, thank you, Mr. Voith. It's all the rage on the Continent this season, you know. It's called The Washer Woman. The chapped hands just add that certain something."

She stirs the laundry with the long wooden paddle, a hard push against tangled sheets and deep water.

"Do you ever wonder what you missed when you took me instead of Jack McGraw?"

"Ferd!"

"No, think about it: trips to the Continent, fashionable clothes, someone else to do all the washing."

Ducklings crash into Ferd's legs, Baby Charley staggering behind in uneven toddler steps, arms raised as outriggers. Ferd sweeps tiny little Francie up and puts her on his shoulders as she squeals in delight. Laughing at him framed in children, her soapy hands once again pushing up against her kerchief, she shakes her head. "Oh, Ferd. It's not always pretty, but it's everything I always wanted."

ഇ

And here suddenly it's warm weather now, children intent on ice cream cones that are melting quickly in the heat. It's a familiar scene: the whole family, sometimes Charley and even Emma, too, stroll along Kennedy Street on a Saturday afternoon after stopping at Rodano's, that paradise of ice cream and penny candy. As they make the turn to walk up Eighth Street to Longfellow, the boys are starting to gobble their cones, getting ready, but this time it is Eleanor who calls out first, "Race you! Race you up the hill to home!" which is her cue to say, "Mark, get set, go!" Charley Boy, Johnny, and Francie are all sprinting in Eleanor's wake. Margaret hesitates for the merest second—too grown up to play?—before dashing after them all, with an even chance to catch up.

She looks around at the little ones, her hands tightening on the pram's handle. "I'll race you! Ready? Ready, set, go! Up the hill to home!"

ဢ

Some time later, Charley Beck appears in the doorway, looking grim. "Your father wants you to come upstairs." Sophie collects them together, offering silent encouragement. They snake their way through the praying throng, which has swelled in number now that early morning Masses are over, and up the stairs, slowly, unwillingly.

Sophie murmurs to Margaret, "Go get Jeanie," who is in her crib after Sophie has given her aspirin and gently cleaned her ear. For her part, Sophie retrieves Tommy, careful not to wake him, letting his head rest against her shoulder. In the bedroom, the other children are already kneeling, joining Emma and Ferd around the bed. Sophie hasn't even realized that Dr. Cavanaugh is here. He looks gray and haggard. Eleanor is pushing Bernie's hands together and trying to get him to put his head down, but Jeanie skitters out of everyone's reach and is craning to see over their heads to understand what's going on.

ဢ

Palm Sunday. The bedroom she and Ferd have shared all these years. So many babies, so much happiness; almost no tears before now. She can't reach them, gathered here by the bedside, as the inevitable marches toward them, upright and intent once again. Here they all are, kneeling around the bed, around her, and she, motionless, inert. Dr. Cavanaugh uses his stethoscope once, twice, pulls away slowly, shakes his head. There is a mournful sound. Slowly, Ferd rises above the wailing, his long slender frame held rigid as he walks from the room. Jeanie follows him, not understanding, eager for attention, trying to show him something—what is it? That she's learned how to snap her fingers, something she's seen the boys do and has been trying to copy for days now. Lookit, Daddy, lookit what I can do! And Ferd firmly takes her by the shoulders, moves her to one side, and keeps walking.

ဢ

Lillie sees her life, sees all their lives, as a vast photograph, as though it all occurs in a single moment. Perhaps it does.

Epilogue

It is well into August now. Charley is deep in the tomato plants, hunting for hornworms. After a small infestation last year, he is vigilant in stalking for the large but hard-to-find caterpillars that he peels up and crushes under his boot. He's come to enjoy this activity that allows him to concentrate without having to think, and to become invisible and out of reach among the laden vines. The caterpillars that are covered in white egg cases he leaves alone, since they carry with them the source of their own kind's destruction. It fascinates him that a parasitic wasp stings the hornworm and deposits her eggs, which feed on the muscle of the worm as they grow, avoiding the major organs so that their host remains alive long enough for them to drill through its skin, spin their own cocoons, and finish pupating externally, finally emerging just as their hollowed-out host collapses onto itself in death. Though the wasp is on Charley's side, he can't help a certain sympathy for the doomed and despoiled hornworm.

Charley sometimes wonders what is burrowing its way through him, hollowing him out, and what will finally emerge in the end. Not a man given much to grieving, especially in the face of an unchangeable reality, he is surprised to discover that he resents having to bear up and carry the weight of everyone else's grief without being allowed the luxury of his own mourning. It is only once, alone among the vines, that his vision clouds unexpectedly and drops begin to fall onto the firm red flesh of the tomato in his hand, and he suddenly finds himself crumpled onto his knees in the dirt, his keening lament loud enough to startle the squirrels.

Today, though, it satisfies just to be invisible. It's a quiet afternoon, as so many are this summer. The older children have developed their own ways to disappear, to the point that it's even hard to find them for meals. Chloe, his angel in a work apron, does what she can to keep the machinery of the household running, sometimes with a hand from Sophie, too. It's no one's fault that nothing can be enough. Not when it is their own beating heart that they are missing.

In the stillness, Charley somehow hears the muffled sound of the kitchen door opening, heavy and slow footsteps on the concrete stairs, and the squeak and slam of the spring porch door. He does not need to see to know that it is Emma carrying a basket of laundry out to the line. He should go out to help, of course. He should. He will. His eye catches a telltale patch of denuded greenery in front of him, and he turns over leaves to track down the culprit. The fat hornworm he finds munching on the underside is free of any egg cases. "Lucky you," Charley says as he peels it from the leaf and drops it on the ground. "It's easier this way."

ജ്ജ

The weather this summer has been astonishingly free of its normal, crushing humidity, and the many shades of green are still fresh, a happy backdrop that highlights the roses and hollyhocks that pose along the street. The good weather seems to cause general high spirits, with people on the streets apt to exchange greetings and neighborly comments more freely than usual. How Lillie would have loved it.

It is people infected with just these high spirits who jostle past Ferd as he stops just beyond the threshold of the District Grocery Store, squinting painfully into the sun of the late afternoon. Behind him, a masculine voice says, "Watch out for this fellow, sweetheart," just as he is bumped into, and a man and woman pass to either side of him; she saying, "Oh! Sorry!" and giggling into her hand, while he turns to tip his hat to Ferd, saying, "Pardon." But as he slides his companion's arm back into his own, he leans down and remarks to her, "Though he could certainly take a step or two to one side and save us all the bother," and she giggles again, her eyes twinkling up at him as the two continue along Kennedy Street.

The jostling continues as Ferd stays where he is and stares after the couple deep in conversation, as they lean into each other in easy companionship. He sees the tall slender man in profile and it is himself, and the sparkling woman laughing up at him, squeezing his arm as she finishes her story, is suddenly Lillie. It's movie night, and he doesn't care, he never cares, what movie they are going to see. The joy of movie night has nothing to do with the movie.

Finally, one hard shove from behind propels him forward, and his feet continue to move beyond those first few steps. He grips a paper sack containing a few desultory purchases, having stopped at the store on the way home to help delay his inevitable arrival there. But no delay is long enough to make time go backward.

Instead, it plods endlessly forward, dragging him along, though he can see no reason why he has to go with it. His numbness is blasted away each morning by the always-fresh electrical shock of anguish, but he stitches it back together and wraps it tight around him in order to find his way out of bed. He is hollow to the point of translucence, and wonders that the jostling he endures today doesn't simply deflate him onto the pavement like an abandoned balloon.

He is not insensate. He sees. He sees how Tommy, generally forgotten in the crush of the motherless household, is gently but purposefully toed aside as he crawls underfoot in the kitchen. He sees that the girls, even in their sadness, are already impatient with the idea that they have some responsibility in running the household. He sees the children look at him with a mixture of diffidence and something akin to fear, and treat him with delicacy from a safe distance. He sees himself retreating each evening after supper to the comfort of his parents' house, where he can fully surrender himself into someone else's care. He sees the genuine concern that Gus and Doro have for him, the gladness they feel in being able to offer the solace that he so obviously needs, and, no one would be willing to admit it out loud, their joy in finally having time with their son again after so many years. He can even see Emma, increasingly ancient and ragged in a way that frightens the small neighborhood children, struggling up and down the steps as she is left, in her dotage and bottomless grief, to somehow manage a household of twelve.

He knows. Somewhere high up in the back of his brain, he knows that he is not the only one who is lost. He simply isn't able to make the rest of himself care. Charley is the one pressing to make him care. It seems not even a week, mere days, after the funeral that they are in the kitchen: Charley with his newspaper, Ferd circling, shuffling, standing and staring, vaguely aware of the chronic rumble of children throughout the house. Above the background noise, he finally realizes that the sound he hears is Charley's familiar chortling over the funny papers. He feels the betrayal might more kindly be delivered with a bullet. He slams his hand on the table and for once speaks so that even Charley can plainly hear: "How could you? How *dare* you? Your only child is not even cold in the ground, and you sit here *laughing*?"

Charley looks up at Ferd, considering him for a moment. His gaze is level but not unkind, and his voice is even. "You have a houseful of children, Ferd. You can't live with the dead." And goes back to reading his paper.

Now the days are weeks, and the weeks are months, and he continues to find ways to delay the trip home from work. He watches his feet plod forward and recognizes that he's made the turn onto Eighth Street. In the back of his legs, he can feel the street begin to angle upward, and he is compelled to pick his feet up with greater force. It's there in his head with the echo of his footsteps: *Up the hill to home! Up the hill to home!* The silly little sing-song started with the ducklings, when they were too big for the pram but still small enough to feel oppressed by the steep hills up to 741 from the south and east. Holding hands in a line, with Lillie somewhere in the middle, they would clomp deliberately, noisily ahead, leaning into the hill, chanting slowly at first, but gradually picking up speed and volume to propel themselves to the top of the hill and into the yard with a final breathless whoop. Later, it is the boys who inevitably turn it into a contest, as hard-fought as though a nickel were involved, with Lillie serving as the starter pistol. *Race you! Race you! Up the hill to home!*

Up the hill to home! The chant reverberates through him, clanging in his ears with each clomping step, so that he doesn't immediately hear the shouts coming from ahead of him. It's the movement that catches his eye, arms and legs pinwheeling with abandon down the hill, so that he finally recognizes the gleeful shrieks of three children barreling his way. They and he notice each other in the same instant, and the children, carried by their momentum and ebullience, forget to pull up, forget to be cautious or distant. Jeanie is the first one to aim for him, yelling, "Daddy, Daddy, Daddy!" as she hurls herself in his direction. They reach him, one right after another, Jeanie, Bernie, and Dorothy crashing into him and wrapping him so tightly that he has to take a step back to stay balanced. He feels them laughing into him, feels it into his bones, tingling up his spine, reverberating through him, until it erupts out of him as a laugh, too. He is startled by the sensation, by hearing the unfamiliar sound it makes, and his mouth clamps shut. But the vibration of the children continues to tickle its way up through him and force its way out as another laugh. He looks down into their open faces laughing up at him. With no thought, he puts the sack down and swoops Jeanie up, swinging her once around to make her squeal, then sets her back down and takes her and Dorothy by the hand. He looks at Bernie, now in possession of the sack, and nods. "Are you ready? On your mark, get set...Here we go! Up the hill to home!"

ꕥ

Emma has lugged the basket out and thumped it down. *Now am I done?* It's the same after every activity. She fixes breakfast. *Now am I done?* She changes a diaper. *Now am I done?* She mends a sock, washes a dish, peels a carrot, each time wondering if it is enough to secure her release. As the silent answer remains the same, she performs the next task and asks again. At night it simply becomes a single repetitive prayer. *Please let me go. Please let me go.* Seventy-six years have faded to nothing against the backdrop of four infinite months.

Now am I done? With the basket at her feet, though, she remains immobile, an automaton whose mechanism has wound down and is frozen in place until the key is cranked again. She remains unmoving even as the noise coming up the street gets louder *laughing* and then louder still *happy as a bird* until it crashes with a whoop into the yard *so full of life and romp* propelled by Ferd and the three children, and she finally turns to look. *Laughing all day long, a perfect tease.* They are all red-faced and breathless, *cheeks as red as red roses* and the children throw themselves onto the grass with arms and legs splayed *as bright and happy as can be* while Ferd bends with his hands on his knees and pulls in air.

Ferd glances up and meets Emma's gaze, which is so unguarded he feels he's caught her in an intimate act, but she doesn't look away. He pushes himself upright and still she holds his gaze, until he feels compelled to walk to her. He glances down at the basket. "Here, let me help you with that." He bends to pick up the top sheet and finds the corner to hand to her. She takes it from him and reaches into the bag hanging from the line for the first clothespin.

Charley finally emerges from the back garden holding a basket of today's tomatoes. He stops for a moment and watches in wonder as Ferd picks up and Emma pins, and they move together down the line. As he finally continues toward the house and supper preparation, he and Ferd look at each other. Charley nods. "Howdy, Ferd. Welcome home."

Acknowledgements

I used a number of excellent print and online resources as I attempted to stay true to the time periods and historical events chronicled in *Up the Hill to Home*. The most exceptional is *Washington at Home*, Kathryn Schneider Smith's beautiful masterwork that explains Washington, D.C. through a survey of its neighborhoods, each one described by a passionate and knowledgeable local. Anyone who wants to truly understand the city of Washington needs to own this book. Another excellent book is *Washington through Two Centuries* by Joseph Passonneau, which illustrates and describes a single large swath of downtown D.C. as it changes over two hundred years, and which was exceedingly helpful to my project.

I started writing *Up the Hill to Home* in my head after I first read my grandmother Lillie May Beck Voith's diary when I was about fourteen. Once I started to put it down on paper many years later, it took me five years to have a completed story. These are the people who materially helped me to get there:

- Norman Anders, husband of Dorothy Cecelia Voith Anders, whose detailed and thorough genealogical research of the Voith family fully predated the advent of this thing called the Internet and saved me years of research and organization.
- My dedicated and unflinching beta readers, especially Steve Groff, who helped me to see my way clear to the ending; Theresa Baker, Laura Jean Ball, Diane Best, Susanne Bledsoe, and Kim Roane; the book clubs of Brookeville, Maryland (Debby McIndoe et al) and Pensacola, Florida (Bonnie Bradley

et al); and a solid handful from the legion of Voith cousins: Joe Voith, Elaine Winch, and the Thomas girls (Carol Comlish, Marti Wallen, Tess Woodruff, Christy Burdette, and Laurie Thomas), who were a book club in their own right.

- Alex Young, who allowed me to take a day a week off from work for several years so I had any hope of finishing this, even though it made his life that much harder.
- My editor, Paula Fleming, who did an amazing amount of work in a very short period of time, and pulled me back from my tendency to go over the top.
- Charley (Boy) Voith, who unfailingly remembers amazing details even when he insists he doesn't remember anything.
- Dorothy Voith Anders, who, with her husband Norman, provided a stunning amount of source material, legwork, and oral histories from herself and her siblings.
- Bernie Voith, who keeps finding more and more unimagined treasures no matter how many times we think we're done.
- And, of course, Jeanie Voith Bort—Mom—inspiration, muse, reader, coach, and #1 fan.

And most especially to my husband Jim, who had no idea in the beginning how this project would turn his whole life on its head, but who was able to keep his sense of humor through it all.

About the Author

Jenny Yacovissi grew up in Bethesda, Maryland, just a bit farther up the hill from Washington, D.C. Her debut novel *Up The Hill To Home* is a fictionalized account of her mother's family in Washington from the Civil War to the Great Depression. In addition to writing and reading historical and contemporary literary fiction, Jenny is a reviewer for *Washington Independent Review of Books* and the Historical Novel Society. She owns a small project management and engineering consulting firm, and enjoys gardening and being on the water. Jenny lives with her husband Jim in Crownsville, Maryland.

To find out more about the people in *Up the Hill to Home* and see photos and artifacts from their lives, visit Jenny's website, jbyacovissi.com.

Apprentice House is the country's only campus-based, student-staffed book publishing company. Directed by professors and industry professionals, it is a nonprofit activity of the Communication Department at Loyola University Maryland.

Using state-of-the-art technology and an experiential learning model of education, Apprentice House publishes books in untraditional ways. This dual responsibility as publishers and educators creates an unprecedented collaborative environment among faculty and students, while teaching tomorrow's editors, designers, and marketers.

Outside of class, progress on book projects is carried forth by the AH Book Publishing Club, a co-curricular campus organization supported by Loyola University Maryland's Office of Student Activities.

Eclectic and provocative, Apprentice House titles intend to entertain as well as spark dialogue on a variety of topics. Financial contributions to sustain the press's work are welcomed. Contributions are tax deductible to the fullest extent allowed by the IRS.

To learn more about Apprentice House books or to obtain submission guidelines, please visit www.apprenticehouse.com.

Apprentice House
Communication Department
Loyola University Maryland
4501 N. Charles Street
Baltimore, MD 21210
Ph: 410-617-5265 • Fax: 410-617-2198
info@apprenticehouse.com • www.apprenticehouse.com

CPSIA information can be obtained at www.ICGtesting.com
Printed in the USA
LVOW12s2142290415

436665LV00005B/162/P